NOW, THIS IS WHEN IT REALLY GETS WEIRD.

I know, I know, dead janitor in disguise, killer history teacher, how much weirder could it get?

Lots. Trust me.

When Dr. DuPont put that sword—well, scimitar—on my neck, I didn't feel scared, like, at all. Instead, I felt that tingle in my chest again, only this time, it was more like this . . . energy.

I reached out, almost like my hands didn't belong to me, and grabbed the hilt of the sword, just above Dr. DuPont's hands on the handle, and yanked, sliding that lethal blade in the space between my arm and my body.

Dr. DuPont was so surprised he didn't even let go of the sword, which was exactly what I had planned, although where that plan came from, I had no idea. Certainly not from that lame self-defense class, where the only thing I'd learned was how to knee a guy in the groin, and trust me, teenage girls already know how to do that. No, this was a different kind of fighting, one so smooth and powerful that I felt like I was standing outside my body, watching myself pull Dr. DuPont right up to me.

I didn't knee him in the groin, although I didn't rule that move out. Instead I . . . ugh, this is so embarrassing.

I head-butted him.

I know, like a soccer hooligan or something. But it worked. He let go of the sword with one hand and reached up to clutch his probably broken nose.

I'd kept my hand on the hilt, and I used it to pull him past me and slam him headfirst into the wall. Now I had a clear shot for the door, but for some reason, I didn't take it. For one thing, all this ninja-style fighting was . . . well, kind of cool. I had no idea how I was doing it, and I wondered if it was another adrenaline thing, like when I was able to push Mr. Hall off me. But it wasn't just that I was having fun. It was almost like I couldn't leave; like I had to finish the fight until one of us was dead.

See? I told you it got weirder.

Other Books You May Enjoy

REBEL BELLE

Rachel Hawkins

speak

An Imprint of Penguin Group (USA)

SPEAK
Published by the Penguin Group
Penguin Group (USA) LLC
375 Hudson Street
New York, New York 10014

USA * Canada * UK * Ireland * Australia
New Zealand * India * South Africa * China

penguin.com
A Penguin Random House Company

First published in the United States of America by G. P. Putnam's Sons,
an imprint of Penguin Group (USA), 2014
Published by Speak, an imprint of Penguin Group (USA) LLC, 2015

THE LIBRARY OF CONGRESS HAS CATALOGED THE G. P. PUTNAM'S SONS EDITION AS FOLLOWS:
Hawkins, Rachel, date.
Rebel belle / Rachel Hawkins.
p. cm.
ISBN 978-0-399-25693-6 (hardcover)
Summary: "Seventeen-year-old Harper Price's charmed life is turned upside down when she discovers she's been given magical powers in order to protect her school nemesis David Stark, who's an Oracle"—Provided by publisher.
[1. Magic—Fiction. 2. Supernatural—Fiction. 3. Oracles—Fiction.
4. Debutantes—Fiction. 5. High schools—Fiction. 6. Schools—Fiction.]
I. Title.
PZ7.H313525Reb 2014
[Fic]—dc23
2013027102

Speak ISBN 978-0-14-751435-6

Printed in the United States of America

Design by Annie Ericsson
Interior images courtesy of iStockphoto

3 5 7 9 10 8 6 4

For Aunt Mimi, Aunt Ruby,
Aunt Audie, Aunt Rona, and Aunt Ann,
rebel belles if ever there were ones.

Chapter 1

LOOKING BACK, none of this would have happened if I'd brought lip gloss the night of the Homecoming Dance.

Bee Franklin was the first person to notice that my lips were all naked and indecent. We were standing outside of our school, Grove Academy. It was late October, and the night was surprisingly cool; in Pine Grove, Alabama, where I live, it's not unheard of to have a hot Halloween. But that night felt like fall, complete with that nice smoky smell in the air. I was super relieved that it was cold, because my jacket was wool, and there was nothing more tragic than a girl sweating in wool. I was wearing the jacket over a knee-length pink sheath dress. If I was going to be crowned Homecoming Queen tonight—and that seemed like a lock—I was going to do it looking as classy as possible in my demure pink dress and pearls.

"Are you nervous?" Bee asked as I rubbed my hands up and down my arms. Like me, Bee was in pink, but her dress was closer to magenta and the bodice was covered in tiny sequins that winked and shivered in the parking lot lights. Or maybe that was just Bee. Unlike me, she hadn't worn a jacket.

Our dates, Brandon and Ryan, were off searching for a parking place. They had been annoyed that Bee and I had insisted on not showing up until the thirty minutes before the crowning, but there was no way I was going to risk getting punch spilled on me or my makeup sliding off my face (not to mention the sweatiness! See above, re: wool jacket) before I had that sparkly tiara on my head. I planned on looking *fierce* in the yearbook pictures.

"Of course I'm not nervous," I told Bee. And it was true, I wasn't. Okay, maybe I was a little bit *anxious* . . .

Bee gave an exaggerated eye roll. "Seriously? Harper Jane Price, you have not been able to successfully lie to me since the Second-Grade Barbie Incident. Admit that you're freaking out." She held up one hand, pinching her thumb and forefinger together. "Maybe a leeeeeetle bit?"

Laughing, I caught her hand and pulled it down. "Not even a 'leeeeeetle bit.' It's just Homecoming."

"Yeah, but you're going to get all queenly tonight. I think that warrants *some* nerves. Or are you saving them for Cotillion?"

Just the word sent all the nerves Bee could have wanted jittering through my system, but before I could admit that, her dark eyes suddenly went wide. "Omigod! Harper! Your lips!"

"What?" I asked, raising a hand to them.

"They're nekkid," she said. "You are totally gloss-less!"

"Who's 'nekkid'?"

I looked up to see the boys walking toward us. The orange lights played up the red in Ryan's hair, and he was grinning, his hands in his pockets. I felt that same little flutter in my stomach that I'd been feeling since the first day I saw Ryan Bradshaw, way back in the third grade. It had taken me six years from that day to make him my boyfriend, but looking at him now, I had to admit, it had been worth the wait.

"My lips," I said. "I must've wiped off all my gloss at the restaurant."

"Well, damn," he said, throwing his arm around my shoulders. "I'd hoped for something a little more exciting. Of course, no lip gloss means I can safely do this."

He lowered his head and kissed me, albeit pretty chastely. PDA is vile, and Ryan, being my Perfect Boyfriend, knows how I feel about it.

"Hope you girls are happy," Brandon said when we broke apart. He had both of his arms wrapped around Bee from behind, his hands clasped right under her . . . um, abundant assets. Bee was so tall that Brandon's chin barely cleared her shoulder. "We had to park way down the effing road."

Okay, I should probably mention right here that Brandon used the real word, but this is my story, so I'm cleaning it up a little. Besides, if I honestly quoted Brandon, this thing would look like a *Cops* transcript.

"Don't say that word!" I snapped.

Brandon rolled his eyes. "What the hell, Harper, are you, like, the language police?"

I pressed my lips together. "I just think that the F-word should be saved for dire occasions. And having to park a hundred yards from the gym is not a dire occasion."

"So sorry, Your Highness," Brandon said, scowling as Bee elbowed him in the ribs.

"Easy, dude," Ryan said, shooting Brandon a warning look.

Ignoring Brandon, I turned to Bee. "Do you have any lip gloss? I completely spaced on bringing any."

"My girl forgot makeup?" Ryan asked, quirking an eyebrow. "Man, you *are* stressed about this Queen thing."

"No, I'm not," I said immediately, even though, hello, I clearly was. But I didn't like when people used the "S-word" around me. After all, a big part of my reputation at the Grove was my ability to handle anything and everything.

Ryan raised his hands in apology. "Okay, okay, sorry. But, I mean, this is obviously pretty important to you, or you wouldn't have spent over a grand on that outfit." He smiled again, shaking his head so his hair fell over his eyes. "I really hope your tastes get cheaper if we get married."

"I hear that, man," Brandon said, lifting his hand to high-five Ryan. "Chicks gonna break us."

Bee rolled her eyes again, but I didn't know whether it was at the guys or the fact that my outfit was over a thousand dollars (yes, I know that's a completely ridiculous amount for a seventeen-year-old girl to spend on a Homecoming dress, but, hey, I can wear it, like, a million times provided I don't gain five pounds. Or at least that was how I rationalized it to my mom.)

"Here." Bee thrust a tube into my hand.

I held it up to read the name on the bottom. "'Salmon Fantasy'?"

"That's close to the shade you wear." Bee's long blond hair was woven into a fishtail braid, and she tossed it over her shoulder as she handed me the lip gloss.

"I wear 'Coral Shimmer.' That is very different."

Bee made a face that said, "I am only tolerating you because we've been best friends since we were five," but I kept going, drawing myself up to my full height with mock imperiousness, "And Salmon Fantasy has to be the grossest beauty product name ever. Who has fantasies about salmon?"

"People who screw fish," Brandon offered, completely cracking himself up. Ryan didn't laugh, but I saw the corners of his mouth twitching.

"So witty, Bran," I muttered, and this time, when Bee rolled her eyes, I had no doubt that it was at the guys.

"Look," she said to me, "it's either Salmon Fantasy or naked lips. Your choice."

I sighed and clutched the tube of lip gloss. "Okay," I said, "but I'm gonna have to find a bathroom." If it had been my Coral Shimmer, I could have put it on without a mirror, but there was no way I was slapping on a new shade sight unseen. Ryan pulled open the gym door, and I ducked under his arm to walk into the gym. As soon as I did, I could hear the opening riff of "Sweet Home Alabama." It's not a dance until someone plays that song.

The gym looked great, and my chest tightened with pride. I know everyone, even Ryan, thinks I'm crazy to do all the stuff I do at school, but I honestly love the place. I love its redbrick buildings, and the chapel bells that ring to signal class changes. I love that both my parents went here, and their parents before them. So yeah, maybe I do stretch myself a little thin, but it's completely worth it. The Grove is a happy place to go to school, and I liked to think my good example was the reason for that.

And it meant that when people thought of the name "Price" at Grove Academy, they'd think of all the good things I'd done for the school, and not . . . other stuff.

Instead, I focused on the decorations. I'm SGA president—the first-ever junior to be elected to the position, I should add—so Homecoming activities are technically my responsibility. But tonight, I'd delegated all of the decorating to my protégée, sophomore class president, Lucy McCarroll. My only contribution had been to ban crepe streamers and balloon arches. Can you say tacky?

Lucy had done a great job. The walls were covered in a silky, shimmery purple material and there were colored lights pulsating with the music. Looking over at the punch table, I saw that she'd even brought in a little fountain with several bistro tables clustered around it.

I scanned the crowd until I saw Lucy, and when I caught her eye, I gave her the thumbs-up, and mouthed, "Nice!"

"Harper!" I heard someone cry. I turned around to see Amanda and Abigail Foster headed my way. They were identical twins, but relatively easy to tell apart since Amanda always wore her long brown hair up, and Abigail wore hers down. Tonight, both were wearing green dresses with spaghetti straps, but Amanda's was hunter green while Abigail's was closer to seafoam.

The twins were on the cheerleading squad with me and Bee, and Abi and I worked together on SGA. Right behind them was Mary Beth Riley, wobbling on her high heels. Next to me, Bee blew out a long breath before muttering, "Maybe no one will notice if she wears tennis shoes under her dress."

Despite Bee's low tone, Mary Beth heard her. "I'm working on it," she said, glaring at Bee. "I'll get better by Cotillion."

Since "Riley" came right after "Price" alphabetically, Mary Beth would be following me down the giant staircase at Magnolia House, the mansion where Cotillion was held every year. So far, we'd only had two practices, but Mary Beth had tripped and nearly fallen directly on top of me both times.

Which was why I'd suggested she start wearing the heels every day.

"Speaking of that," Amanda said, laying a hand on my arm. Even under her makeup, I could see the constellation of freckles arcing across her nose. That was another way to tell the twins apart; Abi's nose was freckle free. "We got an e-mail from Miss Saylor right before we left for the dance. She wants to schedule another practice Monday afternoon."

I bit back a sigh. I had a Future Business Leaders of America meeting Monday after school, so that would have to be moved. Maybe Tuesday? No, Tuesday was cheerleading practice, and Wednesday was SGA. Still, when Saylor Stark told you there was going to be an extra Cotillion practice, you went. All the other stuff could wait.

"I'm so sick of practice," Mary Beth groaned, tipping her head back. As she did, her dark red hair fell back from her ears, revealing silver hoops that were way too big. Ugh. "It's *Cotillion*. We wear a white dress. We walk down some stairs, we drink some punch and dance with our dads. And then we all pat ourselves on the back and pretend we did it just to raise money for charity, and that it's not stupid and old-fashioned and totally self-indulgent."

"Mary Beth!" Amanda gasped, while Abigail glanced around like Miss Saylor was going to swoop out of the rafters. Bee's huge eyes went even bigger, and her mouth opened and closed several times, but no sounds came out.

"It is not!" I heard someone practically shriek. Then I realized it was *me*. I took a deep breath through my nose and did my best to make my voice calm as I continued. "I just mean . . . Mary Beth, Cotillion is a lot more than wearing a white dress and dancing with your dad. It's *tradition*. It's when we make the transition from girls to women. It's . . . important."

Mary Beth chewed her lip and studied me for a moment. "Okay, maybe." Then she shrugged and gave a tiny smile. "But we'll see how you feel when I'm 'transitioning' into a heap at the bottom of those stairs."

"You'll do fine," I told her, hoping I sounded more convinced than I felt. I'd spent months preparing for my Homecoming coronation, but Cotillion? I'd been getting ready for *that* since I was four years old and Mom had shown me and my older sister, Leigh-Anne, her Cotillion dress. I still remembered the smooth feel of the silk under my hands. It had been her grandmother's dress, Mom had told us, and one day, Leigh-Anne and I would wear it, too.

Two years ago, Leigh-Anne had, but for my Cotillion, I'd be wearing a dress Mom and I had bought last summer in Mobile.

"Babe!" I heard Ryan call from behind me.

As I turned to smile at him, I heard one of the girls sigh. Probably Mary Beth. And I had to admit, striding toward us, his auburn hair flopping over his forehead, shoulders back, hands in his pockets, Ryan was completely sigh-worthy. I held my hand out to him as he approached, and he slipped it easily into his own.

"Ladies," Ryan said, nodding at Amanda, Abigail, and Mary Beth. "Let me guess. Y'all are . . . plotting world domination?"

Mary Beth giggled, which had the unfortunate effect of making her wobble even more. Abigail had to grab her elbow to keep her from falling over.

"No," Amanda told him, deadly serious. "We're talking about Cotillion."

"Ah, world domination, Cotillion. Same difference," Ryan replied with an easy grin, and this time, all three girls giggled, even Amanda.

Turning his attention to me, Ryan raised his eyebrows. "So are we just going to stand around and listen to this band butcher Lynyrd Skynyrd or are we going to dance?"

"Yeah," Brandon said, coming up next to Ryan and grabbing Bee around the waist. "Let's go turn this mother *out*."

He pulled her out onto the dance floor, where he immediately flopped on his belly and started doing the worm. I watched Bee dance awkwardly around him and wondered for the millionth time why she wasted her time with that goofball.

My own much less goofy boyfriend took my hand and started pulling me toward Bee and Brandon, but I pulled it back and held up the lip gloss. "I'll be right back!" I shouted over the music, and he nodded before heading for the refreshment table.

I glanced over my shoulder as I walked into the gym lobby and was treated to the sight of Brandon and one of the other basketball players doing that weird fish-catching dance move. With each other.

Since we'd gotten there so late, most everyone who was coming to the dance was already inside the gym, but there were a few stragglers coming in the main gym lobby doors. Two teachers, Mrs. Delacroix and Mr. Schmidt, were also in the lobby, undoubtedly doing "purse and pocket checks." Grove Academy was really strict about that sort of thing now. Two years ago, a few kids smuggled in a little bottle of liquor at prom and, later that night, got into a car accident. My sister—

I cut that thought off. Not tonight.

It was strange to be in the school at night. The only light in the lobby came from a display case full of "participation" trophies with Ryan's name on them. The Grove was excellent in academics, but famously crappy at sports, even against other tiny schools. I know that sounds like sacrilege in the South, but just like any other expensive private school, Grove Academy was way more invested in SAT scores than any scoreboard. We left the football championships to the giant public school across town, Lee High.

I've been up at school at night a few times, and it's always creepy. I guess it's the quiet. I'm used to the halls being deafening, so the sound of my heels clicking on the linoleum seemed freakishly loud. In fact, they almost echoed, making me feel like there was someone behind me.

I hurried out of the lobby and turned the corner into the English hall, so I didn't see the guy in front of me until it was too late.

"Oh!" I exclaimed as we bumped shoulders. "Sorry!"

Then I realized who I'd bumped into, and immediately regretted my apologetic tone. If I'd known it was David Stark, I would have tried to hit him harder, or maybe stepped on his foot with the spiky heel of my new shoes for good measure.

I did my best to smile at him, though, even as I realized my stomach was jumping all over the place. He must have scared me more than I'd thought.

David scowled at me over the rims of his ridiculous hipster glasses—the kind with the thick black rims. I hate those. I mean, it's the twenty-first century. There are fashionable options for eyewear.

"Watch where you're going," he said. Then his lips twisted in a smirk. "Or could you not see through all that mascara?"

I would've loved nothing more than to tell him to kiss my ass, but one of the responsibilities of being a student leader at the Grove is being polite to everyone, even if they are a douchebag who wrote not one, but *three* incredibly unflattering articles in the school paper about what a terrible job you're doing as SGA president.

And you *especially* needed to be polite to said douchebag when he happened to be the nephew of Saylor Stark, president of the

Pine Grove Junior League; head of the Pine Grove Betterment Society; chairwoman of the Grove Academy School Board; and, most importantly, organizer of Pine Grove's Annual Cotillion.

So I forced myself to smile even bigger at David. "Nope, just in a hurry," I said. "Are you, uh . . . are you here for the dance?"

He snorted. "Um, no. I'd rather slam my testicles in a locker door. I have some work to do for the paper."

I tried to keep my expression blank, but I have one of those faces that shows every single thing that goes through my mind.

Apparently this time was no exception, because David laughed. "Don't worry, Pres, nothing about you this time."

If ever there were a time to confront David about the mean things he's written about me, this was it. Of course, those articles hadn't exactly mentioned me by name. I seriously doubt Mrs. Laurent, the newspaper advisor, would let him slam me directly. But they'd basically said that the "current administration" is more concerned with dances and parades than the real issues facing the Grove's students, and that under the "current administration," the SGA has gotten all cliquey, leaving out the majority of the student body.

To which I say, um, hello? Not my fault if people don't attempt to get involved in their own school. And as for the "real issues" facing the Grove's students? The kids who go here all come from super nice households that can afford to send their kids here. We're not exactly plagued with social problems, you know? Which you'd think David would get. He'd lived in Pine Grove practically his whole life, and not only that, he lived with his Aunt Saylor in one of the nicest houses in town.

Or maybe David's issues had nothing to do with "social injustice" at the Grove and everything to do with the fact that he and I had loathed each other since kindergarten. Heck, even *before* that. Mom says he's the only baby I ever bit in daycare.

But before I could reply, the music stopped in the gym.

I checked my watch and saw that it was a quarter till ten. Crap.

David gave another one of those mean laughs. "Go ahead, Harper," he said, sliding his messenger bag from one hip to the other. I know. A messenger bag. And those glasses. And he was wearing a stupid argyle sweater and Converse high-tops. Practically every other boy at the Grove lived in khakis and button-downs. I wasn't sure David Stark owned any pants other than jeans that were too small.

"Only a few more minutes until your coronation," he said, running a hand through his sandy blond hair, making it stand up even more than usual. "I'm sure you'd hate to miss everyone's *felicitations*."

David had beaten me in the final round of our sixth-grade spelling bee with that word and now, all these years later, he still tried to drop it into conversation whenever he could. Counting to ten in my head, I reminded myself of what Mom always said whenever I complained about David Stark: "His parents died when he was just a little bitty thing. Saylor's done her best with him, but still, something like that is bound to make anyone act ugly."

Since he was a tragic orphan, I made myself say "Have a nice night" through clenched teeth as I turned to head to the nearest bathroom.

He just shrugged and started walking backward down the hall, toward the computer lab. "You might wanna put some lipstick on," he called after me.

"Yeah, thanks," I muttered, but he was already gone.

God, what a jerk, I thought, pushing the bathroom door open.

If my shoes had sounded loud in the gym lobby, it was nothing compared to how they sounded in the bathroom. Like the dress, they were a little ridiculous, more for their height than their cost. I'm 5'4", but I was tottering around 5'8" on those bad boys.

Looking in the mirror, I saw why Bee had been so horrified by my naked lips. My skin is pale, so without lip gloss, my lips had kind of disappeared into my face. But other than that, I looked good. Great, even. The makeup lady at Dillard's had done a fabulous job of playing up my big green eyes, easily my best feature, and my dark hair was pulled back from my face, tumbling down my back in soft waves and setting off my high cheekbones.

Yeah, I know it's vain. But being pretty is currency, not just at the Grove, but in life. Sure, I wasn't staggeringly beautiful like my sister, Leigh-Anne, had been, but—

No. Not going there.

I unscrewed the tube of Salmon Fantasy, shuddered again at the name, and started applying. It wasn't as pretty as my Coral Shimmer, but it would do.

I had just slathered on the second coat when the bathroom door flew open, banging against the tile wall so loudly that I jumped.

And scrawled a line of Salmon Fantasy from the corner of my mouth nearly to my ear.

"Oh, dammit!" I cried, stamping my foot. "Brandon, what—"

I don't know why I thought it must be Brandon. Probably because it seemed like the sort of moron thing he'd do, trying to scare me.

But it wasn't Brandon. It was Mr. Hall, one of the school janitors.

He stood in the doorway for a second, staring at me like he didn't know who—or what—I was.

"Oh my God, Mr. Hall," I said, pressing a hand to my chest. "You scared me to death!"

He just stared at me with this wild look in his eyes before turning around and slamming the bathroom door shut.

And then I heard a sound that made my stomach drop.

It was the loud click of a dead bolt being thrown.

Mr. Hall, the tubby janitor, had just locked us in the bathroom.

Chapter 2

OKAY. *Okay, I can handle this,* I thought, even as panic started clawing through my chest.

"Mr. Hall," I started, my voice high and shaky.

He just waved his hand at me and pressed his ear to the door. I don't know what he heard, but whatever it was made him turn and sag against the wall.

And that's when I noticed the blood dripping on his shoes.

"Mr. Hall!" I cried, running toward him. My heels slid on the slick tile floor, so I kicked them off. I got to Mr. Hall just as he slumped to the ground.

His face was pale, and it looked all weird and waxy, like he was a dummy instead of a person. I could see beads of sweat on his forehead and under his nose. His breath was coming out in short gasps, and there was a dark red stain spreading across his expansive belly. There was no doubt in my mind that he was dying.

I knelt down next to him, my blood rushing loudly in my ears. "It's gonna be okay, Mr. Hall, I'll go get someone, everything is gonna be fine."

But just as I reached for the dead bolt, he reached out and grabbed my ankle, pulling me down so hard that I landed on my butt with a shriek.

Mr. Hall was shaking his head frantically.

"Don't," he gurgled. Then he closed his eyes and took a deep breath through his nose, like he was trying to calm down. "Don't," he said again, and this time, his voice was a little stronger. "Don't open that door, okay. Just . . . just help me get to my feet."

I looked down at him. Mr. Hall was pretty substantial, and I didn't think there was any way I was lifting him off that floor. But somehow, by slipping my arms under his and bracing myself against the wall, I got him up and propped against the door of one of the bathroom stalls.

Once he was up, I said, "Look, Mr. Hall, I really think I should get help. I don't even have a cell phone with me, and you"—I looked down at the sticky red circle on his stomach—"you look really hurt, and I think we should call 911, and—"

But he wasn't listening to me. Instead, he opened his shirt.

I braced myself for a wound on his stomach, but I wasn't prepared to see what looked like a bloodstained pillow.

With a grunt, Mr. Hall tugged at something on his back, and the pillow slid from his stomach to land soundlessly on the floor.

Now I could see the gash, and it was just as bad as I'd thought it would be, but my brain was still reeling from the whole "Mr. Hall isn't fat, he just wears a fake belly" thing. Why would Mr. Hall pretend to be fat? Was it a disguise? Why would a janitor need a disguise?

But before I could ask him any of this, Mr. Hall groaned and slid to the floor again, his eyes fluttering closed.

I sank with him, my arm still behind his back. "Mr. Hall!" I cried. When he didn't respond, I reached out with my free hand and slapped his cheek with enough force to make his head rock to the side. He opened his eyes, but it was like he couldn't see me.

"Mr. Hall, what is going on?" I asked, the acoustics of the bathroom turning my question into an echoing shriek.

I was shaking, and suddenly realized how cold I was. I remembered from Anatomy and Physiology that this was what going into shock felt like, and I had to fight against the blackness that was creeping over my eyes. I couldn't faint. I *wouldn't* faint.

Mr. Hall turned his head and looked at me, then really looked at me. Blood was still pulsing out of the gash that curved from under his khaki slacks around to his navel, but not as much now. Most of it seemed to be in a big puddle under him.

"What . . . what's . . . your name?" he asked in a series of soft gasps.

"Harper," I answered, tears pooling in my eyes, and bile rushing up my throat. "Harper Price."

He nodded and smiled a little. I'd never really looked at Mr. Hall before. He was younger than I'd thought he was, and his eyes were dark brown. They were beautiful, actually.

"Harper Price. You . . . run this place. Kids talk. Protect . . ."

Mr. Hall trailed off and his eyes closed. I slapped him again, and his eyes sprang open. He smiled that weird little smile again.

"You're a tough one," he murmured.

"Mr. Hall, please," I said, shifting to get my arm free. "What happened to you? Why can't we open the door?"

"Look after him, okay?" he said, his eyes looking glazed again. "Make sure he's . . . he's safe."

"Who?" I asked, but I wasn't even sure he was actually talking to me. I've heard that when people are dying, their brains fire off all sorts of weird things. He could have been talking to his mom, or his wife, if he had one.

Suddenly there was a loud rattle at the door. I gave a thin scream, and Mr. Hall grabbed at the stall door like he was trying to pull himself up.

"He's coming," Mr. Hall gasped.

"Who?" I yelled. I felt like I had stepped into a nightmare. Five minutes ago my main concern had been whether Salmon Fantasy would clash with my pink dress. Now I was cradling a dying man on the bathroom floor while some crazy person pounded on the door.

Mr. Hall managed to get himself into a sitting position, and for one second, I thought we might actually be okay. Like, maybe the wound that had soaked through that pillow wasn't so bad. Or maybe this whole thing was an elaborate prank.

But Mr. Hall wasn't going to be okay. There was a white line all around his lips, which were starting to look blue, and his breaths were getting shallower and shorter.

He swung his head to look at me, and there was such sadness in his eyes that the tears finally spilled over my cheeks. "I'm so sorry for this, Harper," he said, his voice the strongest it had sounded since he'd run into the bathroom.

I thought he meant he was sorry for dying and leaving me at the mercy of whatever was on the other side of that door.

But then he took a really deep breath, lurched forward, grabbed my face, and covered my lips with his.

My hands reached up to pry his fingers from my cheeks, but for a guy who had barely been able to talk a few seconds ago, his grip was surprisingly strong. And it *hurt*.

I was making these muffled shrieks because I was afraid to open my mouth to scream.

Then I felt something cold—so cold that it brought even more tears to my eyes—flow into my mouth and down my throat, and I went very still.

He wasn't trying to kiss me; it was like he was blowing something *into* me, this icy air that made my lungs sting like jogging in January.

Tears were streaming down my face, and I let go of his hands, my arms falling to my sides. By now, my chest was burning like I'd been underwater for too long, and that gray fog was hovering around the edge of my vision again. As the gray spread, I thought of my sister, Leigh-Anne, and how hard it was going to be on my parents if I died, too.

I don't know if it was that thought, or the fact that being found dead in the bathroom underneath a janitor was not how I wanted people at the Grove to remember me, but suddenly I felt this surge of strength. The gray disappeared as adrenaline shot through my system, and I wrapped my fingers around Mr. Hall's wrists and yanked with everything I had.

And just like that, he was off me.

I took a deep breath. Never had I felt so happy to breathe in slightly stinky bathroom air.

For a long time, I just sat there against the stall door, shaking and gasping. I could still hear whatever was on the other side rattling, but it seemed far away for some reason, like it wasn't even connected to me.

I guess it only took about thirty seconds for me to catch my breath, but it felt like forever. I looked down at Mr. Hall. Lying on his back, his eyes staring at nothing, it was pretty clear that he was dead.

Just as I was taking that in, the rattling at the door stopped.

The burn in my chest had faded to a tingle, and there was this jumping feeling inside my stomach, like I'd swallowed a whole bunch of Pop Rocks. My arms and legs felt heavy, and my head was all spinny.

Slowly, I stood up, careful to keep my feet out of the puddle of blood that continued to spread under Mr. Hall. I glanced down at my legs and saw that my panty hose were surprisingly run-free, despite everything that had just happened.

What *had* just happened?

I forced myself to look at Mr. Hall again. The gash in his stomach was horrible, and big, and sure, it looked like a wound from some sort of medieval sword or something, but that was impossible, right? He probably just hurt himself on some scary janitor equipment. I mean, the floor waxer didn't look like it could slice somebody open, but it's not like I'd ever inspected it for danger.

The more I thought about it, the more comforting the idea seemed. It was certainly better than thinking there was a sword-wielding maniac on the other side of the door.

It had just been a rogue piece of machinery. A blade or a belt or something had snapped and cut Mr. Hall open, and that had been the rattling at the door. He hadn't had time to unplug it, and it was probably spinning down the hall right now. I'd get out of here, and I'd go find a teacher and tell him or her, and everything would be fine.

I looked at myself in the mirror. My skin was almost as white as Mr. Hall's, making the Salmon Fantasy look cheap and too bright.

"It's going to be fine," I told my reflection. "Everything is *fine*."

I walked to the door, and as I did, I had to step over that weird pillow thing Mr. Hall had strapped to his body.

Oh, right. That.

Why did Mr. Hall have a fake belly? My brain felt like it was in a blender as I tried to think up a plausible explanation, hopefully one that would tie in with my possessed machinery idea.

Okay, Mr. Hall was younger than I'd thought. And cuter. Why would he be wearing a disguise? Was he in the witness protection program? A deadbeat dad hiding out from paying child support?

And there was something else. Something weird about him.

I looked back at his body, bracing myself against throwing up or fainting, but I didn't feel anything except that tingle in my chest.

It was something about his face, something that had just felt odd when he'd . . . kissed me? Blown on me? Whatever.

I crept back to him, still careful about the blood, then I reached down and touched his beard. My dad and granddad both have beards, and neither of theirs felt like this one.

Sliding my finger around the edge of his beard, just under his left ear, I saw why.

It was a fake. It was a pretty good one, and it was glued on super tight, but it was still a fake.

Then I glanced up at his balding head and saw a fine stubble covering the bare half-moon of his scalp.

So Mr. Hall hadn't been fat, or bearded, or balding.

"Oh, this is some *bullshit*," I whispered. That's when I knew I was seriously freaked out. I never curse out loud, not even in private. It's just not ladylike.

There was no theory I could come up with to explain any of that, no matter how *CSI: Pine Grove* I was trying to be. No, the best thing to do was to get the heck out of the bathroom and find a teacher, or a cop, or an exorcist. I'd take anyone at this point.

I hurried to the door before realizing I'd left Bee's lip gloss in the sink. My brain was still scrambled, and despite the dead body at my feet, all I could think was that Bee loved that ugly stuff, and I had to grab it before it was, like, confiscated for evidence or something. So I ran back to the sink.

It's funny to think about now, because even though that lip gloss had gotten me into this whole mess, that same lip gloss totally saved my life. If I hadn't gone back for it, I would have been at the door when it exploded into two pieces and slammed into the row of stalls with the force of a small bomb.

And if *that* hadn't flattened me like a pancake, I still would have been directly in the path of the man who came running in with a long, curved blade—a scimitar, I was pretty sure I remembered from World History II with Dr. DuPont—held out in front of him.

So thanks to Bee's lip gloss, I was standing frozen by the sink when the sword-wielding maniac came in and my life stopped making even the littlest bit of sense.

In all the dust from the door flying off, it took the man a minute to realize I was there. He had his back to me as he knelt by Mr. Hall's body. I watched, still as a statue, as he reached into Mr. Hall's pockets, but I guess he didn't find what he was looking for because he stood up really fast and muttered the F-word. I couldn't hold it against him, though. This did seem like a dire situation.

Then he turned around, and I'm sure the look of total confusion on his face was reflected on mine.

"Harper?"

"*Dr. DuPont?*"

I didn't get much time to wonder why my history teacher had just killed a janitor, even though I had this whole joke forming about how Dr. DuPont must *really* hate when his trash cans aren't emptied—you know, to make him see me as a person and not just a potential shish kabob. I learned that in the self-defense class Mom and I went to at the church last spring.

But that joke dried right up in my mouth, because Dr. DuPont crossed the bathroom in two strides, and put his sword against my neck.

Chapter 3

Now, this is when it really gets weird. I know, I know, dead janitor in disguise, killer history teacher, how much weirder could it get?

Lots. Trust me.

When Dr. DuPont put that sword—well, scimitar—on my neck, I didn't feel scared, like, at all. Instead, I felt that tingle in my chest again, only this time, it was more like this . . . energy.

I reached out, almost like my hands didn't belong to me, and grabbed the hilt of the sword, just above Dr. DuPont's hands on the handle, and yanked, sliding that lethal blade in the space between my arm and my body.

Dr. DuPont was so surprised he didn't even let go of the sword, which was exactly what I had planned, although where that plan came from, I had no idea. Certainly not from that lame self-defense class, where the only thing I'd learned was how to knee a guy in the groin, and trust me, teenage girls already know how to do that. No, this was a different kind of fighting, one so smooth and powerful that I felt like I was standing outside my body, watching myself pull Dr. DuPont right up to me.

I didn't knee him in the groin, although I didn't rule that move out. Instead I . . . ugh, this is so embarrassing.

I head-butted him.

I know, like a soccer hooligan or something. But it worked. He let go of the sword with one hand and reached up to clutch his probably broken nose.

I'd kept my hand on the hilt, and I used it to pull him past me and slam him headfirst into the wall. Now I had a clear shot for the door, but for some reason, I didn't take it. For one thing, all this ninja-style fighting was . . . well, kind of cool. I had no idea how I was doing it, and I wondered if it was another adrenaline thing, like when I was able to push Mr. Hall off me. But it wasn't just that I was having fun. It was almost like I couldn't leave; like I had to finish the fight until one of us was dead.

See? I told you it got weirder.

I stood there, crouched in my pink dress while Dr. DuPont turned around to look at me with an expression I can only call incredulous (that was the word I had beat David Stark with in the *fifth*-grade spelling bee.)

Blood was caked all around the lower half of his face. Panting, he looked down at Mr. Hall's body, then back at me.

He laughed, but it was an ugly, wet sound. "So he passed it on to you," Dr. DuPont wheezed. Then his bloody lips curved in a nasty smirk. "Well, *bless your heart*," he drawled in a not very nice (if kind of accurate) imitation of my accent.

He moved sideways, toward the stalls, the sword still pointed at me. "I really can't think of a worse choice," he said, still smiling, "than the bimbo who wrote a paper on the history of *shoes* for my class."

Okay, that stung. I'd worked hard on that paper. And it hadn't been on shoes. It had been about how fashion affected politics. And I may like clothes and makeup and shoes, but I am *not* a bimbo. Dr. DuPont could totally bite me. I almost said that, but then I changed my mind. As crazy as everything had gone, Dr. DuPont might take that as an opening to actually, you know, *bite me*.

"Tell me, Harper, are you going to use your new superpowers to strong-arm some boy into taking you to prom? Or maybe become head cheerleader?" Something in his expression hardened. "Not that you're going to live that long."

Then he lunged again, sword high, but I was ready for him. I spun around so my back was to him, then dropped so the sword passed right over my head. With my hands on the floor, I kicked out my left heel. "I already *am* head cheerleader," I said through clenched teeth as my foot connected with his jaw.

Before Dr. DuPont recovered from my kick, I spun in my crouch and used that same leg to knock his legs out from under him.

He cracked his head against the sink as he went down, and I figured that was the end of it.

I stood up and looked down. There was a ragged tear from the hem of my skirt all the way up to the middle of my thigh.

"Oh, *shoot*," I muttered, giving Dr. DuPont's limp body a dark glare.

Then it occurred to me that I should definitely get out of here and find a non-homicidal teacher. Something in me still didn't want to leave, but I shoved that down. Dr. DuPont had said *superpowers*, and talked about Mr. Hall "passing something on" to me. That must have been what that weird blowing in my mouth thing had been. But I could figure out exactly what had happened to me later. Right now I needed to get out of here before Dr. DuPont came to.

My arms and legs were starting to ache. I'd be black and blue tomorrow, I thought, as I scooted around Dr. DuPont, *and* I'd probably missed the crowning, thanks to all this craziness. I swear, if—

I didn't get to finish the thought. Instead, there was a sharp pain at the back of my head that brought tears to my eyes and ripped a short scream from my throat. Dr. DuPont had grabbed a big handful of my thick hair. Yanking so hard that I was surprised I wasn't snatched bald, he used my hair to pull me back and sling me into the sinks.

My right elbow hit the edge of the counter and a wave of nausea spilled over me.

I was still blinking back stars when Dr. DuPont swung a powerful kick to my stomach.

All the air left my lungs, and I crumpled to the ground, gasping and gagging at the same time. My chest was burning again, this time from lack of oxygen.

I lay there, staring at Dr. DuPont's shiny black loafers as he walked over to the corner and picked up the scimitar he'd dropped.

I'm going to die here, I thought dimly. *I'm going to be stabbed to death by my history teacher with some freaky sword, and no one will ever know what happened to me. And my parents will have two daughters who died at school dances, and my mom's eyes will get sadder, and Dad's face will get thinner, and our house will feel even grayer and emptier.*

Now the pain in my stomach had nothing to do with Dr. DuPont's kick. I closed my eyes as tears burned. Dr. DuPont was talking, but I couldn't really hear him. He said something about the wrong place and the wrong time, and then he said this weird word that started with "pal."

Paladin. What was that?

He might as well have been speaking Greek. All I could focus on was the burn in my chest and the aching of my midsection.

He was right in front of me now. I opened my eyes and saw the sword hanging at his side. The end glittered in the ugly fluorescent light of the bathroom.

I turned my head a little so I didn't have to see him raise the blade.

Something pink caught my eye. It was one of my shoes. I remembered taking them off to help Mr. Hall. Apparently, they'd gotten kicked under the sink.

Dr. DuPont was still talking, but I was focused on that shiny pink shoe that now looked so silly in the midst of all this death and destruction. I reached out and pulled the shoe to me. Dr. DuPont laughed. "Afraid of dying without the right accessories, Miss Price? Nice to see you're still a silly bitch, right to the end."

But I didn't want the shoe because it was pretty, or because it was pink. I rolled onto my back, slowly drawing my knees up. It wasn't the most ladylike of positions, but I was going to need leverage. I held the shoe against my chest. I ran my thumb over its heel, remembering my desire to stomp on David Stark's foot in these shoes. It would've hurt.

I fought to keep a smile off my face as Dr. DuPont raised the sword.

In fact, if I had stomped on David's foot hard enough, the heel would've gone right through. It was awfully sharp.

If Dr. DuPont hadn't been a total drama queen and raised the sword with both hands, he might have actually killed me. He certainly wouldn't have ended up giving me the opening he did.

Because while his arms were high over his head, about to bring the sword down, I pushed myself off the floor and into a spin, the high heel clutched in my hands, sharp point out.

The sword was still poised in the air when I came to an abrupt stop and sunk the heel into his throat, right under his jaw. I'd learned about the carotid artery in Anatomy and Physiology, which was turning out to be a *much* more useful class than I'd originally thought, and while I'd definitely been aiming for it, I was still kind of shocked that I managed to hit it.

I guess Dr. DuPont was, too, because his eyes got really wide, and the sword clattered to the floor. He stared at me, his lips opening and closing like a fish, my pink shoe stuck in his neck. I guess it would've been kind of funny if it hadn't been, you know, completely gross and horrifying.

Dr. DuPont reached up and pulled the heel out of his neck. Blood poured from the hole, pulsing out with his heartbeat.

He looked at the shoe for a long time, like he couldn't figure out what it was. Then he muttered, "Pink." The shoe fell from his fingers and he dropped back on the floor, his eyes wide and staring.

The only sound in the bathroom was my breathing and the steady *plink-plink* of the dripping sink.

Reality took a minute to set in, but when it did, it was bad.

I had just killed a teacher. With my shoe.

I ran over and picked up that shoe, wincing at the streaks of red on the heel. I grabbed a handful of paper towels and wiped it off, and my breathing got faster and faster.

"It's okay," I murmured to myself. "It was self-defense. He had a sword."

I scrubbed at the heel, feeling like Lady Macbeth. Self-defense or not, I'd just killed someone. That was bad. That was *really* bad. I looked in the mirror, and saw that other than flushed cheeks and bright eyes, I looked pretty much the same as I had when I came in the bathroom. Well, except for the line of Salmon Fantasy scrawled across my face. I grabbed a paper towel and began scrubbing at my mouth.

Even my hair wasn't that messed up. *I should tell Ms. Brenda that the next time I go in,* I thought automatically. Then it occurred to me that there was no way to tell my hairdresser that her 'dos hold up even when you're kicking the crap out of sword-wielding teachers.

After I was done getting the blood off my shoe and ugly lipstick off my face, I tossed the paper towel in the trash and looked around. Mr. Hall's body was against the stalls, and Dr. DuPont was lying about three feet away. There were big cracks in the tile from where I'd slammed Dr. DuPont's head into the wall, and the bathroom door lay in pieces on the floor, surrounded by a fine layer of grit and more broken tiles.

Without really thinking, I slid my shoe back on and hobbled over to the trash can, where the second high heel lay on its side.

I guess this is the part where I should have started screaming and/or vomiting, but I just felt . . . numb. Certainly not as horrified as someone who just watched two men die (and one by her own hand. Well, her own shoe) should feel.

That weird feeling, like adrenaline times a thousand, was still flowing over me. That was probably what was keeping the nervous breakdown at bay. As I stepped over the fallen door and out of the bathroom, I wondered why no one had come looking for me yet. I mean, I must have been in there for at least half an hour. Then I glanced at my watch and saw that only eleven minutes had passed since I'd bumped into David Stark.

I walked down the English hall, and the farther I got from the bathroom, the shakier my legs felt. I was almost to the gym lobby, close enough to could hear the band's lead singer say, "Okay, in just a few, we'll be announcing Homecoming Queen, so come on up here, ladies."

That's when I felt something in my stomach shift dangerously, and I turned and ran back down the English hall.

As my heels clattered down the hallway—

Oh God, oh God, don't think about your heels, don't think about your shoe sticking out of his neck!

I realized I should have run down the history hall because

there was no way I could go back in the bathroom with Mr. Hall and Dr. DuPont.

But it was too late now.

Then I remembered that—hello?—there are two bathrooms in the English hall, so I ran into the boys' room across the hall from the girls'.

As I barreled through the door, I heard a startled male voice squawk, "What the hell?" but I didn't even glance at the figure standing by the sink. I ran straight into one of the stalls, actually thankful it didn't have a door.

I had barely hit my knees before everything that was in my stomach came up.

"Holy crap," I heard Sink Guy say, and then he was there in the stall with me, lifting the heavy mass of hair away from my face and neck. It felt so good, and it was such a nice thing to do that I wasn't even embarrassed that some random guy was watching me, Harper Jane Price, SGA president, head cheerleader, Future Business Leader of America, and soon-to-be Homecoming Queen, puking my guts out in the boys' bathroom.

I felt shaky and hollowed out when I was done, but better. Lots better.

"Here," Sink Guy said, handing me a bunch of damp, cool paper towels. I took them gratefully and pressed them against my sweaty face. At the same time, the mystery guy laid a few more of the paper towels against the back of my neck. He was still holding my hair back.

My face buried in the paper towels, I reached up and flushed the toilet.

"Thank you," I murmured into the wad of wet towels.

"No worries. So are you knocked up?"

I looked up and found myself glaring into David Stark's blue eyes.

Of course.

"No," I said, trying to get to my feet in the narrow stall without flashing my panties at him. He reached down and took my elbow to help me. "I was joking," he said. "If there's ever been anyone *less* likely to be on *Teen Mom* than you, I've never met her." He sounded sincere, but I still shook him off.

I walked out of the stall and over to the sink, where I rinsed my mouth out about twenty times. When I was done, David reached into that stupid messenger bag of his and pulled out a tin of Altoids, wordlessly handing me a few.

"Thanks," I said again, hating that I'd had to say "thank you" to David Stark two times in as many minutes.

He just shrugged, but he was looking at me in that weird, almost predatory way he has. With any other guy, that look would mean he was trying to get in my pants, but I doubt David even thinks about those kinds of things. He only gets that look about the stupid school paper, and I knew he was trying to sniff out a story about why "Pres" was tossing her cookies in the boys' room the night of the Homecoming Dance.

"I know you weren't drinking," he said. "Not after—" He broke off awkwardly before clearing his throat. "So, food poisoning?"

"No," I said again, "It's just that they're about to announce Homecoming Queen, and I'm nervous. Stage fright."

I thought it was pretty good as far as excuses go, but David just laughed. "Yeah, right. Pres, you'd make out with a spotlight if you could figure out how. It's gotta be something else."

That hungry look was back in his eyes, and it suddenly occurred to me that the reason I'd thrown up was literally across the hall. My stomach and knees turned to jelly. It was a miracle that David hadn't noticed the broken door to the girls' room when he'd come in here. There was no way he was going to miss it when he left. And David was the smartest person I knew; he was the only thing currently standing between me and valedictorian. David had seen me going toward the girls' room, and when he saw the two dead bodies in there, he'd put two and two together.

And he would *love it*. He'd write a bazillion articles for the paper chronicling my downfall, and the eventual trial, and he'd win awards for it. Do they have a Pulitzer for high school papers?

"Well, whatever is up with you, I suggest you get over it so you can collect your crown," he said, turning to leave.

"Wait!" I cried, grabbing his arm. How could I keep him from going out there?

"What?" he snapped, clearly pretty irritated.

"Um . . . I just, uh, I just wanted to say thank you. Again."

David stared at me like I'd just started speaking in tongues, but after a moment, kind of patted my hand and said, "Yeah, you're, uh . . . no problem."

Then he pulled open the bathroom door. I stayed, frozen, waiting for him to shout or something when he saw the destruction across the hall.

But all I heard were the soft squeaks of his tennis shoes as he walked away.

Oh my God, had he missed it again? Looked like valedictorian was in my grasp after all!

But then, when I walked out of the bathroom, I saw why David hadn't seen anything: There was nothing to see.

The bathroom door was in place and in one piece.

Chapter 4

EVERYTHING after that is kind of a blur, mostly because I was pretty sure I was going insane. I know I walked into the bathroom and didn't even feel all that surprised to see that it was empty, with no sign of the two dead bodies that had been in there just—I checked my watch—six minutes ago. The walls were fine, no cracks or big craters roughly the size of Dr. DuPont's head. I even checked the trash can for the bloody paper towel I'd used to clean my shoe.

The trash can was empty.

That's when I made this weird, high-pitched sound that was kind of a sigh and kind of a gasp. I'm pretty sure I would have had a complete nervous breakdown right then and there if David Stark hadn't poked his head in and said, "Uh . . . Pres? You gonna hurl again?"

I turned to look at him, and the smirk fell off his face. "Holy crap," he said, crossing the room and grabbing my arms. "Harper? What's wrong?"

I saw my reflection in the mirror, and totally understood why he looked genuinely freaked. My eyes were huge and glassy and my skin had gone gray. Not that I really cared. I mean, I'd gone crazy. I was crazy.

For some reason, that thought was way more upsetting than the idea that I'd turned into some sort of superhero who'd killed evil Dr. DuPont with my shoe. That had been traumatizing, I guess, but it had also been . . . well, kind of cool. Like something out of a comic book. But going insane? That was *real*.

"Harper?" David said again, giving me a little shake.

I think I would've caved then and the whole story about Mr. Hall and Dr. DuPont would've come tumbling out in a series of sobs and shrieks. But luckily, Bee chose that moment to push the bathroom door open.

"God, there you are!" she exclaimed, and her voice reverberated off the tile walls, hurting my ears. Behind her, Amanda, Abigail, and Mary Beth crowded into the bathroom, too.

Then they saw David, and all of their normally pretty faces twisted into sneers. I wasn't the only one who didn't like David's editorials.

One of Bee's best qualities was loyalty, but it sometimes had an ugly way of showing itself, especially where David was concerned. "What are you doing in the girls' room, paper boy?" I wondered if I'd ever looked at David like that.

"Are you stalking Harper?" Amanda asked, folding her arms over her chest.

David wasn't holding my arms anymore, and he certainly wasn't looking at me with concern. His usual scowl was back in place. "Yeah, that's it, Amanda," he said, trying to shove his hands into the pockets of his skinny jeans. "I'm a stalker. And what a charming and unique insult."

Amanda rolled her eyes, which was her standard response when she didn't have a comeback, and Bee looked at me. "Whoa, Harper, what's wrong?"

"I think she's sick," David said, stuffing his hands in his pockets, his eyes focused on a spot somewhere over my head.

"Probably because she's been talking to you," Abigail snapped back.

"Abigail," I said, but David just laughed. "Lovely talking to you ladies," he said as he walked out the door.

"Did he do something to you?" Bee asked as soon as he was gone.

I laughed, but it sounded, um, crazy, so I stopped. "No. I just . . . I think I'm coming down with something. He was checking on me. It was nice, actually."

Mary Beth wobbled up to my side and frowned. "Probably only because he wanted something. I don't trust David Stark as far as I could throw him."

That's when I finally noticed the crown dangling from Bee's fingers, the rhinestones shining dully in the florescent lights. "Is that . . ." My voice came out squeaky, so I started over. "Is that the Homecoming Queen crown?"

She looked down like she had totally forgotten about it. "Oh, yeah! Duh. That's why I came to look for you. You totally won!"

She squealed and threw her arms around me. I kind of

hugged her back, but mostly I was just thinking, *I missed it. I've wanted this for years, ever since Leigh-Anne won it two years ago, and I missed it because I was having a schizo freak-out in the bathroom.*

Bee didn't seem to notice that I was less than enthusiastic. "We looked for you, like, everywhere when they called your name."

"Everywhere?" I parroted.

"Well . . . everywhere in the gym. So then Ryan said I should just go up there and, like, accept it on your behalf, so I did, and then I remembered you'd gone to the bathroom, so I came to find you!"

Pursing her lips, Bee tilted her head to one side. "Seriously, Harper, what's wrong? You look really bad. No offense."

I rubbed my hands over my face. "I told you," I said from behind my fingers, "I started feeling sick." I put my hands down and tried to smile brightly, but I had a feeling I looked demented. I *felt* demented.

Bee was still squinting at me when Abigail took the crown from her hands. With a big smile, she reached up and plonked the crown on my head. "Well, there you go, Your Majesty!"

I turned and looked in the mirror. My face was still gray, my eyes were still huge, and the crown looked fake and stupid. Plus it was crooked.

I burst into tears.

All four girls wrapped me in a group hug, and at first I thought they were comforting me, that somehow they understood that I'd had a terrible night, and that I had thought I'd killed a guy, but actually, I was just going insane, and seeing that *effing* crown on my head had been the final straw.

But then Abigail squealed, "Oh, sweetie, I know! It's, like, a dream come true!"

"What do you know about schizophrenia?" I mumbled against Ryan's mouth.

He raised his head, his eyes hazy, his hand still hovering around the hem of my dress. "Huh?"

We were sitting in his car, parked in my driveway. It was after midnight, but still bright in the car, thanks to the truly obscene amount of security lighting my parents have. Somebody tried to break in a few years back, and ever since then, my dad has been more than a little paranoid. But, I mean, if we didn't have this big brick, ivy-covered house that pretty much screams, "HI! THE PEOPLE WHO LIVE HERE ARE TOTALLY LOADED! PLEASE TAKE SOME OF THEIR STUFF! THEY'LL JUST BUY MORE!" he wouldn't have to worry so much.

My crown was on the floorboard. I'd taken it off as soon as we'd left the school, even though Ryan had joked that he expected me to wear it 24/7 from now on. And then Brandon had made a joke about how I should wear it during sex, and said something about properly "saluting" the Queen, which, A) didn't really make that much sense, and B) was dumb anyway.

"It's just something I was thinking about," I said to Ryan now. "Didn't you write a paper on it for AP Psychology last year?"

Ryan blinked. In the dim light of the car, his hazel eyes were nearly black, and he'd loosened the hunter green tie around his neck and shed his suit coat. Normally, seeing Ryan all rumpled and disheveled sent a little thrill through me, but tonight, I was way too preoccupied to appreciate his hotness.

He slid off me and back into the driver's seat, running his hand through his hair. "Um . . . yeah. Well, I mean, to be honest, I used one of Luke's freshman psych papers." Luke was Ryan's older brother, currently off at the University of Florida. When I frowned, Ryan gave me one of those lopsided grins that usually made me smile in return. "Is this about the Committee for Academic Honesty?" he asked. "Because I'd hope dating the committee chairwoman, like, exempted me from that."

"No, it's nothing to do with CAH," I said, rubbing my eyes. "I just . . . wait, Ry, you used someone else's paper? For an *AP class*?"

He sighed and leaned forward, folding his arms on the steering wheel. "It was right in the middle of basketball season, and I didn't have time to write a paper on crazy people. And it wasn't anyone, it was Luke, and since we're brothers, that makes that paper, like, half mine anyway."

He was joking, and I wanted to laugh, I really did. I rolled my lips inward, trying to stop the next sentence from coming out, but it was no use. "Ryan, playing basketball on quite possibly the worst team in Alabama is not going to get you into a good college."

"Oh God," he muttered, slamming his head back against the headrest.

"However," I continued, hating myself, but, as usual, totally unable to stop, "cheating in an AP class will most definitely keep you *out* of Hampden Sydney. Colleges take academic honesty very seriously."

He snorted, but didn't look up. "Can we not do this right now, Harper? I know you're perfect, but—"

"I am not perfect," I muttered, crossing my arms and settling back into my seat. I had hallucinated killing my teacher with a shoe. That would probably do a lot more to keep me out of a good college than Ryan's stolen paper.

"Yeah," Ryan said, raising his head, "you are. Or at least you try to be. I mean, I love you, but why do you have to be queen of everything? Why can't you just . . . *chill*?"

Last year, my mom took me to see a therapist after she found me making decorations for the Spring Fling at three in the morning. Dr. Greenbaum said that my "obsessive need to overachieve" was due to a "fear of being out of control" and that, like Ryan said, I needed to chill. Only she used some fancy term for "chill" and also suggested I start taking Lexapro to help facilitate said chilling. I managed to get out of the meds by wearing blue jeans and a T-shirt to my next therapy session, where I drew pictures of myself crying in a tornado. That seemed to make Dr. Greenbaum happy and she decided I didn't need the drugs after all. And the next time I did school stuff in the middle of the night, I just did it in my closet with the door locked. Honestly, what is wrong with this country when striving for excellence means you need antidepressants?

But then I remembered I actually *was* crazy now.

"Forget it," I said to Ryan. "I don't want to fight about this again. I'm just having a really rough night."

"Are you bummed you missed the crowning ceremony?" he asked, leaning down to pick up my tiara.

Leave it to my Perfect Boyfriend to give me the perfect out. Of course Ryan would assume I was bummed about missing the crowning.

"Yeah," I said, trying to look more wistful than freaked out. "I know it's stupid, but . . ."

"Hey," he said softly, "It's okay to feel disappointed. Here." He took the crown and gently placed it back on my head. "Harper Jane Price, I officially crown you Homecoming Queen." Then he leaned forward and kissed me. It was a sweet, soft kiss, and one for its own sake, and not as a prelude to something else.

That was one of the many great things about Ryan. Just a few minutes ago, we'd been fighting, but once I'd said I was sorry, he was over it. I could be a champion grudge-holder. Briefly, an image of David Stark flickered in my brain, but I pushed it away. David had been nice to me tonight—well, nice for him—so maybe it was time to bury the hatchet. Besides, it was creepy to think about David while I was kissing my boyfriend.

Ryan pulled away, and I smiled at him, laying my hand on his cheek. "You are the greatest boyfriend ever, you know that?"

He shrugged. "Pretty much, yeah." He scooted closer and kissed me again, but this time, it was definitely a prelude to something else; something I was most definitely not in the mood for.

Gently pushing at his shoulders, I said, "It's been kind of a crazy night. Can we maybe . . . not?" I hoped I sounded regretful and not irritated.

Ryan sighed, ruffling the hair that flopped over his eyes, but then he turned to me and smiled. "Sure." Then he glanced down and frowned. "Oh, crap, babe, I'm sorry."

"For what?"

He reached out and touched my leg. "Your skirt. I must've accidently ripped it."

I felt the hysterical tears/laughter start to rise again as I looked to where his finger was slowly running up and down the tear in my skirt. The tear I'd made when I'd kicked Dr. DuPont.

But it was impossible to have that tear, since the whole thing had been in my head because I was crazy now.

Right?

But . . . a little voice whispered in my head, if it had all been imaginary, then why did I still have that Pop Rocks feeling in my chest? Why did I still feel a tremor running through all my muscles, like I could tear off Ryan's car door if I really wanted to?

"Oh, don't worry about it," I said, trying to sound normal even though all I really wanted to do was run inside the garage and try to lift my dad's SUV. You know, for scientific purposes.

We made out for another ten minutes or so, but neither my head nor my heart were particularly in it. Ryan could probably sense that, but he didn't say anything. Finally, he walked me to my door, gave me one last kiss, and then I was breathing a sigh of relief as his taillights disappeared down my drive.

But I didn't go inside. Instead, I sneaked around the back of the house to the tall wooden fence that surrounded our backyard—if you could call the half acre of landscaped gardens a "yard." The fence was eight feet high and covered in thick, thorny pyracantha bushes. Leigh-Anne had dared me to climb it once when I was six. I'd gotten maybe a foot off the ground before the thorns tore up my palms. I still have a thin white scar at the base of my right thumb. Needless to say, I'd never made another attempt to scale the fence.

But now I stood in the dark, my heart pounding in my ears, and a shivery feeling coursing through me.

Just try it, I thought.

It wasn't real, the larger, more sensible part of my brain screamed. *There were no bodies! No collateral damage! Not even a freakin' paper towel!*

I looked down at the tear in my skirt. Sure, it was possible I'd been kicking and punching at thin air because I'd finally gone full-on schizoid. *But*, I thought, *what if . . .*

I was done thinking. I slipped off my pink, teacher-killing heels, threw them over the fence, and felt my muscles tense.

And then I jumped.

Chapter 5

I GRABBED the top of the fence, my hands tangled in the pyracan-tha bushes, my feet dangling off the ground. Okay, so far, no proof of my superhero-ness. Sure, it had been a great jump, but I was a cheerleader; jumping was not new to me. At least I'd missed the thorns this time.

I took a deep breath. Whatever happened next meant I'd know for sure whether or not what had happened tonight was real. Either way, I figured, life was about to get pretty different.

Slowly, I curled my legs up to my chest and lowered my fore-head to the top of the fence. Then I pulled with all the strength in my arms until the top of my head was resting on the gate. My arms didn't even tremble as they held all my body weight.

I uncurled my legs and pushed until I had both arms fully extended and both legs straight up in the air. My dress fell down over my head, so if any of our neighbors were up and about, they saw more than just me going all Russian gymnast on our fence.

Then I brought my feet down to rest on the top of the fence by my hands, so I was basically doing the world's most extreme backbend, a move I'd never been very good at despite all of my years of cheerleading. But now I did it with no problem, feeling like my body was almost out of my control, the same way I'd felt fighting Dr. DuPont. Planting my feet, I let go of the fence with my hands and pulled my torso up so that I was standing, looking down into the garden, my dress falling back down around my knees.

"Well," I murmured, "that answers that."

But just for good measure, I did a front flip off the top of the fence.

I landed in our pool, which was kind of bad planning on my part. I'd jumped just a little too hard and overshot the small patch of grass between the fence and the ridiculously huge expanse of aqua water. Of course, on the bright side, I'd also missed slamming into the concrete patio.

I came up out of the super chilly water not even caring that my new, really expensive dress was ruined. There was a huge smile on my face.

I was a superhero.

"HARPER JANE!"

The smile fell from my face instantly. Oh, crap.

Mom stood just inside the back door, wearing a robe and pajamas. She must have been right in the kitchen to have made it outside so quickly, but Mom had never waited up for me before. Why did it have to be the one night I was diving off the fence?

But Mom must've missed that part of the show because all she said was, "What on earth are you doing in the pool?"

As I hoisted myself up the ladder, she came rushing down the steps of the deck, her bare feet slapping on the wood. "I'm fine," I told her, climbing out of the chilly water.

"You clearly are not," she fired back, whipping off her robe and throwing it around my shoulders. "You're practically blue, and your dress is *ruined*. Have you lost your mind?"

"No," I said, pulling the lapels of the robe closer around me. It was warm and smelled like Lancôme lotion and coffee. "I just decided to come in through the back door so I wouldn't bother you and Daddy. I wasn't looking where I was going, and I tripped." I gave her what I hoped was a sheepish smile and nodded toward my heels which, thankfully, had landed on the pool deck. "Stupid new shoes, you know how it is."

But Mom wasn't an idiot. She frowned at me. "And, what, you just . . . didn't see the pool?"

I glanced over at it, noticing that all the underwater lights were on. It gleamed like a giant turquoise jewel in the darkness of the backyard. There was no way anyone could miss it.

"Mom—"

But she already had me by the shoulders, turning me to face her. "Harper, have you been drinking?"

"*No*," I said, reaching up to squeeze one of her hands for emphasis. "You know I wouldn't do that. I promise."

Mom watched me for a long time. There were new wrinkles around her eyes, and in the dim, greenish light of the pool, she looked almost sickly. All the euphoria that had just been coursing through me seemed to drain out. I had almost been killed tonight. I pictured Mom, sitting at the kitchen table in her robe, waiting for me when I was never coming home, and suddenly, the whole superhero thing didn't seem so great.

"I'm *fine*," I told her again, reaching out to hug her before remembering that I was soaking wet. "Just . . . distracted and clumsy."

I wasn't sure how convinced she was, but she finally smiled and tucked a piece of wet hair behind my ear. "Okay. But you might want to work on that, or Mary Beth won't be the only one taking out an entire row of debutantes."

Relieved, I laughed. "She'll get better."

Mom and I walked back into the house, and I saw that the coffeepot was on and nearly empty. "How long have you been up?" I asked. It wasn't even midnight yet, and that was my curfew.

"Awhile," was all Mom said, but then, from the doorway, I heard Dad say, "She hasn't been to bed yet."

Dad's hair—what little he had left—was sticking up and his eyes were blurry with sleep. As he shuffled into the kitchen, I smiled at his familiar plaid pajama pants and University of Alabama T-shirt. "Why are you soaking wet?" he asked.

"She fell in the pool," Mom explained. Unlike her, he seemed to take that in stride. "Gotta be more careful, kiddo," he told me, walking up to Mom. He put a hand on the back of her neck, pulling her toward him to kiss her temple.

I guess I should be icked out that I have parents who are obviously still so in love—and to be honest, sometimes, I am—but there was also something . . . comforting about it. I thought of

Ryan, wondering if we got married, would we be like this in twenty years?

"So did you win?" Dad asked, and it took me a minute to remember what he was talking about.

"I did," I told him. "But I left the crown in Ryan's car."

Dad squinted. "That doesn't sound like you. Hope you weren't *distracted*. Do I need to get my shotgun?"

"Ew," I said as Mom nudged him with her elbow.

"I don't think any firearms will be required to get Ryan and Harper down the aisle one day," she said, winking at me.

Mom loved Ryan, especially since he'd been so great after everything with Leigh-Anne.

"So now that she's home, will you finally get some sleep?" Dad asked Mom.

The lines around her eyes deepened as she smiled. "Sure will," she said, but rather than heading back to her own bedroom, she walked me up to mine.

"You're sure you're all right?" she asked, hovering in the doorway.

"I will be once I take the hottest shower in the world."

Mom smiled again, but it was faint and kind of sad. And then her eyes drifted to my open closet, where my Cotillion dress was hanging in its plastic bag. "It's such a gorgeous dress," she said softly. "I just wish . . ."

I held my breath, waiting for the tears. But this time, Mom gave a tiny shake of her head and said, "Anyway. You'll be beautiful. Oh, and Miss Saylor called tonight. There's an extra—"

"An extra rehearsal on Monday, I know." Twisting behind me, I reached for the dress's zipper. "Amanda and Abigail told me."

Mom crossed the room, helping me unzip. "You know I think Cotillion is a wonderful thing, but sometimes I wonder if Saylor doesn't take it a little bit too seriously. Before she took it over, the girls had maybe three practices for the entire thing. Now it seems like you have three a week."

Last week we'd had four, but I didn't say that to Mom. "Miss Saylor just wants it to be perfect."

Mom pursed her lips, and for a second, it was like she was Old Mom again. The mom who laughed more, who had a weakness for gossip, who didn't wait up for me before it was even my curfew. "Pine Grove's Cotillion has been going on for nearly a hundred years, and there was never one hiccup until Saylor Stark took it over. Do you know how much mistletoe she makes the Junior League pay for? I tried to tell her that just because our town's Cotillion takes place a month before Christmas, there's no need to re-christen Magnolia House 'Mistletoe Manor.' That stuff is *expensive*."

Saylor Stark, with her gorgeous clothes and her silver hair and her impeccable manners, was kind of my hero. I mean, I put up with her nephew because I liked her so much. But it was nice having old, gossipy Mom back, so I nodded in sympathy. "She's also really strict about where we stand. That's what all the rehearsals are about. Making sure we're all standing in a perfect circle."

"Ridiculous," Mom said on a sigh. "Anyway, go take your shower and get some rest."

"Will do!" I said brightly, waiting until she shut the door to drop my grin. As soon as I heard her footsteps heading downstairs, I shimmied out of my wet dress and dashed into the shower. Once I was out, I threw on some flannel pajamas, snatched up my laptop, and headed into my walk-in closet. There was little chance of my mom coming back, but I didn't want to freak her out any more than I already had tonight. I was *not* going back to Dr. Greenbaum.

The first thing I did was Google "superhero," but that just got me a bazillion way too detailed Wikipedia entries on Marvel comics. A search for "Mr. Hall, janitor, Grove Academy" turned up absolutely nothing, which wasn't too surprising. What *was* surprising was that a search of "Michael DuPont, history teacher, Grove Academy" brought up only his faculty page on the Grove Academy website. That was weird. All of the Grove faculty are super accomplished; most of them are former college professors, and Googling any of them brings up either a book or paper they've published, or a lecture they've given at some academic conference. But there was nothing for Dr. DuPont. Almost like he hadn't existed before he came to the Grove last year.

Chill bumps broke out all over my body, and I reached up to pull a fluffy pink robe from a hanger. Wrapping it around me, I thought back to my fight with Dr. DuPont. He had called me something, some weird word I'd never heard before. "Pal" something.

I typed "superhero pal" into Google, but that just brought up some truly disturbing Batman/Robin fan fiction. So I tried "warrior pal." That got me a bunch of World of Warcraft sites. I sighed, scrolling down, about to give up when a word caught my eye: "Paladin."

That was it. That was the word he'd used. I clicked on the link and a definition popped up. "Paladin: an honorable knight; defender of a noble cause."

"Laaaaaame," I whispered. I much preferred superhero.

An hour later, I'd read pretty much everything the internet had to offer on the subject of Paladins and I was more confused than ever. The word was used to describe everything from high officials in the Catholic church to French knights to a class of warrior you could use in—ew—role-playing games.

But even with all the definitions, one thing remained the same. Paladins were warriors and protectors, charged with safeguarding a specific person or place.

That didn't sound particularly super. I slumped against the wall of my closet, pulling the robe tighter around me and burying my chin in it. Shouldn't I get to fly? Or at the very least, shoot laser beams out of my eyes?

Feeling like a complete moron, I stood up and focused as hard as I could on my closet door. No matter how hard I stared, no laser beams. I even tried muttering "laser" under my breath, but nothing.

That done, I gave a few experimental hops, trying to see if I could levitate even for a second. When that didn't work either, I briefly considered trying to jump out the window, but then I remembered Mom's expression when she'd found me in the pool.

So no lasers, no flying, but superstrength and an ability to kick some major ass. That was something.

I sat back down on the floor of my closet and turned to my computer. I had a couple of tabs open, and when I went to close the one about superheroes, a boldface paragraph caught my eye: "Perhaps the most defining characteristic of the superhero is a willingness to sacrifice for the good of others, even to the point of laying down his or her own life."

A shiver went through me. Mr. Hall had done that, apparently. And I knew that whole spiel about great responsibility coming with great power, but *dying* . . . that didn't seem worth a few measly superpowers. Even laser beam eyes weren't worth getting gutted by a scimitar-wielding history teacher.

But, I reminded myself, technically Mr. Hall hadn't been a superhero. He'd been a Paladin, and that was . . . different, right? And what—or who—had been his noble cause?

What was mine?

The next morning, I woke up early and drove to the library, checking out a bunch of DVDs. I spent the rest of the weekend holed up in my room with all three *Spider-Man* movies, the new *Superman*, and *X-Men* 1–3. I already owned *Batman Begins*, so I watched that, too.

Bee and Ryan both called my cell, and while I talked to Ryan, telling him I wasn't feeling so hot, I let Bee's calls go to voice mail. I felt awful doing it, but it was too risky to talk to her. Lying—okay, not *lying*, exactly—to Ryan was one thing, but Bee was tougher. She'd bought my whole "I got sick" thing Friday, but I'd been lucky. Normally, her Best-Friend Sensor was a lot more finely tuned than that. Besides, it might be too tempting to spill everything, and until I had a better handle on what was going on, that didn't seem like the best idea.

So I dedicated myself to my mission, and by the time Monday

morning rolled around, I had definitely figured some stuff out. First of all, I had gotten totally screwed on the "origin story" front. All superheroes have origin stories, like how Bruce Wayne's parents get killed and he goes to Tibet or whatever, and Superman is an alien, and Spider-Man had that radioactive spider. Me? I kissed a janitor in the school bathroom. Also, from *X-Men*, I learned that the people who seem to know what the eff is going on usually come find you, take you to a secure location, and tell you . . . well, what the eff is going on. So the way I saw it, some organization had clearly sent Mr. Hall to the Grove to protect something or someone. And Dr. DuPont had clearly come to the Grove to take that thing/kill that someone. And then that shadowy organization had fixed the bathroom with . . . um . . . magic or something (okay, so I wasn't clear on everything) so no one would know what happened.

Now, all I had to do was go to school and act normal and wait for them to find me.

Easy. Provided no one else tried to kill me, of course.

Usually, Ryan drove me to school, but when I called him Sunday night, I told him I was going to drive myself Monday.

"Okay," he replied, a little hesitant. "Is . . . Harper, is everything okay? I mean, I've hardly heard from you this weekend; you said you weren't feeling great . . ."

"I'm fine," I assured him. "It's just supposed to be really pretty tomorrow, and I haven't driven my car in, like, forever."

There was a pause, and I waited for Ryan to suggest I just pick him up instead. But then he sighed. "Right, I get that," he said at last. "No problem."

Still, when I hung up the phone, I couldn't shake this feeling that there *was* a problem. I pulled out my day planner, and on my list of weekly activities, added, "Spend more time with Ryan."

Seeing it written down made me feel better and I reminded myself that it wasn't like this was forever. As soon as I understood what had happened Friday night, I could move past it and get back to my normal life. Easy.

Monday *was* gorgeous, one of those perfect fall days that are kind of rare in Alabama. I drove to school with my windows down, the cool autumn air blowing my hair around my face. Now that I knew I wasn't crazy, I felt a lot better. Being a super-hero, or Paladin, or whatever, seemed like a natural extension of the stuff I already did. I mean, didn't I work my butt off to make the Grove a safe and fun place to be? Whatever was at the Grove that needed protecting, chances were I was already protecting it.

As I pulled into the sweet parking place I had by virtue of being SGA president, my good mood swelled. The school looked so beautiful under the bright blue October sky. The Grove was made up of four redbrick buildings with a large courtyard in the center. There were stone tables and benches in the courtyard where seniors ate lunch when the weather was nice. The trees surrounding the cluster of buildings were stunning shades of red and orange and gold, and when the bell tower chimed the half hour, I thought my heart might burst with pride.

I got out of the car, smoothing my hair and readjusting my green headband. Even though the Grove didn't have uniforms, we did have a really strict dress code that ensured everyone always looked nice: no jeans, no T-shirts, definitely no shorts. Today, I had worn one of my favorite outfits, a turtleneck the same green as my eyes, and a plaid skirt with brown knee-length boots and tights. I looked awesome and I knew it.

In fact, I thought it was my awesome outfit that was making people stare at me as I made my way from the parking lot. Then I noticed that they were . . . staring.

That's when I realized that the starers were all holding a bunch of papers stapled together—the school newspaper.

Clutching my books and tossing my head back, I forced a big smile and approached the nearest group. They were sophomores, so they were still a little scared of me. All three immediately went to hide the papers behind their backs.

"Hi!" I said brightly, hugging my bag tightly to my chest.

"Hi," they chorused back. The one in the middle reminded me a little bit of Bee, all fluffy blond hair and big dark eyes, and I was sure I'd seen the other two around campus. Yes, the one on the right—a tall redhead wearing a skirt just a little bit too short—had tried out for cheerleading last spring.

None of the three met my eyes.

"So, is there something in that paper that I should know about?" I asked, trying to sound friendly and jokey. "It's not a hideously unflattering picture of me after cheerleading practice, is it? Or me shrieking at the SGA?"

Translation: I am head cheerleader and SGA president, and I could destroy you all if I wanted to. And that's not even bringing my superpowers into it. I had never used my popularity for evil before—but I'd never been gaped at either. So I figured there was no harm in putting a little of the fear of God into these girls.

The girl on the left cracked first. She was tiny and had white-blond hair, and her blue eyes were huge as she looked up at me. "It's just the . . . uh, special Homecoming edition of *The Grove News*."

My smile froze in place. Surely, he wouldn't have.

"Can I see it?" I asked, still grinning, still upbeat.

The one who looked like Bee shook her head ever so slightly at the tiny girl, but she was already handing me the paper. I took it with trembling hands.

My worst fears were confirmed.

There, on the front page of the special Homecoming edition of *The Grove News*, was a huge, albeit blurry, picture of me leaning on Bee, clearly sobbing my eyes out, as we made our way out of the girls' bathroom. It looked like it had probably been taken with a cell phone, and the headline read, "It's Her Party and She'll Cry If She Wants To?" Under the picture of me and Bee, there was a smaller caption: *Homecoming Queen misses crowning under mysterious circumstances.* My eyes darted over the rest of the article as my heart started pounding. ". . . *hiding in the boys' room . . . violently ill . . . tension between the 'Queen Bee' and her underling, Bee Franklin . . . this reporter . . .*"

By now, I had sort of started hyperventilating as my eyes zeroed in on the byline in bold letters.

David Stark.

Who I was now going to *murder*.

Chapter 6

IT WASN'T just the humiliation of having the entire school know that I was puking and crying in the bathroom during Homecoming, or the veiled insinuations that I'd been sick because I was pregnant or on drugs. It was that the school probably already knew that Mr. Hall and Dr. DuPont were missing. And sure, that bathroom had looked spotless, but it's not like I'd done a sweep for DNA. For all I knew, the police were in Headmaster Dunn's office right now, with big folders full of evidence that two men had died in the girls' bathroom last Friday, and asking if anyone was displaying any "strange behavior." And, oh, look! Here was a convenient picture of me sobbing around the girls' bathroom.

"Are you okay?" the tall sophomore asked. "You look kinda . . . purple."

I snapped my head up and smiled, or at least pressed my teeth together in the semblance of a smile. "I'm fine," I said, but my voice was way too loud. "This is just a silly misunderstanding between me and David. Can I keep this?"

"Sure," the shorter girl who'd handed me the paper said.

"Thanks so much!" I turned around and headed straight for Wallace Hall.

Before I'd gone more than a few steps, I heard Ryan call my name. He was jogging over from the parking lot, a bunch of papers crumpled in his hand. "Hey!" he said once he'd caught up to me. One hand cupping my elbow, he leaned down, studying me. "Are you okay?"

"Of course," I said, trying to look more okay and less homicidal.

"Why didn't you tell me you were sick Friday night?"

"It was nothing," I insisted, shifting my backpack to my other shoulder. "And I didn't want to make a big deal about it. Honestly. This is just another one of David Stark's jerk moves. I can handle it."

Ryan clenched his jaw, looking up toward Wallace Hall. "What is that dude's problem?"

"He's a jackass."

Not taking his eyes off the building, Ryan shook his head. A muscle worked in his jaw and he shoved the sleeves of his dark blue sweater up his forearms. "No, it's more than that. He's always been like this with you, ever since we were little. Back in middle school, I thought maybe he had a thing for you, but—"

"First of all, I highly doubt that. Secondly, sometimes people are just . . . I don't know, born mean or something."

Glancing back down at me, Ryan gave a half-smile. "Maybe. Want me to go kick his ass?"

Ryan was joking; I think the closest he'd ever been to a fight was watching UFC with his brother on Saturday nights. But as soon as he said it, it was like someone had punched me in the stomach, an almost overwhelming sense of *wrongness* washed over me. "No!" I yelped, and Ryan startled.

"Whoa, Harper, I was kidding." He held both hands up in mock surrender. "I'm a lover, not a fighter."

That weird, nauseous sensation subsided, and I rubbed my temples. "I know, sorry. Anyway, let me go talk to David, and I'll see you at lunch, okay?"

"Sure you don't want me to go with you?" An auburn curl fell over Ryan's forehead as he ducked his head to meet my eyes, concern all over his face.

But the idea of him coming with me to see David sent my stomach roiling again. I managed to give a little laugh. "No, I've got this."

Ryan dropped a kiss on my cheek and gave my elbow one last squeeze. "You always do."

He headed across the quad, broad shoulders held back, long legs striding across the grass, and I turned back to Wallace Hall. I don't know what I looked like, but it must have been pretty scary, because everyone was quick to jump out of my way. Most of them were holding papers, though, so they probably all thought I was about to have a nervous breakdown right in front of them. Which actually was a good thing. After that weird thing with Ryan, a lot of my anger had died down. Hearing people whisper behind my back powered it right back up.

As I pushed open the heavy door, I mentally called David Stark every bad word I could think of.

By the time I reached the journalism lab, it felt like sparks were exploding from my head. There were a few articles taped to the door, and even in my rage, I saw that almost all of them had David's byline. Gritting my teeth, I stepped inside.

Thanks to all of the computers lining the back wall, the classroom felt a lot warmer than the hall. No one was working at the computers now, and there were only three people in the room. David was sitting on a desk, laughing with two other newspaper staffers, Michael Goldberg and Chie Kurata.

I'd planned out this whole speech in my head amidst all the bad words—yay, multitasking!—about how what he'd done was not only personally offensive to me, but demoralizing and degrading to the school, because when we make one of us look bad, we *all* look bad. And honestly, how did he expect to get away with this kind of crap? He had to have written the article and printed up the paper over the weekend. That meant he'd done it behind Mrs. Laurent's back, and that had to be a detention-worthy offense at the very least.

But something about seeing him sitting on top of a desk, eating yogurt and laughing with his friends made me snap. I could feel my face get red, and this intense, trembly feeling rose up from the middle of my chest. My intelligent and calm speech flew right out of my head.

"WTF, David?" I asked, storming into the room and throwing the paper on the nearest desk.

He at least had the good grace to look chagrined. "Harper—"

"No!" I said, or at least I meant to say. It came out a little shriek and Michael flinched and looked at his feet. Chie, a pretty, petite Asian girl who'd transferred to our school just this year, raised her eyebrows so high they disappeared underneath her heavy black bangs.

David stood and put his hands up in front of him in the universal sign for "calm the heck down."

But there was no stopping me now. "Why would you do this?" I gestured angrily at the paper. Just over David's head, there was a poster featuring a typewriter and the quote "Journalism Is History on the Run," and I made myself stare at that rather than meet his gaze. Man, laser eyes really would've come in handy now.

He sighed and ran a hand through his hair. He was always doing that, which is why he usually looked like he'd been electrocuted by fourth period. "It was a valid story, Pres," he finally said. "Something was definitely wrong with you that night and I think the student body of the Grove has the right to know if their golden girl is hiding something."

"No, they don't," I fired back. "What was going on that night was none of your business!"

"I was involved that night too, Harper."

"Um, you held my hair while I puked. I don't think that exactly makes you a major player in the night's events, David."

"You held her hair?" Chie asked. She had slid down into one of the desks, twisting around to face us.

He glanced over at her, his mouth turning down with impatience. "Yeah, but that's not the point."

He turned back to me, and he didn't look even a little bit sorry anymore. "When I see a story that affects the school, it's my journalistic duty to report it."

I laughed. "Your *journalistic duty?* Look around you, David." I snatched up the paper from the desk, gesturing around the tiny, hot room with its posters of famous dead journalists and lame quotes. "You write for the tiniest school paper ever. This"— I rattled the paper—"is a glorified newsletter. You don't even send it to a real printer. You just print copies off the secretary's computer! Don't you get it? No one wants you to dig up corruption in the SGA, or uncover health violations in the cafeteria, or write nasty stories about a girl who works hard to make the Grove an awesome place for everyone, even total jackasses like you. I can't believe you would do something like this when—"

I broke off. I was breathing hard, and the paper was crumpled in my hand. Michael had gone to one of the computers, his back to us, but his shoulders tight and his ears nearly as red as his hair. Chie was still sitting in her desk, stunned. Truth be told, I felt kind of stunned, too. I mean, I hardly ever lost my temper, and I'd certainly never done it in public. But here I was, panting, sweaty, my hands smudged with ink. My face was on fire, and I could feel some of my hair sticking to my cheeks and neck.

Was this part of being a Paladin/superhero? Was I like the Hulk, only sweaty instead of green? What was wrong with me?

Okay, I mean, obviously I was freaked out that David's little exposé might get me, um, *thrown in jail forever*, but my anger seemed to run deeper than that. What had I been about to say to him? *I can't believe you'd do something like this when . . .*

When you were nice to me that night.

That's what I had been about to say. I was angry because David Stark had hurt my feelings. I took a deep breath and dropped the paper onto the nearest desk. Then I carefully smoothed my hair away from my face and willed my blood pressure back to a non-stroke level. I straightened my shoulders and looked at David with haughty disdain.

"Anyway," I said, "I expect a printed retraction and apology in the next issue."

David folded his arms over his chest and grinned, clearly deciding to battle haughty disdain with snarky nonchalance. Well, his posture was snarky nonchalance at least, but his eyes were practically burning. "Expect it all you want, Pres. I stand by that story."

If I hadn't already been so rattled, I wouldn't have said what I said next. But David had pushed so many of my buttons that I just smirked back. "Retract it, or I am going to file a formal complaint with the school board."

The grin faltered.

"It would be the second one, right? Didn't someone on the debate team file in September after you accused him of cheating?" I rolled my eyes upward, like I was trying to remember something. "And didn't your aunt say something like if you got one more demerit, she was making you resign from the paper? I seem to recall her mentioning it to my mom at Cotillion practice."

The look of naked fear that skittered across his face made me feel sick. So did the sound of my voice. I sounded so much like Leigh-Anne.

He made me do it, I told myself. *You're not a mean girl, but he made you be one.*

David recovered quickly, but his grin was ugly now. "Fair enough, Pres. Next issue."

"Thank you."

I cleared my throat and picked up my book bag. As I turned to go, David called out, "Harper?"

"What?"

He took a minute, like he was trying to decide if he should say whatever it was he wanted to say. I wondered if he felt like I had, like he didn't want to say something hateful, but I'd made him.

"You know, all the articles aside, I actually thought you were better than this," he finally said. "Nice to know that you *are* just another high school bitch."

Maybe it was that his words were so close to what Dr. DuPont had said right before he nearly murdered me. Maybe it was because a little part of me felt like David might be right. Or maybe it was because I just really didn't like to be called names. Whatever the reason, my right hand shot up to slap David Stark across the face. I didn't even consider my new superpowers, and if those new powers would mean David's head would go flying off.

But it didn't matter. Half an inch from David's cheek, my hand stopped in midair. And it wasn't because I had some crisis of conscience, either. It was like my hand hit an invisible wall right by his head.

He had flinched in anticipation of the slap, but now he opened his eyes and looked at my palm as it hovered next to his face. I wasn't sure which one of us looked more surprised.

I drew back my hand a little, then pushed it forward again. Again, my hand stopped like there was Plexiglas between my hand and his head.

I tried the left hand, making David raise his shoulders and shut his eyes again, but the same thing happened, so now I was standing in front of him with my hands poised on either side of his face.

This time when he opened his eyes, he looked at my hands in confusion. "Um . . . Harper? Are you gonna hit me or not?"

I stood there, looking at my hands and at his face between them. I still really wanted to hit him, but it was obvious that I wasn't going to be able to.

So I dropped my hands and raised my chin. "No, I'm not." I let my tone say, *Because I am totally a better person than you* and hoped he hadn't noticed the fact that my hands didn't seem to work when it came to slapping his face.

"Ooookay," he said slowly, and I heard someone stifle a giggle behind him, so I had a feeling this bizarre little story would run right next to my apology next week.

"I'll see y'all later," I mumbled, grabbing my book bag and trying not to run out of the room.

The bell rang as I ran down the hall, passing the bathrooms. There was no police tape across the doors, so that was a good thing. As I turned the corner to go down the history hall, I glanced in Dr. DuPont's room. Mrs. Hillyard, a substitute teacher

I'd had a few times, was standing at the front of the class. All the stuff in the garden had pretty much convinced me that my fight with Dr. DuPont had been real, but I was still super relieved to see Mrs. Hillyard. There had been a tiny (okay, not that tiny) part of my brain that had been terrified of coming to school and finding Dr. DuPont and Mr. Hall there like nothing had happened.

But they were definitely gone and I was definitely a superhero . . . er, Paladin. Hadn't that thing with David proved it? If I was guardian and protector of the Grove, I couldn't just run around slapping people in the face. My body actually wouldn't allow it; that's how good I was now.

Or maybe it was just David.

That thought leapt into my brain and I stopped in my tracks. Hadn't the Paladin definition said that we were guardians of places or *people*? But why would David need a Paladin unless there was some group dedicated to removing the world of self-righteous jerks, in which case I was *totally* on the wrong side?

Then it occurred to me that there was a pretty easy way of figuring out if it was just David I couldn't hurt or people in general.

I looked around until I saw Brandon by his locker. "Bran!" I called, waving him over. I kind of felt bad about doing this experiment on Brandon. It felt like slapping a puppy. A dumb, perverted puppy, but a puppy nonetheless.

Brandon looked as concerned as he was able to. "Hey, Harper. You okay? The paper said you were sick Friday night, and Bee said she didn't hear from you this weekend, and—"

"I'm fine," I said with a wave of my hand. "Food poisoning. Anyway, would you mind if I tried out an, uh, experiment on you?"

His face brightened and he gave me a look that I guess was supposed to be sexy, but was vaguely stupid instead. "Does this experiment involve nakedness?" he asked, leaning one shoulder against the lockers.

"Brandon, your best friend is my boyfriend. And *my* best friend is *your* girlfriend."

He shrugged, flipping his hair out of his eyes. Brandon's hair was a few shades darker than Bee's, more gold than blond, and while I guess he was attractive in a clean-cut jock kind of way, I'd never go for his type. Too many muscles, too few brain cells. "And?"

Well, at least now I wouldn't feel bad about hitting him. I raised my hand and brought it down on his cheek with a really satisfying SMACK.

He yelped and a bunch of people in the hall turned to stare.

"Sorry!" I said. "You, um . . . there was a bug. Okay, see you later, bye!"

I dashed into my first period class, my hand stinging and my mind whirling. Normally, first period AP European History was my favorite class, but that day, I didn't even take notes. I spent most of the time wondering why I'd been able to slap Brandon and not David. If I was Paladin for the Grove, I shouldn't have been able to hit any of its students.

I wrote in my notebook, *"B said offensive thing, so could be hit as he is jerk."*

That made sense. But then I wrote, *"D also said offensive thing—called me bitch. But could not hit."*

Then under that, *"But you were a bitch to D, so deserved it, so D not jerk, so could not hit."*

Hmmm . . .

Clearly, I needed a test subject, someone totally innocent. If I couldn't hit him or her, then I was right, and it was my job to protect the Grove. If I could . . . ugh, I did not want to think about that.

I glanced around until my eyes landed on Liz Walker. She was sitting one desk over and up from me. I had several classes with her, but we weren't exactly friends. She ran with a group some of us called "the churchy people." Other, less-nice people called them "the Jesus freaks." Basically, if I were looking for one of the nicest people at the Grove, Liz was it.

So that's why I *did* feel bad when I fished a pen out of my bag and chucked it at her, figuring that if I were Paladin of the Grove, it would stop about an inch from all that shiny blond hair.

It didn't.

I flinched as the pen smacked Liz right in the back of her head. She gave a startled cry and whirled around, hand on her head, eyes full of not-so-churchy anger.

"Harper?"

My teacher, Mrs. Ford, was looking at me with total confusion. "Harper," she said again, "did you just . . . did you just throw a pen at Liz?"

Now the whole class was looking at me. I turned on my best smile and said, "Oh my gosh, no, Mrs. Ford! I was just . . . um . . . writing really fast because there was so much information to take in, and I had, like, some lotion? On my hands? Anyway, the pen flew out of my hand and hit Liz." I turned to Liz. "Really sorry about that. Total accident."

"It's okay," Liz said, but she was scowling and rubbing the back of her head.

Mrs. Ford was watching me like I had just sprouted a second head, but she eventually shrugged and said, "Well, be more careful."

"Will do!" I chirped. Then I turned back to my notebook, my heart pounding and my mouth dry. Holy crap.

I had a noble cause, all right. But it wasn't Grove Academy.

It was David Stark.

Chapter 7

I SPENT the next three classes pretty out of it. For the first time in history, I took absolutely no notes. I just sat and stared and thought.

Mr. Hall had been protecting David. Dr. DuPont had been trying to kill David. I now had to protect David. Other people would probably try to kill him. But why? I mean, yes, David Stark was annoying, but that didn't make him worth *killing*. And if Mr. Hall had been protecting him, had he chosen to? Because I sure as heck hadn't chosen this. What would happen if I just . . . didn't? Or could I pass the powers on to someone else?

By the time the bells rang for lunch, one thing was abundantly clear to me:

I needed my mentor-person *right now*. I had figured out as much as I possibly could, so it was time for my Giles or my Professor X or whoever to get here and start explaining.

I slung my bag over my shoulder and started heading to lunch when it occurred to me that it wasn't like my Giles/Professor X could just come sashaying into the cafeteria amidst a hundred teenagers. No, I'd have to be on my own.

The problem was—where? The Grove was so small that there were very few places without students lurking. I stood on the steps of Wallace Hall, looking down at the courtyard, which was already filling up. Any minute now, Ryan, Bee, and Brandon would be here. I looked over to Nash, the building that housed the cafeteria and the fine arts classrooms—and the only building on campus that even *I* had to admit was ugly, all short and squat—and saw Bee coming out the door, a Styrofoam box in her hand. Amanda, Abigail, and Mary Beth were all surrounding her, and she was looking over her shoulder and laughing at someone behind her. Brandon, probably, which meant Ryan wasn't far behind.

For a second, I thought about going over to meet them. I even started down the steps. But when I got to the bottom, instead of heading across the courtyard, I found myself turning left and heading for the chapel that was in the very back corner of campus. Of course! The chapel was only used for assemblies, so it was deserted most of the time. Plus, the back of it faced the woods. If ever there were a perfect place to wait for superhero instructions, that was it.

The chapel was actually really pretty, and it was a shame that we didn't use it very often. It was built out of pale gray stone, and there were stained-glass windows running down each side. As I walked around toward the back, I decided that at the next SGA meeting, I would definitely bring up ways we could use it more. Maybe something at Christmas. Provided I would still *be* on SGA. What if my Professor X person said I had to quit all my extracurricular stuff? Or what if I had to leave school altogether?

If I had powers, would I have to go to some other school for kids who had them, too? Were there any other kids who—

I came to a sudden stop as I reached the back of the chapel. There, sitting on the steps where I'd planned on waiting for my mentor-person, was David Stark.

"Ugh, no!" I cried without really thinking. I'm pretty sure I even stamped my foot.

David's blue eyes widened. "Harper?" he mumbled around a mouthful of sandwich.

"What are you doing here?" I asked, pushing my shoulders back.

He swallowed and stood up, dusting his hands on his pants. He opened his mouth like he was going to say something, but before he could, he suddenly winced, pressing his fingers against his temple.

I immediately took a step forward. "What's wrong?"

David blinked a couple of times, fingers moving against his forehead. "Headache. I've had one for like a week now. Probably spending too much time in front of the computer." Reaching into his pocket, he pulled out a tiny packet of aspirin. As he tore it open with his teeth, he glanced over at me. "Anyway, that's why I'm here. Lunchroom was too loud. So what are *you* doing out here, Pres? Why aren't you eating lunch with your court?"

Darn it, why hadn't I thought up a reason to be out here in case I bumped into anyone?

But then the perfect excuse came to me. I looked down and scraped the dirt with my boot heel. "I just couldn't deal with all the questions about that article you wrote. I was embarrassed."

David watched me for a long moment and I studied him right back. I wanted to see something, anything, that would make David Stark look like someone who needed to be protected by supernatural bodyguards, but he seemed to be a normal high school boy, albeit one with truly terrible fashion sense. Today he was wearing worn-out corduroys with a bright green T-shirt and a too-small navy blazer.

Who are you? I thought. What the heck is so important about David Freaking Stark?

He laughed, startling me. I was so used to David scowling that it was kind of weird to see so many of his teeth. "God, you're the worst liar I have ever seen," he said. "First the whole stage fright thing, now this 'I was embarrassed' act . . ."

"I *was* embarrassed!" I shouted back, but he just kept on laughing. I picked up a small rock and tossed it at him, but it came to a skidding stop six inches from him, and dropped back to the ground. Luckily, David was so caught up in laughing at me that he didn't notice. I'd known it wasn't actually going to hit him, but still, it felt good just to throw something. Then I remembered my Professor Giles X could be watching me right now, and probably wouldn't approve of me slinging rocks at the guy I was clearly supposed to protect.

"I just don't see why the eff that's so funny," I muttered, just in case that person was listening. At least they'd know I'd had just cause.

David's laughter trailed off and he looked at me with genuine curiosity. "Why do you do that?"

"Do what?" I tucked an errant strand of hair back into my headband.

"Say 'eff' or 'G. D.' Why not say the actual words?"

I heaved a sigh and glanced toward the woods. If my Professor Giles X was out there, there was no chance he was coming now. So much for alone time.

I turned back to David. "I just don't think it's . . . necessary to use those words in polite company when there are so many perfectly good euphemisms."

David stared at me. "Dear God, what planet are you from?"

I threw up my hands. "Forget it, okay? I wouldn't expect you to understand anyway. Just like you don't understand why the Grove is important to me, or why I might not want my personal issues blasted all over your stupid newspaper, or why I might have wanted to eat lunch by myself for once."

Oh God, I was doing it again, that shouty, kind of scary thing I seemed to do whenever I had to talk to David for more than five minutes. I needed to go. This idea had obviously been a bust, and there was still plenty of lunch left to hang out with Ryan.

Speaking of whom . . . I pulled my phone out of my bag and saw that, sure enough, Ryan had sent me a text message five minutes earlier. "Where R U?" Then another one from three minutes ago. "R U OK?"

"I gotta go," I said, but David caught my arm before I got very far.

This close, I could see the faint blond stubble on his chin, and when he opened his mouth, I noticed the tiniest chip in his front tooth. "Harper, look, I just want to say . . . earlier today, that whole thing with . . . what I called you, and—"

"No problem," I said, waving my hand, my eyes still on my cell phone as it started blaring "Sexy Back," Ryan's ringtone (he had picked it himself). I didn't really want to answer it when I'd be seeing him in just a few minutes. Plus I didn't want to lie to him in front of David, giving him even more ammo against me. I could just hear him. "Why did you lie to your boyfriend about where you were? Why are you really out here? Did you by any chance murder Dr. DuPont?"

Okay, so that last one was a long shot, but I was not in the mood to deal.

I looked at David, not even trying to hide my irritation as "Sexy Back" finally stopped. "It's fine, okay? I shouldn't have said that stuff about the school board and your aunt. I'm . . . I'm sorry."

My phone started ringing again. Ryan must've been really worried. "Now, I really have to go."

But David wasn't letting go so easily, not of the subject and not of my arm.

"Fine, but what was up with you not hitting me? It didn't look like you didn't want to, it looked like you *couldn't*."

Great, so he had noticed that. "David, look, we can talk about this later, but my boyfriend is looking for me, and I have to go—"

"Harper?"

Oh, *shoot*. I turned just as Ryan rounded the corner. He was holding his cell phone in one hand, a look of total confusion on his face.

"Ryan," I said, trying to make myself smile. I guess I thought if I just smiled a lot, Ryan wouldn't think there was anything unusual about me arguing behind the chapel with David.

But Ryan wasn't even looking at me. He was glaring at David, towering over him by at least four inches. "What the hell is going on?"

David dropped his hand. "Nothing, man," he said to Ryan. "We were just talking about the paper. That's it."

Ryan was looking between us, an unfamiliar expression on his face. It took me a second to realize that he was angry. More than angry, really. He was furious. And Ryan *never* lost his temper.

"Why can't you just leave her alone?" he asked David. Ryan's jaw was clenched, and I'd never seen his hazel eyes look that cold. "I mean, other than being better than you in every class, what has Harper ever done to you?"

David must have been as weirded out by Angry Ryan as I was, because for once, he didn't have a smartass response. His skin went a little pale, and I could see the whites around his blue eyes. "Look, I'm sorry. You're right, I've been a dick, but I swear to God, I wasn't bothering her. I was sitting here first, and she just—"

"Save it," Ryan said, holding up a hand. "Whatever your little war on Harper is about, it's over. I don't want you to write one more damn word about her. I don't want you to talk to her. I don't even want you to *look* at her."

I knew that Ryan was trying to protect me, and maybe I should've been thrilled to watch my boyfriend go all alpha male for me, but instead I felt . . . irritated. "Ryan, I told you I could handle this."

"But you haven't," he fired back, his voice unnaturally loud in the quiet behind the church. The breeze had died down, and there wasn't even the rustle of leaves. It was hard to believe that only a few hundred feet away, kids were eating lunch, talking, laughing. "This guy is a jerk, and you've just taken it for years. I get that you're sucking up to his aunt, and that you want to be nice to people, Harper, but damn. You don't have to be a doormat."

"I'm not sucking up!" I said, just as David moved forward, saying, "Take it easy, Ryan—"

And then everything exploded.

Ryan, sweet Ryan, who had never purposely hurt anyone, shot a hand out to push David away, and suddenly, it was like a screen dropped in front of my eyes. I could see Ryan's hand hit David's chest, saw David stumble back as his glasses flew off.

I saw his head hit the edge of the stone steps of the chapel, blood erupting from underneath his sandy hair. I saw his blue eyes roll up until all I could see were the whites.

Then the vision vanished.

I was moving before I even really knew it, just like with Dr. DuPont. My hand shot out and caught Ryan's wrist, his hand just inches from David's chest. I yanked Ryan's arm down as my knee came up, catching him in the stomach. While he was bent over from that, I leaned down and put my shoulder into his chest and, still holding his arm, flipped him over my back. All six feet three inches, two hundred pounds of him.

He landed on his back. As he landed, I straightened up and put my foot on his throat, pressing down slightly. My fingers were tight around his wrist, and some inner knowledge told me that if I pulled up and twisted in a certain way, I'd break it, along with a few bones in his hand.

And if David hadn't shouted my name, I probably would have.

It was like waking up from a dream. I looked down and saw Ryan's wide, panicked eyes, my boot against his neck. I saw the shocked look on David's face.

"What the hell?" Ryan squeaked, and I immediately dropped his arm, stumbling a few steps back.

Getting superpowers was supposed to be a good thing. You helped people. You didn't nearly twist your boyfriend's hand off.

David was leaning down, helping Ryan to his feet, but all I could do was stand there, numb. That feeling I'd had when I was fighting Dr. DuPont, like I wasn't even in control of my body. *Then* it had been cool. But this? So out of control that I'd hurt someone I loved? That was terrifying.

"Pres?" David asked hesitantly. Both he and Ryan stood there, waiting for me to say something. Dozens of excuses ran through my mind. New energy drink. New, high-tech cheerleading moves. But in the end, no words came out of my mouth, and I just did the easiest thing I could think of.

I ran.

From behind me, I heard someone call my name, but whether it was Ryan or David, I didn't know.

Or care.

I didn't stop to get my bag, which meant that I couldn't drive home, but I knew I had to get out of there.

Stopping just outside the gates, I looked left, then right. The Grove was located in one of the town's nicer neighborhoods, full of tree-lined streets and big houses. My own house was a good three miles away and to the left. So I turned to the right.

I had no idea where I was going, so I figured I'd keep walking until my mentor found me, or the cops came after me for assaulting Ryan.

A cool breeze ruffled my hair and blew my skirt against my legs as leaves skittered down the sidewalk. I didn't realize that I'd started crying until the wind cooled the tears on my cheeks.

"It'll be okay," I mumbled out loud, adding talking to myself to the list of crazy things I'd done today. Not that I cared. "It'll be okay," I said again, louder this time, and the more I thought about it, the more convinced I was that it really would be.

All right, so my superpowers had flipped out on me and nearly made me hurt Ryan. But he and David were the only people who had seen it. Ryan loved me. He'd forgive me as soon as I came up with a reason for what happened. Preferably one that didn't sound completely insane.

And David . . .

If there had been any doubt in my mind that David Stark was involved in whatever was going on with me, it was gone now. I'd flipped Ryan to keep David safe. And something told me that if Ryan hadn't been joking about kicking David's ass earlier, I would have done that ninja thing on him then, too.

But why? That was the thing that didn't make any sense. Okay, it was one of the many, many things about this that didn't make any sense, but it was definitely the most pressing. The *why* would lead to the *who* and the *how*. And that meant I didn't have time for this middle of the sidewalk pity party I was currently throwing. I had to get back to the Grove, and I had to talk to—

Suddenly, pain slammed into my chest, like someone punched me in the sternum. It was so intense that I gasped. Then, as quickly as it had come, it was gone, leaving behind a heavy pressure that made me wonder if my lungs had been replaced with bricks.

I stood there, my hands clenched at my sides, sucking in deep breaths. I had felt this way before.

Right before Dr. DuPont burst through that bathroom door.

"Pres?"

The pain had crowded so much of my mind that I hadn't heard David's Dodge pull up alongside me, which meant I had been *really* out of it, because that thing had to have a hole in the muffler or something.

"Oh God, *seriously?*"

"Look, let me give you a ride home, okay? It isn't safe for you to be walking here by yourself."

The heavy feeling intensified. "Um, David, hate to break it to you," I said, trying to sound normal even though my breathing was speeding up, "but this isn't exactly a rough neighborhood. I think I can avoid getting raped and murdered on someone's croquet lawn, okay?"

He leaned across the passenger seat and for the first time, I saw that he looked genuinely worried. Maybe even a little scared. "Harper—" he started to say.

I stepped down from the sidewalk, and leaned forward, my hands resting on the open passenger window. "What's wrong?"

"It's *that car.*" His eyes darted to his rearview mirror and I turned to look over my shoulder. About a hundred yards away, a black car with tinted windows idled at a stop sign. I figured the suffocating feeling in my chest had something to do with it, and *that* meant it was probably not filled with good guys.

"The car was outside the school when I left," David said in a voice barely above a whisper, like the people in the car could hear us. "It's been following you."

Adrenaline started flooding through my system as I turned back to David and said, "Get out of here. Now. Drive—"

But before I could finish, the black car revved its engine with a roar that drowned out David's crappy Dodge.

And then it was racing straight at us.

Chapter 8

IT WASN'T like I had a lot of time to think about what to do next, so I went with instinct.

I dove through David's open passenger window and scrambled onto his lap.

I know, I know. Between that and the head-butting, I was going to get my southern belle title revoked. But I knew what I needed to do, and it was faster to drive the damn car myself than try to explain it to David. And I knew he couldn't move into the passenger seat in enough time. That black car would be on us in seconds.

David made a sound that was somewhere between shock and outrage as I grabbed the wheel and placed my foot on top of his on the accelerator.

The Dodge rattled, and squealed, and thunked, but, thank God, it lurched forward just as the black car's front grille kissed our bumper. The shock was still enough to send me flying painfully into the steering wheel, and David into my back.

"What the hell?" David yelled in my ear.

My eyes still on the street, I reached down with one hand and unfastened David's seat belt. "Scoot!" I hollered over the clunking of the car and the rush of wind pouring through the open passenger window.

We were hurtling down the oak-lined avenue, branches forming a leafy arch overhead. My hands were slick with sweat as I clutched the steering wheel, and my calf muscle was already aching from how hard I was mashing David's foot on the gas pedal. There was still a trace of that disconnected feeling I'd had when fighting Dr. DuPont and Ryan, like I wasn't completely in control of my body, but this time, I was definitely feeling more there, if that makes any sense.

I glanced in the rearview mirror and saw that the black car was only a few feet behind us. We'd gotten a head start, but they were driving a much better car. Already, the Dodge was shuddering like its frame was about to fly into pieces, and we were only going seventy miles an hour.

Then it occurred to me that we were going seventy miles an hour on a street where the speed limit was twenty-five. I sent up a quick prayer that there were no little kids riding bikes anywhere nearby, and pressed my foot down even harder.

David gave a grunt of pain as my heel dug into his foot. "Sorry!" I yelled. "But come on! Scoot!"

I could tell he was trying to get out from under me, but the only way to do it quickly (and so I could maintain our speed *and* my concentration) would be to actually put his hands under my butt, lift me off him, and slide. Instead, he was trying to slide out from under me without touching my butt, or hips, or really any area that could be considered inappropriate.

That wasn't going so well. It's not like I weigh very much—I'm maybe a buck ten—but David is a slight guy, and I was pretty firmly wedged onto his lap. While I appreciated this rare show of chivalrous behavior, now was not the time for David to worry about my delicate sensibilities.

Especially since I'd just realized this was a dead-end street.

"Scoot, scoot, SCOOT!" I yelled at David.

"I AM SCOOTING!" he shouted back.

Then he looked out the windshield and saw the same thing I had: the large grove of trees at the end of the street that we were headed straight for. At seventy-five miles an hour.

He used three different versions of the F-word, and before I knew it, his hands were on my butt and he was sliding into the passenger seat. I landed on the nubby seat with a grateful sigh. Now the steering wheel wasn't pressed into my chest, and David's bony knees weren't cutting into the back of my thighs. Cheap upholstery had never felt so good.

David was several inches taller than me, so I had to slide down a little to maintain my pressure on the accelerator, but we never swerved or dropped our speed.

"Thank you!" I said, but David didn't seem to hear me. He was running a shaking hand over his paper-white face and mumbling to himself.

"Buckle up!" I shouted.

That he heard. I buckled my seat belt, too, and then looked over at him as the trees got closer and closer.

"Why are you smiling?" he shouted, terror all over his face.

I was smiling? I could see my reflection in his glasses, and he was right. I was smiling kind of big, actually. And then I realized why. Because even though this was scary and dangerous and so, so illegal . . .

It was fun. I felt in my element and in charge. I'm always happiest when I'm excelling at something, and, to quote one of those World of Warcraft websites I'd stumbled onto, these bad guys were about to get *pwned*.

The smile turned into a laugh as I gripped the steering wheel tight in my left hand and reached down with my right.

"I've always wanted to do this!" I shouted.

The end of the street was only a few dozen yards away. The black car was right behind us.

I pushed down as hard as I could with both feet on the brake pedal, and at the same time, I jerked the emergency brake up and spun the car hard to the left.

And it worked! Okay, so it wasn't a total success. The black car was so close to us that it hit us as we spun, crunching in the back door on my side. David gave a low groan, but whether that was for his car or the fact that we had been literally seconds from death, I wasn't sure.

The rear of the car fishtailed, taking out at least three mailboxes as I righted the Dodge and sped off in the opposite direction, back toward the Grove. I had an idea.

I glanced in the rearview mirror and saw the black car had done a similar spin and was now following us again, although we had a much bigger lead this time.

It wasn't going to last long, though. I could see sparks shooting up from the rear tire. It had probably gotten crunched along with the back door. The Dodge also seemed to have trouble shifting into fifth gear, and I heard a grinding sound that couldn't be good. I only hoped I had enough time . . .

We shot down the street, the car wobbling now and much harder to control. We passed one house where a woman in a flowery shirt and hot pink capri pants dropped her garden hose and stared at us in openmouthed shock. I cringed. Mrs. Harris, who was in the Junior League with my mom. I really hoped she hadn't recognized me.

We passed the Grove, and I was super thankful there was no one loitering outside the gates.

"Two more miles, two more miles," I muttered to myself. The Dodge was only going around fifty miles an hour now, and the black car was gaining on us.

Another sound caught my attention over the rushing wind and dying car. "Sexy Back" was playing somewhere. Somewhere nearby.

I looked around until I spotted my book bag at David's feet. "You got my bag?"

By this point, David was huddled against the passenger door, staring at me with naked horror. He shook his head, like he hadn't understood the question before blinking a few times and saying, "Oh . . . um, yeah. I thought you might need it."

"Why did you follow me?"

David looked over his shoulder at the black car. "Huh? Oh, well . . . I wanted to, uh, ask you some more questions about what the hell is going on with you." He turned back around and wiped his glasses on the bottom of his T-shirt. "Of course, *I* thought you were on drugs. I didn't realize you were actually an assassin or something."

He was lying, I could tell. Maybe it was a Paladin thing, or maybe I was finally seeing through him the way he always seemed to see through me.

"Bull," I said.

"What?" He looked at me with wide eyes.

"Bull," I repeated. "You didn't want to ask me more questions about the paper. Why did you follow me?"

"I'm not lying!" he insisted, glancing behind him again.

"Yes," I said calmly, even as the black car got closer, "you are. Why did you follow me?"

The black car thumped our bumper, but I wasn't worried anymore. We were only a few houses away now.

"Because you were crying!" David shouted, his voice cracking with fear, and, I thought, anger. "You were upset and I felt bad about the stupid article, and then that weird shit happened with Ryan, and even if I don't always agree with the things you do at school, you do try and you didn't—"

He broke off and sagged against the seat, closing his eyes. "I just . . . I don't like crying girls, okay?"

We were quiet for a second while I took that in.

"That was very nice of you, David," I finally said. "Now hold on because I'm about to drive into a fence."

"Yeah, okay," he muttered, his eyes still closed. "You do that."

Then his eyes shot open. "Wait, what?"

My house was there on the right, and I swung the Dodge straight through our fence.

We crashed through with enough force to rattle my bones and shatter the windshield into roughly a million spiderweb cracks. But that was okay. I didn't need to see now.

I kept pulling the wheel to the right, which meant that I missed our pool, driving David's car straight to the back corner of our yard.

The black car wasn't so lucky. Not only did it hit the water, it had been going so fast that it hit it with all the force of driving into a brick wall. I could hear the splash, and as I looked in the rearview mirror, I saw the huge wave that came out of the pool.

The Dodge came to a shuddering halt, bumping against something solid that I thought might be my mom's new birdbath.

Whoops.

I put the car in park and turned it off, plunging us into silence. Well, not total silence, since I was breathing pretty hard and David kept mumbling, "Please don't let us be dead, please don't let us be dead."

"David," I said, reaching over to grab his arm. He reached over with his other arm and covered my hand with his.

"Pres?" he said, opening his eyes, which still looked very wide and very blue in his pale face. "We're not dead," he said, almost like he was talking to himself. "How did we not get dead?"

I smiled at him and squeezed his arm. "Because I'm awesome."

He stared at me and his smile got bigger and brighter as the fear drained out of his face. "We're not dead!" he said, like he just now got that we were still sitting in his gross—and now completely busted—car instead of playing harps in the sky or whatever.

I was smiling back, my grin probably exactly as crazy as his. "We're *so* not dead!"

He laughed and the sound was so full of relief that I found myself laughing, too.

He turned to me, still grinning. I was grinning back when he reached out, grabbed the back of my neck, and pulled me to him.

Chapter 9

For one horrifying second, I thought he was going to kiss me. I wasn't really sure how I'd react if he did. I mean, I knew that if he kissed me, it would be a kiss of the "I am so glad I am not dead that I would kiss a flesh-eating zombie were it sitting in this car beside me" variety more than the sexy "I only write mean articles about you because I am secretly in love with you" type.

But it was only a hug. And if I maybe spent a second or two thinking that he actually smelled really nice, or that he was much more solid than he appeared, so what? I was traumatized by all the car chasing/nearly dying.

Luckily, it didn't last long, but when I pulled back, I noticed that my heart was pounding and there was this weird fluttering sensation.

Butterflies.

No, I thought to myself. Near-death flutters of anxiety. That's all.

Then I noticed that David was staring out the shattered windshield, looking as weirded out as I felt.

Oh my God, what was wrong with me? I could barely muster

up the enthusiasm to make out with my own super hot boy-friend, and I was . . . oh dear God, was I blushing? Ugh.

Ugh ugh ugh.

Yup, the car chase had clearly addled my brain.

I was about to say something mean to David, you know, to restore equilibrium, when his eyes got big and he blurted out, "Bad guys in the pool!"

Huh? Was that like thinking of baseball when—OH! Right!

I pushed open my door and leapt out into my yard, taking deep breaths, hoping the cool air and sight of people drowning in my pool might get my hormones or whatever back under control.

I had knocked over Mom's birdbath. It lay in three big pieces right under David's bumper. And then, of course, there was the giant hole in our fence. But those were really the least of my problems. This biggest issue was the black Cadillac currently sinking into my pool.

No sound came from the car, and there didn't appear to be any activity inside, so I guessed the impact had knocked out the driver and any passengers he or she might have had.

David was standing next to me, watching the car as the aqua water bubbled and churned around it. "So are we, um, are we gonna let them drown?"

I was glad he said that. We.

I had killed Dr. DuPont, and I didn't feel bad about that. I couldn't. He had been seconds from killing me when I jammed that shoe into his neck. But whoever was in that black car . . . well, I didn't know what they'd wanted. My gut told me they had been bad guys, but that still didn't make me feel great about letting them drown in my pool.

I was also more than a little worried about explaining this whole thing. All evidence of my fight with Dr. DuPont had mysteriously vanished, but I wasn't sure how whoever had worked that particular mojo could cover *this* up. I expected our neighbors to start congregating in the street any minute now, like they did when the power went out.

David gave a huge sigh and ran his hands over his hair. "Well, this is weird. And awful."

"Yup." My skirt had gotten twisted around my hips somewhere in all of this, and I started straightening it. Anything to avoid looking at the pool.

"Who are you?" David asked me for the second time that day. "International assassin? Ninja? Vampire slayer, maybe?"

I lifted my head. "No, I'm a—"

There was a slight popping sound from the pool, and David and I both turned our attention back to the water.

Which was now empty.

And with one loud crack, the hole in my fence was suddenly gone. I didn't even have to look behind me to know that the screech of metal was David's car repairing itself. In just a few seconds, all evidence of the insane car chase, the crash, all of it, was gone. Then the only sound in my backyard was the singing of birds and the rustling of the leaves.

"That really happened," David said softly. "All that shit, it . . . disappeared, right? I didn't hallucinate that?"

My adrenaline seemed to vanish as completely as the Cadillac, and it was all I could do not to collapse in a heap on the grass. It was one thing to see the aftereffects of stuff disappearing. It was another to see an entire car—with people inside—poof out of existence.

"Yeah," I replied. "That happened."

"Do you know why?"

When I turned to him, David was still staring at the pool, the fingers of his right hand pressed against his temple again.

"No. But . . . David, something seriously weird is going on."

The hand at his temple moved up to tug on his hair as David made a sound that was part sob, part laugh. "You think? Jesus, Harper. You . . . you flipped Ryan Bradshaw like a pancake. You drove a car like Jason Bourne. And then this . . ." He waved his hand at the water. "I don't . . . I mean . . ." His words trailed off and he sank down into a crouch, eyes still fixed on the pool.

Walking over to him, I pulled at the shoulder of his jacket. "Okay, I get that it's weird, and while I totally respect the need for a PTSD moment, we really need to talk."

His eyes moved up to my face, still kind of unfocused. "About what? Why bad guys are chasing you, and why freaking *magic* is apparently real?"

"I actually think the bad guys might be chasing *you*, but yeah."

David staggered backward, and sat down heavily on the grass. As he did, he nearly overturned Mom's statue of two little girls reading on a bench, but I was able to grab it before it fell.

His sleeves, too short as usual, fell back from his thin wrists as he rested his elbows on his knees, hands tugging at his hair. "Hold up, what? You think those guys were after *me*? Why?"

"I don't know. Do *you* know why?" I towered over David, my shadow falling on his body.

Dazed, David shook his head. "I can't—"

And then I saw it. Something flickered across his face and he flinched.

"You do know," I said, yanking him to his feet. "David, what is it?"

He swallowed heavily. "Nothing. It's nothing."

At that moment, I really hated that my superpowers prevented me from shaking the crap out of him. I settled for balling my fist up in the front of his shirt and pulling him down to meet my eyes. "David, look around you. This? *This is crazy-sauce.* And if you know anything that could help me figure out why I'm suddenly Wonder Woman, I need to know it right. Effing. Now."

I actually said the word that time, and David's eyes went so wide I wondered if that had shocked him more than the disappearing Cadillac.

But he never got a chance to answer me.

"Yoo-hoo!" a voice called out from the other side of my fence, and David and I both went still.

"Is that?" I hissed.

"My Aunt Saylor." He gulped.

The back gate swung open, and suddenly Saylor Stark was standing there, a pair of Chanel sunglasses pushed down her nose as she took in the sight of me, shaking and sweaty, clutching the front of her nephew's T-shirt.

"Oh my," she said, and two syllables had never contained so much dismay. "What exactly is going on here?"

David and I practically leapt apart as Saylor moved into the yard, her high heels sinking slightly. The late afternoon sunlight flashed on her silver hair as well as the silver and turquoise jewelry around her neck. Other than a slight grass stain on the hem of her beige trousers, she looked as immaculate as ever.

"I was over at Anne Beckwith's, and I *thought* I saw your car tearing down the street, David James Stark," she said, pushing her sunglasses back into place with one finger. "But I told myself, 'Of course not, Saylor. David would never drive so irresponsibly. Besides, he's meant to be in school right now.'"

She turned her head to me. "As are you, correct, Miss Price?"

"Yes, ma'am," I said feebly. "I . . . I felt sick, and David offered to drive me home."

I couldn't see her eyes behind her dark glasses, but I had a feeling they were very cold. "Really?" she said. "How odd. Because right after I had the thought that David would never, ever drive his car in such a manner, I noticed that *he* was not the one behind the wheel."

Oh God. Of all the people to see me doing my Dale Earnhardt, Jr., impression, it had to be Saylor Stark.

"She asked to drive it," David said, speaking up for the first time. He still seemed a little out of it, and his voice wasn't as strong as normal, but he was still good at thinking on his feet. "She'd never driven one like it before, so she, uh, wanted to."

As one, the three of us looked over at David's pathetic Dodge. Even without its fender and back door mangled, it didn't exactly scream, "DRIVE ME."

Maybe David wasn't that great at thinking on his feet. And

why did he even own a car like that, anyway? Saylor surely could've afforded something nicer. It was probably a point of pride with him, like his weird thrift shop wardrobe.

"I'm sorry, Aunt Saylor," he continued. "I shouldn't have ditched school, but Harper, uh, was sick. And you're always going on about good citizenship."

I tried not to let surprise show on my face. That was actually a pretty good save. Certainly better than "chicks really want to get behind the wheel of my Stratus." And the fact that he'd been able to do it after nearly getting killed *and* dealing with what appeared to be magic was impressive.

"Good citizenship doesn't have to come at the cost of your own morals, David," Saylor snapped. "You know better than to skip class, and I am very disappointed in you. And of course, we haven't even gotten into the completely reckless way you two were driving. I think you and I will be having a long talk when I get done with Cotillion practice this afternoon, young man."

Saylor's gaze swung back to me. "Speaking of, Miss Price, if you're feeling so ill, maybe you'd better sit today's rehearsal out."

"But we're supposed to practice the prayer today," I said, blinking. "I'm leading the prayer."

Her smile was brittle. "I'm sure Miss Franklin will do a fine job filling in. And maybe by Wednesday's practice, you'll be feeling more yourself."

Sick for real now, I could only nod. Behind my parents, Saylor Stark was the last person in the world I wanted to disappoint. And there was no mistaking that tone. Not only had she caught me skipping class, I was skipping class *with her nephew*, whom I had clearly sucked into my downward spiral. If she knew that I'd also made him an accessory to what *might* have been murder . . .

And that's when it hit me. David was Saylor's *nephew*. He had lived with her his whole life. If people wanted to kill him, surely Saylor would know why. But how exactly did you go about asking something like that? *Hi, Miss Saylor, are y'all by any chance in the witness protection program? Or hiding from wizards?* She wouldn't just take the prayer away from me after that. She'd kick me out of the entire Cotillion. Maybe even out of the entire *town*.

As she dusted imaginary dirt from her slacks, I watched Saylor, trying to see if there was any sign that she knew why David and I had been speeding down the street. But between the huge sunglasses and Saylor's Perfect Southern Lady ability to repress any and all emotions, I couldn't tell.

David, shaking off his daze, moved toward his aunt. "Let Harper do the stupid prayer," he said, sounding a bit more like himself. "This isn't her fault."

Saylor's head shot up. "First of all, you will not call the Cotillion prayer 'stupid.' Secondly, you should be at school right now, not drag racing down Ivy Lane. Thirdly, I have told you that you need to be more careful. And going a hundred miles an hour in a car that is on its last legs is hardly careful. What if you'd had another one of your headaches?"

David scowled at her. "My headaches are no big deal," he said, but Saylor held up her hand.

"We are not having this argument in Miss Price's backyard. You're coming with me."

He flung one long arm out toward his Stratus. "My car—"

"You can pick it up in the morning. Harper, I'm sure your parents won't mind if David leaves his vehicle here."

The way she said it left no doubt that refusing was not an option. "It's fine," I said. "And honestly, it's still another few hours until practice, and I'm sure if I took a quick nap and had a sandwich, I'd be fine, too." I ended with a little laugh, as if by sheer force of will, I could make her see the funny side to all of this.

That smile again, the one that felt like a threat. "I'll see you on Wednesday, Harper," she said, and I could practically hear a gavel go down. I'd been found guilty of Unladylike Behavior, Nephew Endangerment, and, if the look she shot my boots was any indication, Improper Footwear.

And if she ever found out about Ryan . . . oh God, *Ryan*. I had to call him. I had to explain. "Say good-bye to Harper, David," Saylor trilled as she began making her way toward David's car, moving on the balls of her feet to keep her heels from sinking again.

David's eyes met mine, and I could tell the shock was definitely wearing off. He was getting that same predatory look he'd had at the Homecoming Dance. "Tomorrow. You and me. *We need to talk*," he said in a low voice.

I couldn't help but roll my eyes. "Duh. But . . . I need to smooth things over with Ryan before I'm seen having sneaky conversations with you. So let me find you tomorrow, okay?"

"Pretty sure ninjas and magic and dead guys trump your boyfriend's insecurity," he hissed, leaning in closer.

"And pretty sure *you* now know I could kick your behind, so why don't you let *me* handle this?" I whispered back. That wasn't true, of course. If David hadn't been rattled, he would've remembered this morning, when I hadn't even been able to slap him. But at least I got a little satisfaction out of seeing him go pale.

"Fine," he said through clenched teeth.

"Thank you," I huffed back.

"David!" Saylor called again, and this time, there was a definite edge to her trill.

"Tomorrow," he said again, pointing at me.

"Tomorrow," I agreed.

Chapter 10

"So ARE you mad at me about yesterday?"

I gave a shuddery sigh as I slid into the passenger seat of Bee's car the next morning. Thank God, she'd made a Starbucks run before coming to pick me up. I took a scalding sip of my latte, then nearly choked on it.

Bee always got me a skinny vanilla latte. This was a triple espresso that was so strong, I was surprised my teeth hadn't melted. Then I noticed how rigidly she was sitting in her seat, and that the rap music she liked was especially aggressive today.

For a second, I sat there, trying to figure out why I *would* be mad at Bee. I'd spent the night tossing and turning, worrying about why Ryan wasn't answering my calls. I must have called him at least ten times, but he'd never picked up. And when I hadn't been worrying over that, I was thinking of Saylor Stark, the look on her face when she'd seen me grabbing her nephew. God, what if she'd heard me use the F-word?

Then I remembered. Bee had done the Cotillion prayer for me yesterday, and she'd sent like three texts last night that I hadn't responded to.

"Of course I'm not mad at you," I said, but I must not have sounded very convincing.

"You seem like you are. Harper, you always answer my texts. And a couple of people said you had a big fight with Ryan yesterday and ditched school."

My heart stuttered in my chest at that. Oh God, had Ryan *told* someone what happened? Did the entire school know I'd flipped him like a freaking omelet?

But no. No, if Ryan had told anyone, it would have been Brandon, and Brandon would've told Bee, and Bee definitely would've mentioned that first. I tried to keep my sigh of relief quiet before replying, "I told you, I was sick."

I reached out to turn the radio down, but Bee slapped my hand. "No touching my tunes until you 'fess up. Were you really sick, or did you have a fight with Ryan?".

"I was sick," I insisted again. "Remember the night of the Homecoming Dance? I . . . I must have some kind of bug."

Bee frowned. "Something was definitely up that night," she murmured, and for the first time, I noticed that while she might have been asking if I was mad, she was the one who seemed pissed.

"What's that supposed to mean?" My brain was racing. Oh my God, had Bee put Mr. Hall's and Dr. DuPont's disappearance together with my pukeage?

A muscle worked in Bee's jaw, and finally she spit out, "Mary Beth was going home for her free period yesterday, and she said she saw David Stark coming out of your backyard. She said he looked really weird, and then later, she saw Ryan leaving school, and he was super upset, and . . ."

She trailed off and my fingers tightened around my coffee cup. "Go ahead."

"Mary Beth said that you and David have always been kind of . . . sparky. So she thinks there's something going on with the two of you."

I frowned at the "sparky" bit. David and I did not have . . . sparks. What we had was a feud that had been running since we were both in diapers. Something Bee of all people should have understood.

"Is that what you think, Bee?" I asked.

She shrugged. Today, Bee was wearing a huge pair of sunglasses that seemed to hide half her face. Her hair was done up in a high ponytail, and I could see a muscle twitch in her cheek, like she was grinding her teeth. "Explains a lot. Like why you've been so freaking weird lately."

Then she glanced at me. "Explains what was going on in the bathroom the night of Homecoming."

It was way too early in the morning for this conversation, I decided, drinking a little more espresso. It still tasted like battery acid, but I needed the caffeine. I already had a slight headache.

"I'm not going to pretend to understand why you suddenly have a thing for David when you have *Ryan Bradshaw* as a boyfriend," Bee continued, yelling over the music. I went to turn it down, but she pushed my hand out of the way. "What pisses me off is that you didn't tell me about it."

"There's nothing to tell!" I shouted. "I'm not cheating on Ryan, I don't have a thing for David, and I was *sick* yesterday. That's it! Not fighting with my boyfriend, not pregnant, and not any of the other hundreds of things you and Mary Beth probably guessed while y'all were talking behind my back. Oh, and by the way, David was at my house with his aunt. I'm guessing Mary Beth left out that little tidbit."

Guilt, or maybe hurt, flickered over Bee's face. "Do you think I'm a total dumbass?"

My head was pounding, and my face felt hot. "Right now, yeah, I do!"

Bee whipped into a parking place and braked so hard that I jerked forward in the seat.

She pushed her sunglasses up to glare at me. "I caught the two of you in the bathroom and you burst into tears."

"That was actually a little *after* you found us," I muttered, but she was on a roll.

"I know you want everyone to think you're perfect, but you don't have to pretend with me." She thunked her head back against the gray leather, and a few girls walking by shot curious glances at the car. "Or at least I thought you didn't."

She slumped back into her seat, shaking her head. "I tell you everything," she said softly. "*Everything.*"

I put my drink back in the holder and took her hand. "Hey," I said softly. "I tell you everything, too. I promise." Guilt tasted more bitter than the espresso, but I told myself that it wasn't technically a lie. After all, I wasn't lying to her about Ryan and David. Not really. Still, for just a second, I thought about how nice it would feel to tell someone—someone who loved me, someone who wasn't David Stark—about what was going on.

But it was too bizarre, and for all I knew, it might also be dangerous. Until I had a better idea of who was after David and why, the best thing I could do was keep things as normal as possible.

So I leaned forward and said, "Ryan and I did have a little argument yesterday, but it was nothing. We'll be fine. I plan on making up with him as soon as I see him today. And there is nothing going on with me and David Stark."

She swiveled her head to face me. Bee's eyes had always been both spooky and beautiful, almost startlingly dark against the peachiness of her skin and the wheat blond of her hair. Now, they were narrowed and wary. "Promise?"

I held up my hand. "Pinky swear."

After a pause, she giggled and hooked my finger with hers. The little silver ring Brandon had gotten for her—complete with a pink cubic zirconia that we will not talk about—dug into my skin. "Pinky swears are sacred, you know."

"I do," I said, sitting up primly. "So I don't use it lightly."

Her grin turned into something like a leer. "So when you and Ryan make up, is it gonna be hot?"

Rolling my eyes, I disentangled our pinkies. "Perv."

That sorted, we got out of the car. Then, out of the corner of my eye, I caught sight of David standing outside Wallace Hall, waving at me. He was wearing a bright purple argyle sweater over a white button-down and jeans, so he wasn't exactly inconspicuous.

As subtly as I could, I flicked my hand at David behind my

back. I knew we needed to talk, but with Bee on high alert where he was concerned, now was not the time.

"I can't believe we still have a sub in history," Bee said, snapping my attention back to her.

"Oh, is, uh, Dr. DuPont out?" I asked, trying not to imagine him standing in front of me, my shoe sticking out of his neck.

"Apparently," Bee said, nodding across the courtyard. Mrs. Hillyard, the substitute teacher from yesterday, was hurrying up the steps into Wallace.

"But Dr. DuPont was a jackass anyway," she added. "Didn't he give you a hard time?"

You could say that. "Oh, not really," I replied, just in case there were undercover police officers hiding in the bushes or something. "I actually kind of liked him."

"Liked who?" Brandon asked, coming up to join us. "Me? Because I can tell you one thing, Miss Harper here is not a fan of the Bran Man."

"And I'm not a fan of you calling yourself that," Bee muttered, even as she let him take her hand and swing it.

"No, I'm serious!" Brandon insisted, flicking his blond hair out of his eyes. "Yesterday, she full-on smacked me in the middle of the hall. For no reason!"

"Oh, I'm sure," Bee said sarcastically.

"It's true," Brandon insisted before shooting me a sideways look. "Is that why Ryan's out today? Did you smack him around, too?"

That was way too close to the truth for comfort. Frowning, I asked, "He isn't here today?"

"Not yet," Brandon said, nodding toward the parking lot. Sure enough, Ryan's car wasn't in its usual spot. Heart sinking, I did my best to look concerned, but not panicked.

"Maybe he's running late," I offered.

David chose that moment to walk over to us, and next to me, I felt Bee stiffen a little.

"Harper, can I talk to you for a sec?"

"The bell's about to ring," I said to David, hoping he heard that as *Friend Time, not right now.*

He frowned. "We really need to talk about yesterday." He had gotten my message, and now he was sending one of his own: *I don't care.*

"What happened—" Bee asked, but I was already tugging her away.

"Your apology was more than sufficient," I called breezily over my shoulder. "We're fine."

I could feel David glaring at my back, but I kept pulling Bee toward the school. Yes, yes, David might be my noble cause, but Bee was my best friend. There was a chance I'd already screwed up the boyfriend thing. I didn't want to screw up what I had with Bee, too.

"You sure you don't want to talk to him?" she asked once we'd walked through the front doors.

"Positive," I replied. "I told you, it's nothing more than the usual me and David Stark Mutual Disdain Society thing acting up again."

Bee pulled her lower lip between her teeth, stopping just in front of the main office. I thought she glanced back outside toward the parking lot and Ryan's empty spot. But all she said was, "See you at lunch?"

"Absolutely!" I chirped, doing my best to ignore David as he stormed past us.

Nothing happened the rest of the morning, but that didn't stop me from jumping every time the bell rang. I also went out of my way to avoid the English hall, wondering if I'd ever feel safe at school again. There were no Pop Rocks in my blood, and there was no summons to the headmaster's office to talk about Dr. DuPont, but I stayed on edge. Ryan's absence didn't help. Was he hurt, or too freaked out to even look at me?

By the end of first period, I'd made up my mind to call him, one more time. Cell phones were a major no-no during school hours, but I decided to risk it in the bathroom.

I'd just turned down the corridor when a hand shot out of the nearby janitor's closet and hauled me into the dark.

Chapter 11

WITHOUT MAKING a sound, I went to slug my attacker, only to have my hand freeze in midair.

Of course.

"Are you insane?" I hissed, batting David's hand away. It didn't touch him, obviously, but it still made me feel better.

"I told you we'd talk today," he whispered.

"Right. Talk. Like normal people, not . . . skulking around in broom closets."

"Skulking? Really?" David raised his eyebrows, and even in the dim light, I could see the smirk forming.

"First of all, I'm not taking crap about word choice from the guy who uses 'egregious' in every article he writes. And secondly, this"— I gestured to the cluttered shelves, the cleaning products, the damp mops—"definitely warrants the use of skulking."

Rubbing his hand over his eyes, David heaved a sigh. "Fine. We're skulking. And since the bell rings in five minutes, we need to skulk fast. Tell me everything."

I shifted my weight from one foot to the other. "It's . . . kind of long. And intense. And not something that can be spilled between classes in the janitor's closet."

"Try," David said, his teeth clenched.

Frowning, I put my hands on my hips. "Fine. On the night of the Homecoming Dance, a janitor passed some kind of superpower on to me before he died. Then I killed Dr. DuPont with my shoe, but when I came back to the bathroom, everything had disappeared and I thought I was going crazy, but then those bad guys chased us yesterday, and they also disappeared, so I'm not crazy, but there's something *super* crazy going on, and I think it's connected to you since I'm totally incapable of hurting you. That's why I couldn't slap you the other day even though, trust me, I really, really wanted to."

I took a deep breath. "So there. That's the fast version. Any questions?"

David stumbled backward, sitting down hard on an upside-down bucket, then shook his head. "I . . . I think my brain actually shut down," he said. He braced his elbows on his knees, leaning forward with his steepled fingers covering his mouth.

"After yesterday, I thought whatever you said, I'd be good. I mean, dude disappeared. And my car magically repaired itself. I should be unshockable, you know?"

David still wasn't looking at me, so I knelt down in front of him as gingerly as I could, trying not to touch the ground or accidentally flash him. "I know," I told him. "It sounds insane. It *is* insane."

His eyes fixed on mine. "You killed someone," he said, his voice barely audible. "With a shoe."

"He had a sword," I fired back and then, to my shock, David burst out laughing.

"A sword. Our history teacher attacked you with a sword in the bathroom and you killed him." He dropped his head into his hands, only to raise it a second later. "Wait. You said a janitor passed these powers on to you. A janitor who died. Mr. Hall?"

Surprised, I nodded. "Yeah. Had you noticed that he was missing?"

But David was pressing his face into his hands again, moaning. "Oh my God, oh my God."

"What?" When he didn't answer, I tugged on his sleeve. Apparently that much I could do. "What do you know about Mr. Hall?"

When David lifted his face, he was pale. "He rented the little house at the back of our property."

I rocked back on my heels. "Mr. Hall *lived* with you?"

"Not with me, but more or less in my backyard, yeah. He . . . he took off a few days ago. Or at least that's what my aunt thought. I even asked her if we should, like, report it or something, but she said he was a grown man, he could come and go as he pleased."

Now David's skin had taken a bit of a greenish cast, and I grabbed one of the extra buckets, just in case. "I was at school Friday night, working on the paper," he said, almost like he was talking to himself. "Dr. DuPont . . . do you think he was after me, and killed Mr. Hall when he got in the way?"

"I don't know," I told him. "But that makes sense. And you're sure nothing like this had ever happened to you before?"

Briefly, he was the old David again. "Are you asking me if I'm sure no one has ever tried to kill me before, Pres? Trust me, nothing like this has ever happened."

"That you know of."

That wiped the smirk right off his face. "Oh God. You're right. If you hadn't told me, I never would've known about Friday night. Mr. Hall and Dr. DuPont and you and swords . . ."

He trailed off, and for a long moment, he sat there, totally quiet, twisting his fingers and breathing. Then he glanced back up at me, he nodded. "Okay. Processed. Now what do we do?"

As bizarre as it sounds, I wanted to . . . I don't know, hug him. He'd taken all this weirdness and done the same thing I'd managed to do with it: take it in, feel crazy for a little bit, and then deal.

Maybe David Stark wasn't completely useless.

"When Dr. DuPont tried to kill me, he called me a 'Paladin.'"

"Like Charlemagne," David said, almost to himself.

"What?"

Shaking his head, David said, "Charlemagne. He was this French king—"

Irritated, I cut him off with a wave of my hand. "I know that. I was in AP European History, too. But what does he have to do with Paladins?"

"He had a group of knights called Paladins. I don't remember anything about them having superpowers, though."

Well, that was something, at least.

As briefly as I could, I filled David in on what I'd learned about Paladins so far. When I finished, he nodded. "So you think I'm your noble cause."

"I really hope you're not, but it's looking like that's it. Which is why, yet again, I'm going to ask you if there's anything you can think of, any reason people would care about you enough to want to kill you. I know you write annoying articles, but if I haven't wanted to murder you yet, I don't know why anyone else would."

He gave a little snort of laughter. "Fair enough. But I'm telling you, Harper, there's nothing. I'm just . . . a guy."

But he was flexing his fingers, and I knew there was something he wasn't telling me.

"David," I told him, reaching out to touch his knee before I thought better of it. "Seriously. Whatever it is, no matter how random you think it might be, you need to spill, and you need to do it *now*."

His blue eyes blinked behind his glasses, and for a second, I thought he was going to give me the brush-off again. But then he sighed, tipping his head back to study the ceiling. "It's so stupid I can't believe I'm even going to tell you. But . . . the debate club thing. The article saying that Matt Hampton had stolen the other team's questions . . ."

I nodded. That had been a pretty big deal a few months back. David had snuck the article into the paper after hours, which had seriously pissed off Mrs. Laurent. But not because it was underhanded. The match David was talking about? It hadn't even *happened* yet. That debate had been scheduled for the Saturday after David wrote the article.

He didn't have any excuse for why he'd made it up, and I honestly think he'd have gotten expelled if it hadn't been for his aunt's influence. I still couldn't believe Mrs. Laurent let him stay on the paper, but I guessed that could be chalked up to Saylor, too.

"I know everyone thinks I wrote that article to be a dick or whatever. But the thing is, Pres, when I wrote it . . . it was like I was sure it had happened. I knew it. I couldn't tell you how or who told it to me, but I was positive it had happened. I never would've written it if I hadn't been."

I took that in. "Okay. So maybe you . . . I don't know, dreamed it. I've had dreams that seemed completely real, and—"

But David was already shaking his head. "No, I've always had weird dreams. Like, seriously intense, crazy dreams. I even talked to Aunt Saylor about taking me to the doctor for it, but she said vivid dreams ran in our family."

"Huh," I said, filing that away for later. David didn't seem to notice.

"But this wasn't like those. This was something I . . . I knew."

"So you thought something was true, and it ended up not being true. That's not exactly a superpower, David. And certainly not worth chasing you down over."

David drew his legs up, pressing his heels against the edge of the bucket as he rested his elbows on his knees. "That's what I thought. That maybe too many late nights had finally gotten to me."

I found myself nodding in sympathy.

"But then, the day after the academic hearing, Matt Hampton caught me in the bathroom. Tossed me against a wall and asked who had told me about the questions. He had stolen them, Pres,"

David said, his expression grave. "He was going to use them. But . . . hadn't yet."

Okay, that was a little more interesting. "So you . . . you can see the future?"

David rolled his eyes. "Okay, it sounds really stupid when you say it like that."

"David, we're huddled in a supply closet talking about killer history teachers and superpowered knights. Telling the future, honestly, doesn't make it any weirder. In fact, it makes it somewhat clearer. At least now we know why someone might want to kill you."

David snorted. "Yes, my ability to not predict debate club outcomes is incredibly impressive."

The bell rang. It startled both of us, and we shot to our feet. Kneeling down, I'd been a few inches below David, but when we stood up, we were suddenly way too close, and I found myself stumbling backward away from him.

Once again, my chest tightened, and there was that weird fluttering sensation that was like butterflies. But it couldn't be butterflies. I did *not* have butterflies over David Stark.

But he backed up, too, a weird look on his face. Then he cleared his throat. "Okay," he said. "I'll check out Mr. Hall's house today. See if there's anything there. What are you planning on doing? Other than keeping people from killing me." His eyes widened. "Oh man, how are you supposed to do that? Mr. Hall lived with us and worked at the school. We can't be that . . . that . . . *close* all the time."

I nodded in agreement. "And logistics are the least of it," I muttered, thinking about Ryan and Bee, both of whom had reasons to want me and David to spend less time together. Then something else occurred to me. Mr. Hall had died defending David. Bled out on the bathroom floor from a giant *scimitar* wound. Was I expected to defend David to the death? *My* death?

Something must have shown on my face because David squinted at me. "What?"

I shook my head. We could get into how far my protective services extended later. "Whenever you're in danger, I can sense it. There's this . . . jumpiness and pain and stuff. I can't exactly miss it. Besides, this town's not that big, and we only live a few blocks apart. And I am here at school every day. As for the rest of it, we'll . . . I don't know. Once we figure out what's going on, maybe we can figure out some way to stop it."

"Good plan," he said, even as he gulped nervously. "Look, you said the internet didn't yield much in terms of answers. But if this Paladin thing is ancient, maybe we should use . . . I don't know, older sources."

"By which you mean books?" I asked, quirking an eyebrow.

"Exactly." Now that some of the color was returning to his face, he looked more like the David I was used to. "When the debate club thing happened, I checked out a book from the library about . . ." He trailed off and cleared his throat a little. "Um, you know, people who see the future and stuff. Here."

He reached into his backpack and pulled out a thin black book, handing it to me. *They Saw the Future!* was emblazoned on the cover in bright purple foil.

I studied it for a second, pressing my lips together. "It's like you *want* me to make fun of you."

Scowling, David went to take the book back, but I held it out of reach. "No, you're right. There might be something in here. It's better than nothing."

David didn't look much happier, but he nodded. "Right. I've marked some of the pages I thought were the most interesting. Plus we can go to the library this afternoon and—"

"No," I said automatically. I'd already been caught spending one afternoon with David Stark. If we got caught two days in a row, even if it was in an unsexy place like the library . . .

David scowled, and I hurried on. "I only mean not *today*. I have . . . family stuff."

I wasn't sure David was going to accept that for an answer, but in the end, he gave a terse nod. "Okay. Maybe this weekend then."

Today was Tuesday. Surely by Saturday, things with me and Ryan would be sorted out. "Saturday is fine," I said, bending down to scoop up my backpack. "And that was a good idea. The book thing."

"Maybe the next time you pay me a compliment, you can try not to sound like you're about to hurl." He smirked, a tiny dimple appearing in one cheek.

I rolled my eyes.

"Okay," he said, going to open the door. "I'll pick you up at around nine on Saturday."

I shook my head. "I'll pick you up. One ride in that deathtrap you call a car was plenty, thanks."

"You know, it actually wasn't a deathtrap until someone decided to drive it down a residential street at roughly a bazillion miles an hour."

"To save your life," I threw over my shoulder as I left the closet.

Luckily, David had enough sense to let me leave first. Also luckily, I only got one girl looking at me as I shut the door behind me. I gave her my brightest smile. "Wanted to make sure everything was spick-and-span in there!"

Chapter 12

I DROVE past Ryan's house on the way home that afternoon. His car was there, but I didn't have the guts to go up to the house. Instead, I went to the library. Maybe I could find out some of this stuff on my own, and then I wouldn't need any more alone time with David.

Except you're supposed to protect him, I reminded myself as I searched the shelves. *That will probably require plenty of alone time.*

Unless there was some way out of this whole thing. With that thought in mind, I grabbed two different biographies of Charlemagne. Between those and *They Saw The Future!*, maybe I'd figure *something* out.

Mom and Dad were both at work when I got home from the library, and aside from Bee texting me a few times, my phone was depressingly quiet, and I was, well . . . depressed. It seemed almost impossible to believe that yesterday, I was driving to school, happy and excited about my newfound superpowers. And now, after only a few days, I'd already killed a man (possibly more than one, actually, if the pool thing had worked), jujitsued my boyfriend, and made Saylor Stark, the one woman I lived to impress, think I was some kind of hot-rodding skank. And now David knew about them. David, who practically made a habit of ruining my life, knew the biggest secret I'd ever had.

To keep my mind off all of that, I paged through the books. Unfortunately, they were about as helpful as the internet had been. The Charlemagne book mentioned Paladins, naming them as some kind of elite bodyguard force for the king. There was even a picture of them, looking entirely too skinny to be badass killers. As I studied the reproduced painting, I was at least grateful that their lame burgundy suits no longer seemed to be the official uniform. Burgundy washed me out, and velvet made me itch.

Other than that, there wasn't much there. The book referenced the Paladins guarding the king, but it never mentioned noble causes or superpowers, so it seemed kind of useless. After all, I was pretty sure David Stark wasn't a king.

But that thing with the debate club, no matter how stupid he thought it was, had to be important. It wasn't like whether or not the debate club cheated was a major, world-changing event, but still. If David could see the future, no matter how small or insignificant those visions seemed to be . . . yeah, that might be something people would kill for.

Tossing that book aside, I picked up *They Saw the Future!* It was one of those Time-Life books they used to sell on TV. I was pretty sure my Aunt Jewel had a few, but I'd never seen this one before. I opened it up, scanning the chapters, muttering their titles aloud. "'Visions of Doom,' 'Seen Too Late,' 'Dreams of Destiny' . . ."

David had put a little Post-it flag beside that chapter in the table of contents.

He'd marked another one, too. "Oracles." I flipped the book to the page listed, snorting with laughter when I saw the picture taking up most of the page. It was a scantily clad girl, wearing what appeared to be a large, transparent handkerchief, her head thrown back, her eyes closed. "Okay, you weren't marking this one for the information," I murmured, but when I turned the page, I saw that David had actually put more flags on the pages not featuring half-naked ladies.

"'Historically, Oracles came into their power in their teen years,'" I read next to one marker. "'The visions often did not reach full potency until the Oracle was between eighteen and twenty years of age.'"

I turned another page, and found more little paper flags. "'The original Oracles at Delphi were controlled by five men known as the "Ephors," elected men who served as a sort of Parliament. Oracles were strictly female.'"

"Well, there you go then," I said quietly. Unless David had a secret bigger than the debate club thing, it was looking like we could dismiss any chance of him being an Oracle.

But then another flag caught my eye. "Oracles were greatly prized commodities, and it was rumored that most of the great leaders of the world—Genghis Khan, Elizabeth I, Charlemagne— all had Oracles at their disposal."

The hair on the back of my neck stood up. David wasn't a girl, that was for sure, but I knew Paladins were connected to Charlemagne. And if Oracles were, too . . .

I reached out for the Charlemagne book, flipping it back to the page on Paladins, my eyes scanning for anything about Oracles. There was nothing, but once again, I found myself staring at the illustration of the Paladins in their fancy little uniforms. Their fancy, burgundy uniforms embroidered with gold thread in the shape of—

I grabbed the psychic book again. There, over the picture of the half-naked Oracle, was a little symbol, like a skinny figure eight, turned on its side. It was the same shape embroidered on the Paladins' uniforms.

"Holy crap," I muttered under my breath.

"Harper?"

Startled, I looked up from the book. Ryan was there. Standing in my doorway. And he was smiling at me.

Okay, so the smile was kind of tentative, and he seemed a little . . . wary, hovering there by the door, but still. He was *here*.

I immediately pushed myself into a sitting position, shoving the books away and wishing I was wearing something a little more flattering than my sweats and one of his old basketball T-shirts. But his expression softened when he saw "Grove Academy Raiders" scrawled across my chest. "I wondered where that shirt ended up," he said, lips lifting. There were shadows underneath his eyes, and his wavy hair seemed a little poufier than normal. It was the closest I'd ever seen Ryan to looking "rough" since the time he'd had the flu sophomore year.

"Oh my God, Ryan, I am so sorry about yesterday," I blurted out. "I was afraid you were going to hit David, and I don't know, get suspended or something, and I . . . freaked out. Did I hurt you?"

Sighing, Ryan came in and sat on the edge of my bed. "I really wish I could say no, because it kind of hurts my masculinity to admit my tiny girlfriend kicked my ass."

"I didn't kick it so much as *throw* it," I said, wanting him to laugh. *Needing* him to laugh.

And he did. Kind of. It was more a huff of breath than his normal laugh, but I would take it. "Where did you learn how to do that anyway?" he asked. His eyes searched my face, and I twisted my fingers in the bedspread.

"Self-defense class. I guess I took it a little more seriously than I thought." Lifting my head, I tentatively moved my fingers closer to his. "Is that why you weren't at school today? Because I hurt you?"

Ryan shook his head. "I was a little sore, yeah, but I . . . I needed some time to think." Hesitantly, he reached out and took my hands between his. His hands were warm and big, dwarfing mine. "Harper, believe it or not, the kung fu isn't really what I wanted to talk about. I mean, it's part of it, but . . ." He paused, looking down at our joined hands. "I just . . . things are weird with us."

"No, they're not," I said immediately, and when he quirked an eyebrow, I sighed and rolled my shoulders. "Okay, yes, the past few days have been a little intense, with Homecoming and all, and Cotillion coming up, and the, uh, flipping you bit."

Ryan shook his head, a tiny crease appearing between his

brows. "No, it's been going on a lot longer than the past few days."

Okay, now I was confused. Sure, my superpowers had been throwing things off since Friday, but before that, everything with me and Ryan had been fine. Better than fine. We were happy.

"I'm not blaming you," Ryan was saying. "You had a really rough year with—with your sister and everything, and I know getting college stuff together is freaking you out—"

"No, it's not," I said, and the corners of Ryan's mouth turned down.

"And that's another thing. Lately, it's like I can't say anything without you contradicting it."

"I don't—oh. Sorry."

Ryan ran a hand over his hair, ruffling it. "I love you," he said at last. "You know that. But it's . . . it's like we're speaking two different languages most of the time. Harper." He tugged on my hand. "If there's something going on with you, you can tell me, okay?"

For a second, I really thought about telling him. I wasn't sure how I was going to spin it, exactly, but there had to be something I could say. Some way of letting him know it definitely wasn't *him*, it was me. And then a funny expression crossed his face. "Is it David Stark?"

Maybe it was because the question was so unexpected, or maybe because it *was* David Stark—in a way—but whatever the reason, my reaction was . . . not great.

I made this kind of spluttering sound that was kind of like a laugh, but mostly involved me nearly spitting all over Ryan. "W-what? What would David Stark have to do with anything?"

"You guys seemed pretty . . . intense yesterday," Ryan said, dropping my hand.

"Yeah, we were *intensely arguing* over him writing that stupid article," I said even as I had a sudden vision of me and David, laughing in his car. Hugging. God, we had *hugged*.

Now Ryan was frowning. "But you're always arguing with him. Or talking about him. Or competing with him. And sometimes I wonder how you can be so obsessed with someone you supposedly hate."

"I'm not obsessed," I corrected before I could stop myself, and his mouth tightened. "Forget it," I said quickly, rising up on my knees to scoot closer to him. "I promise you, David Stark is . . . nothing to me." And he wasn't. I mean, he may have been some future-telling guy I was supposed to protect, possibly unto *death*, but other than that . . .

Ryan seemed less than convinced, so I leaned forward and pressed my lips to his. He hesitated for a second, but then, finally, he kissed me back. As his hand slid up to tangle in my hair, I moved forward, still on my knees. Ryan's other arm tightened around my waist, and I sank into the kiss, trying for a few seconds to turn my mind off.

It was nice. I know you're probably supposed to use words like "hot" or "amazing" to describe your boyfriend kissing you, and we've had plenty of make-outs I could describe that way, but "nice" was good, too. Comforting. Stable.

When we pulled apart, Ryan had that happy, glazed look that told me all thoughts of David Stark and my ninja moves and basically anything else had been obliterated.

Smiling, he leaned forward, pressing his forehead to mine. "So we're good?" he said, and I realized we hadn't really talked about anything. He'd brought up stuff, I'd denied it, and then we'd made out for a little while. It was becoming something of a pattern.

But that probably means we're good at conflict resolution, I thought.

"We're better than good," I told him, smiling back.

Still rubbing one of my hands, Ryan glanced down. "So what were you reading so intently it made you use a four-letter word?"

Before I could stop him, he picked up *They Saw the Future!* Both of his eyebrows went up as he studied the Oracle. "Whoa."

I snatched the book back, half shoving it under my bed. "Doing some research. Essay on ancient Greece for a college application thingie."

I'd been so happy to see Ryan that for a few minutes, all thoughts of Paladins and Oracles and whatever the heck was going on with me and David Stark had fled my brain. But looking at the picture reminded me that while things may have been better in Boyfriend Land, the rest of my life was only getting twistier.

Chapter 13

THANKS to a little more making out, Ryan seemed willing to let the subject drop, and I think he'd totally forgotten about it by the time we heard the garage door opening. "Your mom," he said, moving back.

"Yeah, we better get downstairs." Mom loved Ryan and I think she already thought of him as her son-in-law, but that still didn't mean she'd be okay with the two of us alone in my bedroom.

We made it to the living room before she came in, both of us striking nonchalant poses, me on the couch, him in my dad's chair. "Har—oh, you have company," Mom said as she came in the living room. She glanced back and forth between us and decided no rules were being violated. "Excellent!" she said. "Four hands to help me with groceries."

Once we'd helped Mom unload the car, Ryan decided to head home. After one last kiss, he drove away, and I went back into the kitchen. As I did, I spotted the space where David's car had been yesterday. He'd gotten it this morning, apparently—I'd left the gate unlocked for him, but I hadn't seen him. Still, it reminded me that while things with my boyfriend might be okay for the time being, things with the Starks definitely were not.

But I had an idea. While Mom put groceries away, I rummaged around in the pantry, grabbing flour, some spices, and a can of crushed pineapple. Dumping those on the counter, I fished out a mixing bowl and some measuring cups and went to work.

"What are you doing?" Mom asked, setting the paper bags of food on the counter.

"Making a cake," I replied. I measured out a tablespoon of vanilla as Mom walked over to the bowl, taking in the assembled ingredients. "Hummingbird cake? Fancy. Who's the lucky recipient?"

"Miss Saylor." Reaching in one of the drawers, I pulled out the biggest spoon I could find.

Mom gave me a careful look. She knew what hummingbird cake meant. "And what did you do that requires a 'sorry I screwed up' cake?"

I was already lucky the school hadn't called Mom and told her about me skipping class, so I decided to keep it as simple as possible. "David and I had a thing the other day."

Mom heaved a sigh. "Harper . . ."

"We weren't fighting," I quickly added, earning me a snort of laughter.

"That's a first, then."

"We had a disagreement, that's all. Miss Saylor saw us, and I thought a cake would smooth things over a little bit." Which it would, hopefully. And it would give me a good excuse to go tell David about the connection I'd made between Paladins and Oracles.

With a rueful smile, Mom walked over to the fridge and pulled out the eggs and sugar for me. "Well, in that case, let me help. You're a good baker, but you're not the best one in this family."

Mom cracked the eggs in a separate bowl while I lifted two bananas out of the fruit basket on the counter. We fell into a comfortable silence as she whisked and I mashed. And then, when I leaned over to scrape the bananas into her eggs and sugar mixture, Mom gave a little chuckle. "Do you remember how bad Leigh-Anne was at baking?"

I watched her out of the corner of my eye as I started to stir. It wasn't that I didn't want to talk about my sister, but I never knew how it would go. Sometimes, Mom could look at pictures of her and tell stories, and it was fine. We'd smile or laugh, and then move on to some other topic.

Other times, her voice would get tight, and her lip would tremble, and then the tears would come. And even though I knew it was awful of me, when she got like that, all I wanted to do was run away. To ignore it.

But there were no tears in Mom's voice now. "Yeah," I said carefully. "The baking soda brownies."

Mom's chuckle turned into a real laugh. "Yes! Oh God, I knew I should've tasted them before we started wrapping them up for the bake sale."

Now I smiled, too. "Yeah, but even though they were terrible, Leigh-Anne sold all of them, remember? Said they were special 'vitamin brownies' and that's why they tasted so bad."

"And then you told her she shouldn't lie at a church bake sale," Mom added, holding the mixing bowl as I dumped the wet ingredients into the dry.

"Right." I nodded. "But she said the more brownies she sold, the better it was for the church, so God would understand."

We both laughed again, and then that silence fell, this time a little heavier than before.

"That's the Leigh-Anne I wish people would remember," Mom finally said. Her voice wasn't tight, and her lips were steady, but sadness clung to every word. "I wish people could focus on her, not . . . not how she died."

I wanted that, too. More than anything. But Leigh-Anne's death hadn't only been a nuclear bomb going off in the middle of my family. It had been a scandal. A source of gossip. The pretty and popular Homecoming Queen getting drunk on prom night, wrecking her car, killing herself and nearly killing her boyfriend? It wasn't something people would easily forget.

They wouldn't forget no matter how much Mom wished, or how hard I tried to make up for my sister's one stupid decision. Not that I thought running SGA or organizing charity bake sales could wipe out the memory of that night. But maybe I could . . . I don't know, reset the balance.

Clearing my throat, I turned away and grabbed a few cake pans from the cabinets. I focused on pouring the batter, waiting for Mom to leave the kitchen and go up to her bedroom, the way she almost always did when we started talking about Leigh-Anne.

But to my surprise, she started unwrapping the packages of cream cheese for the icing. "I hope Saylor appreciates all the trouble you're going through."

"It's not that much trouble," I insisted, sliding the cake pans into the oven. "I've been meaning to make hummingbird cake for The Aunts for a while now."

At the mention of The Aunts, Mom rolled her eyes affectionately. "Well, don't let them know you gave their cake away to Saylor."

The Aunts were actually my great-aunts, but since my grandmother—their sister—had died when I was a baby, they'd kind of adopted me as a granddaughter by proxy. They got together at my Aunt Jewel's house every Friday afternoon to play cards, and I usually tried to stop by, but between school and Cotillion, I'd been too busy lately. It had probably been nearly a month since—

Suddenly, what Mom said registered. "What do you mean? Don't The Aunts like Saylor?" They'd never said anything to me about her, and trust me, if The Aunts weren't crazy about someone, they didn't exactly keep it a secret.

Mom shrugged as she started to whip the cream cheese and sugar together. "Saylor's monopoly on all major town events has never sat well with them. Especially since she's still a relative newcomer and a Yankee."

Now I rolled my eyes. "She's been here for nearly eighteen years, and she's from *Virginia*."

"You know The Aunts don't consider Virginia the South." Triumphantly, she pushed the bowl of icing toward me. "Can you take it from here?"

"Sure, thanks," I replied, but my mind was still on The Aunts. I didn't know why I hadn't thought of it before. If there was something weird about the Stark family, they would know it. They knew everything. Seriously, why had I wasted any time searching the internet when I had them? I made a mental note to stop by Aunt Jewel's on Friday—and to buy more cake ingredients.

Mom and I chatted while the cakes baked, and once they were done, I stuck them in the fridge to cool and went to my room to make myself a little more presentable. That accomplished, I headed back to the kitchen to find Mom frosting the cake for me.

"You're seriously going to take this to Saylor tonight?" Mom asked, nodding to the microwave clock. "It's nearly seven."

"Which is perfect timing," I insisted. "After dinner, but before people start getting ready for bed."

Mom looked up, a strange expression flitting across her face.

"Harper, you know . . . you don't have to prove anything. Not to me, or Saylor Stark, or this entire town. You could just—"

"Chill?" I suggested, thinking of Ryan.

Mom didn't laugh. "I worry about you. You've always taken things so seriously, and—" She broke off with a little laugh. "While I'm proud of all you've accomplished, it's not like the fate of the world depends on dance decorations or when you bring people cake. Or Cotillion."

I tried to shrug that off. Again, what was wrong with a little dedication? But Mom's words seemed to lodge somewhere inside my chest. She was right that the *whole* world didn't revolve around what I did at the Grove, but she also didn't know about David. About whatever I *was* now. What if the entire fate of the world did depend on me taking this cake to Saylor Stark?

With that thought in mind, I decided to pick out one of Mom's nicer cake plates. Just in case.

"I promise, once Cotillion is over, I'll start dropping some things. I'll need to focus on college stuff by then anyway."

Mom didn't seem particularly comforted by that, but she helped me move the cake onto the holder. "I hope Saylor appreciates all of this."

Sighing, I lifted the cake. "You and me both."

Chapter 14

DAVID'S HOUSE was only a few blocks from mine, so it didn't take long to get there. People who aren't from the South imagine we all live in these big plantation houses like in *Gone with the Wind*, but the truth is, those are few and far between. And if you *do* see one of those big wedding cake houses, chances are it was built in the past fifty years.

But Saylor Stark's house was the real deal. Built in 1843, it was the oldest house in Pine Grove. According to The Aunts, it used to have a name. Ivy Hall, or Moss Manor. Something silly like that. The name had even been worked into the iron of the giant double gates. But Saylor had had new gates made when she moved in, something that, again according to The Aunts, was a supremely bad idea. "Houses are like boats," Aunt May had sniffed. "They should always keep their original names."

I didn't know about all that, but I did know that the Stark house was one of the prettiest I'd ever seen. It wasn't as grand and imposing as Magnolia House, but it was pretty in its own way. There was a wide front porch covered in ferns and white rocking chairs, and lamplight spilled out of the big windows lining the front of the house. Ivy crept up one brick wall, and the curving driveway was made, like the one at Magnolia House, out of crushed shells rather than gravel. I parked behind Miss Saylor's Cadillac, and, gingerly taking the cake, headed up the brick steps to the front door. I was about to ring the doorbell when I heard Miss Stark say, "Done with that paper."

"I can't," David replied. I'd heard that tone of voice before. I didn't have to see David to know that he was clenching his teeth and scowling.

"You can and you will," Miss Saylor fired back. "No more late hours, no more riding around in fast cars with girls—"

"Oh my God," David groaned. "Like Harper Jane Price is some kind of bad influence on me."

"I want you to stay away from that girl," Miss Saylor said, and I nearly reeled.

That girl?

Since when was I someone people called That Girl? That Girl didn't wear pearls. She wasn't SGA president. She didn't volunteer her time on teen counseling hotlines. I was most definitely *not* That Girl.

"I don't know what's going on with you," David said, his voice getting louder. I had the impression that was because he'd moved closer to the front door. "But since when do you care where I go or who I spend time with?"

"I have always cared," she replied. "But I worry about you. I'm your aunt, David; that's allowed."

"Whatever," David replied, and I cringed. Saylor Stark didn't seem like the kind of woman you could say "whatever" to. "I'm nearly eighteen, and the last time I checked, that means I get to see who I want to see and go where I want to go. And right now, I'm going to the library."

Wait, what?

Suddenly, the front door swung open.

Shoot.

David took a step forward, nearly bumping into me. His eyes widened as he pulled himself up short. "Whoa, sorr— Pres?"

And now Saylor was peering around his shoulder, and there I was, holding a stupid cake, which suddenly seemed less like a peace offering and more like a really bad idea.

"I was bringing this by to say sorry for yesterday. To both of you," I added as Saylor moved forward. "You know, for the . . . the car driving and the recklessness, and the—the grabbing . . ."

With my free hand I started making this clutching gesture. I was talking about grabbing David's shirt, but it looked like I was milking a cow.

Or worse.

My face red, I thrust the cake at David, who nearly stumbled backward. "Anyway, it's hummingbird cake, and I know that's your favorite, Miss Saylor, so . . . enjoy!" Ugh. It wasn't like me to be this . . . awkward. And then, to make matters worse, I tripped a little in my hurry to get back down the steps and out of there as quickly as I could.

But I'd barely gotten to the driveway before Saylor called, "Harper!"

I turned around. "Yes, ma'am?"

Saylor waved her hand at me, diamonds catching the street-lights. "Have you eaten dinner yet?"

My palms were sweaty and I did my best to discreetly wipe them on my skirt. "No, ma'am."

"Well, neither have we. I made chicken and dumplings. Why don't you come on in and eat with us. Then we can try out this lovely looking cake."

In all the years I'd known the Starks—and that was basically all my life—I'd never actually been inside their house. The temptation to see inside . . . well, I couldn't resist.

"That would be nice, thank you," I said, walking back up the steps. As I did, I noticed a set of wind chimes hanging from the porch roof. They were silver and shiny, and there was something weird about the shape of them. Musical notes?

Before I could look any closer, Saylor had an arm around my shoulders, guiding me into the house. It smelled a lot like my Aunt Jewel's house—that comforting combination of scented candles, coffee, and something cooking. But that was where the similarities ended. While Aunt Jewel's house was neat and full of light and space, the Stark house was so full I found myself nego-tiating around couches and ottomans. Every room was full of furniture, vases, picture frames, weird little porcelain statues of farm animals. It was like she'd raided every garage sale between here and Mobile.

Thankfully, Saylor's dining room was the one room that wasn't overstuffed, and I took a deep breath as Saylor gestured to one of the chairs around a long wooden table. "Sit down, honey," she told me. To David, she said, "Give me a hand."

While they disappeared into the kitchen, I sat down and took in Saylor Stark's dining room. Like the rest of the house, it seemed slightly . . . crowded. Even the wallpaper was busy, covered in a pattern I couldn't quite make out. There was a heavy curio cabinet in the corner, filled with all kinds of knickknacks, and more pictures on the wall. I scanned the faces, wondering if any of them were David's parents. Most of the pictures did seem to be of young, shiny-haired, smiling people, but none of them actually looked like David.

Frowning, I leaned forward, trying to see more clearly. But before I could, David came back in, a small stack of plates and some silverware in his hands.

"We need to talk," I whispered quickly, darting a glance at the door to the kitchen. "After dinner. I think I found out some—"

"Here we are!" Saylor trilled, carrying a steaming pot. After sitting it on a terra-cotta trivet in the middle of the table, Saylor took the seat at the head of the table, David to her left, me to her right. The smell from the pot was mouth-watering, and I suddenly realized I'd been so nervous about Ryan that I hadn't eaten lunch.

"My aunts make chicken and dumplings," I offered. "My mom tries, but she can never get them quite right."

Saylor gave me an indulgent smile. "The secret is white pepper. I bet your aunts know that. Which reminds me, I need to call your Aunt Jewel. Can't have Cotillion without her famous punch!"

I tried to hide my shudder. I loved Aunt Jewel, but her punch—a truly dreadful concoction made from white grape juice, ginger ale, Hawaiian Punch, and practically a pound of sugar—made my teeth hurt. Still, I nodded at Saylor. "She'd like that. And actually, speaking of Cotillion—"

But before I could say anything else, Saylor held one manicured finger up to her lips. "We can talk about that later. Let's say grace first."

She reached out her hand and took mine, lifting her other hand to David. He took it and then held his other hand out to me.

I laid my palm in his.

When I was eleven, my family was visiting my uncle's farm and Leigh-Anne dared me to touch an electric fence. It had been stupid, but I did what my big sister asked. The shock had blown me off my feet and made my whole arm numb for nearly an hour.

What happened in Saylor Stark's dining room felt a lot like that. Power surged through me, and every nerve in my body screamed. Saylor's rings felt almost unbearably hot against my skin, and for one dizzying second, I thought I could smell something burning.

A screen dropped in front of my eyes, just like that day behind the church with David and Ryan. But this time, I couldn't make any sense of the images. Girls in white dresses, a pool of red liquid on a hardwood floor. Chunks of glass—no, *ice*—flying through the air. And over the hum of whatever power was linking me and the Starks, the sound of screams. So much screaming.

Almost as suddenly as they'd begun, the images stopped, and suddenly, my hands were at my sides and I was staring at Saylor's dining room table, my breath sawing in and out of my lungs.

"What—" I said, but Saylor was already getting up, moving so quickly her chair slammed into the wall, scuffing a black mark into the wallpaper.

"David!" she cried, and I turned to see that he was slumped on the floor, head in his hands. I thought the lights were reflecting off his glasses, but then I realized that that wasn't it. His eyes were solid white.

As Saylor crouched next to him, cradling his head, David began to speak. "The night of the swans," he muttered. "Power restored, a new era rises, but one must fall. One must give everything. Night of the swans . . ."

"Shhh," Saylor murmured, smoothing his hair away from his face.

My own face still felt hot and when I glanced down, I saw that all the hairs on my arms were standing up.

David's eyes fluttered shut, and with a sigh, he sagged against the carpet. As he did, Saylor gently pulled her hands back and rocked on her heels.

Saylor Stark had always been one of the most beautiful women I knew, but now, she looked old and almost . . . haggard. And her eyes, when they studied my face, might have been the same warm blue as David's, but they were steely and hard and full of something I didn't have a name for.

"You're our new Paladin," she said, and despite all the awfulness of what had just happened, relief so intense it nearly took my breath washed over me. After all this time waiting for my Professor X, it was Saylor Stark. We were going to be fine.

"Well." Saylor rose to her feet. "We are totally effed."

Chapter 15

SHE SAID the actual word. Saylor Stark said the F-word.

From his place on the carpet, David started to stir. "What happened?" he muttered, trying to sit up. As soon as he did, he flinched, lowering his head back into his hands. "Did I have a stroke? Is that why I think you said what I think you just said?" he asked Saylor.

"You know," I said, ignoring David. "You know what I am."

She didn't answer. Instead, she walked into the kitchen. I heard the rattle of ice, then a cabinet opening and closing.

David still sat on the carpet, knees drawn up to his chest.

"Are you okay?" I asked, sliding out of my chair and onto my knees. The thick carpet scraped my skin as I edged forward.

"No," he replied. "I feel like my head is about to explode."

I moved a little closer to him. He looked so pale and wretched that I was tempted to smooth his hair back the way Saylor had. Instead, I fisted my hands in my skirt. "I know that was intense, but hey—your aunt knows what's going on. That's awesome, right? We can get some answers."

David raised his head. His pupils were so huge his eyes looked almost black. "Actually, Pres," he rasped out, "my aunt being in on this makes it a hell of a lot weirder."

Saylor came back in, holding a small glass full of a dark amber liquid. She sat down at the table, threw back the drink, and then looked at the two of us again.

Then she got up and made another drink.

Once that one was down, she finally said, "I'm not really your aunt, David. If that makes things easier for you."

David went very still, and for a moment, everything was so quiet, I could hear the ticking of the grandfather clock in the hallway.

Then she turned to me. "I thought it might be you. I knew that Christopher was gone, I . . . I felt him go. And then you and David both looked so shaken up yesterday that I wondered if maybe . . ." Sighing, she set her glass down. I stared at the perfectly set table, the silverware still in neat rows, napkins folded, and fought the urge to burst into hysterical giggles. Or tears.

Shutting my eyes, I tried to focus. "Christopher?"

David murmured, "Mr. Hall. That was his first name." When I opened my eyes, David was still looking at the ground, arms encircling his knees.

Saylor tipped her head back. The light from the chandelier caught her earrings, sending scattered rainbows across the shiny surface of the dining room table. "What happened?"

I told her about the night of the Homecoming Dance as briefly as I could. When I was done, a single tear trickled out from under Saylor's closed eyes. "It's my fault," she murmured. "I knew the wards needed to be stronger the closer we got, but I couldn't think of a way to do it. And I hoped . . ." She opened her eyes then, focusing on David. "I hoped," she said again, and then she was standing up.

I half expected her to go make another drink. Instead, she wandered to the window, hands braced on her lower back. "I'm guessing you two will want the whole story, then."

David was still grayish, but when he rose to his feet, there was steel in his voice. "You think? If you're not my aunt, then who the hell are you? Why do I live with you?"

Saylor took a deep breath. "Technically, I kidnapped you."

I felt David jump at that, and wasn't sure anything had ever been more painful than watching him try to think of some way to respond. "My parents?" he asked, his voice strangled.

"Dead," Saylor replied, blunt. "Murdered by the same people who are after you now."

She dropped her head, pinching her nose between her thumb and forefinger. "I'm messing this up. There's so much to tell you, and I don't even know where to start. Christopher would've been better at this, Christopher was—" Saylor broke off. "It doesn't matter. The point is you're an Oracle."

"But that's impossible," I said. "Everything I read said that Oracles are always girls."

Saylor whipped her head around to me. I think for a second, she'd forgotten I was there. "You've already started researching this?"

"A-a little," I told her, standing up. "Dr. DuPont used the word Paladin, so I started there. Then when I talked to David, he mentioned his . . . his dreams, and we started putting things together."

The look Saylor gave me was part pride, part appraisal. I'd seen it before at Cotillion practice. "Clever girl," she said in a low voice. "Maybe you'll be better at this than I thought."

Then she heaved another sigh and came back to the table, bracing her hands on it. "But what you read was wrong. There *can* be male Oracles, although there's only been one besides you, David. In the eighth century, there was one named Alaric, and—"

David gripped the back of a chair, his jaw set. "I don't want a history lesson," he ground out. "You're telling me you're not my aunt, my parents are dead, and I'm an *Oracle*. The eighth century doesn't really mean shit to me right now."

"David," I said, tugging his jacket.

"It's all right," Saylor said, her eyes still on David. "You have every right to be upset. More than upset. But we are running out of time, and now that there are . . . ," her gaze flicked to me, "unforeseen complications, I need you to listen. I need you to understand. I don't need you to forgive me right now, but please. Hear me out."

David paused, nearly vibrating with anger and energy. But eventually, he sat.

Saylor closed her eyes briefly and then continued. "Unfortunately, Alaric was nowhere near as powerful as all of the women who came before him were. His visions were muddy, unclear. More what could be than what *would* be."

"That seems . . . lame," I said, going back to sit in my chair.

"That's a word for it, yes," Saylor replied. "And the problem is, you can't have more than one Oracle at once. One has to die for another to be born."

Dumbly, I nodded. "So if you get stuck with a dud Oracle—"

Saylor cut me off with a wave of her hand. "You have to kill it in order to bring forth the next one. But obviously Alaric wasn't about to let himself be killed. Instead, he attempted a . . . well, a ritual on himself. One that would make his powers increase ten-fold so that his visions would be clearer."

"Did it work?" David's hands were still wrapped tightly around the top of his chair, but his shoulders weren't up around his ears anymore and some color had returned to his face.

Saylor patted at her hair, leaning back. "It did. But it worked too well. Alaric didn't just improve his visions. He gained new powers. Alarmingly strong ones. At that time, Alaric . . . I suppose you could say he belonged to Charlemagne. And Charlemagne had set up a cadre of knights to protect Alaric that he called the Paladins. But until Alaric did his ritual, they were just ordinary men. After the ritual, Alaric was able to make them . . ." She trailed off, her eyes moving over me. "Well, you. Not just knights, but supernaturally gifted warriors, all of them loyal to Alaric to the point of death."

I swallowed, not liking the sound of that.

Saylor sat forward in her chair a little, hands clenched in front of her. "But the ritual had an unintended side effect. That much power, it's . . . it's more than a human brain can handle. It more or less burned Alaric up from the inside, twisting him into something evil. Charlemagne eventually ordered him executed."

"But he had a whole posse of bodyguards with superpowers," David muttered, sinking into his chair.

Saylor nodded. "Exactly. Between Alaric's powers and the

dozens of Paladins guarding him, it took over a hundred men to kill the Oracle. An entire village was destroyed in the process, and there were only two Paladins left when it was all over."

"So once Alaric was dead, what happened?" David asked. His mouth was still set in a hard line, but his eyes were curious.

"A group of powerful men met and decided that the Oracle should no longer belong to any one ruler. She—and they were only ever women after Alaric—should be kept safe somewhere, guarded. The two remaining Paladins volunteered for the task."

"Okay," I said slowly. I really wish I'd brought some paper and pens. This seemed like a situation where a chart could help. "So what are you then?"

The corners of her mouth turned up. "When Alaric took Charlemagne's knights and turned them into Paladins, he also took Charlemagne's two court magicians and gave them powers as well. Granted, they only got a fraction of the magic that Alaric possessed, but it was enough. They called themselves Mages. And that, Harper, is what I am."

In the silence that followed, I heard a car drive down the street and the distant hooting of an owl. "So you're a witch?" David finally asked, the tips of his ears red.

Saylor smoothed an imaginary wrinkle from her pantsuit and gave a dismissive sniff. "That is an ugly word, David Stark. Mages don't ride around on broomsticks or conjure up things. We use potions, minor spells to assist the Oracle and the Paladin in their work."

"So there's one Oracle," I said, flinging a hand out toward

David. "And now there's one Paladin." I pointed at myself. "How many Mages are there?"

"Two, usually," Saylor answered, fiddling with the edge of a placemat. "The Ephors—those are the men who took charge of the Oracle—believed in keeping things traditional. Since there were two original Paladins, two original Mages, they've always tried to maintain that balance. You said the bathroom was spotless after the fight with Christopher and Dr. DuPont, right?"

When David and I both nodded, Saylor said, "That was alchemy." Then she frowned. "Incredibly dangerous alchemy, though. That spell is a sort of temporal shift. It returns the setting to what it looked like before the trauma. Cara never would've tried something like that."

When David and I both asked, "Who?" Saylor waved a hand. "The other Mage when I was with the Ephors. She was old then, though, and that was nearly twenty years ago. They must have someone new."

David, who had been worrying at one of his fingernails, dropped his hand. "A temporal shift. Why doesn't that make the people that got killed . . . undead?"

Saylor turned her glass over and over in her hand. "I told you, our powers are very limited. Control over the human body and soul . . . that's very far beyond us. Fixing a gate or a broken section of tile in a bathroom is one thing. Erasing something as permanent as death is . . ." She broke off, pushing her glass away. "In any case, the main purpose of the Mage is to serve as a kind of . . . battery, I suppose, to the Oracle. That's what happened tonight. When the three of us joined hands, you finally got the burst of power you needed."

And we'd seen David's vision, too. Except even now, it was fading from my mind, like trying to remember a dream. What had David said?

I glanced over at him and saw that he also appeared to be deep in thought. But before I could ask any more questions, Saylor stood up.

"Which leads us to now. And to you. Both of you. Eighteen years ago, we were living in Greece. That's where the Ephors keep the Oracle, Paladin, and Mage. We'd had the same Oracle for . . . oh, years. Since before I was called. And when she died, she gave us one last prophecy. That the next Oracle born would be a boy. So they ordered Christopher to kill him. You," she said to David.

I took a sip of my lemonade. The ice had melted, and it tasted bitter now, but my mouth was so dry I didn't care.

"When an Oracle dies, she always gives the place and time where the new one will be born. Christopher and I were sent to get you."

For the first time, shame washed over Saylor's face. "Alchemy." She fumbled in her pocket, bringing out a small blue jar of lip balm. "This is a salve. A potion that lets the Mage do minor mind-control spells. I compelled your mother to hand you to me. She did it with a smile."

I thought the back of the chair might crack under David's hands, but he didn't say anything.

"We were halfway back to Greece when I realized I couldn't

do it," Saylor continued, tears in her voice. "Christopher couldn't, either. We'd made a vow to protect the Oracle, no matter what. And so we . . . we stole you."

She stood up again, brushing at her slacks. "Mages don't have particularly powerful magic, so we try to steal it whenever we can find it. Back in the 1800s, there was a witch who lived in this town. I don't know why, but for whatever reason, she threw up wards all over the place. Makes it hard for anyone to get in if they mean to do harm. So it seemed like the perfect hiding spot."

Saylor busied herself with some of the knickknacks on the sideboard, picking up a porcelain shepherdess and putting it down beside a Swarovski hedgehog. "And of course, I made sure I got on every committee I could, the more excuse to put up extra protection symbols. I even put one on you," she said, pointing to David's arm. Startled, he pushed up the sleeve of his T-shirt, and sure enough, there was a tiny scar on his arm, almost like a birth-mark, in that same shape of a figure eight on its side.

"But then," Saylor said, "I guess you figured that out. Still, they worked. Oh, the first year, there was a man the Ephors sent who got through, but Christopher sorted that out, and I put up that ugly statue in the park. After that, there were no more inci-dents until recently."

My brain actually ached. I didn't know that was possible.

I rolled my neck, hoping that might help. "So why now, then? Why after nearly eighteen years are all your spells and wards not working?"

Saylor gave a rueful smile. "They were only ever a Band-Aid. The closer we get to Cotillion, the weaker they'll become."

David's head shot up. "Cotillion?"

"Night of the swans," I said, suddenly remembering. "That's what you said when you had your little"— I waved my hand— "fit."

"Vision," Saylor corrected while David shrugged his shoulders, uncomfortable.

"What's happening the night of Cotillion?" It was stupid, I know, but as soon as I said it, a weight seemed to settle in my chest. Cotillion. The night I'd been looking forward to for so long, and now even *it* was part of this insanity?

Saylor went to take another sip of her drink, but it was empty. I didn't drink alcohol, but I felt her pain as she frowned at the ice cubes in her glass. I could use a drink, too. "Before the last Oracle died, she not only gave us the location of the new Oracle, she also named a specific night when the new Oracle would be tested. At the end of this test, the Oracle would either be the most powerful Oracle yet, or . . . or he would be dead."

That word—*dead*—seemed to hang in the air around us. David dropped into a chair, his hands clutching the knees of his pants as he slumped forward.

Saylor reached out, to touch him, I think, but her hand only hovered a few inches in front of him before she drew it back. Clearing her throat, she continued, "So that's why I took over Cotillion and moved it to that night."

"Why not cancel it altogether?" I shifted in my seat. "Take David out of the country that night or something."

But Saylor just shook her head. "Certain events, they're like fixed points in time. Destined. This is one of them. David has to go through this test, whatever it is, and nothing can stop it. All we can do is . . . be prepared."

"So what does all this mean?" I finally asked. My voice sounded dry and unused, and my mind was racing, trying to process all of this. Magic, and Greece, and stolen babies . . . it was like my life had suddenly turned into a really bad soap opera.

"It means that you've been given a sacred duty," Saylor said. Her voice sounded different, and there was hardly a trace of Southern accent in it at all. "From this day forward, you will be tasked with protecting the Oracle at all costs. He'll be your sole focus until the day you, like Christopher, have to lay down your life for him."

Saylor reached for my hand, and I gave it to her without thinking. "So, Harper Jane Price. Are you ready to accept your destiny?"

Chapter 16

I WITHDREW my hand. "No, thank you."

Saylor and David both stared.

"I appreciate your offer very much," I continued. "But I'm afraid I have to refuse."

Saylor rose to her feet, an expression somewhere between anger and disbelief spreading across her face. "I'm not inviting you to a garden party, Harper. I'm asking you to accept the role destiny has handed you. I'm asking you to use the powers you've been given."

But I was already shaking my head. "No. No, this is not my destiny." Heart hammering, I could feel blood rushing to my face and I knew that my chest and neck must be splotchy. "I have my own life, and things . . . things I want to do. I can't follow him"— I flung my arm out at David—"and keep him safe forever. What am I supposed to do about college? Or—or getting married and having kids and—"

Breaking off, I took a deep breath and held up my hand. "You know what, no. Forget it. It doesn't matter, because I'm not going to be a Paladin."

Saylor rolled her lips inward, eyes narrowing. It was an expression I'd seen on her face dozens of times, usually when Mary Beth was screwing up at Cotillion practice. "It's not something you get to decide," she said. "You already *are* a Paladin. The moment Christopher passed his powers on to you, you accepted this responsibility."

"But I didn't," I fired back. My throat was tight, and I could feel the tears pricking my eyes. Great, splotchy *and* I was about to be snotty. "This was done to me. I didn't choose this. And so now, I'm choosing *not* to do it."

I looked down at David who was still sitting on the floor, watching me. "I'm sorry," I told him. "I obviously don't want you to die. I mean, I know I've said that I did a few times, but I didn't really mean it. And it was only when you were being especially provoking, so—"

"Harper."

I turned back to Saylor. "No," I said again, but she continued like I hadn't spoken.

"This isn't something you can walk away from." Saylor's back was ramrod straight, shoulders tense under the bright coral of her jacket. "Do you know how important Oracles are? Wars have been fought over them. And now the Ephors are coming after David again, and I don't know what they want to do with him."

"You can do magic!" I shouted back and despite all of it, there was some tiny part of me still horrified I'd shouted at Saylor Stark. But I shoved that down and kept going. "You can make wards to protect him, and—and make things disappear. You don't need me."

Walking forward, Saylor gripped my arms, tight enough to hurt. "We do," she insisted, giving me a little shake. "There have to be three, Harper. Three people, working together. The Oracle, the Paladin, and the Mage. One part of that missing . . ."

"And what?" I asked, my gaze flying back to David. He was standing now, but his face was blank and I had no idea what he was thinking.

"It won't work," Saylor said, and for the first time, I saw how desperate she really was. Her voice went softer even as her grip got tighter. "Harper, Christopher and I risked everything to save David. We did not get this close to lose him now."

I struggled out of her hands. As I did, my eyes fell on the wall behind her and all of those skinny sideways figure eights, the symbol of the Paladin. Something surged in my blood, but I shut my eyes. No. No, I was not doing this. I was walking away. I *could* walk away.

But standing there, shaking with some power I couldn't even name, that seemed easier said than done.

I thought of my mom and dad. Of Ryan and Bee and all those college brochures in my desk at home. And the shaky feeling started to recede.

Taking deep breaths through my nose, I tried to get myself under control. "Tell me why," I said at last. "Tell me why it's so essential that I give up my whole life to keep David safe."

Saylor blinked and took a step back from me. "He can see the future, Harper. The only person in the entire world who can. Don't you think that's worth protecting?"

Rubbing my hands over my face, I fought the urge to scream. "Yes, but not at the expense of *my* life."

There was the lip roll again. "And what is it you plan on doing with your life that's so important, Harper? Is it more important than ensuring the safety of the only Oracle?"

"Yes."

We both turned to look at David. His hands were shoved in his pockets, his gaze on the floor. "Harper's life is important, Aunt—" He broke off, shaking his head. "And she's right. She can't just follow me around forever. That's not fair to her. Or to me. I mean, I might actually want to get a girlfriend at some point, and no offense, Pres, but I think you might salt my game a little. Wait, do I have to be celibate, too?"

Saylor rolled her eyes. "David, take this seriously."

Even from a distance, I could see the steeliness in David's eyes as he took Saylor in. "I am. Trust me. And that's why I'm saying this whole thing is crazy. Paladins and Oracles and ancient Greece . . ." Sighing, he lifted one hand to rake it through his hair.

"You keep doing—what did you call them? Wards?—and I'll try really hard not to tell the future anymore, and Harper will go back to her regular life of committees and dances and being a pain in my ass."

Saylor opened her mouth to reply, but David held up his hand. "You said the three of us have to work together. Well, it's two against one here. This?" He made a circle with his finger between the three of us. "This isn't happening. And now if you ladies will excuse me, I'm going upstairs and taking some aspirin."

With that, he turned and walked away. Saylor and I listened to his heavy tread on the staircase, both of us jumping a little when his door slammed.

Dropping into the nearest chair, Saylor covered her face with one hand. "I meant what I said, Harper. There's no walking away. From the moment you entered that bathroom, your fate was sealed. His, too." She picked up her head and nodded in the direction of the stairs.

I didn't answer her. Instead, I took my keys from where I'd laid them by my plate. The chicken and dumplings had coagulated into a beige blob and I wondered how I'd ever thought they looked appetizing.

"Thank you for dinner," I told her even though I hadn't eaten a bite. "Also, I think—" My voice broke, so I cleared my throat and tried again. "I think it would be best if I pulled out of Cotillion this year." I wasn't sure how I was going to explain that to my parents, but I also knew that I wanted no part of whatever was going to happen that night.

Saylor's gaze stayed steady on me. She might not have been related to David by blood, but her eyes were nearly the same shade of blue. For a second, I thought she was going to try the sales pitch again. Instead, she gave a little nod. "I understand."

My knees were shaking as I went to leave the dining room. I was just to the doorway when Saylor said my name again.

"Yes, ma'am?" I asked, turning to face her.

"Thank you so much for the cake," she said, and in that moment, she was the Saylor Stark I'd known my entire life, all perfect silver hair and straight white teeth. "You're a doll."

Chapter 17

I spent the next few days avoiding David. Or maybe he spent them avoiding me. Either way, I hardly saw him, and when our paths crossed, both of us were quick to look the other way. Once, as I watched him cross campus, his shoulders up around his ears, I felt a twinge of . . . something. At first, I thought it was maybe the beginnings of that gut-wrenching pain that meant he was in trouble. But it wasn't that. I think it was sympathy. Or pity. As hard a time as I was having wrapping my brain around *Saylor Stark* being some kind of witch, David must have been having it a million times worse.

But I'd done the right thing in walking away from them. From all of it. No matter how awesome I thought superpowers would be, they weren't worth giving up my life for.

Still, as I perched on a stool in my Aunt Jewel's kitchen that Friday afternoon, I couldn't stop thinking about how worried David looked every day, how just that morning, someone had slammed a locker in the hallway, and he had nearly jumped out of his skin.

It was true, what I'd told Saylor; I didn't want David to get killed by bad guys, obviously. But I still couldn't see how it was even feasible for me to watch over him forever.

So why did I feel so bad?

"Harper, a bird is going to land on that lip if you keep pokin' it out," Aunt Jewel said. She sat at the table with her two sisters, my Aunts May and Martha. The three of them were doing what they did every Friday afternoon—playing cards and smoking. Since I wasn't married, I didn't get to play with them, and smoking was out until I was widowed.

Not, I thought as I fanned the smoke away from my face, that that was ever going to be an issue. Smoking was so seriously gross.

"I'm not poking out my lip," I replied, even though I was pretty sure I had been.

Aunts May and Martha were twins, but seeing them with Aunt Jewel, the three could have easily been triplets. All of them had the same iron-gray hair, permed within an inch of its life, and all three wore the same type of brightly colored elastic-waisted pants, usually paired with floral sweaters, or, like today, holiday-appropriate sweatshirts. Aunt May's had a turkey on it, while Aunt Martha was wearing pumpkins. Aunt Jewel had what appeared to be a giant pie stitched on the front of hers.

Sipping sweet tea, I watched them play rummy and insult each other. "Martha, I know you're not going to take that ace," Aunt May said as my Aunt Martha did just that. May scowled as she flicked ash into an ugly clay dish I'd made for that purpose at summer camp seven years ago.

"You are evil, Martha," she said, drawling her twin sister's name out so that it sounded more like "Maawwtha."

Aunt Martha gave a smug smile and arranged her cards. "Harper, baby, do you hear your Aunt May being ugly to me?"

"Don't drag Harper into this," Aunt Jewel said as she laid down another card. She was the eldest of The Aunts, and the other two tended to listen to her. "We never get to see her, and now the two of you are going to spoil her visit by fussin'."

I hid a smile behind my glass. Actually, sitting in Aunt Jewel's cozy, yellow kitchen, watching the three of them argue with each other, was one of my favorite things. They could get downright nasty over cards, but there was never any doubt that they were sisters who loved one another.

I wondered if I could ever think of the word "sisters" and not feel a steady ache in my chest.

I sat my tea on the counter behind me. "I'm fine," I told them. "Also, Aunt May, if you pick up that four Aunt Martha discarded, you can get a run."

Jewel and Martha groaned as, hooting, Aunt May scooped up the card. "You should come by more often, Miss Harper," she said.

Aunt Jewel began gathering the cards back up, and Aunt Martha looked over at me. "Speaking of, what brought you by today, sweetie? Not that we're not thrilled to see you, of course, or that we aren't pleased as punch to have a hummingbird cake"— she nodded toward the heavy glass platter on the counter—"but you're usually so busy."

"Too busy," Aunt May chimed in. "Girls today have so much going on. School, and sports, and dances, and committees . . . it's too much!"

"Don't say that," Aunt Martha told her, lighting another cigarette. "Our Harper is responsible and has a good sense of community. What's wrong with that? And least she's not one of those Teen Moms."

The other aunts clucked in sympathy. A few months back, Aunts Martha and May—they lived together—had gotten a satellite dish and discovered the joy/horror of reality TV.

"Or one of those crackheads, like on that show where they make people feel bad about taking drugs," Aunt Jewel offered. "Did you see the episode with the girl who did something called huffing? With the cans of cleaning—"

I hated to interrupt, but once they got going on car crash TV, they might never stop. "I have been busy," I broke in. "And that's kind of what I wanted to talk to y'all about."

All three of my aunts put their cards down and swiveled in their chairs to face me. There were few things they loved more than people coming to them for advice. It helped that they were really good at it. "It's about Cotillion," I said, and Aunts Martha and May exchanged a look, while Aunt Jewel exhaled a cloud of smoke.

"That Cotillion," Aunt Martha spat out. "I suwannee." That was her way of saying "I swear." Aunt Martha belonged to that generation of ladies who thought any type of swearing—not just saying the bad words—was not the thing to do.

"You don't like Cotillion?" I asked, surprised. All of them had done it, and so had my grandmother, my mom, my sister . . .

Besides, The Aunts lived for tradition and propriety. Cotillion should be one of their favorite things ever.

"We did," Aunt Jewel said, stubbing out her cigarette as she stood. Ladies never smoked unless they were sitting, after all. "Until that woman took it over."

More grumbling. I scooted forward on the edge of my stool. "Saylor Stark?"

Aunt Jewel rolled her eyes. "Such a silly name."

"Before she came, Cotillion was held in the spring. Which is when it's *meant* to be held," Aunt Martha said, laying her hands in her lap. "Girls are supposed to come out in the spring; everyone knows that. That's why it used to be called the Chrysalis Ball."

"And now it's what? The Mistletoe Ball?" Aunt May asked. She gave a derisive sniff. "That doesn't even make sense. Unless she has y'all running around kissing people."

"She would," Aunt Jewel muttered, plucking a piece of lint from the pie emblazoned across her chest.

"Who ran it before?" I asked.

"Cathy Foster," Aunt Jewel answered promptly. "And she did a lovely job of it, too. I never understood why she handed it over to a stranger."

"I never understood why Saylor Stark was so bound and determined to be in charge of Cotillion, anyway," Aunt Martha said. "Apparently, she'd run one back in her hometown in Virginia."

Another round of frowns and clucking. "The whole thing was odd," Aunt May mused, leaning back in her chair. "Cathy loved running Cotillion, and as far as I knew, she planned on passing it on to her daughter. Then Saylor Stark showed up, had one lunch with her, and suddenly, *she* was in charge."

"Same with the Pine Grove Betterment Society," Aunt Martha reminded her. "I thought Suzanne Perry was going to run that until the end of time. But it was the same thing. Saylor Stark marches her behind over to Suzanne's house with a rum cake, and suddenly she's in charge of the PGBS, too."

I fidgeted on my stool, thinking about my conversation with Saylor. She'd called herself a Mage, but it seemed like "witch" was just as good a term. And she'd obviously used some kind of power on Cathy Foster and Suzanne Perry. And now that I knew why she'd taken over all of those things, my beloved Cotillion included . . .

"Do y'all know anything else about the Starks? Anything . . . I don't know, kind of odd? Out of the ordinary?"

Aunts May and Martha exchanged another glance as Aunt Jewel got another glass of sweet tea. "Whole family is strange if you ask me," she said, frowning. "Saylor appearing in town like she did, with that brand-new baby. And buying up Yellowhammer."

Right, that had been the name of the Starks' house. I knew it was kind of dumb.

"When we were growing up, people used to tell ghost stories about that house," Aunt May mused. "They said a witch lived there a long time ago. Or something like that." She waved her hand, raining ashes down on Aunt Jewel's yellow gingham table-cloth. "Of course, you can't swing a possum without hitting a haunted house in these parts, so I'm sure it was nothing."

Aunt Martha shook her head. "I always thought it was odd that she didn't have a husband. I'm telling you, I don't think that boy is just her nephew."

"Hush, Martha," Aunt Jewel admonished. She went back to the table and began dealing cards again. "I'm not Saylor Stark's biggest fan by any means, but no matter who she is to that boy, she's done the best she could by him. And he's turned out nearly as smart as our Harper!" Leaning forward, Aunt Jewel gave me a shrewd smile. "You're still going to whup him for valedictorian though, right, baby?"

I smiled back. "Absolutely."

They started to play again, and while I was already about to go into a diabetic coma, I poured myself some more tea anyway. "Are there any other weird things that've happened here in town? Not only related to the Starks, but . . . I don't know. People seeing things. Stuff disappearing, like . . . magic kind of stuff?"

All three of them exchanged a look this time, and then Aunt Martha very gingerly put her cards down. "Harper, have you been doing the huffing?"

"No," I said, setting down my glass so fast that tea sloshed out onto the counter. I reached behind me for a paper towel and continued. "I was just wondering. For a research project. I'm doing a—a paper on local superstitions."

Mollified, The Aunts resumed their card game. "Oh, well, in that case, of course there have been odd things," Aunt May said.

"There's that window in the courthouse that supposedly shows a man's face if the sun hits it the right way."

"And they say the choir loft at First Baptist is haunted," Aunt Martha added, pulling out another cigarette from her pack. "Although I think it's just pigeons up there, and the janitorial staff isn't doing their job."

"You know, sweetie, now that you mention things disappearing, there *was* that man years back," Aunt Jewel said, not looking up from her cards. "Real particular. Several people saw him lurking around town, dressed all in black, very suspicious. He was renting a room over at Janice Duff's boardinghouse. One night, Janice hears this awful ruckus up there, and when she goes in, she swears up and down that she saw him dead on his bed with a big sword in him."

My neck prickled as Aunt May nodded. "That's right. I talked to her about it the next week at church. She said it wasn't a regular sword either, it was one of those big curvy ones. Like in the old movies about sheikhs. What do they call those things?"

"Scimitars," I croaked, my mouth dry.

"That's right, a scimitar. Anyway, she calls 911, havin' an absolute fit, but when the police get there, the man was gone."

"And more than that," Aunt May said, discarding a five of clubs. "There was no trace he'd ever been there. No blood, no clothes, no suitcase. Bed made up all pretty and everything."

"Most everybody thought Janice was having a nervous breakdown. Happens when some women go through"— Aunt Martha dropped her voice to a whisper—"The Change."

My hand was shaking as I poured myself another glass of tea.

This time, I was pretty sure it wasn't from the sugar. Closing my eyes, I took a deep breath and hoped The Aunts wouldn't notice.

Not my problem, I tried to tell myself.

Aunt Jewel picked up a discarded card, and then turned a bright smile on me. "Anyway, does that answer your question, baby?"

I swallowed. "Sure does."

Chapter 18

"I'M PREGNANT."

"Huh?" Looking up from the pair of shoes I'd been pretending to study, I turned to face Bee. "What did you say?"

"Finally!" Bee said, tossing her head back with an exaggerated eye roll. "I said your name three times already, and when that didn't grab your attention, I decided to go dramatic."

Smiling, I tossed one of those little stockings you get to try on shoes at her. "Well, it clearly worked. I take it you are not actually carrying Brandon's spawn, then?"

Bee snorted and lifted one foot, turning her ankle so that I could admire the shoe from all angles. "No, thank God. My mama would kill me. Now what do you think of these?"

We were at the Pine Grove Galleria, our typical Saturday-afternoon destination. Today's trip was especially important since we were picking out our shoes for Cotillion. Or Bee was. I hadn't worked up the nerve to tell her I'd quit Cotillion yet, but since we were already on our third store, I was going to have to do it soon. I just wasn't sure how to break it to her in the middle of Well Heeled. The store was relatively deserted and I didn't see anyone we knew; the only other customers were a little girl, who was probably around ten, and her mom. Still, I was beginning to wish I'd just said something in the car on the way here.

Dutifully, I continued to inspect the white high heel she'd slipped on. "Pretty," I told her.

Bee frowned. "But not perfect."

"I . . . don't you think they're a little high?"

Sighing, Bee slid her foot out of the shoe and put it back in the box. "Probably. I'm good in heels, but I don't want to pull a Mary Beth."

Next to us, the little girl was trying to talk her mom into buying her a pair of red sparkly ballet flats, but the mom was holding her ground. "We're picking out *church shoes*, Kenley," she said, exasperated, and I had to hide a smile.

Bee stood up and reached out, picking up a strappy sandal. She ran her fingers over the jeweled straps. "This is pretty. It would look good with your dress. Doesn't it have sparkles?"

I tried to keep from sighing longingly. Yes, my dress had sparkles. Subtle ones, but sparkles nonetheless. And a little bustle and a short train, and about a hundred silk-covered buttons . . . and I would never wear it.

I'd been trying to work up the nerve to tell Bee all afternoon. First, I'd sworn I'd say something on the ride to the mall. And when we'd walked inside, I had been all set to say, "Actually, Bee, I've decided not to do Cotillion this year."

Now we were on our third store, and I knew it was now or never.

I took the shoe from Bee's hand and set it back on the shelf. "It would look good, but . . . I'm, um, not doing Cotillion after all."

Bee's mouth dropped open a bit, but no sound came out. Turning away from her, I moved over to a display of scarves. I'd never worn a scarf in my life, but I made a big show of pulling one out and examining the pattern.

"Why not?" Bee asked from behind me.

I put the first scarf back and pulled out another, and once again thought about telling Bee the truth. *I can't do Cotillion because I have superpowers, but they suck. Because something is going to happen there that night that I don't want to be involved with.*

But I couldn't say any of that. So instead, I played the one card I'd promised myself I would never, ever play. "Leigh-Anne," I said. "It's . . . too hard. Thinking about the year *she* did it . . ."

Bee didn't say anything for a long time, and I wasn't sure I had ever felt worse than I did at that moment. Damn it, I'd given up the whole Paladin thing. So why was it still messing up my life?

Bee appeared at my elbow. "Okay," she said, tucking her hair behind her ears. "Then I won't go either."

I dropped the scarf. "Bee, you can't—"

"I can," she said, even as she threw one last lusting look at the shoes. "We always said we were going to do Cotillion together."

Bee may have been the only person on earth more excited for Cotillion than I was, but she gave me a brave if entirely fake smile. "It'll be fine. We'll do, like, one of those anti-prom proms, only it'll be an anti-Cotillion Cotillion. We'll wear black dresses and hang out at my house watching bad movies and drinking bad punch."

"It'll be hard to find worse punch than my Aunt Jewel's," I said, and Bee's smile got a little more real.

"We'll manage," she said. Then she stopped to pick up the scarf, placing it back on its shelf. "Now let's go to the food court and eat our weight in Cinnabon."

"You are the bestest best friend in all the world," I said, looping my arm through hers.

"I know," she said, squeezing my arm against her side. "And you in no way deserve me."

I didn't. Not even a little bit, and the truth of that lodged in my throat so that all I could do was squeak, "Yup."

As we made our way through the mall, Bee and I chatted about Ryan and Brandon, and it could have been any other Saturday, if it weren't for the constant gnawing of guilt. Staying away from the Starks was the best thing to do, which meant staying away from Cotillion. I didn't want to ruin that for Bee, but it wasn't like I'd asked her to give it up.

Suddenly, Bee came to a stop, pulling me up short, too. "Oh."

"What?" I asked, following her gaze. And when I saw what she was looking at . . .

"Oh," I echoed.

Mary Beth was standing in front of the Starbucks in the food court, sipping an iced coffee and smiling up at Ryan.

He was leaning against the wall, hands in his back pockets, and he was smiling down at her. There was even . . . head-tilting.

My boyfriend was leaning and head-tilting at another girl. And not any girl. Mary Beth Riley, who practically had a neon sign flashing "TAKE ME NOW, RYAN BRADSHAW!" over her head.

"Is she chewing on her straw?" Bee asked quietly, and I narrowed my eyes. She was. She was *totally* chewing on her straw and smiling and head-tilting and—

Before I could think it through, I was walking over to the Starbucks, Bee trailing a few steps behind. "Ryan!" I called, smiling broadly.

He swiveled his head at the sound of my voice, but there was no guilt in his face. Mary Beth, however, jumped a little.

"Are you following me?" I asked him, coming in close to slide my arm around his waist. "I told him Bee and I were doing some shoe shopping today," I informed Mary Beth, who gave me a sickly smile.

"Actually, no. I was here to pick up my tux. Check me out, renting a full six weeks early."

"You're a good boyfriend," I conceded. And he was, which was why I couldn't stand idly by and let other girls chew straws at him.

A thought occurred to me. Ryan said he was picking up his tux for Cotillion. Ryan was supposed to escort me to Cotillion, and while the night wasn't as big a deal for guys as it was for girls, I knew Mrs. Bradshaw was on the committee at Magnolia House. She expected her son to go. And if I wouldn't go with him . . .

Bee must have been thinking something similar, because she turned to Mary Beth. "Do you have an escort for Cotillion?"

A sudden flush spread up Mary Beth's neck. "Not yet," she answered, and I saw her gaze flit to Ryan.

I moved in a little closer to him. Okay, this Paladin thing had already derailed my life enough. Turning Saylor Stark down was supposed to mean getting my life back, not ruining Cotillion for my best friend and handing my boyfriend over to Mary Beth Riley.

Bee glanced over at me, a little smile tugging the corner of her lips. "Bummer. I mean, it seems like all the decent guys at school are taken, and really, what are the chances of someone suddenly becoming available?"

The great thing about best friends is that they know you really well. And the terrible thing about best friends is that . . . they know you *really* well. Bee knew that the thought of Ryan taking Mary Beth to Cotillion was killing me. And what better way to get me to change my mind about Cotillion than to dangle that possibility?

I met Bee's eyes. "You know what? After we grab some food, why don't we go back to the store and get those shoes? The more I think about it, the more I think they *would* be perfect with my dress."

Bee grinned. "I think that sounds like an excellent idea."

I watched Mary Beth watch Ryan, longing all over her face. And I remembered that while Ryan might not have seemed guilty, he had been leaning. Exactly the way he used to lean against my locker door back in ninth grade. No, there was no way I was letting this happen. Operation Get My You-Know-What Together was starting now.

So I smiled at Bee, hugged my boyfriend, and said, "Me, too."

Chapter 19

THAT MONDAY, I found myself back at Magnolia House. Saylor's eyes had widened a little when I'd walked through the door, but she hadn't said anything, other than, "Good afternoon, Harper. I trust you'll be ready to take over the prayer again?"

I had, and it had gone well. Unfortunately, the rest of the practice was going less smoothly.

"Oh, for Heaven's sake, Miss Riley!" Saylor snapped yet again.

As Mary Beth stammered out apologies, I rubbed my ankle and tried not to grimace.

Cotillion practice had only started half an hour ago, and this was Mary Beth's third fall. The first one had been before we'd even put on our heels, and the second one had nearly taken out the potted fern by the bay window, but this third one had been on me.

As usual.

Normally, I stuck up for Mary Beth when she stumbled, but after the stuff at the mall with Ryan, I was feeling less than charitable.

I was also feeling slightly unsettled. David was currently

slumped in one of the tiny velvet chairs in the sitting room, his legs out and crossed at the ankle. Even though I couldn't see his face behind the Kurt Vonnegut paperback he was holding, I had a feeling his expression was somewhere between boredom and disdain. It was the first time I'd been this close to him since that night at Saylor's, and even though I was doing my best to ignore it, it was almost like I could feel this thread stretching between us.

"Ladies," Saylor said, clapping her hands. "I realize you're all very busy and preoccupied, but Cotillion is one of the most important nights of your life. It's when you present to the world both the kind of woman you are and the kind of woman you would like to be."

"I am the kind of woman who would like to be done with this shit," Mary Beth muttered. She'd taken off her heels and they dangled from her fingers, bumping my shoulder blades. I rolled my back irritably, hoping she'd move them away. And stop talking. That also would've been nice.

Saylor didn't give any indication she'd heard Mary Beth. I'm pretty sure if she had, we would have seen Magnolia House's first murder. Instead, she clasped her hands in front of her and turned her gaze on me. "For example, Miss Price. What kind of woman do you want to be?"

The question threw me, and I suddenly realized that this was a test. Apparently, walking away from Paladin-dom wasn't going to be that easy.

I knew the things I wanted to *do*—make my school better, go to college, become the second female governor of the state of

Alabama—but I had a feeling that wasn't what Saylor was looking for. "I . . . I want to be a good woman," I said finally. "One who does the right thing, not only for her community, but for herself. Who follows her heart even if it's not the most popular thing to do."

There were a few giggles behind me. I knew how lame that answer had sounded, but it was true. Doing the right thing didn't seem like all that much, but look at Leigh-Anne. Look at what doing one wrong thing had cost her. Lame or no, that was my answer. And I hoped Saylor heard what I was really saying.

Across the room, I caught a little glare of light. I realized David had lowered his book, and was watching me, his lips pressed in a thin line. I wondered if he thought I was talking about him.

"That was a lovely answer, Miss Price," Saylor said. Her voice sounded . . . different. A little lower, and without those clipped tones she usually used. Then she gave a little shake of her head and clapped again.

"All right, now we're going to practice descending the staircase accompanied. On the actual night, your escort will lead you down these stairs. There is a trick to walking gracefully on the arm of a man, and luckily, my nephew, David, has graciously volunteered to assist us."

"If by 'graciously volunteered,' you mean 'was threatened and coerced,' then yes, I did," David said, unfolding himself from that tiny chair.

A muscle twitched in Saylor's jaw, but she let the remark pass.

"Go ahead and line up at the top of the staircase," she said, pulling that little blue pot of lip balm out of her pocket. "Oh, and Mary Beth, if you could come down here for a moment."

"Ugh, what now?" Mary Beth sighed, but she went.

"Remember, girls," Saylor called as David loped up the stairs, passing Mary Beth. "You are to lay your hand gently on the forearm, not loop your arm through his. This is Cotillion, not a square dance."

"I actually think square dances are less shameful than this," David muttered at the top of the stairs. Still, he held his arm out gallantly to Elizabeth Adams, keeping his spine straight and shoulders back. As they made their way down the staircase, I watched Saylor and Mary Beth. They had gone into the alcove by the front door, and Saylor was talking to her while holding her hands and looking into her eyes.

Once Elizabeth was at the bottom of the staircase, David jogged back up to take Abigail Foster's arm, then, once she was done, Amanda's, then Bee's. There was only one other girl between me and Bee: Lindsay Harris. According to The Aunts, every girl in town had done Cotillion when they were young, but now, fewer and fewer girls did it every year. It was becoming one of those traditions that some people thought was a little too old-fashioned, a little embarrassing.

Once Lindsay was safely at the bottom of the stairs, David came up to me, crooking his elbow. "Shall we?"

But before I could rest my hand on his forearm, Saylor called, "Actually, David, I'd like for Miss Riley to go first."

"Sure," David said, shrugging and raising his eyebrows.

I was left to hover there awkwardly as Mary Beth walked back up the velvet-covered stairs, her white heels still hanging from her hands. When she reached the top, she took a deep breath, slid the heels on, and took David's arm.

David made his way down the steps as carefully as if she'd been made of glass, but he shouldn't have bothered. Mary Beth didn't just walk. She floated. She glided. She practically levitated down those stairs.

As she passed me, I got a hint of rose, and then they were there at the bottom of the steps. With a little squeal, Mary Beth clapped her hands and bounced up and down on the balls of her feet. Even David seemed impressed.

Magic. Whatever Saylor had done to the lady who'd run Cotillion before, or the former head of the Pine Grove Betterment Society, she'd done it to Mary Beth, too. If you asked me, it seemed like kind of a waste of something so super powerful, but if it kept me from being trampled, I guess it was all for the good.

No reason to feel bad about ditching my Paladin duties, then. What would it matter if the occasional guy broke through Saylor's wards? Maybe she'd already made them stronger.

Now that Mary Beth had finally made her first successful run down the stairs, it was my turn again. David offered his arm, and I laid my palm as lightly as I could on his sleeve.

"We need to talk," he said in a low voice as we started to descend.

"We don't," I replied through clenched teeth.

I could feel his forearm tense under my hand. "Except that we *do*."

From her position at the bottom of the staircase, Saylor watched the two of us. Anyone observing would've thought she was making sure we were moving at the right pace while using the appropriate posture. But I knew better.

So when David turned to me again once we were done, I hurried off to the little powder room off the main foyer.

Like everything else in Magnolia House, it was done all in shades of burgundy and green. A tiny wicker table by the door held a basket of scented lotions and a small bowl of potpourri, and there were tiny framed pictures of Magnolia House throughout the years on the walls. It wasn't actually an antebellum house—they'd built the place in the thirties—but it was still a pretty exact replica of the big places that had once filled Pine Grove. They even kept antique furniture in the bedrooms upstairs.

I was studying one of the pictures when I realized what else was covering the walls—dark green wallpaper with a familiar pattern. My vision swam with skinny golden figure eights. My hands started shaking as I turned on the little gold faucet shaped like a swan. I splashed my face with cold water and was taking a deep breath when the door suddenly opened and David was standing there.

He went to shut the door, but I pushed past him before he could. Or at least I tried to. Even though my hands only shoved against the air half a foot from him, David still got out of the way, letting me into the hallway.

"No more skulking," I hissed, shooting a glance back at the main foyer. This corridor was nearly blocked by the main staircase, so David and I were partially hidden. "We don't have anything to talk about. Not anymore."

David made a move toward me. I thought he was going to grab my arm, but then he seemed to think better of it. "I need to talk to someone about this," he said, and there was almost something pleading in his voice.

Since I'd never heard David Stark plead for anything ever, I hesitated. Then I remembered how desperate I'd been to tell someone, anyone, about what had happened with Dr. DuPont.

So I stepped back a little farther into the shadows. "What is it?"

Sighing, David tugged at his hair before reaching into the pocket of his jeans. "This." He handed me a crumpled piece of paper, and I saw that it was an e-mail.

"This is the third one of these I've gotten this month."

From the foyer, I could hear Saylor announcing the next rehearsal, and I knew I didn't have much longer before I'd be missed. As quickly as I could, I scanned the e-mail.

Dear Mr. Stark: We here at the University of West Alabama are pleased to inform you that you have been selected for our Distinguished Student Scholarship. Recipients of this scholarship must first submit to an in-person interview with a representative from the university. We would be happy to schedule this interview at any time that is most convenient for you. Kindly contact us so that we might set up a time as soon as possible.

Underneath that there was a phone number and a name, Blythe Collier.

Handing him the paper, I glanced over my shoulder. "Okay, what's so weird about that? That's a legit scholarship. I've heard of it."

David leaned close enough for me to see my reflection in his glasses. "Yeah, it's legit, but you have to *apply* for it, Pres. They don't *offer* it to you. And there's no interview for it."

I flexed my fingers. "So someone might be trying to lure you out of town."

"Maybe." He was a little sheepish as he shoved the paper back into his pocket. "I know it sounds stupid—"

"David, you're really going to have to stop saying that. And look, I admit, maybe this is a bit fishy, but why tell me? Why not tell Saylor?"

Snorting, David tugged at his hair. "Can you blame me for not trusting her right now, Pres? She's lied to me my entire life. She's not even my actual aunt."

His voice rose on the last word, and I touched his arm. "Shhh. I know. But . . . she's in this with you. I'm not."

David looked down at me. "I'm not asking you to go full Paladin on this. But I . . ." He broke off and sighed. "God, I might actually choke on these next words. I trust you. And I wanna check this out, but I'm not stupid enough to go check it out myself, and I think I might . . . need you."

No. No. Tell him no. You are not his Paladin and this is not your issue anymore.

But I watched David chew a thumbnail, his skin pale. His other hand, shoved in his pocket, jangled change nervously, and he looked more freaked out than I'd seen him yet. That had to be the only reason I heard myself say, "E-mail her. Make an appointment. And I'll . . . I'll go with you."

Chapter 20

"This is ridiculous. You know that, right?" David glared at me as he slid into the passenger seat, fastening his seat belt. "You could've come up to my house. Or I could've gone to your house. Basically, there were at least three options that didn't involve me walking three blocks from my house and you dressing like Carmen Sandiego."

I adjusted my sunglasses and pulled my hat a little farther down. "I'm not . . . look, you were the one who didn't want your aunt to know we were doing this. And I think it would be better if people didn't see us together." Especially since I'd begged off hanging out with both Ryan and Bee, telling them I was studying for the SATs.

David settled into his seat and immediately reached out to flip the radio on. My finger itched to push his hand away—I could be as bad as Bee when it came to people touching my radio—but music was probably better than awkward silence or bickering.

The drive out of town was pretty. Fall had come to Alabama in full force, the leaves orange, gold, and red. Overhead, the sky was that pure, impossible blue that only happens in the fall, and if I rolled down the window, I knew I'd smell wood smoke.

Nearly every other house we passed had some kind of Thanksgiving decorations in the window or on the mailbox. I counted three papier-mâché turkeys, two cling-form Pilgrims, and at least half a dozen cornucopias. Pine Grove definitely went all out for the holidays.

It wasn't until we were about a mile out of town that David finally turned down the radio. "We're going to feel really stupid if this is a totally legit scholarship offer, aren't we?"

I glanced over at him. "I won't, but you should. Who turns up to a scholarship interview in skinny jeans and a *Doctor Who* T-shirt?"

Reaching down, David slid the seat as far back as it would go before resting his heels on the glove compartment. "You mean like you did? Because there are few things less conspicuous than a teenage girl rocking a sombrero."

"It's not a—forget it. My choice of headgear is not the important thing. We need to figure out what we're going to do once we get there. I mean, if this *is* an attempt to lure you out of town to kill you or kidnap you or whatever, we should be prepared."

David shifted in his seat. "Isn't that your area?"

Uncomfortable, I shrugged. "I guess so."

Silence fell over the car again.

"Are you going to kill him?" David finally asked. "Or her?"

That was my job, right? Or it would be, if I were actually going to be a Paladin. Which I *wasn't*.

"We can question whoever it is," I said. "See how many of them there are, what their plans are."

"You heard Saylor. Their plans are probably to kill me."

"Yeah, but maybe we could get more of a sense of why. Is it the whole 'boys make crappy Oracles' thing, or is there more to it? For example, maybe you've been writing horrible articles about other people."

Snorting, David wrapped his arms around his knees. "No, you're the only person I torture in that particular way."

Why do you? I suddenly wanted to ask, but I bit back the question. David and my tangled personal history wasn't the issue here.

"Have you had any more . . . you know?" I lifted one hand off the steering wheel and wiggled it. "Visiony things?"

"Prophecies? No. Nothing since that night."

I made the turn into Merlington, driving down an oak-lined street. "Well, that's part of it, right? Being a boy means not having great visions." Overhead, the trees cast shadows on the car, covering David's face in dappled sunlight.

David shrugged. "Unless I do some kind of crazy spell on myself that makes me Mega Oracle."

I turned to look at him, nearly running a stop sign. "You wouldn't do that though, right?"

David dropped his feet from the dash, pulling at the hem of his T-shirt. "Seeing as how I wouldn't even know where to start on something like that, let's go with no."

He wasn't looking at me, but something in his voice wedged

under my skin like a splinter. "But even if you did know how," I said, "you . . . you wouldn't, right? I mean, you heard what Saylor said. That spell gave Alaric awesome visions and power, but it also fried up his brain and ended with lots of dead people."

David sighed, scrubbing a hand up and down the back of his neck. "Yeah, I got that part. Still, it sucks having visions that are so half-assed, you know? And no matter what Aunt—" He stopped, dropping his hand back to his lap. "I'm never going to stop doing that, am I?"

"You can still call her your aunt, David," I said, surprised at the gentleness in my voice. "I mean, she did raise you."

He made a noncommittal sound in reply before settling back in his seat. "All I'm saying is, being able to see the future but not really see the future is frustrating as hell. I get why someone would try a spell like that."

We drove past the big brick sign reading "The University of West Alabama," and I turned down the narrow street leading to campus. The library was at the end of the road, rising out of the bright green lawn like some kind of medieval church. I could already make out the stained-glass windows. "Well, the next time you start thinking like that, try to remember that Alaric ended up dead thanks to that spell."

David turned to me as I pulled into a parking space. In his glasses, I had to admit, I did look a little Carmen Sandiego-ish, so I tugged off the hat. "Okay, before we go in, anything else I should know?"

Unbuckling his seat belt, David dropped his gaze. "No."

"You are the worst liar in the entire world." As I shifted the car into park, a couple of girls walked past the car, long hair blowing in the breeze. Other than them, I didn't see anyone else in the parking lot.

"I'm not lying," he said, but I waved him off.

"Look, I know we're not exactly best friends, but we *have* known each other more or less since the womb. Remember in second grade when you spilled all the blue paint, and tried to say you hadn't? You're making the exact same face."

David rolled his eyes. "And what face is that?"

I jutted my jaw out and gave my best David scowl. "Kinda like this," I said through clenched teeth, and he gave a surprised laugh.

"Okay, I do *not* look like that. That looks like . . . I don't know, Dick Cheney."

"No, this is totally how you look when you lie," I insisted. "You did it with the blue paint and you're doing it now."

David's grin slowly faded and his fingers fiddled with the edge of his T-shirt, pulling it up over his bicep a little. Since when did David Stark have biceps? How did you get any muscle tone when all you did was type and be annoying?

"Trust me, Pres," he answered as he opened his door. "That's it. No more to tell."

He wanted me to trust him, and Saylor wanted him to trust her, and I just wanted this whole thing over with.

So why are you here? a little voice whispered inside my head. Instead of chasing that thought, I got out of the car and hurried after David.

He was looking at his phone. "Okay, so the appointment is in ten minutes on the second floor of the library. Which would be . . ." He pointed to the large Gothic building. "Here."

I stared at it, waiting to feel that sudden tightness in my chest that told me David was in danger. But there was nothing but the breeze brushing my hair into my face and the slight chill of early November. No vise around my heart, no Pop Rocks.

"Should we go in?" David asked, and I nodded.

Walking inside, the familiar old building smells of mildewed carpet and burnt coffee assaulted my nose, but other than that, everything felt . . . fine. Normal. Maybe this *was* a routine scholarship interview.

The office David had been told to go to was on the library's second floor. As we made our way up the stairs, everything was completely silent except for the squeak of David's sneakers on the stone floor. "Do you feel weird?" he asked.

I shook my head. "No. I feel . . . weirdly unweird, actually."

Slanting me a look, he gave a half-smile. "Only for us would unweird *be* weird."

It was easy enough to find 201-A. It was the first office right off the stairs, and when David knocked on the door, a pretty, petite brunette opened it, smiling at us. There were deep dimples on either side of her shining white teeth, and despite the imminent danger we might be in, I couldn't help wondering where she'd gotten her lipstick. That was a seriously gorgeous—ugh, no. Focus.

"Hi, there!" she said brightly. "David?"

It was hard to imagine anyone looking less like an assassin, especially since she was decked out in a pink and green Lilly Pulitzer dress.

David startled slightly, and I wondered if he was thinking the same thing. "Yeah," he finally said. Then, clearing his throat, he tried again. "I mean, yes, I'm David Stark."

The brunette reached out and shook his hand. "I'm Blythe," the woman—girl, really—said, pumping David's hand enthusiastically.

Then her eyes slid over to me. "Oh!" she said. "You brought a friend!" The dimples deepened, and she leaned forward with a conspiratorial wink. "Or is this your girlfriend?"

Rude, I thought, but then I realized we hadn't exactly come up with an excuse as to why I was here with David.

David slung an arm across my shoulders, and I automatically slid my arm around his waist. Seeing as how we were standing a few feet apart, I'm not sure if any two people have ever held each other more awkwardly.

"Yup," I said. "Girlfriend."

"So my girlfriend," David agreed, and I would've dug my fingers into his ribs if I'd been capable of it.

But if Blythe noticed our extreme awkwardness, she didn't acknowledge it. "Well, y'all come on in!" she said.

Once her back was turned, David glanced over at me. I knew what he was thinking. How could a girl who appeared to speak only in exclamation points possibly be a hired killer?

"I have to say, David, we have heard so many great things about you," Blythe said, going over to her desk. As she riffled through it, she added, "Oh, and could y'all shut the door, please?"

David turned to do that while Blythe kept talking. "You do not even know the trouble we've had trying to get in touch with you."

His hand still on the doorknob, David turned back to Blythe. "Yeah, you guys have sent a bunch of e-mails."

Blythe gave a light, trilling laugh. "Oh, trust me, it's been a lot more extensive than some e-mails." Suddenly her face brightened as she found whatever it was she'd been looking for.

"Oh, here we go!" she said chirpily. She was holding a letter opener, one that looked far longer and far sharper than necessary for opening mail.

For a second, all I could do was stare dumbly at the blade, wondering why I wasn't feeling the chest tightening and the Pop Rocks, and all of that.

Blythe planted one foot on the edge of the desk, launching herself up and over, and I realized why I hadn't felt like David was in danger.

She was lunging for *me*.

Chapter 21

LIKE IT had that night with Dr. DuPont, my body started moving before my mind had time to catch up. David shouted, but I was already bracing myself, throwing up an arm to deflect the blow. Blythe landed on me, hard, and I felt something icy arc along the skin below my elbow. Then the ice turned into searing heat, and I saw a flash of red. *Oh my effing God*, I thought, almost from a distance. *She stabbed me. A girl in Lilly Pulitzer stabbed me.*

Gritting my teeth against the sudden blossom of pain, I reached up with my other hand, trying to grab her wrist, but she moved faster than I'd anticipated, snaking out one foot to hook around my ankle and send me crashing to the ground.

As she did, I managed to grab the hem of her dress, yanking her off balance, too. We fell together, my head thwacking the base of one of the chairs. I saw stars, and then another flash of silver as the blade darted at my throat. Without thinking, I grabbed at the letter opener, my palm closing around it. I could feel metal cutting into my skin, but the agony was nothing compared to the adrenaline and fear racing through me. Above me, Blythe had her teeth bared in a snarl. Sweat dotted her forehead and her upper lip, and strands of hair came loose from her pony-tail to cling to her cheeks. Her face was pale, dark eyes huge in her head, and I realized that despite her being the one with a weapon, she was scared. Terrified, even.

Blythe might have had the element of surprise on her side, but she wasn't a Paladin. I gripped the blade even harder, forcing her hand away from my throat. Red rivers were running down my forearm now, but I didn't care. I'd deal with the pain later.

I decided to go with the same move that had surprised Dr. DuPont. Jerking my head forward, I smacked my forehead as hard as I could against her nose. The letter opener dropped to the floor as Blythe raised both hands to her face with a watery cry. Pushing myself up on my elbows, I went to shove her off me, but before I could, there was a crash and the sound of breaking glass.

Blythe slid off me, boneless, and collapsed on the floor. Behind her, David stood clutching the remnants of the desk lamp. His eyes were wild and he was practically panting.

Wincing, I pushed myself up, taking care not to put any pressure on my injured hand. Now that the fight was over, the pain was even worse. I only had to glance at the gash bisecting my palm to know it was going to need stitches. Even as I stared down at Blythe, I was wondering how I could explain this particular injury to my parents.

"Jesus," David said, looking down at the blood dripping from my hand and arm. "Are you okay?"

When I stared at him wordlessly, he amended, "I mean, obviously you're not, but . . . are you going to be?"

"I-I think so," I told him, but to be honest, I felt a little faint. Not from the blood loss and the pain—although they were part of it—but from how close that blade had been to my throat. How all my supposed superpowers hadn't counted for much when someone got the jump on me.

There was a little white cardigan hanging from the back of Blythe's chair, and I grabbed it, wrapping it as tightly as I could around my bleeding hand. The wound in my arm still hurt, too, but it wasn't as deep and it had already stopped bleeding.

"Why didn't you feel anything?" David asked. "Isn't that part of your whole deal? Like with the guys in the car?"

Staring down at Blythe, I shook my head. "Seems like I only feel that when someone's after you. She was trying to kill *me*."

David blinked. "So . . . your superpowers don't help you defend yourself, too? That seems kind of unfair."

It seemed a heck of a lot more than kind of unfair to me, but I didn't say that to David. "Give me that lamp. Or what's left of it," I said. When he did, I ripped the cord out of the base, then nodded at Blythe, who was beginning to groan a little. "Help me get her in a chair."

Once we did, I threaded the cord through the slats in the back of the chair, tying her hands tightly behind her back. Blythe stayed unconscious through the whole thing, blood dripping steadily from her nose, leaving bright red splotches next to all those little pink and green daisies on her dress.

"I can't believe no one heard all that," David said, gesturing to the blood on the carpet. Frowning, I looked up from the cord.

"Yeah, me neither. There aren't many people here, but you would think someone would've heard me nearly getting murdered."

Chewing on his thumbnail, David was still staring at the letter opener. It was lying on the carpet, edge gleaming in the fluorescent lights. "This is insane," he said at last.

I gave the knot one last tug and sighed. "Yes. As has been established."

Now that I was certain she was pretty securely tied to the chair, I stepped back next to David and studied our captive.

"She seems . . . younger," he said at last. "I thought she was too young to work at a college before, but now that I really *look* at her . . ."

She was young. Barely out of her teens, I'd guess. I looked at her crooked nose, wondering if I should feel guilty. But then I thought of her leaping over that desk, blade in hand.

Nope. No guilt here.

Moaning, she started to stir. "What are we going to do?" David whispered.

"Question her," I replied. My blood continued to drip steadily on the beige carpet, and underneath the fluorescent lights, David looked greenish. Outside, the leaves of a giant magnolia tree beat softly against the window.

"We can't . . . are you going to kill her?" I didn't think it was possible for David to look any more wretched, but as he turned to me, hands clenching and unclenching at his sides, I was worried he might throw up.

And I didn't know how to answer him. I honestly hadn't

thought about that. Meet this chick, question her, get a little more info on what was going on—that had been my whole agenda. But David was right, it wasn't like we could just leave her here. And she *had* tried to kill me. Before I could think through that any further, Blythe's eyes fluttered open.

They rolled around in her head for a second before coming to land on me. "You are a heck of a lot tougher than you look," she said, her voice thick.

I folded my arms over my chest. "Who are you?" I'd seen enough movies to know this was the part where the bad guys usually laughed and started spitting in people's faces, but the girl nodded at her name tag.

"Like it says on the freaking pin. Blythe." There was no hint of a Southern accent in her voice now.

"Yeah, right," David muttered next to me, but I ignored him.

"I don't mean your name." I'd only ever interrogated one person—a freshman cheerleader named Tori Bishop. Of course then, I'd been asking about some car wash money that had gone missing, not my potential murder. Still, I figured the technique would be basically the same. Clenching my jaw, I narrowed my eyes at Blythe. "I mean . . . what are you? You're not a Paladin—"

Blythe snorted and then winced. "Obviously. And since I'm clearly not an Oracle"— she jerked her head at David—"why don't you use the process of elimination?"

"You're a Mage," David said, mimicking my pose. "Like my— Like Saylor Stark."

Blythe surged against the cords holding her, eyes suddenly

fierce. "No, I am nothing like Saylor Stark. I do my damn job. I am loyal to the people who gave me this power."

"The Ephors?" I asked as David said, "How long have you been a Mage?"

We glared at each other, and Blythe's gaze flicked back and forth between us. The corner of her mouth lifted in a smirk, cracking the dried blood under her nose. "Which one of you am I supposed to answer first?"

After a moment, David rolled his eyes. "Her," he said, gesturing toward me. "Answer her first."

But instead of answering, Blythe kept looking at the two of us. "How old are you guys?"

"Seventeen," we answered in unison, and Blythe made a kind of gurgling chuckle. Seriously, I never wanted to break someone's nose again, even if they *were* trying to stab me. It had some majorly gross aftereffects.

"Me, too," she said. While she'd seemed young, she hadn't looked *that* young. David glanced over at me, and although telepathy wasn't part of the Paladin-Oracle bond, I still knew what he was thinking: *How effed up is this?*

Tightening the cardigan around my hand, I stared Blythe down. "You haven't answered my question."

Heaving a sigh, Blythe leaned back in the chair. "Yes, the Ephors," she said, and while she didn't add "you idiot," it was clearly implied. Then she looked at David. "And as for your question, about six months."

"How do they find you?" I found myself asking. Suddenly, I was really regretting not asking Saylor more about all of this. It would've been nice to know that Mages could be just as homicidal and dangerous as Paladins in their own way.

Blythe looked up at me, tilting her face. "You know those tests you take in school? The things that judge aptitude for certain careers?"

"I worship those tests," I said, leaning back against one corner of the desk.

A lock of hair had fallen into Blythe's eyes, and she huffed out a breath. "Me, too. There are questions woven into that thing that alert the Ephors to people who have Mage potential."

David stepped back a little, nearly tripping over a jar of pens. It must have fallen during the fight with Blythe. Righting himself, David rubbed one hand over his mouth, studying Blythe. "But a Mage's power can be passed on, right?"

Sighing, Blythe rolled her neck. "Yes, but it helps to find someone with a few natural abilities if you can. If the Ephors have time, which they did in my case. The Mage before me knew she was dying for months. Plenty of time to prepare."

Over Blythe's head, David and I locked eyes. That was an interesting little fact. I wondered if it worked the same way for Paladins. But before I could ask, Blythe jerked her head in my direction and said, "Now would the two of you get on with the killing me part already?"

"We're not going to kill you," I heard myself say, and when Blythe looked up at me, eyebrows raised, I hastily added, "I mean, not yet. So long as you tell us what we need to know."

The letter opener was near the door, so I picked up the nearest weapon I could lay hands on: a stapler.

I lifted it, going for "menacing." I admit it lacked a certain elegance, but hey. It was worth a shot.

David placed his hand on my arm and pushed it back down. "What?"

"Just . . . that's embarrassing for all of us," he replied.

Blythe gave another one of those laughs that made me shudder. "This is such a freaking mess," she muttered before fixing me with her dark eyes. "You don't even know what's really going on here, do you? What's your name, Paladin?"

"Harper Price," I said, good manners automatically kicking in over sense.

"Do you want to give her your address, too?" David muttered, but Blythe's gaze stayed on me.

"Well, listen to me, Harper Price. Me, the people I work for . . . we don't want to hurt David. We want to *help* him."

I opened my mouth, but David replied before I could say anything. "Help me?" His voice was tight with anger, and he reached up to tug at his hair, never a good sign. "You killed the man who was sworn to protect me."

"That wasn't me—" Blythe said, but David acted like she hadn't spoken.

"You tried to run me over," he said, eyes wide behind his glasses. I could see a flush creeping up his neck.

Scowling, Blythe struggled a little against the cords. "Okay, that *was* me, but technically I was after *her*—"

"And then, to top it off, you lure me out of town and try to stab Harper right in front of me."

By now, David was nearly shouting, and again, I wondered

why no one was running in. Surely we'd made enough noise to bring someone up here. I mean, this was a library, for goodness' sake.

"If you're trying to help me, why would you—or the people you work for—do any of that crap?" David rocked back on his heels, waiting for an answer, and I would've felt sorry for Blythe had it not been for the whole stabbing thing. Being on the other end of a David Stark Glare was a truly unpleasant thing.

Blythe sat up as straight as the cords would allow, leaning forward. "Because," she said, clenching her teeth, "those people— that janitor, your so-called aunt—they were holding you back, David. You have a destiny, and I'm here to help you fulfill it."

Chapter 22

THERE WAS a pause. In it, I could hear the ticking of the little clock above Blythe's desk, but nothing else. No sounds from downstairs, nothing from the parking lot outside. Finally, David took off his glasses and scrubbed a hand up and down his face. "I am so effing sick of that word," he muttered, and I found myself nodding. "Destiny" was not my favorite word these days either.

"The Ephors wanted to kill David," I told Blythe. "Because of his . . . boy parts and stuff."

David lifted his head at that, and I think he mouthed, *Really?* at me, but I was watching Blythe.

She held my stare, grinning, and between the blood, her ridiculously young face, and the Lilly Pulitzer, it was more than a little unsettling. "So you're not totally ignorant, then. Awesome. Yes, at first the Ephors thought that David's 'boy parts' would make him a bad Oracle. After all, the only one they'd ever had didn't exactly work out for them."

"Alaric," David said, polishing his glasses on the bottom of his shirt.

"The very same," Blythe said with a little nod. "So you can

imagine why they were very anti–boy Oracle for a while there. But"— Blythe's smile went from slightly unhinged to smug, but still seriously unhinged—"that was before they found *me*."

David still had his glasses dangling from his fingers, but at that, he put them back on and squinted at her. "What does that mean?"

"No offense or anything, but Saylor Stark has nothing on me as far as the alchemy game goes," Blythe said, settling back into the chair. For the first time, I honestly believed she was seventeen. "I mean, Saylor can do a mind-control potion on what? One, two people at a time, max? I've got this whole *freaking* library under my thumb right now." Smirking, she tried to cross her legs, but the way we'd tied her to the chair made that impossible. She settled for bringing her knees tighter together. "I got a job here as a volunteer, and every Friday, they do this big potluck thing. One potion in a batch of brownies, and bam. I have an office, an official e-mail account . . ."

My hand was starting to feel a little numb, so I loosened the cardigan around it. As I did, I saw Blythe's gaze flick to her sweater, a tiny frown creasing her brow. "So that's why no one came up here when we fought," I said, getting it at last. "Alchemy."

Tearing her eyes from her blood-soaked cardi, Blythe nodded. "I didn't want to be disturbed."

"So what does your badass alchemy have to do with David?" I asked, looping the sweater around my hand again. Blythe grimaced.

"I liked that sweater," she said, and while I could appreciate an attachment to clothes, I was quick to snark back, "I liked my hand."

Blythe rolled her eyes. "You were the one who grabbed the knife."

As she said it, some of the adrenaline started to wear off, and a wave of nausea swept through me as I remembered the blade so close to my throat, the blinding pain of wrapping my palm around it. How close to death had I actually been? Moments, definitely. And for the second time in my life. Third if you counted the car chase.

I was pretty sure Paladins weren't supposed to feel scared or sick, but that was fine. I wasn't *really* one. Was I?

That wasn't something I wanted to think about right now, so I scowled at Blythe. "Answer my question," I said. "What does your . . . magic or whatever have to do with David?"

David had moved across to Blythe's desk, and he leaned back against it, bracing himself on his hands as he waited for Blythe to answer. That put him a little bit behind her, and I could tell she was trying to look at him out of the corner of her eye.

"Boy Oracles can be just as awesome as girl Oracles. Heck, they can be *better*." Behind her back, she flexed her fingers. "And—look, can y'all loosen these things? I can't feel my hands."

David made a move forward, but I held up my hand. "Answers first."

The look Blythe gave me was weirdly approving. She shrugged and continued, "If you know the right kind of alchemy to use—which, hi, I do—you can . . . I don't know, like, *supercharge* him. Make it so that he can see further into the future. And more. And it's not even that difficult of a spell, really. Some alchemy requires, like, lizard innards and stuff, but this is just saying some—"

"We know about the spell," I interrupted, clenching my hands at my side. "It made Alaric insane and ended with a whole bunch of people dead and a whole village destroyed."

Disgust flickered over Blythe's cherubic face. "Because he wasn't a Mage. The spell itself isn't bad. It was just that Alaric didn't know what the heck he was doing. I would. I mean, I *do*. And there's so much you could do once the spell was in effect."

"Like what?" David asked, and even though she couldn't look right at him, Blythe swiveled her head in his direction.

"Come with me and I'll show you," she said, her voice lower than before, almost like a purr.

David straightened a little, and I saw him swallow hard. "Um . . . no. Thank you," he said, and it was all I could do not to roll my eyes. Boys, honestly.

"Okay, so the Ephors want David all Super Oracle. Got it. That really doesn't sound all that bad, I guess."

Blythe's eyes narrowed as David startled. "Pres?"

I kept going. "And of course, once they have a Super Oracle, it makes total sense that they'd want to kill, you know, *the person sworn to protect him*."

Gripping the arms of Blythe's chair, I leaned down, getting in her face. "Oh, wait, except it doesn't make sense at all. If you guys want David to be more powerful, why kill Mr. Hall? Why kill *me*?"

For the first time, Blythe seemed unsure. She dropped her gaze, and David stepped forward, coming to stand behind me.

"Because the spell is dangerous," he said softly. "Why else would Harper need to be out of the way?"

My head shot up. Saylor had said that spell ended up destroying Alaric. As David's Paladin, would I need to protect him from that?

Blythe's big brown eyes widened in appreciation. "No," she said, shaking her head. "It's not—well, there is a *slight* danger element, maybe. But, hi, crossing the freaking street can be dangerous. And like I said, Alaric wasn't a Mage. He wasn't *me*. So it wouldn't *be* dangerous. Just because he screwed up the spell doesn't make it a bad spell. Just a bad . . . spellcaster."

I might have bought that if her gaze hadn't slid from David to the bright splash of blood—mine or hers, I wasn't sure—on the carpet. "I would do it right."

My head ached, and my hand and arm were still stinging, and I felt this weird desire to curl up on my bed and cry. Or sleep. Instead, I tightened my hold on Blythe's chair. "So that's the test David has to face at Cotillion? You're going to do some spell on him that will either soup up his powers, or turn him into a crazy person."

From behind me, I heard David make some kind of noise, but I didn't turn around to face him. One problem at a time.

The dried blood around Blythe's face cracked and flaked when she smiled. "Look, I am trying to help you guys out. Just . . . just go with it, okay? Don't fight me, don't try to stop me. David will have awesome powers, the Ephors will have an Oracle again, and we can all be buddies. The three of us, working together, kicking ass, taking names . . . all that."

"We already *have* a Mage," David said, coming to stand beside me. I could feel him trembling, but his voice was steady. "Saylor Stark."

Blythe blew a breath out, ruffling her bangs. "Who can maybe do a couple of weak mind-control spells. Boring. I'm offering you everything. All the power you could ever want."

Flexing his fingers, David just watched her.

I shook my head. "Okay." Setting my hands on my hips, I faced Blythe. "Interrogation over."

It might have been the bad lighting, but I thought her olive skin went a little pale. "So this is the part where you kill me, huh?"

I should. Everything in my blood was urging me to kill her. Somehow, I knew that if I gripped her head the right way, jerked her neck just so, she'd be dead in less than a second. No blood, no fuss, and almost no pain at all. But even as my fingers curled into my palms, as cold sweat trickled down my back, I knew I couldn't do it. Self-defense was one thing. This felt like . . . murder. Besides, there was something else I could do with Blythe.

"We need to take her to Saylor," I told David. "She'll know what to do." I wasn't a hundred percent sure that was true, but I was positive that I sure as heck didn't know what to do.

David must've felt the same way because he shoved his hands in his pockets and rocked back on his heels. "Yeah. We definitely need an adult."

It wasn't that funny, but the whole afternoon had been so stressful that I burst into giggles. Surprised, David rocked back farther, but, after a second, a slow grin spread across his face.

"Wait, are you two really a thing?" Blythe asked, making David's grin disappear.

"No," he said quickly, and I shook my head so hard it was a wonder I didn't sprain something. "No," I echoed. "No, no, no, no. Vast worlds of no."

I think Blythe would've said something sarcastic in reply, but David didn't give her the chance. "We need to get you out of this building without anyone seeing it. You have anything for that?"

Blythe slumped in her bonds, dimples vanishing, big brown eyes going dull. "If I say no, are you going to staple me to death?"

David bent down and picked up the letter opener, tossing it to me. It was slick with blood—*my* blood—but I still caught it easily with my good hand. "No," he told her. "If you say no, Harper gets her turn with that."

It was a tone I'd never heard David use, and considering how long I'd known him, that was saying something. He sounded steely and grown-up, and threatening. Almost like someone who could be a superpowered . . . something.

But this was *David Stark*. The only threatening thing about him was his toxic level of obnoxiousness.

Still, it worked on Blythe. She jerked her head toward her desk. "Top drawer. Bottle of nail polish. Dab a dot on all of us, we're as good as invisible."

I moved to the drawer, and pulled it out before something occurred to me. "David, why don't *you* get it?"

He crossed the room in a couple of strides and rifled through the open drawer. When I didn't double over in pain, I gave a little nod. "Okay, it's safe."

Blythe was watching me from under her bangs, her brown eyes sparkling. "Smart girl. But, honestly, if I had some kind of deadly potion, wouldn't I have used that on you instead of a letter opener?"

David snorted, turning the bottle of nail polish over in his long fingers. "She has a point, Pres." As I snatched the bottle from him, he reached up to smooth his hair, making him look . . . well, he was never going to be entirely presentable, but at least *better.*

After dotting the back of all of our hands with the nail polish, David and I managed to untie Blythe, get her out of the chair, and tie her back up without her attempting to murder me. We navigated her down the stairs, and sure enough, even though we passed several people, no one so much as glanced in our direction. It was eerie.

We were at the car before David asked, "Why don't Mages have potions that can kill people?"

I wasn't sure if Blythe's expression of disgust was for the question or for the way I kind of manhandled her into the backseat. "We're not that powerful. A little mind control, some temporal disturbances . . . those we can pull off. Anything to do with human life is a little trickier. But I'm working on it, trust me."

"Is that how you survived the car crash into my pool?" I asked her, but Blythe just fidgeted on the seat, trying to tuck her dress underneath her.

"I actually poofed out of there before the car hit."

"You can just 'poof' out of places?" David leaned his forearms on the roof of the car, looking in at Blythe. "Can you also just poof into places?"

I handed David the keys—my hand still hurt too much to think about wrapping it around a steering wheel—and slid into the passenger seat, buckling my seat belt. "David, maybe *don't* give the tiny psychotic witch ideas, okay?"

As David pulled out of the parking lot, I leaned back and closed my eyes, taking a deep breath through my nose. *We'll take her to Saylor. Saylor will know what to do.*

The more I repeated it, the better I felt. In fact, as David got closer to Pine Grove, I was feeling almost . . . proud. My first real mission as a Paladin, and I had captured the enemy, learned something about the other side's plans, and managed not to get too horribly injured. Of course, I'd still need to go to the hospital. My hand would need stitches, which meant coming up with a good excuse for my parents. But when I slid the sweater sleeve off my hand, I could see that the wound was already beginning to heal. It was puckered and red and ugly, but mostly closed. I turned my hand back and forth, marveling at it, and David glanced over.

"Whoa," he murmured, and I nodded.

The "Welcome to Pine Grove" sign loomed in the distance, and I actually smiled a little bit. Yes. Today was definitely one for the win column.

David must've felt the same, because as we sped into town,

he looked over at me and said, "You know, Pres, this was actually . . . I don't want to say fun because of the attempted stabbing, but—"

"No," I said. "I get what you mean. We did good work today. And once we get her—"

I turned to the backseat, ready to face Blythe's sullen expression and found myself staring at . . . nothing.

The backseat was empty.

Chapter 23

THE CAR shook and shimmied as he slammed on the brakes and swerved off the road. Throwing it in park, he turned around in his seat and joined me in staring slack-jawed at the spot where Blythe had been. "How?"

"She's a Mage," I offered, too stunned to think of anything else. Saylor had said their magic was pretty low-level. Making yourself disappear was not what I considered low-level magic.

David made a sound that was somewhere between a laugh and a groan, and lowered his forehead to the seat.

"She wasn't kidding about her alchemy game, was she?" he asked, his voice hoarse.

As I looked at the empty backseat, all I could see was Blythe leaping over that desk, Mr. Hall bleeding to death on the bathroom floor. They weren't trying to kill David, they were trying to kill *me*, and I had let one of my would-be assassins go. One who had way more power than I'd prepared for, at that.

After a beat, David turned to me. "You wanna drive around for a little bit?"

Wordlessly, I nodded. David turned my car down one of the side streets leading toward Pine Grove Park, and we drove until we reached the little hill above the playground.

We sat in silence while watching kids scampering over the brightly colored playground equipment. A little girl climbed up the same slide where, when we were eight, I'd shoved David off the ladder. Or had he shoved me? I couldn't remember. And there, on the swing set, a boy sat on the swing where Ryan had given me my first kiss.

Shutting off the ignition, David leaned forward on the steering wheel. "She wants you dead," he said.

I looked at my hand again. "Yeah, I got that."

He let out a heavy sigh, dropping his forehead to the steering wheel. "So what do we do now?"

I wished I had an easy answer. I wished I could pretend none of this was real, and that everything could go back to the way it was. But now there was a lot more on the line than my social life. My actual *life* was at stake here, and while the idea of hiding under the covers, preferably until Rapture, was appealing, it didn't seem to be an option.

Sitting up straight, I pushed my hair away from my face, gathering it into a loose knot. David's backpack was at my feet, and I fumbled through it until I found a notebook and a pen. Skipping past a bunch of sketches at the front—which, hey, were actually pretty decent. I stopped, looking more closely at a few. There was Chie, his friend from newspaper, her dark hair curling around one ear, hand playing with her bangs. And there was Bee, laughing. Bee did this thing when she laughed of tipping her head all the way back, mouth open and teeth flashing. David had captured it perfectly, and I couldn't help but smile.

I flipped to another page, and there was me. I took up nearly the whole sheet of paper, standing next to a wall of lockers, my head slightly down, face in profile. I was smiling, but my shoulders were tense and I was clearly twisting my ring around my finger.

Clearing his throat, David pulled the notebook back and flipped to a blank page. "I like drawing people," was all he said before once again placing the notebook back in my hands.

Something seemed to have settled over the car, something heavy and weirdly tense, like the air before a storm.

"When did you draw—" I asked, but David tapped the blank paper in front of me.

"So what was all that stuff Blythe said?"

Taking the hint, I nodded and picked up a pen. "Okay. So the Ephors want to do a spell that makes you Mega Oracle." I jotted that down. "And they're doing it at Cotillion."

David was studying me over the rims of his glasses. "Are you . . . making a flow chart?"

"Shut up. Also, why is it that prophecies are always so vague and mystical? I mean, would it kill you to be able to say, "Oh, the bad guys are coming on *this* day at *this* place and they're going to do *this* thing? 'Night of the Swans,' honestly . . ."

A ghost of a smile flittered across David's face. "I'll try to make things more specific the next time I have terrifying visions of the future, Pres."

I caught myself smiling back before returning my attention to the notebook. "But now we know what this test you have to face is. She's going to try the spell on you. So all I have to do is keep that from happening."

David nodded, but he didn't seem any happier. "Unless she kills you first."

I swallowed around the sudden lump in my throat. The cold sweat was back, too. You know, if the universe is going to give you superstrength and superspeed and fighting skills you never had, it should also give you some kind of anti-fear power.

"Saylor has wards up all around town to protect you, right? Well, we'll see if she can whip up some for me, too." My voice was light as I said it, but the hand holding the pen shook a little, and David was still frowning.

"You're serious," he said after a moment. "You really want to do this. Be my Paladin. Fight the forces of evil during your Cotillion."

I laid the pen on the notebook and met his eyes. "It's the only choice. These people want me out of the way—"

"Dead," David interjected, and I scowled at him.

"Yes, dead." I tucked my hair behind my ears. "Why do you keep bringing that up?"

"Because I want you to get it," he snapped back, his hands squeezing the steering wheel. "Because the idea of someone— anyone—*dying* for me makes me feel sick, and the thought of *you* dying for me is . . ."

Breaking off, he squeezed the steering wheel again, fingers flexing almost convulsively. "Pres, this is real. It's real, and it's scary, and it's so messed up, I don't even know where to start. You could die. I could die. People are actively trying to hurt us. And I feel like we both need to . . . acknowledge that. Use words like 'dead' instead of cutesy euphemisms."

Cold sweat was still prickling all over my body. Outside the car, on one of the benches, a harried young mom in jeans and a black turtleneck called out something to her kid, probably "Be careful!" My own mom had sat on that same bench, saying the same thing to me.

I thought of Mom's tired smile, of her sad eyes, and the big hole that Leigh-Anne had left in our house. If something happened to me . . . Blinking against the stinging in my eyes, I picked up the pen and started to write again. I would have to make sure nothing *did* happen to me.

"You're right," I said, and David didn't say anything for a long time.

Then, finally, "It hurt you to say that, didn't it?" Out of the corner of my eye, I saw him lean back in his seat.

"The words nearly choked me, yeah."

He snorted, and I went back to writing. "So, yes, people want me dead. They might do a spell that makes *you* dead. Happy now?"

David reached around the headrest to stretch his arms. "Will you start saying the real F-word with more regularity, too?"

"Don't push it," I replied, as outside, a gust of wind sent dead leaves rattling against the car. Cotillion was only three weeks away. Three weeks didn't seem like nearly enough time to plan for something this big. Heck, last year's Spring Fling had taken me over two *months* to prepare.

Glancing up from my notebook, I took in David as he slouched in his seat. Once again his hair was all mussed and his glasses were slightly crooked, and he was obviously thinking over something pretty hard. His brow was furrowed and his fingers drummed against the steering wheel.

"What are you fretting about so hard over there?" I asked him.

He worried at his lower lip for a moment before answering. "Remember when I told you about those crazy dreams I always had?"

"Yeah."

"Well . . . one of them was about you."

My heart thudded heavily in my chest, but I made my voice as light as I could. "Ew. So don't want to hear about that."

Now he did smile, but only a little. "No, not like that. You asked me the other day why it was that you and I could never seem to get along. And, I mean, yes, part of it was competition."

"Egregious," I muttered, and now his smile was a little wider.

"Felicitations," he replied, and some of the tightness in my chest eased. "But part of it—" He broke off and thumped his head back against the steering wheel.

"God, this is so dumb." He sat up again, his eyes on the ceiling. "When I was like five or six, I dreamed that you killed me."

"Okay," I said slowly, and he swiveled his head to look at me.

"I always knew a dream was a stupid reason not to like you. But now . . . Pres, apparently I can see the future. What if—"

I cut him off with a wave of my hand. "No. Saylor said you were only now starting to come into your powers. You probably didn't even have them when you were five."

He nodded, but his knuckles were white around the steering wheel. "Only . . . you weren't angry in the dream. Neither was I. It was like we were both . . . sad. I woke up crying and everything."

The hairs on the back of my neck prickled. Even as he said it, it was like I could see it. Me and David, staring at each other, tears streaming down both of our faces. There was something in my hand . . .

But wait. No, there was no way that could happen.

Making a fist, I pulled my arm back and swung at his face with everything I had. David gave a startled cry and flattened himself against the other side of the car, but the punch never landed. Instead, my fist came to a halt six inches from his nose.

"See?" I said, and relief washed over his face.

"Right." David gave a shaky laugh. "You can't hit me."

"I can't so much as pinch you," I replied. "So killing you? Totally off the table. Now let's drop that, and get back to the real problem, namely this."

I thumped the notebook with my pen, dismayed to see that everything Blythe had told us didn't even take up a whole page. "You need to call your Aunt Saylor."

"She's not—"

"I know, I know." Lifting a hand, I waved him off. "But you know what I mean. We need to talk to her as soon as possible and tell her what happened. Call her and tell her to meet us—" I checked my watch. It was only a little past one in the afternoon. Hard to believe it had only been a few hours since we set off for Merlington. "Tell her to go to Miss Annemarie's Tearoom."

David already had his phone out, but he paused, lifting both eyebrows. "And you want us to talk about this in Little Old Lady Land why?"

Miss Annemarie's was a Pine Grove institution. A tiny room filled with china, chintz, and more ceramic cats than anyone should ever own, the tearoom catered almost exclusively to senior citizens. It was one of The Aunts' favorite places to go for lunch, but today was Saturday, and they only went on Wednesdays.

"I want to talk this out in a neutral area," I told David. "And, no offense, but ever since that night, your house gives me the creeps."

He nodded, sympathetic. "Yeah, I get that."

"Plus, everyone at Miss Annemarie's is ancient, so there's less chance of being overheard."

"Good thinking." David went to dial, but before he did, stopped, ducking his head a little so he could meet my eyes. "So we're really doing this. You're going to fully accept Paladin-hood or whatever."

The way I saw it, my only foolproof way of getting out of this thing alive was getting rid of Blythe and ensuring the spell didn't happen at Cotillion. It had taken the Ephors seventeen years to find her; who knew how long they'd have to search for a new Mage? Besides, no Blythe, no spell, no need to kill David's Paladin.

But all I said to David was, "Harper Jane Price doesn't quit. Ever."

David's lips quirked. "Yes, I believe I've picked up on that over the years."

He turned back to his phone, punching in Saylor's number. As he talked to her, making plans to meet in a few minutes, I watched the kids playing and tried to tell myself I wasn't making a huge mistake.

Chapter 24

"You SHOULD TRY the oolong," Saylor told David as she unfolded her menu at Miss Annemarie's. As I'd anticipated, the tearoom was nearly empty, with the exception of two women sitting by the front window, both of them easily in their eighties. Outside, the wind had picked up, and gray clouds moved swiftly across the sky. Miss Annemarie's was situated in the town square, right next to the jewelry shop where The Aunts bought all my Christmas and birthday presents. In the middle of the square, there was a statue of one of the town founders, Adolphus Bridgeforth. David was glaring at Saylor over the top of his menu. "I hate oolong," he told her. "It tastes like leaves."

"It *is* leaves," I noted, opening my napkin over my lap.

"Touché," he muttered, a faint smile hovering on his lips.

Saylor was watching David, and the look on her face wasn't quite sadness and it wasn't exactly longing, but it was some mixture of the two. Then she folded up her menu, slid the corner of it under her saucer, and folded her hands on the table, fingers clenched.

Her diamonds winked in the light from the tiny lamp in the

center of the table, and now her expression was as placid as all the china cats dotting the restaurant. Seriously, Miss Annemarie could give Saylor a run for her money in the glass knickknacks department. "Well," she said at last. "I assume the two of you had a reason for bringing me to Miss Annemarie's."

I squirmed a little bit in my rose-patterned damask chair. I'd made my chart and I thought I had a good idea of what I wanted to tell Saylor, but there was no escaping the fact that David and I had kind of screwed up today. Even though I knew Saylor wasn't the person I'd thought she was, old habits die hard, and I hated the thought of disappointing her.

Maybe David picked up on that, because he leaned over the table, and in a very low voice, said, "Something happened today."

Saylor didn't move, but her eyes flicked to my hand. We'd stopped on our way back into town to get bandages and antibiotic cream for my cut, and the majority of my palm was swathed in gauze. "I can see that."

As quietly and quickly as he could, David told Saylor about Blythe, pausing only when Miss Annemarie tottered over to take our orders. When he was done, Saylor sat very still, her face totally blank. But her hand was clutching her fork so hard, I was afraid she might actually bend the metal. "And the two of you decided to tackle this by yourselves why exactly?" she asked, voice syrupy sweet, eyes blazing.

I took a sip of ice water, stalling for time, but David already had an answer. "Because I don't trust you," he said. "Her," David added, gesturing to me with a teaspoon, "I trust."

Miss Annemarie reemerged with our food—chicken salad for me and Saylor, a club sandwich for David. As she set it down on the table, Miss Annemarie smiled at me. "How are your aunts, Harper?"

"Fine, thank you," I said, hoping that would be enough. I loved the old ladies in my town, but dear God, they could *talk*. And Miss Annemarie didn't show any signs of quitting. "And your parents?"

"Also fine, thank you, Miss Annemarie."

The old woman sighed and shook her head, chins wobbling. "They've been so strong after your sister passed. Such a tragedy."

I forced a tight smile. "They have, yes."

"I'm keeping y'all on my prayer list," she murmured, patting me on the shoulder before shuffling back to the kitchen. Now the two women by the window were looking over at us, squinting like they were trying to recognize me. *Yes,* I wanted to say, *I am Leigh-Anne Price's sister. Yes, that Leigh-Anne, the Homecoming Queen who wrapped her car around a tree when she was totally smashed.*

"You okay?" David asked in a low voice.

Clearing my throat, I speared a mayo-coated grape with my fork. "Yup. Now, back to what we were saying about Blythe. She told David that they didn't want to kill him anymore; now they want to do a spell on him. Apparently it's the same one—"

I didn't get to finish. Saylor's hand was shaking so badly she nearly dropped her tiny cup of oolong.

She put it back in the saucer amid a clatter of china. "Alaric's ritual."

"That's the one," David said around a mouthful of club sandwich. "But Blythe said it only went so badly with Alaric because he wasn't a Mage. She thinks if she tried it—"

"Don't even finish that sentence, David Stark," Saylor snapped. Outside, the wind blew harder, rattling the big window, and all three of us jumped. "Didn't you hear what I said the other night? That ritual drove Alaric mad. It resulted in the deaths of hundreds. It turned him into a monster."

Saylor laid her hands flat on the table, and I could see they were trembling slightly. "No matter what this girl said, it's the ritual itself that's dangerous. Alaric had to be put down like a dog. And you said this Blythe girl was . . . what was the term you used, David?"

He swallowed before answering, "Super psycho bitch batshit."

Saylor's upper lip curled. "Ah, yes. Charming. And only seventeen, right?"

When we both nodded, she closed her eyes and took a deep breath. "The temporal shifts, the vanishing spell . . . those are things Mages just don't do. They're too dangerous, too risky, too . . . big. And she's using them all over the damn place. What must they be thinking, using someone so young to attempt something so insane? And *why*?"

I shook my head. "She claimed she could do it better than Alaric, and that David and the Ephors could work together afterward. Apparently surviving this ritual is the test David has to face the night of Cotillion."

"Which I'm still in favor of just skipping altogether," David said, dumping three packets of sugar into his cup.

Saylor stirred her tea with more force than was probably necessary. "I told you, there is no skipping it. This event is preset. Destined."

David and I both groaned a little at that word, but I had to admit, it made sense. "Think of it this way," I told David, tossing my hair over my shoulder. "At least we know when it'll happen. We have a set date to prepare for."

If the way David glowered at his tea was any indication, he wasn't exactly buying that, but he gave a little shrug. "Okay."

I shot a look over at the old ladies by the window, but they were deeply involved in their crème brûlée and not paying any attention to us. "Miss Saylor, could you get back to that part about putting Alaric down like a dog?" I glanced over at David. He wasn't looking at me, but was tracing little patterns on the tablecloth with his fork. "You said almost all of his Paladins died protecting him. So who killed Alaric?"

Saylor was quiet for so long that I didn't think she was going to answer. And then, finally, "The other two Paladins."

David's fork stopped moving on the table, snagging on the gingham. "How? If their 'sacred duty' is to protect—"

"Alaric was a danger to himself in that state." Saylor reached out, her hand hovering over David's for a moment before she pulled it back. "Which meant the inherent contradiction in that overrode the Paladins' instinct to keep him safe."

Lowering her head, Saylor pinched the bridge of her nose. "If we were at my house, I'd be able to show you. I have books, illustrations, things you'll need to see."

Giving up the pretense of eating—my mouth was too dry, my

stomach too jumpy—I pushed my plate away. "Well, we're not at your house. If I'm going to do this, I need to do it . . . my way."

"There is no your—" Saylor said, but she broke off as the front door to the tearoom rattled open, bringing another puff of wind and the smell of rain. As her eyes widened, I heard a familiar voice say, "Jewel, honestly, no soup is worth going out on a day like this."

My heart sank as I heard Aunt Jewel reply, "Oh, hush, it's not even raining."

"Yet," Aunt May snapped.

Turning slowly in my chair, I took in my aunts, all huddling in the doorway of the restaurant. The three of them were all dressed in nearly identical black slacks, orthopedic shoes, and bright sweaters. Aunt Martha saw me first, her eyes widening in pleasure. "Oh, look, girls!" she trilled. "It's Harper Jane!"

Smiling weakly, I raised my hand in a little wave as they started to bear down on me. As they did, the front door opened again, and there, right behind The Aunts, was my mom.

Chapter 25

MOM LOOKED toward The Aunts and, finding them, saw me. Her brow wrinkled in confusion. "Harper?" she said, walking toward the table. Compared to the aunts in their party-colored sweaters, Mom looked a little wan in her silky cream blouse and tan slacks. Her hair, a few shades lighter than mine, was mussed from the wind.

"Mom!" I said, trying my best not to sound guilty.

"Hillary, you didn't tell us Harper would be here, too," Aunt May said. Mom shook her head. "I . . . didn't know she would be. You did say you were going out with Bee today, didn't you, Harper?"

It wasn't really a question; Mom knew exactly what I'd said. Still, I wondered why she looked so befuddled. I mean, she'd caught me having lunch in Miss Annemarie's Tearoom with Saylor and David. It wasn't like she'd found me smoking crack in an alley.

"Plans fell through," I told her, wrinkling my nose like "What can you do?" "But then I ran into Miss Saylor, and she asked me out to lunch with her and David."

Next to me, David lifted his hand in greeting, and Saylor picked up her teacup, taking a swallow. Only seconds ago, she'd been rattled and freaked out. Now she looked like she always did: cool, collected, Queen of Pine Grove.

"It was so sweet of Harper to join us," she said. "Boys never really appreciate this place."

No one under seventy-five really appreciated Miss Annemarie's, but Mom nodded. Still, that crease between her brows didn't ease.

"Why don't we pull a table over?" Aunt Jewel asked, tugging at the hem of her purple sweater. "I'm sure Annemarie won't mind, and then we can all have lunch together."

"No!" I said, way more sharply than I should have. The crease between Mom's brows deepened, and even Aunt Jewel seemed surprised.

"We're about to finish up here," Saylor covered smoothly. I saw The Aunts and Mom drop their gazes to our nearly full plates. "And, Harper, didn't you say you were meeting Miss Franklin after lunch?"

"I did," I said, nodding. "So . . . I wouldn't want Miss Annemarie to go to the trouble of bringing a table when we're about to leave."

Mom was intent as she watched me. It reminded me of when I was little and she was checking me to see if I was sick. I half expected her to lay a hand on my forehead. "All righty then," said Aunt Jewel, clapping her hands together. "Y'all finish your lunch, and we'll go grab a table. Your Aunt May is absolutely perishing for Annemarie's crab bisque, else we'd be eating at Golden Corral like we usually do on Saturdays."

Cursing Aunt May's sudden highbrow craving, I got up and gave each of them a quick hug. "I'll stop by later this week," I promised, breathing in The Aunts' familiar scent of Youth Dew, hairspray, and smoke.

When I got to Mom, she hugged me back, but concern was still stamped all over her face. "Harper, are you sure you're—" She gasped then, grabbing my hand and lifting it to her face. "What on earth happened to you?"

Gently as I could, I took my hand back, fighting the urge to hide it behind my back. "I broke a glass this morning. Stupid. But it's fine! The bandage makes it look worse than it is."

I think Mom would have asked more questions if Aunt Jewel hadn't leaned over and taken my hand, inspecting it over her glasses. "Did you put peroxide on it?"

The Aunts would pour peroxide over a severed leg; it was their cure-all.

"Yes, ma'am."

Sniffing, Aunt Jewel gave me my hand back. "Well, then you'll be right as rain. Now come on, let's get a table before May dies of soup deprivation."

They steered Mom toward a table in the corner, and I sat back down, taking a deep breath. Once I was sure my family was out of earshot, I leaned into Saylor. "That's why we have to do things my way. I have a family here. Friends. A life. I have to keep those things. I have to make it through this as—as normally and inconspicuously as possible."

Saylor raised one perfectly groomed brow at me. "And how exactly do you plan to 'inconspicuously' stop this Blythe from doing a spell on David at Cotillion?'"

"I'll . . . figure it out," I said, shooting a glance at my mom and The Aunts. Aunts May and Martha were arguing over the tea list, and Aunt Jewel was regaling Mom with a story that apparently required a bunch of hand gestures. Watching them, a wave of affection washed over me. "There has to be a way to keep me not killed, keep David un-bespelled, and still live my own life."

If Saylor Stark were the type of woman who chewed her lip, I think she would have at that moment. As it was, she tapped her teaspoon against her saucer. "I'll put up more wards around the town, wards geared specifically toward you. Of course, that won't do you any good the night of Cotillion, if David's vision is anything to go by. And you have to train with me. At my house, every day."

"Train how?" I asked, thinking again of Blythe and the letter opener. What training would've prepared me for *that?* "Do you know how to fight? I mean, no offense, Miss Saylor, but you *aren't* a Paladin. And you don't exactly seem like the . . . fighting type."

Saylor leaned back in her seat, raising one silver eyebrow. "You're right, I'm not a Paladin. But I worked next to one for nearly thirty years, and I was there with Christopher when he trained under the Ephors. Now, if that isn't good enough for you, you're welcome to go to the judo classes at the community center."

Chastened, I poured another cup of tea. "I'm sorry. I'd . . . I'd love to train with you, Miss Saylor, but every day—"

"We only have three weeks," Saylor interrupted, sitting up straight. "And that is not nearly enough time to get you ready for something like this."

"Trust me," David said. "If anyone can handle pressure, it's Pres."

I appreciated his vote of confidence, but Saylor was right— three weeks was nothing.

On the other hand, three weeks was *nothing*. I could do this. I could find some way to balance my regular life with my Paladin responsibilities. Maybe all those other Paladins gave up their lives to protect Oracles, but they probably weren't as good at organizing and multitasking as I was.

"I can do that," I told Saylor, and as I said it, I realized that I could. I just had to be careful with scheduling and do, as Bee would say, a leeeeeettle bit of lying. And, I resolved, it was also time to start telling a leeeeeeettle bit of the truth to someone. "But I'm going to do it my way."

Saylor's brows drew together. "What does that mean?"

"It means we're in trouble," David said, but when he looked at me, he was grinning.

Chapter 26

On Monday, I put my plan into action. Bee, Ryan, Brandon, and I were having lunch in the courtyard underneath one of the big oak trees. Ryan leaned against the trunk, long legs stretched out in front of him. Brandon had Bee in his lap, and if Headmaster Dunn saw that, they'd both end up with detention, but I refrained from mentioning it. Next to me, Ryan nudged my hip with his.

"Harper?"

"Hmm?"

Smiling, Ryan balled up the rest of his sandwich, tossing it at the nearest trash can. It bounced off, of course, and I made a note to remind him to pick it up later. "You are a million miles away," he said, snaking an arm around my waist and pulling me closer.

"It's nothing. Thinking," I said, ducking my head and laying it on his shoulder. I was usually against PDA of any kind, but after neglecting Ryan all weekend, I felt like I owed him a little extra demonstration. He must've appreciated that, because he pressed a kiss to my temple.

"You're always thinking," he said, more affectionately than accusatory. "And I'm always wondering what about."

I lifted my head. "We've known each other for eight years, been dating for two, and you don't know what I'm thinking?" I was teasing, but Ryan, still smiling, shook his head.

"Never," he said. "No idea what goes on in that giant brain of yours."

I wasn't sure why the words stung, but they did. He was still grinning guilelessly, his hazel eyes bright, his auburn hair tumbling over his forehead, and he was still so handsome it made my chest tight.

So he didn't know what I was thinking. Ever, apparently. Big deal.

I snuggled in closer, and said, "I have a lot going on right now."

From Brandon's lap, Bee giggled. "You always have a lot going on, Harper. It's, like, your thing. When you die in a hundred years, they'll probably write on your gravestone, 'Here Lies Harper Price—Damn It, She Still Had Stuff to Do!'"

Ryan and Brandon laughed, but I couldn't stop the shiver that ran through me. A hundred years or three weeks? And damn it, I *did* still have stuff to do. Starting now.

"Hey, guys?" I said to Brandon and Ryan. "Could I talk to Bee alone for a sec?"

"Sure," Ryan said, automatically rising to his feet.

"Are you going to talk about your periods or something?" Brandon said, frowning.

"You're disgusting!" Bee shrieked, slugging him in the shoulder.

Even Ryan frowned with distaste. "Dude, really?"

Brandon grabbed Bee by the waist, lifting her with him as he stood up, pressing a smacking kiss to the side of her neck. Once she was on her feet, Bee's cheeks were red, her blond hair a fuzzy halo around her head. "Go," she told Brandon, playfully shoving at him.

The boys loped off, and Bee and I watched them go. Shaking her head, Bee sighed. "I don't know why I put up with him."

Me neither, I thought. But I needed Bee on my side for what I was going to say next, and ragging on her boyfriend was not going to accomplish that.

Once the boys were out of sight, Bee turned to me, sympathy in her big brown eyes. "Look, you and Ryan are perfect together," she said. "Don't worry about that."

I blinked at her. "What?"

Tucking her hair behind her ears, Bee tilted her head. "Isn't that what you wanted to talk about? Ryan saying he never knows what you're thinking? I know how you can obsess over stuff like that, but it doesn't mean anything. Brandon probably doesn't even know I *have* thoughts."

Impulsively, I reached out and wrapped my arms around Bee, squeezing her tight. "That wasn't what I wanted to talk about, but your best friend skills are seriously off the charts."

Laughing, Bee hugged me back. "I try."

We pulled apart, but I held on to her elbows, keeping her at arm's length. "Ryan and I are fine, promise," I told her. "But I actually needed to tell you . . . kind of a secret."

Bee chewed on her lower lip. "I thought we didn't have secrets from each other. Wasn't that what the pinkie swear was about?"

I linked my pinkie with hers again. "It was, and it is. That's why I'm telling you this now. But, I'm warning you, it's . . . weird."

Bee's pinkie tightened around mine. "I can handle weird, Harper."

Seriously hoping that was true, I tugged her to sit down next to me under the oak. "It's about Saylor Stark . . ."

A few hours later, once school was out, Bee and I stood on the Starks' front porch. She stared up at the house, her eyes wide, mouth slightly agape. "You're totally serious about this?"

Ringing the doorbell, I nodded. "One hundred percent."

We could hear the bell echoing throughout the house, and as it did, Bee straightened her skirt self-consciously. "But . . . Saylor Stark? Seriously?"

"Seriously," I replied. The door swung open, and David stood there, dressed in a yellow sweater and his green corduroy pants. He looked like he should be on PBS, talking to a puppet about the alphabet. Still, I had to admit, yellow was a good color on him. It brought out the gold in his hair, and—

I stopped myself. *The gold in his hair?* Since when did I care about David Stark's hair except to note when it was trying to escape from his skull? These past few days were clearly messing with my head.

"Hey, Pres," David said, and then his gaze swung to my right. "And . . . Bee. You're here. With Harper. At our house."

His brows practically disappeared as he turned back to me. "You . . . brought Bee to—"

"Training, yeah," I said quickly. While David stared at me like I'd grown a second head, I breezed past him, pulling Bee after me. "I couldn't keep everything a secret from *everyone* forever, so I let Bee in on what's been going on."

Now David's jaw was hanging open slightly. "You told her—"

"That Saylor is training me and you in martial arts, yes." I moved into the foyer, heading toward the back of the house.

"Martial . . . arts," David repeated slowly, closing the door behind him.

It was stupid. Ludicrous, even, the idea that Saylor Stark was some kind of secret kung fu master, teaching me and David the ancient art of hand-to-hand combat, but I had to tell Bee *something*. It would give me an excuse to be around the Starks, *and* it would get Bee on my side. When I'd told her, I hadn't had to fake my blush or the embarrassment that colored every word.

"That's . . . super bizarre," Bee said once I'd finished.

"Now you see why I've been so secretive about it. I mean, learning to kick people in the head and stuff? It's not exactly how people see me."

Bee had pulled a long strand of hair over her lips and mouthed it thoughtfully. "I get that, Harper, but this just . . ." She shook her head, blond hair moving over her shoulders. "It seems so not you."

"I know it does, but I wanted something that was different. Something for me. Leigh-Anne was a cheerleader, and Home-coming Queen and did Cotillion, and this just felt . . . mine."

The words spilled from my lips almost too easily, and sur-prised, I realized that's because they were . . . kind of true. I was enjoying this. All right, maybe "enjoying" was a strong word, but as soon as I'd committed myself to helping David, to fully being a Paladin, a kind of rightness had set in.

And maybe that's what Bee saw on my face, because she made a clucking noise and reached out to briefly squeeze my hand. "You could use something that's all yours. Although I have to admit, this is not exactly what I would've expected. But I guess it's a good thing to learn? And it *will* look stellar on your college apps."

After that, it had been no problem persuading Bee to help me keep this a secret from Ryan. She totally got why I'd be embarrassed if he found out, and she'd sworn to carry my secret to her grave.

What I hadn't expected was for her to ask to tag along. All I'd wanted was to give her something slightly close to the truth so there would be at least one person kind of in on what was going on. But no excuse had rushed to my lips, and so now here I was, reporting for my first day of Paladin training with Bee Franklin at my side.

David was clearly biting his cheek, and his eyes were bright. "Right, yeah, my . . . my aunt teaches martial arts. To me and Harper. Which is why we've been hanging out a little more."

Bee gave a delicate snort. "Seems like a dangerous thing, teaching the two of you how to kick ass. What if you end up murdering each other?"

David and I exchanged a glance. "Risk we're willing to take," he said at last. "Let me go get Aunt Saylor. She's gonna need to, uh, be prepared for this."

David went into the kitchen, and Bee glanced around. "Miss Saylor's house looks exactly like I imagined." I remembered thinking the same thing when I was here last. It seemed like an entire millennium had passed between that day and this one, so it was hard to believe it had been almost a month.

Saylor bustled out of the kitchen, hands clasped in front of her, all smiles, all business. "Miss Franklin! What a surprise." That last bit was directed at me, but I gave her a little shrug. *My way.*

"So Harper has told you about our little secret," she continued, waving us toward the French doors leading to the balcony.

"She did," Bee said, her eyes taking in every nook and cranny of the house. "And to be honest, I think it's great, Miss Saylor. A young lady today should be able to protect herself."

Behind Saylor's back, I stuck my tongue out at Bee and mouthed, *Suck-up.*

She gave a shameless grin and followed us out into the backyard.

I don't know what I'd expected. Some yoga mats. Maybe a punching bag. And Saylor did have those things. But she also had three dummies set up on stands. Against one of them, there was a sword at least as long as my leg, and Bee stared at it, mouth agape.

"Oh, wow. Y'all are . . . hard-core."

"Yes, yes," Saylor said, bustling over to the sword and picking it up. "This is for . . . inspiration. We obviously don't want to involve weapons. At least not yet."

"Yet?" Bee asked, but Saylor was already heading back into the house with the sword. "Now," she said when she came back.

"One of the things Harper has been learning is how to stay on her guard so attackers can't surprise her."

"Right," Bee said, nodding like that was a totally normal thing for Saylor to be teaching me.

And I have to hand it to my best friend. For the next hour, she watched Saylor Stark throw various things—knives, pots, and more ceramic lambs than any one woman should own—at me from various directions while I was blindfolded, and at no point did she run away screaming, calling us all crazy people. She sat in the grass, legs folded, serenely watching the president of the Pine Grove Betterment Society lob a knife at the Homecoming Queen.

"Good job, Harper!" Bee called out when I batted the knife away, striking the hilt with the side of my hand. "Way to hustle!"

It was the exact same thing she shouted at Brandon when he practiced basketball, and for some reason, it made me smile. Same when, after I spun away from a particularly heavy china cat tossed at my midsection, Bee launched into one of our cheers, complete with shaking her fists like there were pom-poms in them.

After I'd deflected enough things, Saylor finally called it quits. We were both sweating and breathing hard, Saylor from throwing, me from the tension of spending an hour trying not to get whacked.

"Good job, Harper," Saylor told me, untying the blindfold. "And you, Miss Franklin. You were very . . . supportive."

Bee stood up, dusting off the back of her pants. "Thank you, Miss Saylor." Then she nodded her head at the sun porch. "I thought you were training David, too. Why didn't he get stuff thrown at his head?"

David, who was leaning on the French doors, arms folded over his chest, said, "I've already passed this stage. Have my dodging-stuff badge. Belt. Whatever."

I shot him a look, and his chin trembled with the effort of not laughing.

But Bee accepted that. "Okay. Well, that was . . . interesting. Thanks so much for letting me watch, Miss Saylor."

"Any time, honey," Saylor cooed, even as she gave me a glare that plainly said, *Never again.*

"Are y'all done now?" Bee said.

"I have a few more things to go over with Harper, but it's more theory than training." Right. Saylor had wanted to show me the spell Blythe was planning on doing.

"In that case, I'll go ahead and skedaddle," Bee said.

"I'll walk you out," I told her as I wiped the sweat from my face with an embroidered towel that smelled like lavender.

Once we'd gotten to the driveway, Bee turned to me. "Right, so that's kind of nuts," she said.

I grimaced. "I know."

"But," she added, screwing up her face, "it's also kind of awesome. You looked so fierce, all—" She lifted her hands, doing a few chops and slices that I guess were an imitation of me deflecting stuff.

"Shut up," I said, laughing as I batted her hands down.

"Seriously, I get why you're keeping this secret, but . . . I don't know, I'm proud of you. Homecoming Queen, debutante, President of All the Things, *and* a secret ninja. Best best friend ever."

"Harper!" Saylor called from the porch. "Are you coming?"

Sighing, I gave Bee a quick hug. "No rest for the ninja," I said. "And thanks, Bee. For not thinking this was *too* weird."

Her cheeks flushed a little, and she glanced down. "To be honest, Harper? I didn't believe you. That's why I wanted to come today, to, like—"

"Call my bluff?"

Nodding, Bee pulled her sunglasses down from the top of her head. "Which makes me the *worst* best friend ever."

"No," I said quickly, shaking my head. "I've been out of it lately; I understand."

"Harper!" Saylor called again, her voice a little sharper this time.

"Go," she said, giving me a friendly shove. "Get your ninja on."

I reached out to link my pinkie with hers. She squeezed it back. Smiling sheepishly, Bee ducked her head, blond hair swinging over her collarbone. "I forgive you for being a bizarre combination of totally perfect and totally weird."

I laughed at that, and as Bee drove off, my heart felt lighter in my chest.

Chapter 27

THAT WEEKEND, I finally had a date with Ryan. Between training with Saylor, preparing for Cotillion (both the normal and the supernatural parts of it), and keeping up with all my regular stuff, I hadn't exactly been a model girlfriend. Hence tonight's date, which included a movie of his choosing and, since his parents were at their lake house for the weekend, some alone time at Ryan's place. I actually couldn't remember the last time we'd . . . been alone, and I told myself it was anticipation making my hands tremble as I brushed my teeth that evening, not nerves.

When I came downstairs, Mom and Dad were both sacked out on the couch, watching some true-crime TV show. "Hey," I said, pausing in the doorway.

Dad's arm was around Mom's shoulder and both of them had their feet propped up on the coffee table. Even their ankles were crossed the same. "Hay is for horses, Harper Jane!" Dad called out, and I rolled my eyes, but smiled.

"Fine. Good evening, parental types."

Mom looked over her shoulder at me. "You look pretty. Where are you off to?"

Preening a little, I smoothed my fitted sweater over my stomach. "Date night with Ryan. I'll be back by midnight."

There was a splash of light across the pale blue of the wall as Ryan's car pulled into the driveway, and I was already turning to meet him at the door when Mom said, "Ten."

I paused, sure I'd misunderstood her. "Ten what?"

"Ten is when you need to be home. The movie starts at what? Seven? That's plenty of time to get back."

Dad kept his eyes on the TV, but his fingers were drumming on Mom's shoulders. "Um . . . seriously?" My purse was on the end table nearest the couch, and I twisted to grab it.

Mom's eyes met mine, and I could swear there were hollows under hers, new wrinkles in the corners. "Yes, seriously. Ten o'clock, Harper."

Outside, Ryan's door thumped shut, and I could hear his steady tread coming up the front steps. "It's always been midnight," I insisted, hating how petulant I sounded, but . . . I had plans for tonight. Boyfriend maintenance plans. And I hadn't had to be in that early since middle school.

The doorbell rang then, and I cast a quick look toward the front door. "Mom, my curfew has always—"

"I don't care what we've always done," Mom snapped, her voice slightly shrill. "I'm your mother, and tonight, I want you back in this house by ten. Is that clear?"

Ryan had better manners than to press the doorbell again, but

I could practically feel him out there waiting for me. Too bad he wasn't the only one I clearly needed to spend more time with. Knowing that snottiness wouldn't get me anywhere, I nodded. "Okay," I said, doing my best to seem okay. "See y'all at ten."

Mom sagged back onto the couch, relief obvious on her face. Dad, too, seemed to relax a bit, lifting his hand in a wave. "Be safe, kiddo."

I brooded the entire way to the theater. Pine Grove only had one, and it only showed two movies at a time. I'd let Ryan pick tonight—I almost always chose what we saw—and of course, he'd gone with the action film. I'd rolled my eyes, pretending to be exasperated, but really, I wanted to see it, too. I had plenty of moves in my Paladin arsenal, but it wouldn't hurt to add a few more.

We already had our tickets and had stepped into the lobby when I told Ryan about Mom's new curfew. Frowning, he shoved his hands in his back pockets. "Whoa. Okay. I just . . . I kind of wish you'd told me that before we'd come here."

The lobby reeked of burnt popcorn and spilled Coke, and it seemed even more crowded than usual for a Saturday night. The place was always full—when you only have one movie theater in your town, that happens—but tonight it was packed, and I suddenly felt a little claustrophobic. "Why?" I asked Ryan as someone bumped into me from behind.

Rolling his shoulders, Ryan stepped a little closer to me. "Because if I'd known I was only going to have a few hours with you, there are a lot of other things I'd rather be doing than watching a movie."

Maybe it was that unexpected bout of nervousness I'd felt about that very thing earlier. Maybe I was still irritated with my mom and looking for someone to take it out on. Or maybe I was honestly a little pissed off at Ryan. "So, what, if you'd known you'd have to choose between a date and fooling around, you would've chosen the latter?"

"Whoa, Harper." Ryan lowered his voice and looked around us. "Keep your voice down." Only a few yards away, our old Sunday school teacher, Mrs. Catesby, was buying a box of Junior Mints, and I should have been horrified at the thought that she might have overheard me, but I wasn't. Not even a little bit.

Ryan, on the other hand, was. "That's not what I'm saying. I'm saying that I've hardly been alone with you since when? Before Homecoming?"

"I've been busy," I insisted, and Ryan rolled his eyes at me.

"Yeah, I know. With school and Cotillion and whatever other stupid shit is more important than your boyfriend."

I could not believe this was happening. I was fighting with my boyfriend in public. Across the way, I could see Abigail and Amanda, huddled near the ladies' room. They saw me, too, and as they lifted their hands in greeting, Mary Beth emerged from the bathroom. Her eyes landed on Ryan first, and there was no mistaking the . . . it wasn't even lust, it was honest to God *love*, or at least a very deep case of like.

"Don't call the stuff I do stupid," I told him, this time pitching my voice near a whisper. I tried to keep my face blank so the other girls wouldn't be able to tell we were fighting, but they were already heading this way.

"I'm sorry," Ryan blew out on a long breath. "But, God, Harper, sometimes I feel like your whole life is a checklist, and I am way down at the bottom. And, you know, every once in a while, you throw me a bone to keep me happy."

I flinched at that, hard. Not only because it was insulting, but because it was way too close to the truth. "You're not at the bottom," I said, and then Abigail, Amanda, and Mary Beth were there, and I was frantically blinking back tears and faking a huge smile.

"Hi, girls!" I said with forced brightness.

"Hey, Harper," Mary Beth replied, but her eyes were on Ryan. "Are you guys . . . okay?"

"We're fine," Ryan and I said in unison, too quickly. Abigail and Amanda exchanged a look, and I stepped closer to Ryan, slipping my arm through his. His forearm was like a rock under my fingers, and I could still feel the tension humming through him. Even though he was smiling at the girls, I knew they could sense it, too.

There was an awkward silence before Abigail said, "Is Ryan trying to drag you to that stupid *Hard Fists* movie?"

"Groooooosssss," Amanda drawled. "I hate stuff like that. Ryan, be a good boyfriend and take your girlfriend to *The Promise*. Y'all can sit with us."

"Mandy," her twin said, elbowing her in the side. "They probably want to sit alone at the movies."

Mary Beth swallowed, and her shoes must have been really fascinating for all the attention she was paying to them.

"Oh, please," Amanda said, delicately picking out a piece of popcorn and tossing it in her mouth. "Like Ryan and Harper are the make-out-in-the-theater type. That would be like . . ." She screwed up her elfin face. "My parents doing that or something. No offense, guys."

I waved her off, but under my other hand, I could swear Ryan got even tenser. More people were coming in the door now, and as I moved closer to Ryan to avoid the crush, he stepped the tiniest bit away. Ignoring that as best as I could, I held on to his sleeve tighter. "Actually, I want to see *Hard Fists*."

Amanda and Abigail both snorted in disbelief, but Mary Beth's lips lifted in a little smile. "It does look kind of badass," she offered, and Amanda and Abigail swung identical frowns at her.

"Ugh, no, it does not, Mary Beth. All that violence and blood and . . . bleh." Amanda shuddered.

"Maybe you need a Y chromosome to properly appreciate the amazingness of *Hard Fists*, Amanda," Ryan said. Then he nodded at Mary Beth. "Or maybe you just need to be a cool chick like MB here."

MB? Since when did Ryan have a nickname for Mary Beth? It wasn't like anyone else called her that.

Mary Beth's face flushed, and while I thought pink was supposed to look terrible on redheads, she actually looked really pretty with a little color in her cheeks. And there was a softness in Ryan's grin as he looked down at her that I recognized. He used to smile at me like that.

For once, the pain in my chest had nothing to do with David

or danger or magic. This was straight-up teenage angst, and it *hurt*. I mean, fine, if he suddenly liked Mary Beth, whatever, but did he have to do it in front of Amanda and Abigail?

Wait a second. Whatever? My boyfriend was smiling at a blushing girl, and I was embarrassed because my friends were watching?

Standing there in the theater, with what felt like my entire town hemming me in, I let that thought sink in. I wasn't hurt that Ryan might have a thing for someone else. I was scared of what that might make other people think about *me*.

That was . . . effed up.

Suddenly, the lobby was too hot and the smell of popcorn was making me slightly nauseous, and all I wanted to do was go home. What would happen if I turned around and walked out? Would Ryan come after me, or would he shrug and go watch the "badass" *Hard Fists* with MB? And why didn't that thought make me want to tear MB's pretty auburn hair right out of her head?

"Harper?" Abigail asked, laying a hand on my arm. "Are you okay?"

I hadn't realized I was staring at the floor, my eyes tracing the golden concentric circles stamped on the grubby navy carpet. Lifting my head, I did my best to smile, but from the look on Abi's face, I wasn't pulling it off. "Yeah," I said, "it's just hot in here."

"It is," Abigail agreed. "I mean, look at Mary Beth, she's practically a tomato."

Mary Beth's cheeks *were* more red than pink now, and Amanda tried to disguise a giggle as a cough.

Tired of this, tired of them, I tugged on Ryan's sleeve. "In that case, we better go ahead and get into the theater before we all boil to death out here."

I took a step forward and as I did, I looked up into the crush of people waiting to get their sodas and Gummi Bears. I could recognize nearly every face, either from school or church. And then Matt Sheehan, a senior at the Grove, stepped aside, and I found myself staring into a very familiar—and very crazy—pair of brown eyes.

Blythe.

Chapter 28

I FROZE, my hand still on Ryan's sleeve. My heart was somewhere south of my knees, sweat immediately prickling my brow. The crowd shifted, a group of preteen girls sliding in front of Blythe. When they moved on, she was gone.

Rising up on tiptoes, I frantically searched the lobby, looking for some trace of her. "Who are you looking for?" Ryan asked, lifting his head to glance around, too.

"Did you see a girl?" I said, still scanning the mass of bodies moving through the theater.

"I . . . see lots of girls," Ryan replied, bemused.

"No, a specific girl. A tiny one with brown hair and dimples."

"Lauren Roberts?" Abi asked, naming a girl in our math class.

"No," I told her, twisting to look behind me. "But like her. About that height, same hair. Like Lauren Roberts with a major case of crazy eyes."

She could be *anywhere*. She was short enough to pass through the crowd unseen, and damn it, *I* wasn't tall enough to see over all these people.

"Does this chick owe you money or something?" Ryan joked, finally sounding like himself again. But I was too panicked to be happy about that.

The glass doors opened, and as they did, I spotted a few people leaving the theater. I caught the briefest glimpse of a long brown ponytail, and then the door swung shut. It might have been Blythe, but I couldn't be sure.

Whirling on Ryan, I grabbed his arm again. "I'll be right back. Go on into the theater and I'll find you in a few minutes."

"Whoa." Ryan flipped his hand, fingers encircling my wrist. "Where are you—"

I tugged out of his grasp, forgetting about my superstrength, so instead of taking my arm back gently, I more or less wrenched it from him.

Surprise, hurt, and more than a little bit of anger all warred on his face, but I didn't have time to worry about that right now. Blythe was here, and I had to find her before she found me.

"I'll be right back," I said again, then dashed out the front doors of the theater before Ryan had the chance to say anything else.

The November night was cold and clear, and my breath puffed out in front of me as I stood on the sidewalk, looking left, then right. The theater took up one whole side of the square; the other three sides were taken up with little boutiques, Miss Annemarie's, the jewelry store, and Pine Grove's sad attempt at a coffee shop, the Dixie Bean. Other than the theater, the rest of the square was relatively deserted, since most of the shops closed around five. Miss Annemarie's and the Dixie Bean were probably the only things open, but there was no one on the sidewalks, and no sign of the little group that had just left the theater.

I jogged across the street, heading for the center of the square. The statue of Adolphus Bridgeforth, one of the founders of Pine Grove, glowered down at me. The Pine Grove Betterment Society, led by Saylor, had raised the money for it about five years back. I knew that if I looked closely, I'd see wards etched into the stone base. Saylor had been very thorough where David's protection was concerned.

Next to him, the little fountain splashed away merrily, the night wind blowing a few stray droplets on me. Every nerve in my body felt tense and coiled, the hair on the back of my neck standing up.

You're a Paladin, I reminded myself. *You have all kinds of kick-ass abilities and she doesn't.*

But then I remembered how easily she'd gotten the jump on me before.

To Adolphus's right, there was a little flower garden surrounded by a tiny white picket fence. A bronze plaque on the fence said that the garden had been planted by the Pine Grove Betterment Society just last year. Sure enough, as I got closer, I could see tiny golden wards on all the fence posts.

Giving another quick glance around to make sure no one was looking, I reached down and, easy as picking a flower, plucked a stake from the fence. The hole glared at me accusingly, and I slipped the pointed piece of wood behind me as I backed away from the center of the square. I hated vandalism more than anything, but I needed a weapon. Besides, Saylor had put that fence up, so when you thought about it, the fence was practically mine.

In a way.

Keeping the stake low at my side, I headed back toward the theater. There was a parking lot behind it. Maybe that was where Blythe had gone. As I hurried in that direction, a tiny voice in my head kept up a running commentary. *So if you find her, you're simply going to stab her to death with a piece of wood in the parking lot? And hope no one sees? Because tiny girls getting staked behind the Royale Cinema seems like something people would notice.*

But if I got rid of—no, *killed*, I needed to say killed—Blythe now, all of this ended. No Cotillion showdown, no chance of my whole town being wiped out, no chance of David dying. This was my chance.

Or it would have been, if she had been in the parking lot.

There were a few people straggling in, but both of the movies had already started, so the parking lot was more or less empty. Still, I kept my stake hidden at my side as I walked the rows of cars, ducking down to look under them, even peering in the windows.

No Blythe.

When I got to the last car on the row, I sighed, nearly letting the fence post drop from my hand. This was stupid. It probably hadn't even been her. Maybe the stress of the past few weeks was finally catching up with me, and I was going crazy *in addition* to becoming a Paladin.

I should go back into the theater, find Ryan, and figure out some way to salvage this evening. The fence post clattered to the ground, and I turned back to the theater.

And suddenly I heard the sound of running feet. As I whipped around, I could have sworn I saw brown hair disappearing around the corner, back toward the square.

Dropping to my knees, I scrambled for the fence post. Not caring who saw me dashing through downtown Pine Grove wielding a damn stake, I took off after her. My boots clicked hard on the pavement, and I could hear the wind and my own blood rushing in my ears.

Was there a flash of movement over by Miss Annemarie's? I ran in that direction.

But just as I reached the tearoom, the door swung open. I didn't even have time to register that someone was coming out of that door before plowing directly into him.

Something warm splashed all over me, and for one horrifying, dizzying moment, I thought I'd plunged my stake into an innocent person's heart. But, no, I'd managed to lower it at the last second, and I could hear the wood clatter harmlessly to the pavement. As for the hot liquid currently seeping into my cashmere sweater, from the smell, it was the crab bisque that my Aunt May was so fond of.

My breath was sawing in and out of my lungs, burning with the sharp night air, as I stumbled back from . . . David.

Bisque was dripping from the front of his tweed jacket, the crushed plastic container still clutched against his chest. He looked down at himself and then back at me. "Pres? Is this some kind of Paladin thing? Was the soup poisoned or something?"

I didn't answer; I was too busy looking for Blythe, but there was no sign of her. She was gone.

Dropping my hands to my knees, I bent forward, taking deep breaths, trying to slow the slamming of my heart.

"I thought you had a date tonight," David said, and I don't know why that's the thing that did it. The tears that had pricked my eyes earlier suddenly came back full force, and to my absolute horror, I burst into tears.

"Whoa, whoa, Harper," David said, the plastic container tumbling to the sidewalk. He gripped my arms, holding me slightly away from him and ducking his head to look into my face. "What happened?"

"I was on a date, but Ryan and I got in a fight, and he likes Mary Beth—*MB*—I think, but it's like I don't even *c-care*, which makes me a-a horrible person, and then I saw Blythe, or I thought I did, and I vandalized a *fence*, and now we smell bad, and that s-s-soup wasn't poisoned, I just ran into you, and—"

I didn't get any further before David carefully wrapped his arms around me. He held me like I was a bomb he was afraid was seconds from going off, keeping our bodies as far apart as he could while still technically hugging me.

"It's okay," he said, patting my back once. He apparently decided that was a good move because he did it a few more times. And the weird thing was, it *was* kind of a good move. I lowered my forehead to his tweed-covered shoulder and let myself be patted until my tears slowed to a trickle. A few weeks ago, if you had told me that being held in David Stark's arms was one of the nicest things I'd ever feel, I wouldn't have laughed at you. I would've been too busy choking on my own horror.

But leaning against him, crying into his stupid tweed, I thought I could maybe stay there forever. It was such a relief to be able to sob and have someone know all the reasons why.

Once I was calmer, I lifted my head to find David watching me with an expression I'd never seen before. Before I had time to figure it out, he reached behind him and opened the tearoom door. "Well, I'm going to need another order of soup to go, so why don't we go inside and have a cup of tea. Tea fixes stuff, right?"

I looked back across the square at the theater. Ryan was in there, waiting for me. Or sitting next to Mary Beth and not worrying about me at all. Besides, I smelled like crab.

So giving one last glance to the theater, I nodded and followed David inside.

Chapter 29

DAVID AND I sat at the same table in the corner where The Aunts and my mom had had lunch last week. Miss Annemarie brought us a stack of napkins along with our tea, and we both did our best to blot the bisque from our clothes. As we did, I told David about Blythe.

Taking a sip of his tea, he mulled that over. "So you think she was following you just to, uh, mess with you?"

I dropped a sugar cube into my Earl Grey. "I guess. If she was even there. And it's okay, you can say the F-word."

To my surprise, David shrugged. "I don't know, I've kind of become fond of the euphemisms. The other day, I said 'mother trucker' when I dropped a book on my toe, and I have to admit, it was every bit as satisfying as the actual curse."

"See? I told you there were acceptable alternatives."

Raising his teacup in a salute, David inclined his head. "You were right." Then he widened his eyes in mock surprise. "Hey! Saying that didn't even burn my tongue! We're making progress, Pres."

I tossed one of the crumpled-up napkins at him. "Ha-ha."

He tossed the napkin back, but there was a smile playing around his lips.

I sipped my tea, feeling the warmth of it in my toes. The tearoom was always so overstuffed and tacky during the day, but at night, it felt cozy. There were tiny lamps in the middle of all of the tables, and we were the only people in the place. Everything smelled pleasantly spicy—well, everything except me and David—and the atmosphere was almost . . .

No, I wasn't going to say romantic. There was nothing romantic about Miss Annemarie's Tearoom. Or David Stark for that matter.

"What?" David asked. He was frowning slightly, the dim light making shadows underneath his cheekbones. There was the lightest smattering of freckles along the bridge of his nose, and I wondered why I'd never noticed those before.

I looked at him, eyebrows raised. "You shook your head," he said. "What were you saying no to?"

"Oh." I took another sip of tea so that I wouldn't have to answer right away. "I was thinking how crazy this night has been."

Leaning back, David stretched his arms over his head. "Yeah, I was planning on *eating* crab bisque tonight, not being doused in it."

"Oh, please. That jacket cost you what? Two bucks at Goodwill? I will never get the smell out of this sweater."

David reached down and gripped the lapels of his jacket, straightening it. "Hey, I like this jacket."

"That makes one of us," I replied, tucking my hair behind my ears.

David and I had been snarking at each other since we learned how to talk, but tonight, our barbs seemed less pointed. I wouldn't go so far as to call them affectionate or anything, but there was a definite lack of sting.

"We need to tell Saylor about tonight," I told David.

He was turning his teacup around in his hands, steam drifting up to fog his glasses. "I will, when I get home."

Silence stretched between us. Not awkward, really, but heavy somehow. Laden with something I couldn't name. "I'm sure he doesn't like her," David said.

"What?"

"Ryan," he clarified before draining his cup. "You said you think he likes Mary Beth. I bet you're wrong."

"Oh, right. That." Now that the moment had passed, I felt my cheeks flame at the memory of how I'd vomited up all of my feelings out there on the sidewalk. I should've just told him Blythe freaked me out. There was no need to drag my personal life into all of this.

"Don't get me wrong, Mary Beth is . . . well, she's not objectionable or anything, but she's not . . ."

My hands were tight around the teacup, the heat radiating on my palms. "She's not what?"

David tugged at his lapels again before leaning back in his chair. "You."

The lamplight shone on David's glasses, but behind them, his eyes were very blue and intent, and then I suddenly couldn't meet them anymore.

Thank God for Miss Annemarie, who chose that moment to

waddle over to the table, a plastic bag in hand. "Here you go, sweetie," she told David, handing him the soup. "Try to be more careful with this batch. I'm closing up now, so this is your last chance."

"Oh, r-right," David said, fumbling slightly with the bag. "Thanks, Miss Annemarie."

Our tea was gone, so we both got to our feet, thanking Miss Annemarie again. "Don't mention it," she said with a wave of her hand. "It's nice to have young people in here at night for once. Most of the other kids, they all go somewhere fancy on their dates. Like Ruby Tuesday."

I waited for David to insist we weren't on a date, but he gave Miss Annemarie a little smile and a nod. I didn't say anything either, and as weird as it seems, it was like by letting Miss Annemarie think it was a date, it had somehow . . . become a date.

I shook my head again. Crazy thought. Stupid.

After the warmth of Miss Annemarie's, the square seemed even colder. I shivered a little as the breeze made my still-damp sweater cling to my body.

"Here," David said, handing me the takeout bag. "Hold this."

I did, and he slipped out of his tweed, revealing an actually halfway-decent button-down dress shirt underneath. He slid the coat over my shoulders before taking the bag back.

"Thanks," I said, a little awkwardly. I never thought I would be grateful for the scent of crab bisque, but as I pulled the coat tighter around me, I was glad that was all I could smell. I felt weird enough as it was without adding nice boy smell to the mix.

David and I walked down the sidewalk, our arms a few inches apart.

"Do you want me to drive you home?" he asked as we passed the antique store.

"I should probably get back to the theater," I said. "Ryan . . ."

I let that trail off, and David shoved his free hand in his pocket. "Right. Ryan."

We had reached David's car by now, but both of us were sort of hovering beside it. "So," he said.

"So."

David rocked on his heels, frowning slightly. "Is it me, or are we being weird?"

I laughed, nerves making it sound high and thin. "We are being weird. Which is saying something for us."

Grinning, David let his shoulders drop a little. "Okay, good. It's only . . . I should've said something to Miss Annemarie about us not being on a date, but—"

"No," I rushed in to say, slipping my arms into his jacket. "That would've been awkward, too, and probably bad manners to correct her."

"Right!" he said, a little too loud. "It would've made her feel bad, and we don't want to do that. Not when she's made me delicious soup. Twice."

"Exactly," I said, feeling like my voice was a little too loud, too.

His mouth lifted in a half-grin, revealing a flash of teeth and making me realize for the first time that David Stark had surprisingly nice cheekbones. "You actually look pretty good in tweed,

Pres," he joked, reaching out to straighten the lapel of my—his—jacket.

"No one looks good in tweed," I insisted, going to push his hand away. But as I did, our skin touched, and the little pulse that went through me had nothing to do with prophecies or magic.

David must have felt it, too, because his eyes suddenly dropped to my mouth. I saw him swallow.

Oh my God, David Stark wants to kiss me. In public. In the middle of the street.

I waited to be horrified by that thought, but for some reason, horror wasn't coming. Neither was awkwardness or being freaked out or any of the other perfectly acceptable reactions to David Freaking Stark wanting to kiss me.

Instead, I felt myself swaying forward a little on the balls of my feet. But before anything profoundly stupid could happen, a car drove by, some country song blaring out the windows, and David and I stepped away from each other.

My heart was pounding, and I shoved my shaking hands into the pockets of the jacket. "Okay," I said at last. "So I'm going to go back to the theater, and you go home and eat soup and talk to Saylor about Blythe, and I'll see you Monday."

David wrapped one hand around the back of his neck, rubbing the back of his head so that even the hair *there* stood up. "Monday," he repeated, jangling his keys in his pocket. "And speaking of, do you think Bee could maybe sit out on training that day?"

I raised my eyebrows. "Probably. Why?"

He shrugged, sheepish. "I thought you and I might try something. Something prophecy related," he quickly added.

"Right, of course," I said, like it hadn't even occurred to me he could be talking about anything else.

"Awesome," he said. "So Monday."

"Monday," I repeated, and just when I was afraid we were going to stand there echoing each other all night, David finally gave a little wave and got in his car.

As he drove off, I started walking back to the theater, my head so full it ached. So much for a normal Saturday night.

The idea of searching a crowded theater for Ryan was more than I wanted to deal with, so once I got back to the Royale Cinema, I took a seat on one of the padded benches in the lobby and waited. I thought about Ryan sitting in the dark, maybe next to Mary Beth, and tried to summon up some kind of righteous indignation. Here I was, trying to keep this entire town safe, trying to save my own freaking life, and my boyfriend was sitting in the movies with another girl.

But righteous indignation wouldn't come. Neither would devastated betrayal or hurt disbelief. Mostly, I wanted the movie to be over so I could go home and wash the crab bisque out of my hair.

Finally, the doors opened and people began spilling out into the lobby. Ryan was there, but there was no sign of Mary Beth. His eyes roamed until they found me. Crossing the room in long strides, Ryan looked a little relieved, but also fairly irritated.

"There you are," he said, standing in front of me. "I texted and called you like a hundred times."

Rising to my feet, I fished my phone out of my pocket. Sure enough, I had about a dozen missed calls. I'd forgotten that I'd put the phone on silent.

"Have you been here this whole time?" Ryan continued, folding his arms over his broad chest.

"No," I said, but before I could get any further, Ryan frowned.

"Why do you smell like an aquarium? And what are you wearing?"

Oh, crap. I'd forgotten to give David back his jacket. "Someone spilled soup on me," I said, which, hey, was pretty close to the truth. "So that's why I didn't want to go in. Because of the smell."

"And the jacket?" he asked. "Did you knock down a random professor and steal it?" He was smiling a little now. I'm sure the sight of me, bedraggled and covered in soup, was amusing.

And then his smile faded. "I've seen that jacket," he said slowly, eyes moving over me. "That's . . . David Stark has a jacket just like that. I remember the stupid elbow patches."

Ugh. Why hadn't I given the damn coat back? "Yeah," I said lightly. "He was the one who spilled the soup on me."

Ryan's expression was stony. "So you ran out of the place looking for some girl, and then you found David Stark, but he spilled soup on you in the middle of Pine Grove Square, and gave you a jacket?"

"Yeah," I said on a nervous laugh. "Pretty much. Weird night, huh?"

Heaving a sigh, Ryan glanced behind him. "Weird. Sure."

We hardly said anything on the drive home, and when he

pulled in my driveway, Ryan didn't even shut off the car. "I'll call you tomorrow," he said, and all I could do was nod and tell myself he wasn't kissing me good night because I smelled like a Red Lobster.

When I walked through the front door, it was 9:45. Mom and Dad were exactly where I'd left them, although Dad was now asleep, his head tilted back, softly snoring. Mom sat up as I closed the door. "You're early."

"Movie wasn't very long," I said.

Mom clearly had more to say, but I jogged up the stairs before she had a chance. I'd desperately wanted a shower, but once I was in my room, the idea of getting undressed was exhausting to me, so I just slumped down on my bed, bisque, tweed, and all.

It had been one week since I'd sat at Miss Annemarie's and told Saylor Stark that I could be a Paladin and a regular girl. That nothing had to change.

"Nothing does," I muttered to myself. So tonight had been bad. And odd. And, I thought, remembering sitting across from David in the lamplight of the tearoom, unsettling.

But it was one night. And we only had two more weeks of this left before Cotillion.

I could do this. I *would* do this.

I drifted into sleep, David's jacket still wrapped around me.

Chapter 30

"AGAIN," Saylor said, her tone of voice exactly the same as it was during Cotillion practice. But this time, instead of walking down a flight of stairs in heels, I was practicing sword fighting. Also in heels.

To tell the truth, whacking things with a sword felt really good today. Ryan hadn't called on Sunday, and then at lunch, Amanda and Abigail had been talking about *The Promise* and how good it was. "I still can't believe you missed it to see something called *Hard Fists*," Abi had said to Mary Beth.

Mary Beth had darted a glance at me as Amanda elbowed her twin, and I pretended to ignore all of them. I also ignored the stab of guilt that pierced my chest when I saw David in the halls. I had not almost kissed him, I reminded myself. He had almost kissed *me*, and if he had, I would have pushed him away and made all sorts of shocked sounds, and not kissed him back, even a little bit. I was positive of that.

Then, when I got to Saylor's, I'd been treated to a lecture on how possibly chasing Blythe had been foolish and irresponsible.

So yes. Smacking things with sharp metal felt good. Or it had for the first hour at least.

"I don't see why I have to practice so much," I said, wiping sweat from my forehead with the back of my hand. It was a chilly day, but the sun still beat down on me, and I'd been getting quite a workout. The sword was heavy in my hand, and my muscles ached. Still, the dummy I'd been slicing looked a heck of a lot worse.

"Practice makes perfect, Miss Price," Saylor trilled.

"I know that. Heck, I practically *invented* that. In fact, if I decided to do something so low-class as get a tattoo, it would probably be that. What I mean is"— I took another swing at the dummy—"is that I don't have to practice this. You said that when Mr. Hall passed his powers on to me, he also passed on his knowledge. And the knowledge of every Paladin before him."

I swung the sword in an arc over my head, going in to slice the dummy up under the ribs. "I don't have to practice. I can . . . I don't know, do this."

Saylor gave a long suffering sigh and took another sip of sweet tea. "And all of that is true. But practice never hurt anyone. And while your brain knows all of these things, your body is still unused to them." She nodded at the dummy. "Hence the practice. Now again."

"Why swords anyway?" I asked even as I did what she said. Spinning, I hit the dummy in the neck, then pulled the sword out and dropped into a low spin, whacking the flat of the blade against its legs. "They're not exactly the most convenient weapons.

Shouldn't I have"— I grunted as I brought the sword down with both hands—"a gun?"

Saylor poked at the ice in her glass with a bright pink straw. "Modernized weapons won't work for Paladins."

I swung around, the sword making a slight *zing* in the air. "Like, we're not supposed to use them or—"

"The original magic that created Paladins didn't take things like guns, or grenades, or—or rocket launchers into account. Therefore, you can't work with those nearly as well as you can with a sword."

I took that in, turning the hilt of the sword over in my hands. "Okay. But a rocket launcher sounds a lot more useful than a sword."

It took another fifteen minutes, and my thighs and calves had joined my shoulders in screaming, before Saylor said I could quit. I wanted to fling the sword to the ground and sink into a lawn chair next to her, but instead, I put the sword back in the house and wheeled the dummy back onto the patio.

When I did sit down, Saylor rewarded me with one of her rare grins. "Good girl."

She handed me a bottle of water, and I gulped half of it down. "You're doing well," Saylor said as I drank. She frowned, her eyes narrowing behind her sunglasses. "Unfortunately, I'm not sure that it'll be enough."

I lowered the bottle. "What do you mean?"

"You're learning quickly," she acknowledged. "But what the Ephors are intending . . . I never thought I'd face something like that with an untrained Paladin at my side."

"I didn't exactly expect to spend my Cotillion battling the forces of evil, either," I reminded her, and the frown deepened.

"I understand that, Harper. But . . ." She sighed. "As successful as you've been, to be honest, I have no idea how to . . . to train a Paladin. I never had to before. We all have our roles. David is the Oracle, I'm the Mage, and Christopher was the Paladin."

"We'll be okay," I said, wondering how I managed to get the words out without choking. "We'll get through Cotillion and then . . ." I trailed off.

It wasn't like I hadn't thought about what came after Cotillion. Whatever this big prophecy was, it would be settled. But David would still be an Oracle (or dead). I would still be a Paladin (or dead). Right?

Saylor was watching me. "Harper, do you fully comprehend what being a Paladin means?"

I sat up a little straighter in my chair. "Right now, it means making sure crazy Blythe doesn't kill David and inadvertently make a crater where our town used to be."

"But do you understand what that means giving up?"

Now I really didn't want to look at her. I got up out of the chair and started doing the stretches she'd shown me. "Once Cotillion is over, I won't have to give up anything," I said. "Blythe will be gone—dead—the spell won't have worked, and I can get back to normal life."

"Harper, this *is* your normal life now. No matter what happens at Cotillion, you are a Paladin, linked to me, linked to David. Forever. And that means that eventually, you'll sacrifice everything," Saylor said. She didn't insist it. Didn't say it with force, like she was trying to make me believe it. It was a fact.

I faltered, nearly losing my balance. Taking a deep breath, I moved into another stretch. "I don't believe that," I said. Overhead, the sun was so bright, the sky a steely blue.

Suddenly Saylor was standing in front of me. We were nearly the same height, so she was looking right into my eyes. "I don't have a family," she told me evenly. "Or a home. Even my name isn't real. That's what I gave up to keep David safe. Myself. It's what Christopher gave up, too. And it's what you'll give up as well, whether you want to admit it or not. My every waking moment is dedicated to keeping that boy alive."

My arm was very heavy as I lowered it. Everything in me felt heavy. "I don't want that," I said, hating how . . . petulant I sounded. But I couldn't help it. "After Cotillion, what will he even need protecting *from*? The Ephors want to kill *me*, not him."

"Harper, remember what I said about the Paladins protecting Alaric from himself."

As though I'd forgotten about that. "That's not going to—"

"Hey," David called, and Saylor and I both jumped. He was standing inside the back door, watching us. "Did I miss the sword show again?"

He said it jokingly, but somehow I knew he'd overheard us.

I hadn't seen David since Saturday night, and I gave a small sigh of relief. Standing in Saylor's backyard, wearing a sweater that was two sizes too big and jeans that were a size too small, he just looked like David. I wasn't noticing his hair or his eyes or his hands. Whatever that had been between us had clearly been a fluke of the hug and the lamplight and him actually acting like a decent human being.

Still, when he said, "Pres, you wanna come upstairs and work on that thing with me?"

Saylor's eyes narrowed a bit. "What thing?"

"Project for the newspaper," I said. "Can't let major supernatural happenings get in the way of journalism, right, David?"

"Yup," he said with a little nod.

"I thought you weren't on the paper, Harper," Saylor said, sounding unconvinced.

"I'm not," I told her, grabbing my coat from the back of a lawn chair. "But David and I are trying to work together more at school. You know, so no one gets suspicious of us hanging out."

Saylor's blue eyes moved from David to me and back again. "All right," she said. "Don't be too long. I still have a few more things to go over with you before we're done for today, Harper."

"Aye aye," I replied, giving her a tiny salute.

David headed for the stairs, and I followed. We were about halfway up when he stopped and turned back to me, lifting his eyebrows. "'Aye aye?'" he whispered, his mouth lifting in a crooked grin, and . . . oh.

Suddenly, the fluke felt a lot less fluke-y.

Hoping the light was dim enough to hide my blush, I muttered, "Shut up," and pushed past him up the stairs.

Chapter 31

DAVID'S ROOM was a lot like I'd pictured.

I mean, not like I'd ever spent a huge amount of time thinking about David Stark's room, but if you'd asked me to describe it, I think I would've been pretty dead on. There was the totally sensible wooden-framed bed, complete with a blue comforter. There was a matching desk piled high with notebooks and computer stuff, and not much on the walls except for a few maps. I paused in front of one of them.

"Where is this?" I asked.

It wasn't a continent I recognized. David looked up from gathering a pile of laundry. "Oh. Um, that's Middle Earth."

I could've sworn he was blushing, but in the interest of working together, I decided not to give him a hard time about it. Instead, I nodded and moved over to the bookshelf. There was a corkboard posted above it with a few newspaper articles pinned to it, and three photographs. Two were nature shots—a tree that I thought was the oak in Forrest Park, and the pond behind Grove Academy—but one showed David sitting on a stool in front of a blue backdrop. There were three other kids in the photo. I recognized all of them from the newspaper staff. Chie, the pretty Asian girl I'd seen hanging around David, was leaning on his shoulder.

"Are you guys a thing?" I asked, tapping the picture. It suddenly occurred to me that I knew next to nothing about David's social life. He'd always hung out with the same handful of kids in school, all the same kids that were on the newspaper staff now. And since David and I had basically declared ourselves mortal enemies in preschool, our circles didn't overlap often. But I never saw him at school dances or at the movies or anything. I'd certainly never seen him with a girl. But Chie *had* looked weirded out about him holding my hair when I puked at Homecoming.

"Huh?" he asked, squinting at the picture. "Oh, no. We're friends. That was . . . goofing off with the camera in newspaper."

"I think she likes you," I said. He gave a noncommittal grunt in reply, shoving his laundry basket into the closet.

Since that was a dead-end street, I crouched down in front of the bookcase. Like mine, it was overstuffed, but whereas I'd at least made an attempt at organizing titles, David had books shoved in every which way and stacked on top of one another.

There were a bunch of fantasy novels, and classics, as well as several biographies of journalists. I picked up a book about Ernie Pyle and started thumbing through it. "So you're really into this whole newspaper guy thing."

David pushed the closet door closed. "Yeah. I always thought that's what I'd do for a living one day."

I put the book back and turned to face him. "You still can."

He snorted, leaning back against his footboard. "Yeah, I'll

be one heck of a journalist. I can predict the stories before they happen."

I wanted to say something encouraging. Something like, "Hey, you still can! So what if you might be a supernaturally powered crazy dude!"

But even I couldn't fake that much pep. "We'll work it out," I said.

David looked at me, and there was that expression again, the one he usually got right before he wrote a terrible article about me. "You really believe that, don't you?"

I walked over to his desk and sat in the chair. "The only alternative is to sit here and whine about it, and I don't think that's going to accomplish much. Now. What is it you want to try?"

David rubbed his hands up and down his thighs. "I want to try to have a prophecy."

Confused, I sat up straighter. "Don't we need Saylor for that? She's your battery or whatever."

David shook his head. "I don't want her to know about this. And I think . . . I think just the two of us ought to be enough to get some kind of vision. It's worth a shot, at least."

I wasn't exactly opposed to the idea. Some hint of what was coming could be helpful. But I still didn't get why David was so set against telling Saylor.

He must've read that in my face because he sat on his bed, propping his elbows on his knees. "I know I have to trust Saylor again. Eventually. And I will."

I didn't know how to answer that, so I just nodded.

"Okay. Let's prophesize."

Relief washed over David's face. "Right." He sat up, clasping his hands in front of him. "So where should we . . ."

I got out of the chair and attempted to sit as gracefully as I could on the floor. "Here," I said, holding my hands out.

After a pause, David sat across from me, folding his long legs. But he didn't take my hands. Instead, he stared at them like he'd never *seen* hands before. "It probably *will* only work with Saylor," he said. "Surely you and I have held hands before. In PE, playing red rover or something. And nothing happened then."

I thought back, trying to remember if I'd ever held hands with David Stark, but nothing came.

I opened and closed my hands at him. "Maybe we did, but that was before I got all superpowered, so it doesn't matter. Now come on."

Still, he sat there, hands clenched in his lap. "We hugged!" he exclaimed, lifting his head. "In your car, when we didn't die, and the other night, with the soup. We hugged, and I didn't have some crazy-ass vision."

Neither had I. But I'd had a potential case of the butterflies I was trying very hard not to think of right now. And then I noticed the red flush creeping its way up David's neck and wondered if he was trying to squelch the same thing. "That was just a hug, and we were both fully clothed."

He shot me a weird look, and the flush on his neck got redder.

"I mean our—our skin didn't touch," I hurried on, and now, oh God, I was blushing, too. "So maybe this thing needs skin-on-skin contact. Or hand-on-hand. Or . . ."

Frustrated, I reached out and grabbed his hands. "Please shut up and think future-y thoughts."

"I wasn't the one talking," he reminded me, but before I could give any kind of comeback, I felt the low buzz of electricity start between our palms. It was nothing like that first night with him and Saylor, the power of it nearly blowing us out of our chairs. But it was there. Weak and full of static, like a TV channel that was trying to come through.

David closed his eyes and I did the same. Our hands were warm, and as David's fingers tightened on mine, a picture began to form behind my eyelids. There was a flash of white, another of red, and I thought I could hear screams again, but they were so faint, I wasn't sure. More red, and stairs. A bunch of greenery crumpled on the ground, and silver—

Suddenly, the picture was gone, and David wasn't holding my hands. When I opened my eyes, I saw him standing across the room, next to his bookshelf.

"What is it?" I asked, rising to my feet.

Shaking his head, he turned back around, and his face wasn't so much pale as it was gray. When he still wouldn't answer, I grabbed his arm.

"Remember what you said to me about how I had to start saying 'dead'? Well, you have to start saying things, too. Namely, important things, no matter how dumb you think they are."

He turned to face me, and his mouth opened and closed a couple of times. "I saw you, in a white dress. You were lying on the steps, at Magnolia House, bleeding. And I . . . I saw you die."

Chapter 32

I ONLY *thought* I'd taken Cotillion practice seriously before. Now that I knew what the night was really about, I was nearly fanatical in getting everything right.

That Thursday afternoon, Saylor was MIA at Cotillion practice. She hadn't said where she would be, only that she needed me to be in charge. So I walked up and down the stairs of Magnolia House and did my very best not to imagine myself lying dead on them. Like I'd told David that afternoon, Blythe and Saylor had both said that boy Oracles could see what *could* happen, not necessarily what *would*. Of course I *could* die the night of Cotillion. We'd always known that. But I wasn't going to, because that night was going to go off perfectly, no matter how many times I had to correct the girls' placement. Where they were standing was important since Saylor and I were trying to create an easy exit should stuff go badly.

But the third time I snapped, "Move three steps to your *left*, Mary Beth!" she whirled on me.

"Oh my God, Harper, it *doesn't matter*. You don't have to pick on me just because I sat next to your boyfriend at a movie."

It was almost like the air had been sucked out of the room. Or maybe that was from everyone trying not to gasp all at once. Ryan and I hadn't talked about Mary Beth and the movies, or David and the jacket. I think both of us were willing that entire evening away. He'd come over a couple of evenings, and we'd sat in the entertainment room my dad had set up in the basement, watching movies and occasionally kissing, but things still felt fragile and awkward between us. *Nine more days*, I kept reminding myself. *Nine more days, and all of this is over.*

But now here was Mary Beth, throwing it in my face. Bee moved closer. "You sat where with who?" We were practicing in our dresses today, and Bee looked like a seriously pissed-off bride as she stomped to my side. "You went to the movies with Ryan?" she asked Mary Beth.

Bee was one of the sweetest people I knew, but she was also super scary when she got angry. It didn't help that she was over six feet tall in her heels.

Mary Beth went a little pale. "No!" she bleated. "I-I sat next to him after Harper ran out to hook up with David Stark."

Now everyone did gasp, and David, who was in his usual spot, slouching behind a paperback book, sat up.

Bee turned confused eyes on me. "You and David . . ." She trailed off, and I looked around, wondering where the hell Saylor had gotten off to.

"No," I told Bee. "I ran into him. Literally." Pitching my voice lower, I added, "And you know why I've been spending time with David."

She nodded, but didn't look particularly reassured. From his spot in the corner, David called, "The only hooking up Harper did was with a pint of crab bisque. She ran into me, I spilled soup, and then I gave her my jacket. Like a gentleman. That's all there was."

He pulled his feet up onto his chair, propping the heels of his Converse on the edge of the seat, and disappeared behind his book again. But Mary Beth only narrowed her eyes at him and then turned back to me.

"Whatever. Everyone knows that you and David have been flirting since, like, third grade, and all those mean articles are his way of pulling your freaking pigtails. And you have *Ryan Bradshaw* for a boyfriend, and it's like you don't even care!"

The other girls were all circling around us now, like this was some bizarre game of Duck-Duck-Goose, and I could feel my face flaming. The only thing I hated more than a scene was people getting involved in my personal stuff, and this was both.

"You don't know anything about me and Ryan," I told Mary Beth, trying to keep my voice calm.

"I know that all he is to you is another . . . achievement." Mary Beth seemed close to tears now, her voice tight and squeaky. "Look at the way you treated him Saturday night. You just ran out of the theater. No explanation, no apology. And then you show up two hours later wearing David's jacket?"

My hands were shaking, and I realized I was balling them into fists. Afraid I'd wrinkle my gloves, I yanked them off, trying not to pop any of the buttons as I did. "I saw someone I needed to talk to. And I don't have to explain myself to you, Mary Beth."

"Who did you need to talk to that badly?" She was only a few inches taller than me, but Mary Beth drew herself up to her full height. Her hands were clenched in front of her, gloves wrinkling.

Bee was at my elbow now, her brows drawn together, confusion and suspicion obvious on her face.

"Just this girl," I said, hating the words the second they were out of my mouth. Why hadn't I thought of an excuse? Something that sounded the least bit plausible?

Maybe it was because I was tired of making excuses. Tired of lying to everyone about everything. Even Bee, who I'd let in closest of all, still didn't have any idea about what was really going on.

"It was a scholarship chick," David piped up from his corner. He was standing up now, shoving the book in his back pocket. "Harper and I are up for the same scholarship, and I'm gonna be honest, I was trying my best to suck up. Pres—Harper here ran out to talk to her, too. Hence spilling the soup." He folded his arms across his chest. "Now can we please stop being crazy and get back to prancing around a mansion in wedding dresses?"

Next to me, I felt Bee relax a little. It was a plausible story, and at that moment, I could've kissed David. Well, no, not really. I was in no way thinking about kissing David Stark.

That seemed to put an end to it, and I was about to tell the girls to start from the top again. But before I could, Mary Beth pressed her lips together. It was like I could actually feel her steeling herself for what she was going to say next. "You're exactly like your sister, Harper." The words came out fast, almost like she was afraid to say them. "You act like you're perfect, but inside, you're totally screwed up."

I'd been punched and stabbed and slammed into a bathroom wall. None of that hurt nearly as bad as Mary Beth's words. I felt them everywhere, rattling my teeth, pounding into my bones. I half expected to look down and find myself covered with bruises.

I felt an arm go around my shoulders. Bee's fingers dug into the exposed skin of my upper arm. "Mary Beth," she said, her voice shaking a little, "I don't know what the hell has gotten into you, but that was *so* out of line."

"Seriously," Abigail and Amanda muttered together. They wore identical frowns, two pairs of brown eyes glaring.

"In fact," Bee continued, pulling me closer, "I think you should leave now."

"Happily," Mary Beth said, kicking off her heels and pulling a pair of sneakers out from under the little sofa by the door.

"Are you okay?" Bee asked once she was gone, and I made myself smile, even though I could feel how shaky it was.

"Fine," I told her. "Mary Beth has had a thing for Ryan for a million years, and she's jealous. It's . . . it's no big deal."

Bee wrapped me in a quick hug, her collarbone pressing against my chin. "It is a *big* deal. Everything she said was so freaking offensive. The stuff about your sister, and David . . ."

She trailed off. Over her shoulder, I could see David, his face concerned, lips thin. I hadn't run out on Ryan to go "hook up" with David, but hadn't there been . . . something? Wasn't that nearly as bad as if I had kissed him?

"And you and Ryan are good, right?" Bee pulled back, a slight crease between her brows.

"We're great," I said, and David suddenly turned away, pulling his book out of his back pocket. The stairs rose behind him, and all I could think was, *He saw me dead there.* I needed to get out of this dress. I needed to get out of Magnolia House.

"I think I'm gonna go ahead and go home," I told the girls.

Most of them nodded sympathetically, but I saw a gleam in some eyes. Of course. Harper Jane Price was about to have a nervous breakdown in front of them. Who wouldn't want to see that?

"Let me drive you," David said, but I shook my head even as Bee glared at him and said, "I'll drive her."

"I can drive myself," I told them, and when they both went to protest, I help up my hand. "Promise. I . . . need a break."

I think Bee would've kept arguing, but I told her I would text her as soon as I got home and headed for the door before she had a chance.

I got behind the wheel of my car, meaning to head home. But when I got to the turn for my house, I went left instead of right. There was someone I needed to talk to.

Chapter 33

I DON'T KNOW what Ryan was expecting when he opened the door, but me basically launching myself at him was probably not it, if his "Whoa!" was anything to go by.

I stood in his front door, dressed in my Cotillion gown, my arms locked so tightly around his neck that I was holding my elbows, toes dangling off the ground. After a beat, he wrapped his arms around my waist.

Ducking my head, I pressed my cheek to his neck, wanting to breathe in the safe, familiar scent of him, wanting to climb inside his soft gray T-shirt, wanting to *hide* in him.

"Harper, are you all right?" he asked, and I shook my head, pressing closer.

He gave a sighing laugh, breath brushing my ear. "Well, whatever it is, it'll be okay. Actually, wait." Ryan set me back on my feet, looking me up and down, appraising. "Are you running away from a wedding? Because that might be less okay."

I swatted at him with a watery chuckle. "This is my Cotillion dress, thank you very much."

His hazel eyes went wide. "Ah. I thought I wasn't supposed to see you in that."

Waving that away, I stepped past him and into the house. "Oh, who cares?"

I walked down the hall to Ryan's room. His parents would still be at work, so we could safely hang out in what was normally a forbidden zone.

"'Who cares?'" Ryan echoed, following me. "Who are you, and what have you done with my girlfriend?"

Ryan's room used to be his brother Luke's. It couldn't have been more different from David's room. No maps of Middle Earth, for one thing, and not many books. There was a flatscreen mounted to the wall, and a gaming station. Ryan had been in the middle of some basketball game, but he crossed the room and turned the television off.

"So do you want to talk?" he asked, sounding a little unsure. "Or are you here so we can . . ."

He trailed off, but his gaze slid behind me to his bed.

"Talk," I said firmly, sitting on the edge of the mattress. "For one thing, it takes too long to get this dress off and back on."

That made him smile and took a little bit of the disappointment out of his eyes. "Okay. Can I at least do this?"

Sitting next to me, Ryan took my face in his hands and lowered his mouth to mine. Even as I reached out to clutch the front of his T-shirt, I was thinking of that first kiss on the swings at the park. The way my heart had leapt into my mouth, how every hair on my body seemed to stand on end.

It was only natural that Ryan's kisses didn't make me feel like that anymore. We'd been together for two years now. Those kind of sparks only belonged in new relationships, didn't they?

Or was Mary Beth right? Was I holding on to Ryan because he was another *thing* for me to have? Another achievement on Harper Jane Price's list of accomplishments? 4.0 GPA, SGA President, Homecoming Queen, Haver of Best Possible Boyfriend.

"Um, Harper?"

Ryan pulled back, his hands falling from my back. His eyes were kind of hazy, but he was starting to frown.

"What?"

"It's customary to kiss back when a guy is kissing you."

Ugh. I'd done it again. "Sorry," I said, ducking my head in my best attempt to seem apologetic. "I was thinking."

Sighing, Ryan sat back. "Of course you were."

"You're right. Things are weird right now," I said. "It'll be better after Cotillion." That was becoming my mantra. Problem was, I wasn't sure if that was actually true. Whatever was going to happen at Cotillion, Saylor said it would change things. Would it be for the better?

Ryan reached out and took my face in both hands, a mix of exasperation and love on his face. "You always say that," he said, his thumbs tracing my cheekbones. "It's always going to get better someday. Sometime in the future, things won't be so crazy." Leaning forward, Ryan dropped a kiss on the tip of my nose. "But the thing is, Harper, we can't *see* the future. So how can you have any idea if it's going to get any better?"

Irony, thy name is Ryan.

"Do you like Mary Beth?" I asked suddenly. One of Ryan's pillows sat next to me, and I pulled it to my stomach.

Ryan rocked back from me, his hands lifting from my face to hover somewhere in the air around my shoulders. "Where did that— No. I mean, I like her, but not . . ."

"Right," I said, twisting my hands in my skirt. It wasn't that I didn't believe Ryan. He wasn't a bad liar like David, he just . . . didn't. Ever, as far as I could tell. But there was something kind of unsure in his voice, something that lodged under my skin.

"Do you like David?" Ryan asked, dropping his hands to his thighs.

"No," I said immediately. "We're maybe not as hostile as we used to be, and he's finally backed off on the paper thing, but that's it as far as we go."

But I kept thinking of sitting across from David at Miss Annemarie's, the way he'd said Mary Beth wasn't me. And the more I thought about it, the more confused I felt, which sucked since I'd come to Ryan's specifically to stop feeling so confused. To feel *normal*.

Yes, David and I were closer now than we had been. But that was only because he was the only person other than Saylor who knew the whole truth. Of course I'd feel the odd warm fuzzy for him. So there was an obvious solution here.

"Hey, you wanna help me with something?" I asked Ryan, rising to my feet.

He quirked one auburn brow. "Is it the buttons on that dress? Because if so, then yes, very much so."

It was flirty and jokey and I should find it charming and not slightly irritating. I reminded myself of that as I smiled back. "Not exactly. It's research."

The corners of Ryan's mouth turned down and he flopped back on his bed. "Now that sounds like a great, sexy time right there," he told the ceiling.

"It's going to be fun," I insisted, sweeping a pile of *Sports Illustrated* magazines off his desk chair and turning on his computer. "It features death and destruction and other things boys like. It'll be like *Hard Fists*, only more . . . historical."

Ryan was still lying on his bed, arms folded behind his head. He laughed. "Oh, man, *Hard Fists*. I hate that you missed it. There was this one part where this dude killed another dude using, shit you not, a ladle, and Mary Beth said—"

He broke off, and I pretended to be really involved in finding the perfect search engine. "So what kind of death and destruction research?" he said, finally.

"This king, Charlemagne. He had a bunch of knights who died fighting a—" I broke off, suddenly realizing that I couldn't exactly get into all the Oracle stuff. "A bad guy," I finished lamely. I'd read everything I could on Charlemagne's Paladins on the internet, but there was hardly a mention of Alaric. Still, it couldn't hurt to look again.

I rummaged around on Ryan's desk, sifting through more *Sports Illustrated*s, a bunch of loose change, and a stack of video games. "Don't you have a notebook or some paper or something?"

By now, Ryan had shifted on the bed, turning so that his feet were braced on the headboard. He was tossing the mini basketball that sat by his bed on the wall above. Catching it, he tilted his head. "You're seriously going to do homework."

I paused, my hand still resting on a video game, the box reading *War Metal 4*. "It's not really homework. More like an . . . extracurricular project. I thought it might be fun if you were more involved in the stuff I do."

"Why?" Ryan asked, tossing the ball again. "It's not like you're all that involved in the stuff I do."

He didn't say it accusingly, and didn't even seem that put out by it. It was just a fact. "I cheerlead at your basketball games," I reminded him.

He shrugged. "You were doing that before we even started dating. It's no big deal, Harper, I'm just saying we don't have to be all up in each other's business." He gave the basketball another thump before grinning at me. "Unless it's in the carnal sense."

This time, I didn't even try to hide my irritation. "You spend too much time with Brandon," I muttered, and Ryan gave a bark of laughter.

"Right, because he knows what the word 'carnal' means. But please . . . don't keep trying to fix us, Harper. We're not broken."

But the thing is, we felt broken. Really broken. And the scary thing was, I wasn't sure how we'd even gotten here in only a month. I'd been so busy worried about saving David, saving Cotillion, saving *myself*, that I hadn't noticed my relationship was also in need of a hero. Could I fix that, too?

Ryan kept thumping the basketball behind his bed and I watched him, my Cotillion dress crumpled and uncomfortable, and thought about the scariest question of all: Did I want to?

Chapter 34

W HEN I got to school the next morning, Bee was waiting for me in the parking lot. Leaning against her car, blond hair whipping in the wind, she frowned as I walked up to her. "You never texted me last night, and I called you like a hundred times."

It took me a second to remember that I'd promised to text her, and why. Oh, right, the ugly scene at Cotillion practice. "Ugh, I'm sorry. I went over to Ryan's last night, and I left my phone in the car."

Bee pushed away from her car, tugging her knit hat a little farther down over her forehead. "Are you guys okay?"

The words "Of course!" immediately leapt to the tip of my tongue, but I bit them back. Bee deserved better than that. "We're trying to be."

Kids were walking past us and up the stairs into Wallace Hall. I caught a glimpse of Mary Beth's reddish hair before she disappeared into the building. Bee must've seen her, too, because she paused on the steps. "Mary Beth had it totally wrong yesterday. You and Ryan are perfect together, and you know that."

"Are we?" I heard myself ask, and Bee's head jerked up like I'd smacked her.

"What?"

"It's only . . ." I thought about last night, sitting in Ryan's bedroom, me on the computer, him tossing his basketball, sitting four feet apart, but feeling like there was an ocean between us. "I love Ryan, but—"

"There are no buts," Bee said, taking my hand. "You said it yourself. You love him." She shrugged. "That's all that matters."

"You're right," I said, even though I wasn't really sure that she was. And when she added, "Besides, you guys have to get married, and then Brandon and I will get married, and we'll all live next door to each other, and our kids will play together . . ."

She was smiling, and when she bumped my hip with hers, I knew she wasn't totally serious, but I couldn't make myself smile back. I wasn't an Oracle, but even I knew that future was . . . wrong.

Bee lowered her head. "You know, I was thinking last night. Don't get me wrong, your lessons with Saylor are really awesome. I mean, the other day, when she taught you how to disarm someone with a knife? Even *I* wanted to learn that."

I smiled at the memory of last week, Bee sitting in the grass of Saylor's backyard, her long legs stretched out in front of her, cheering me on as Saylor put me through my paces.

"And I get why you're keeping it a secret," Bee went on once we were inside the school. The burnt-hair smell of the ancient heaters assaulted my nose, and the squeak and click of hundreds of shoes filled my ears. "But . . . Harper, if it's making people think you and David Stark have something going on, is it worth it? I mean, do you even *need* any more lessons? You looked pretty freaking skilled the last time I watched you."

"After Cotillion," I told her, giving her my favorite saying. "I have a couple more lessons, and then I'm totally giving it up. Trust me."

But once again, there was that niggling thought. Even if I did manage to keep Blythe from doing her crazy spell and save the town, what would happen then?

No. One day at a time.

Bee nodded, but she was still chewing her lower lip. "Okay. So, hey, since we don't have Cotillion practice today, wanna hit up the Dixie Bean after school?"

A pair of freshman girls walked by, their arms linked tightly. They were laughing, heads close together, and something about them made my throat ache. "I have to meet Saylor today."

Bee's face fell a little, so I hastily added, "Do you want to come with me again? I think today we're learning this cool move that knocks people out. You know, like that *Star Trek* thing." I pinched the air with my hand, hoping Bee would laugh.

She just shook her head. "That's okay. I think the twins are free, so . . ."

"Oh." I dropped my hand. "Right. Well, y'all go to the Dixie Bean. Put extra whipped cream on your mocha for me."

She smiled at that, but it didn't reach her eyes. We made our way to our lockers. "I suwannee," I joked. "Next year? I am so going to be one of those stereotypical seniors who stacks her schedule with easy classes." As I said it, I tried to push away the image of me bleeding out on the steps of Magnolia House. I *would* have a senior year.

"But I guess that's the thing with junior year. Between college stuff, and regular school, things are so—"

"Really busy right now," Bee filled in, switching her backpack to her other shoulder. "I know. And it looks like things are about to get busier for you." She inclined her head toward my locker, or rather, to the pale purple sheet of paper taped there.

That color paper only meant one thing. The headmaster wanted to see me.

"What?" I said dumbly, ripping the paper from my locker.

"It can't be bad," Bee offered. "I mean . . . you're you."

My hand was trembling a little as I pushed the piece of paper into my coat pocket. "Yeah, he probably wants to talk to me about SGA stuff. See you at lunch?"

Brandon came through the front doors then, whooping Bee's name, and I never got a reply.

Turning away, I headed for the main office, Headmaster Dunn's secretary waving me through when I held up the little piece of purple paper. The office smelled like coffee and leather, and the walls were covered in all of his various diplomas and awards for education.

The headmaster himself was a short, squat man with droopy green eyes and a fringe of reddish hair circling his bald head. I took a seat in the chair opposite his desk, and gave him my best

Harper Jane Price smile. "You wanted to see me, Headmaster? Is this about SGA?"

In a way, it was.

His face folded with concern as he leaned over his desk. "Harper, I understand that you're very committed to this school and to your studies. But perhaps you've overextended yourself."

"I . . . what?" The leather chair squeaked under me as I sat up straighter.

He pulled out a manila folder and began paging through its contents. "According to your teachers, your grades have been slipping. And you've been tardy to class . . . let's see . . . three times in the past few weeks?"

Okay, so yes, I had gotten a B on my last history test, and I turned in one paper—*one*—late in English. As for the tardies, the first time had been after the janitor's closet with David. The second had been because I thought I felt that David's-in-danger feeling, but actually, I just hadn't eaten breakfast. The third time had been because David texted me that he'd seen some weird dude lurking outside the school, but it had been the new lawn guy.

Not like I could tell Headmaster Dunn any of that. "I had female troubles."

But even that, the Gold Standard Excuse to Give to Male Teachers, didn't work. Headmaster Dunn went on like I hadn't said anything. "I think it's possible you're suffering from stress."

"*I am not stressed!*" My fingers dug into the sides of the chair, clutching so hard I was surprised I didn't tear a gash in the leather.

He might have believed me if the words hadn't come out in a hysterical shriek.

As it was, he heaved a huge sigh. "In your best interest, Harper, I'm removing you from the SGA."

"You're . . . you're what?"

"Also, I'm going to advise Coach Henderson to give you a break from cheerleading until next semester."

"But it'll be over next sem—"

Headmaster Dunn's jowls wobbled as he shook his head. "And I think the Committee for Academic Honesty can do without you, at least until Christmas."

Now I was making high-pitched whimpering sounds.

I watched him write down and subsequently cross out every single activity I did for the Grove. Future Business Leaders of America? Gone. Key Club? Gone. Annual Christmas bake sale chairperson? Crossed through *twice*.

"There," he said with satisfaction once he was done erasing my entire life. "Now see? You'll feel so much better."

"But . . . college," I said weakly. I didn't care what Saylor said. I could still do that, right? How could I *not* go to college? "They'll see that I dropped out of all this stuff my junior year, and they'll think I can't follow through, and all I do is follow through, so—"

"Harper," he said sternly. "You are bright and talented and driven, and any college would be lucky to have you. But as your principal, it's my job to guide your academic pursuits. And I think all these things you do here at the Grove are getting in that way of that."

He ripped the paper in half, the sound making me wince.

"But now you're free. Concentrate on your classes. That will do more to get you into a good school than all the extracurricular activities in the world."

I stood up, my legs numb. All I could do was nod.

"And, Harper," he added when I opened the door, "maybe take some time for yourself now, okay?"

Chapter 35

THE DAY before Cotillion, I sat on Saylor's sun porch, staring at a textbook.

Today's lesson involved the history of the Ephors and ancient Greece, even though I'd thought our last session before Cotillion might involve more fighting and training. But Saylor said it was important for me to conserve my strength, hence the studying. The day felt pleasant and fallish, and the sunlight was warm between my shoulder blades as I studied.

"This," Saylor said, pointing to a picture of a stone fort at the edge of a cliff, "was the home of the Ephors. Or was. I have no idea if that's where they're still operating from."

I ran my finger over the imposing building. It was huge and vaguely medieval-looking. There were even bars on the windows, and below, the Mediterranean, so blue it almost hurt to look at, crashed against a rocky shore.

"It's . . . beautiful doesn't seem like the right word."

"It's not," Saylor agreed, taking another sip of lemonade. "It's awe-inspiring and terrifying and lovely to look at, but not beautiful."

There was a wistfulness in her voice, and I glanced up. "You miss it."

It wasn't a question. Saylor's eyes were practically misty as she looked at the photograph.

"It was all I knew for a very long time. And don't get me wrong, Pine Grove is very nice, but it's not . . ." She trailed off, her fingers brushing the edge of the page. Then she cleared her throat and sat up a little straighter. "Anyway, that's the seat of the Ephors. And how many are there?"

Sighing, I leaned back in my seat. "Five. They used to be elected by the Greek people, but now they choose their own successors. And they pass their power on via super creepy kissing, just like Paladins."

Saylor frowned. "That's not exactly how I'd put it, but yes."

When I didn't say anything, Saylor reached out and closed the book. "You seem distracted today."

There was absolutely no humor in my laugh. "Kind of have a lot on my mind right now, Miss Saylor."

"David told me there was an issue at Cotillion practice yesterday. Something with you and Mary Beth?"

A breeze swept through the open door of the sun porch, making the wind chimes ring softly, and even though I wasn't that cold, I wrapped my arms around myself. "It wasn't a big deal. But what was you not being there supposed to accomplish exactly?"

Leaning back in her chair, Saylor folded her arms. "Yesterday was actually another training lesson for you. I wanted to see how you did leading the girls by yourself."

I snorted. "Oh, well, everyone turned on me and started

snarking about my boyfriend and David, so that went super great."

"What about David?" Saylor asked.

"Let's just say it hasn't escaped anyone's notice that we're spending a lot of time together, and people have the wrong idea, and . . . " I trailed off. "Anyway, I can fix it."

Before Saylor could reply, David suddenly appeared in the doorway, leaning his head out. "Say— Oh. Pres. Hi."

"Hi," I replied, turning all my attention back to my book. But he walked onto the sun porch, standing in front of me. "Is everything okay? After yesterday?"

I lifted my head then. David's outfit today was another winner: a shrunken black V-neck sweater over a bright purple collared shirt, with blue and violet plaid pants. I didn't even know where one purchased plaid pants. Still, looking at him, I smiled. Say what you would about David's wardrobe—and I'd said a lot over the years—he was always a hundred percent committed to it.

"It was fine," I told him. "I went over to Ryan's and we worked things out, so . . . yeah, right as rain. Except for saving both of our lives and this entire town, of course." I thumped the book in front of me.

David blinked a couple of times, the effect slightly owlish behind his glasses. "Oh, good. Not about us maybe dying, but you and Ryan. That's . . . that's good."

"It is," I said, rubbing my eyes. I felt like I hadn't slept in years.

Silence fell and it lasted a second too long before David turned to Saylor and said, "Anyway, wanted to let you know I was home."

"Anything to report?" Saylor asked, and even though I wasn't looking at him, I knew David rolled his eyes.

"Nope. No one tried to kill me, I've had no bizarre visions of the future, and now I plan on making myself some pizza rolls. We good?"

"Go," she said, waving a hand at him.

But there was affection in her voice, and her eyes followed him out the door.

"You love him," I said, and she swung her gaze back to me.

"I do." She smoothed her hands over her thighs, flattening imaginary wrinkles from the linen.

"Even though he's not your family."

Saylor laughed, a surprisingly husky sound. "Don't you love people who aren't your family, Harper Jane?"

"Of course I do. But you love him for more than the whole Oracle thing. You love him because he's David."

Saylor sighed, looking behind her. The sun was starting to go down, and her backyard was filled with soft golden light. Even in November, things were still green and blooming.

"Yes," she said at last. "I love him because he's David. That boy can be a pain in the backside, don't get me wrong, but he has a good heart. And he's actually handling this a heck of a lot better than I thought he would. Look at him. Whole life turned upside down, and he's in there making pizza rolls." She gave a fond snort. "He's a good boy. So, yes, I love him, whether he can see the future or not."

My throat felt weird, so I opened the book again, flipping pages and trying to focus on the words in front of me. *Ephors were* said to have magical powers of their own, but many people thought they were simply draining that power from the Oracles themselves and—

"Harper, do *you* care about him?"

Closing my hand around my glass of lemonade before it could plummet to the patio, I shook my head. "David?"

"He was the boy we were speaking of, yes," Saylor answered dryly. "And not just because he's the Oracle, but because he's David."

I made a big show of resituating my lemonade glass on the table, wiping stray droplets from the book. "Of course I don't," I said, even as my heart hammered in my ears. "You've seen the two of us together. All we do is argue."

"Passionately," Saylor said.

"There is nothing . . . *passionate* about me and David. I've spent most of my life despising him and while I'll admit that this—this situation has made me appreciate him a little more, there's nothing going on between us."

I made myself meet her eyes, which wasn't easy, seeing as how just thinking about him was making my skin feel weird and too tight.

"Nothing going on," I repeated, but Saylor only squinted at me.

"Do you know, if it weren't for your respective positions, I'd hope you were lying to me. I'd hope you felt the same way about David he's felt about you all these years."

I couldn't keep myself from snorting. "You want me to loathe him?"

Saylor wrinkled her nose. "Is that really how you think David feels about you?"

I couldn't have this conversation right now. Not when there were about a million other things going on that were way more important than feelings.

"Please don't tell me he's only been writing horrible articles about me because of a secret crush," I said, getting out of my chair and going to stand by the window. A cardinal flew into the birdbath, a bright splash of red against all the green. Something about that bright red bothered me, reminding me of . . . something. Something in David's visions. There had been red in that, a wave of it. Blood? The thought made me shudder.

Saylor came up behind me, watching the bird, too, and I suddenly remembered the other thing she'd said. "What do you mean that you'd be happy if we liked each other were it not for our 'respective positions'? Is Paladin-Oracle romance frowned upon or something?"

She sighed. "There's nothing expressly in the rules about it, but it's generally acknowledged not to be the best idea. The relationship between Paladin, Oracle, and Mage is complicated enough without dragging the heart into it. And there's always the chance that personal feelings can interfere with duty."

The late-afternoon sun shone on her silver hair as I looked over at her. Saylor was still staring into the backyard, but her eyes were far away.

"Miss Saylor," I said slowly. "The spell. What if . . . what if Blythe's right and it just powers him up? No crazy times or power twisting his brain or any of that?"

Saylor kept staring in the backyard. In the fading light, I could see some of her fuchsia lipstick had bled into the tiny wrinkles around her mouth. "If that's the case, it would be a miracle. The Ephors believed—I believed—there was a reason Oracles were almost never male. They're . . ." She sighed. "It's an ugly word, but they're aberrations. And if Blythe does this spell on David, he'll be every bit as lost to us, do you understand me? That much power, it will burn him up and eat him alive until he's not David anymore, but a powerful, dangerous creature that absolutely must be put down."

David's dream. Both of us crying, something in my hand, him dying because of me . . .

Goose bumps had broken out over my whole body, and they had nothing to do with the cold. "I understand."

Chapter 36

ACROSS TOWN, my friends were all at Bee's house, putting on their dresses together, laughing and doing each other's makeup. I imagined them stepping into their white shoes, slipping on gloves, while I got ready by myself. I'd told Bee that Mom wanted it to be just us, a kind of mother-daughter bonding thing. Really, I just wanted to be alone.

Once I was done, I turned to stare into the mirror. The dress was every bit as beautiful as it had always been, but it was a smidgen too big. I'd lost weight these past few weeks. And then there was my face, pale even under the makeup. One way or another, everything would change after tonight.

The door opened behind me, and Mom walked in. As soon as her eyes landed on me, she drew in a soft breath. "Oh, Harper."

I fiddled with my pearls. "It looks good, right? I wasn't sure about these sleeves, but with the gloves . . ."

Mom crossed the room in a few strides and rested her hands on my shoulders. "It's better than good. It's beautiful."

And it was. Or it would've been if I could stop thinking of it as the dress I might die in. The dress I would be wearing when I screwed this whole thing up and got everyone I loved and everything I knew blown off the map.

I swallowed those thoughts down, trying to smile. "You look amazing, too," I told Mom. She was wearing a soft pink dress that brought color to her cheeks and made her dark eyes shine. Tears sprang to my eyes, and I turned around to hug Mom before she could notice.

"I'm so proud of you," she whispered against my temple.

I gave a watery chuckle. "Why? All I'm doing is walking down some stairs and trying not to spill punch on my dress."

But Mom shook her head and pulled back. "No," she said, holding me at arm's length. "Not just for Cotillion. For the girl—no, the woman—you've become."

Now I didn't have to worry about hiding tears. We were both a little weepy.

"I'm sorry for being so overprotective these past few weeks," Mom told me. She smelled like Mary Kay makeup and hairspray, and I hugged her again.

"I'm sorry, too," I told her, and nothing had ever been truer.

There was a soft knock at the door, and when Mom and I turned, Saylor was standing there. She was already dressed for Cotillion, too, wearing a navy dress, with a white rose corsage pinned to the bodice.

"Saylor?" Mom asked, confused.

Saylor met my eyes, and I nodded.

Satisfied, Saylor walked into the room and reached into her

handbag. She pulled out the little pot of lip balm. "Hillary, don't you look lovely?"

Saylor's smile was bright as ever, and her accent seemed thicker than normal. "Where did you find that dress?"

I could tell Mom was still a little puzzled, but manners trumped confusion. "Nordstrom," she answered, brushing a hand over the skirt. "I think it's supposed to be a mother-of-the-bride dress, but I guess that's appropriate."

She gave a nervous little chuckle, and Saylor laughed, too. "Mine is the same. But that color . . . here, let me get a closer look."

And then she touched Mom's hand. The scent of roses wafted over me as Saylor held on to Mom and looked deep into her eyes. "You are going to stay home tonight, Hillary. You and Tom both. You don't feel well, and you can't bring yourself to ruin Harper's special night. Tomorrow, you'll wake up and you'll be so sorry to have missed it, but you'll know it was the right thing to do."

Mom swayed on her feet a little, and I gripped her other arm. But after a moment, she gave a faint nod. "I don't feel very well. I think I'll stay home tonight."

Saylor gave her hand a pat. "Good girl. Now go on and change into something more comfortable."

Mom didn't walk out of my room so much as float. "Thank you," I said to Saylor, even though watching my mother leave made my heart twist painfully.

But Saylor was still staring out the door. "Harper, if Blythe's spell goes badly tonight, it won't matter that your parents aren't actually at Magnolia House."

"I know." I looked around my bedroom, wondering if this was the last time I'd see my purple bedspread, or the silver and cherrywood jewelry box that had been my grandmother's.

"Everyone in this town is in danger if—"

"*I. Know*," I repeated. "And I know that my aunts will still be there, and my friends, and my boyfriend."

Turning back to the mirror, I pinched my cheeks in a last-ditch effort not to look quite so much like death. Honestly, white really is a difficult color for anyone to wear. "But I had to do something."

I thought Saylor would argue that, too, but she just sighed and sank down on the edge of my bed. "Don't we all."

"Have you been to Magnolia House yet?" I asked. "Any sign of . . . anything?"

She shook her head. "Everything is as it should be at the house, but Blythe is here."

The words sent a shiver racing through me. "How do you know?"

"I felt my wards giving way this afternoon," Saylor said, glancing up as she rummaged in her handbag. "I don't know how she did it, but it has to be her."

"What could she even be planning?" I asked, going to sit next to Saylor. "Is she just going to march into Magnolia House and start her mojo?"

Saylor shook her head. "I don't know. She'll need to be

protected from you while she's attempting the ritual, but she doesn't have a Paladin on her side. And the ritual itself is surprisingly simple. It won't take her long."

Dr. DuPont, shoe sticking out of his neck, suddenly flashed through my mind. That had been six weeks ago. Six weeks to completely reorder my entire life.

And possibly end it.

"Hired assassins then maybe? Disguised as cater waiters?"

"That's a possibility," Saylor acknowledged with a nod. "Keep an eye on them."

Crossing over to my dresser, I picked up my lip gloss. I wasn't forgetting that tonight, at least. "I will," I said, swiping on a coat of Coral Shimmer.

Saylor watched me in the mirror. "Of course, there's always the possibility she'll try to kill you before she starts the ritual. That would probably be the easiest thing to do."

My heart sank, and the hand holding the lip gloss trembled. "Well, yeah, there's that."

Rising from the bed, Saylor came to stand behind me, her hands on my shoulders. "You can do this," she told me. "I know you can."

"I have been rocking the training pretty hard," I admitted, and Saylor tightened her grip.

"I've known you since you were a tiny little girl, Harper Jane Price. You are driven, and smart, and sharp, and there's no other Paladin I'd rather have fighting for David tonight than you."

It was all I'd ever wanted her to say. Okay, so I hadn't exactly

wanted the Paladin part, but Saylor Stark praising me about anything was good enough for me. Reaching up, I took one of her
hands and squeezed it.

"Are you ready?" she asked as the doorbell rang downstairs.

Ryan.

"As I'll ever be."

Chapter 37

THE GRAVEL and shells crunched under Ryan's tires as he pulled the car up to Magnolia House. My heart thumped steadily in my chest as I stared at his headlights. How many times had I looked at this house and thought it was the prettiest place in the world? How many times had I pictured myself living there, sweeping down those wide front stairs in a Scarlett O'Hara gown?

Now staring at it, all I could think was that not only would I never live in Magnolia House, but that I might actually die there. Tonight. I tugged at my gloves. They were damp and wrinkled, and I realized my palms were sweating.

I was so busy fiddling with the row of pearl buttons, trying to get the stupid gloves off, that I didn't notice Ryan watching me until he reached out and began undoing the buttons himself.

"Here," he said softly. His fingers were surprisingly gentle as they pulled the buttons through their little loops, and for the first time in a long time, something swelled in my chest as I watched him. It wasn't love. Or at least, it wasn't the boyfriend kind of love. But it was warmth and affection and this . . . I don't know, gratitude.

Ryan was a good guy. He always had been. Once he'd finished half the row, he tugged at each finger until the glove slid off my hand. "Thanks," I said as he handed it back to me. One hand free, I went to work on the other glove myself, even though I could feel his gaze like an actual weight on the curve of my neck.

"We're done, aren't we?" he asked. I raised my head, the left glove still half on, half off.

For a second, I thought about pretending I didn't know what he was talking about. Maybe if I smiled at him and made a joke about the gloves, I could stop this from happening. But did I want to? Was there room for Ryan in my life—short as it might be—now?

I knew there wasn't.

But even more, I wasn't sure there had ever been room for Ryan. Not really. Not the way he deserved. Still, I couldn't make myself say anything.

Ryan wasn't stupid. He knew what my silence meant. His throat worked, and his eyes were shiny. "Well, we had a good run of it," he said, broad shoulders shrugging inside his tux jacket. He looked the handsomest I'd ever seen him, like he was meant to wear formal wear every day of his life.

I laughed, but it sounded sad. "You make it sound like we're getting divorced."

He laughed, too, dashing at his face with the back of his arm. "Hey, we've been together nearly our entire high school lives. That's, like, twice the length of a lot of marriages."

Smiling, I reached out and took his hand. "I love you, Ry."

Sniffing, he nodded toward the house. "I know that. But I'm

not an idiot, Harper. There's someone in there you wanna be with more than you wanna be with me."

I actually recoiled at that. "W-what are you talking about?"

Ryan rolled his eyes. "Harper, you and David Stark have been circling each other since kindergarten."

My mouth suddenly felt dry, and I busied myself taking off my glove. "David and I . . . maybe we have ended up being friends after all, and I guess we have some stuff in common—"

"He gets you, Harper. That way you throw yourself into everything you do, he does that, too. And he's a walking encyclopedia like you, and I bet he doesn't even play video games—"

"I like *War Metal 4*," I insisted, but Ryan shook his head.

"It's okay, Harper. I actually feel kind of . . . good. You know, doing the noble thing, stepping aside in the face of True Love . . ."

He was trying to joke, but my throat suddenly went tight. If Ryan had any idea what was really going on between me and David, that it was so much more complicated and so much worse.

"Ryan," I said feebly, but he shook his head.

"It's okay," he repeated even though he sounded a million miles from "okay." "Just go."

I felt like there was more I should say. We might have only been together for two years, but Ryan had been a huge part of my life.

But in the end, I just nodded again. It was better like this. So with one last little wave, I got out of the car and walked into the house.

Saylor was hanging her coat in the front closet when I walked in. "Where are your gloves?"

I stared at her. "Seriously?"

She rolled her eyes, exasperated. "You sound like David. And while I know there are"— she glanced around us—"more pressing matters at hand right now, it's still important that you look the part. Now I'll ask you again, where are your gloves?"

Adrenaline had made me jittery, and my hand shook slightly as I gestured back out the door. "I left them in Ryan's car."

Saylor lifted an eyebrow. "And is Mr. Bradshaw coming inside?"

"I-I don't think so. We broke up."

Closing her eyes, Saylor rolled her lips inward. "Was tonight the best time for that?"

Anger flared up in me. "I don't know. I'm not sure there is a best time for your boyfriend to dump you."

"You and Ryan broke up?"

Bee had just walked in the front door, Brandon a few steps behind her.

"Kind of?" I said before shaking my head. "No, not kind of. We broke up, yes."

I don't know what kind of expression people make after they've watched a puppy get stomped, but it had nothing on Bee's face in that moment. "Right before Cotillion?" she asked, shocked. "You broke up with your boyfriend half an hour before the most important night of your life?"

Taking a deep breath, I picked up the hem of my dress, moving closer to Bee. "First off, this is not the most important night of our lives. There are going to be lots of important nights. And secondly, he actually broke up with me, and it's . . . it's okay."

"It's so not okay," Bee said, her dark eyes watery. "You can't possibly be okay. Harper—"

Behind me, I could hear the kitchen door opening. A couple of men in black pants and white shirts came through, carrying a small table between them.

I met Saylor's gaze. The cater waiters. They didn't seem particularly assassin-like, and they weren't even looking in this direction. But then, Dr. DuPont hadn't seemed scary either until he'd had a scimitar at my neck.

"We'll talk about this later," I told Bee as there was another bustle from the kitchen. The door swung open again, and this time, my Aunts Martha and May swooped in. May was carrying a giant silver punch bowl, while Martha had a ladle tucked under her arm.

"I am older than you, Martha," May insisted. "It is not right that you're making me carry this all by my lonesome."

"You are two minutes older," Martha replied, "and that punch bowl hardly weighs a thing. Besides, Mother left it to you, so it's *your* responsibility to carry it."

May grumbled at that, but then Martha saw me, raising the ladle in greeting. "Oh, Harper! You look so pretty! May, doesn't Harper look pretty?"

"I can't see her over this stupid bowl," May muttered, staggering toward the table the waiters had set up.

Despite everything pressing down on me, I laughed. "Where's Aunt Jewel?"

"She's wheeling the cooler of punch in," Aunt May said, finally getting the bowl situated in the center of the table.

Right. The punch. I thought again of David's vision, the wave of bright red washing over everything. "Where's David?" I asked Saylor, and she nodded upstairs.

Maybe he had some valuable, punch-y insights.

Bee was still standing in the doorway, her arms folded. "Why do you need to see David?"

I opened my mouth, but nothing came out. Thankfully, Saylor covered for me. "With Mr. Bradshaw and Harper's sudden and unfortunate situation, Harper will need an escort. I always bring David as a spare just in case these things happen."

It was probably the last thing Bee wanted to hear, but at least it made sense. I turned away before I could see her scowl, and headed up the stairs to David.

Chapter 38

WHEN I walked into the bedroom, David was standing in front of the window. His tux jacket lay crumpled on the bed, and his bow tie hung around his neck. From the look of his hair, he'd been pulling at it, and one hand was in his pocket, jangling some loose change.

"Nervous?" I asked, and he spun around.

"Are you—" he said, and then he saw me. "Oh. Wow."

I'd had that reaction from a lot of people. Mom, Ryan, the saleswoman at the bridal shop. But hearing *David* say it, seeing *David*'s eyes go wide, made me suddenly self-conscious. I had to stop myself from twisting the silk skirt in my hands, and Ryan's words rang in my head.

Harper, you and David Stark have been circling each other since kindergarten.

And maybe we had. But it's not like any of it mattered anymore.

So I put my shoulders back and walked over to David. "You've seen the dress before."

"It looks different tonight—" David said, but I just kept talking.

"Any sign of . . . well, anything?"

Shoving his hands back in his pockets, David turned to look out the window. "No. But . . . I can feel it. She's here. Or close by."

I could feel it, too. An awareness shivered along my skin, like I was being watched. For all I knew, Blythe was already in the house, waiting around a corner.

"Do you want to see if you can have a vision?" I asked, offering him my hand. He took it, but this time, there was no spark, no frisson of electricity. His hand was warm and soft in mine and he absentmindedly ran a thumb over my knuckles. Now there *was* a spark, but I didn't think it had anything to do with our powers. Still, I'd had a boyfriend up until about ten minutes ago, and things were way too screwed up to start pulling romance into it now.

And added to the fact that I might have to kill David one day . . .

I pulled my hand back from his, moving a little bit away. "Well, speaking of visions, the one you had with me and Saylor. Do you remember all the red in it?"

He screwed up his face, thinking. "Yeah. A bunch of red stuff, really bright. At first I thought it was blood, but it's the wrong color."

Leaning against the giant four-poster bed, I clasped my hands behind my back. "Can I say something insane?"

Snorting, David turned his gaze back out the window. "Tonight would be the night for it."

"I think . . . I think it's my aunt's punch. In the vision."

David frowned. "That sugary stuff that makes your brain hurt? I . . . yeah, I guess it was that color red."

"Do you think it means anything?" I asked, looking out the window with him. More cars were pulling up now, and I could hear the soft murmur of voices as people began milling around downstairs. Soon all the girls would come up here to huddle together in one of the other bedrooms, waiting for Cotillion to start. Would Blythe wait, too?

"I doubt it," David said, and at first, I thought I'd spoken my question out loud. But, no, he was talking about the punch. "If shit goes down, it seems likely the punch will spill, right?"

I didn't want to think about shit going down, people running and screaming, my aunt's punch sloshing to the floor.

"Ryan isn't coming," I told David. His head jerked up, but I didn't elaborate. "So you'll have to escort me. Which is probably for the best since it'll keep me close to you for . . . whatever."

"Right," he said, and then his lips lifted in something close to a smile. "Whoever would've thought we'd end up going to Cotillion together?"

I smiled back. "That? *That's* what's bothering you about this night?"

His laugh was low and husky, but nice, and I suddenly wished I'd spent more time getting to know David instead of always competing with him. Somehow, in these past six weeks, we'd become friends. It might've been nice to have him as a friend all along.

I heard the discordant sounds of the band starting up

somewhere downstairs, and I glanced at the delicate silver and diamond watch around my wrist. "Damn," I muttered. "I guess it's time to get started."

David started pacing again, hands still in his pockets, practically vibrating with nervous energy. I remembered when that used to annoy me. Now, all I wanted to do was wrap my arms around him and tell him everything was going to be okay. I wanted to rest my cheek against his collarbone, and have him tell *me* we were going to get through this. But the music was getting louder now, turning into a recognizable song.

"I'm going to go see where the other girls are and check things out one last time," I told him. "Escorts need to start lining up on the stairs in"— I checked my watch again—"about ten minutes."

David stopped pacing, dropping his head into his hands with a sound somewhere between a laugh and a groan. "God, what is the point of being able to see the future if you can't actually *see the future*? I keep . . . it's like digging through sand. I can't see anything,"

"Hey," I said, pulling one of his arms down. "It's okay. You know what Saylor said. The closer you get to eighteen, the clearer the visions are going to get."

He looked at me, eyes wild. "Harper, I saw you die. I saw you in that dress, bleeding to death on those stairs." He pointed viciously out the door. "So don't tell me it's going to be okay."

I swallowed hard. "Saylor said not every single one of your visions comes true. This one won't. I won't let it."

I must've sounded braver than I felt because David gave me a tiny smile. "You would be too stubborn to die."

"I am, trust me."

We stood there, staring at each other. I didn't even realize we were holding hands until I turned to go and had to disentangle myself.

I was already to the door when he called, "Harper."

"Wha—" was as far as I got, because in a few long strides, David crossed the room and pulled me into his arms. I was so stunned that it hardly even registered that he was kissing me until . . . oh. *Oh.*

This kiss didn't make my stomach flutter; it made my skin sing. It made me raise myself up on tiptoes so I could kiss him back harder. It made me want to kiss him anytime, anyplace, even if we were in the middle of Main Street.

I tangled my fingers in his hair, and his hands gripped the silk around my waist before sliding around my back, holding me so tightly that it should have hurt. But it didn't, not even the littlest bit.

When we broke apart, we stared at each other, dazed and breathing hard. "I just . . ." He took three more quick breaths. "I needed to know."

"Oh God," was all I could manage to say. This was what was between me and David Stark? This was what seventeen years of snarking and fighting and competing had been covering up?

His eyes dropped to my lips. "I think we should do it again, though. To be sure."

He barely got the last word out before I was pulling his mouth back down to mine. Any idea I'd had that maybe it had been the shock, or the fact that it was my first kiss with someone who wasn't Ryan since ninth grade, flew right out the window.

This time, I nearly shoved him away when the kiss ended. "This," I panted, pressing a hand to my abdomen, "is really inconvenient right now. We— No!"

David had been moving closer to me, but froze as I held up my other hand. "Okay, so now we know. And we will deal with that later. Provided we don't die."

He shook his head, like he was trying to clear it. "Now that I know, I really, really don't want to die."

The smile that broke out over my face had to be the goofiest, giddiest thing ever, and I quickly tried to suppress it. Tonight was about being a stoic superhero type, not a flustered teenage girl. I cleared my throat. "Me neither. So let's make sure that doesn't happen, okay?"

He took another step closer, but I was already moving toward the door. "Wait here until it's time to go to the stairs. Keep an eye out for Blythe, and . . . stay."

And then I made myself walk out of the room. Shutting the door firmly behind me, I leaned back against it and blew out a long breath. This was absolutely the last thing I needed. I had been single for all of fifteen minutes, I had an insane tiny witch person trying to kill me, and she was going to attempt a spell that might take David away from me for good. Now was not the time to feel all swoony and weak of knee.

Still, I couldn't stop smiling as I walked onto the landing, peering down at the room below. It was nearly full now, and I noticed nearly everyone had a cup of Aunt Jewel's punch. It was the weirdest thing to me how everyone openly acknowledged that it was terrible, but kept drinking it anyway. Manners in action, I guess.

Scanning the crowd, I looked for anyone who seemed out of place, but these were almost all faces I recognized. There was no sign of Blythe, no sign of anything out of the ordinary.

"Harper?"

Miss Annemarie stood at the top of the stairs, an empty punch cup in her hands, a faint pinkish mustache on her upper lip.

"Miss Annemarie," I said, straightening up. "What are you doing up here?"

She placed her cup on the little marble-topped table on the landing. Downstairs, I could hear the string quartet playing something stately and elegant. "Looking for the little girls' room. The one downstairs has a line you wouldn't believe."

There was a small powder room off the main landing, and I walked toward it. "It's right here," I told her, opening the door.

"Oh, goody," Miss Annemarie said. And then with a shove way harder than any octogenarian should be able to give, she pushed me inside.

Chapter 39

I STUMBLED over the hem of my dress, and tripped, smacking my head painfully against the low sink. Stars exploded in my vision, and I heard the door slam behind me. Other than a thin crack of light around the doorframe, it was totally black, and only Miss Annemarie's heavy breathing told me she was right behind me. I heard the whisper of something swinging at me and flopped onto my back, kicking out blindly.

There was a clink of metal and a soft grunt of pain, and then the bathroom light blazed on. Miss Annemarie stood over me, searching the floor for the knife she'd dropped. "Dear me," she said softly in the same tone of voice she used when she spilled tea.

"Miss Annemarie!" I gasped. "You? *You're* the assassin?"

She glanced over at me, her eyes cloudy. "Have to kill Harper Price," she said, almost conversationally. And then, spotting the knife wedged behind the toilet, "Ah!"

Her girth made it hard for her to bend down, and I crouched there against the far wall, watching her struggle. All my Paladin instincts were urging me to rush forward, pin her to the floor, and snap her neck. But . . . this was Miss Annemarie. She wasn't a Paladin, she was just an old lady. An old lady who wanted to kill me, but still.

I got up slowly, sliding up along the wall, but as soon as I was on my feet, she reared back up, one meaty fist swinging for my head. I dodged it easily, grasping her hand in mine. "Miss Annemarie!" I said again, and it was like she couldn't even hear me. The look on her face was dazed, dreamy. She looked like . . . she looked like Mom had this evening.

Mind control. A shudder ran through me. So that's how Blythe was going to get rid of me. By sending the last person I'd expect to—

And then I looked closer at the pink stain over her upper lip. Punch. She'd been drinking Aunt Jewel's punch.

As had nearly everyone downstairs.

Oh my God.

Blythe had gotten her job at the university by making a mass mind-control potion, slipped into their potluck lunch. She'd done the same thing here, only with my Aunt Jewel's punch, and suddenly that part of David's vision made perfect sense.

It also meant I was perfectly effed.

Armies of cater waiter assassins I'd been prepared for. Some hired thugs, sure. But people I knew and loved, all turned against me? I couldn't kill those people. I couldn't even *hurt* those people.

Miss Annemarie jerked her head toward mine, trying to head-butt me, but I'd perfected that move. I ducked, and then reaching out with my right hand, tried the thing Saylor had taught me. I pressed right above Miss Annemarie's carotid artery, and she dropped like a stone.

I did my best to haul her inert body out of the way, and flung the door open. There was no murmur of voices downstairs now, no violins. Everything seemed deathly quiet, and when I eased out of the bathroom and peeked over the landing, I saw everyone just . . . standing there. Arms at their sides, abandoned punch cups on the floor. What I didn't see were any white dresses.

I checked my watch. Of course! While I was fighting Miss Annemarie in the bathroom, the other girls had probably gone upstairs. And they wouldn't have had any of the punch since red juice plus white dress equals disaster.

Moving as silently as I could, I crept down the hall to the bedroom where we'd been told to assemble. The door was closed, but when I opened it, I was greeted by a sea of white dresses. "Harper!" Amanda and Abigail cried, and I waved my hand.

"Shhh!" The girls all stared at me, but everyone went quiet. "Look, there's been a little delay," I said, trying to keep my voice low. "First of all, has anyone in here had the punch?"

"Do we look stupid?" Mary Beth asked, narrowing her eyes. Her cheeks were nearly as red as her hair. "You and Miss Saylor both practically threatened to kill us if we touched the stuff."

Breathing a sigh of relief, I pointed at them. "Wait here."

Dashing down the hall, I ran to the bedroom where I'd left David. He was putting on his jacket when I opened the door. "Am I late?" he asked when he saw me standing there.

Without answering, I grabbed his hand, tugging him out of the room.

When I got back to the girls' room, I practically threw him

inside. "All of you stay in here until I come back," I instructed. "Don't let anyone in, and don't let anyone out."

"Harper," Bee said, moving forward, but I stopped her with a hand.

"Not now, Bee."

"But—"

"Seriously!" I snapped. "I'll be . . . I'll be right back."

Something flickered across her face, but I shut the door before I could put a name to it. I had way more important problems now. Namely that I didn't know what to do next. I had to keep Blythe from David, but that meant I had to find Blythe. She was obviously here, but where? Should I just stand guard over this door, or should I make my way downstairs, fight it out?

And then the choice was made for me. There was the pounding of feet on the stairs, and suddenly, people were swarming the landing, all headed for me. The knife Saylor had given me rested cold against my thigh, but the first person to leap at me was my Aunt May, and I couldn't even think about using it.

Aunt May, my sweet Aunt May, who taught me how to knit, who bought me a piece of candy every time we went to the store, jabbed a cocktail fork at my eye. I ducked, my back still against the door, and then Mrs. Green, the children's librarian, reached down and tried to tug at my ankle. I shook her off, but even as I did, someone else was grabbing my hair, and another hand closed on my wrist, and I was fighting and kicking, but there were so many of them, and they had me backed up against the door.

"Harper!" I heard someone cry from inside the room. I

thought it was Bee, but I couldn't be sure. More hands were on me now, and someone had a pie server nearly at my throat.

I shoved it away, trying to close my fingers around that spot that had worked on Miss Annemarie. I had to get to Saylor. I had to find Blythe. I had to get out of this before I was killed with some elaborate cutlery.

"Bee!" I shouted through the door, Dr. Greenbaum's nose crunching under my elbow. "Is the door locked?"

"Yes!" came her muffled reply. "But, Harper—"

I would have to hope it held. One thing I knew for sure was that Blythe wasn't upstairs. I'd been in all the rooms, and she wasn't in the crush of people surrounding me. Taking a deep breath and muttering, "I'm really sorry about this," I pushed both arms out as hard as I could, fists clenched.

The three people nearest to me fell back, stumbling into the people behind them. I heard someone cry out as they tumbled down the stairs, and I prayed with everything in me that it wasn't one of my aunts. I let every Paladin instinct I had take over as I pushed the crowd back, back, farther down the stairs. There were lots of them, but not a one had my powers. I tried not to look at faces as I whirled and kicked, as I flipped people over my shoulder, as I spun and knocked people off their feet.

Finally, a clear path opened up and I sprinted down the stairs. I heard footsteps behind me, but I didn't turn around. "Saylor!" I screamed. "SAYLOR!"

I ran through Magnolia House. Somewhere in the fight, my dress had gotten ripped, and I nearly tripped over the hem again as I pushed my way into the kitchen.

Saylor was there, up against the counter. Brandon lay at her feet, and there was a rolling pin in one of her hands. The other lay across her abdomen.

"That young man attacked me," she said, her face the color of oatmeal.

"It's the punch," I told her, locking the door behind me. "She put a mind-control potion in the punch, and . . . Saylor, I can't kill people I know. People who don't even know what they're doing."

She grimaced, disappointed in me, I thought. But then she drew her hand back and I saw that it was slicked with blood. For the first time, I saw the knife at Brandon's side. "He got in a good blow before I hit him," she said, her tone surprisingly light for someone discussing being stabbed.

"Saylor—" I said, stepping forward, but she shook me off.

"It's nothing. I have a potion that can heal this right up. David. Is he all right?"

"For now," I said as the kitchen door rattled and shook. "I locked him in with the girls. They didn't drink the punch."

Saylor's mouth wobbled. "One valuable piece of advice, it turns out."

"Can you reverse this?" I asked.

The thumps on the kitchen door were getting louder, but Saylor shook her head. "As long as Blythe is here, they're under her control."

Sighing, I ran a shaking hand over my face. "But where is Blythe? I didn't see her anywhere in the crowd and—"

Pain ricocheted through me, so strong that I felt like I had been stabbed. I bent over, panting, my vision shaking.

No, not my vision. The house. The entire house rumbled and quaked, little bits of plaster falling from the ceiling. "David!" I gasped.

Saylor moved forward, clutching my dress. Her hand left streaks of blood down the skirt. "You said he's with the girls? All of them?"

I nodded, closing my eyes. I could see the sea of dresses in front of me, see David's bewildered face as I'd slammed the door.

"Yes," I said. "All seven of them."

"Harper." Saylor's eyes were huge with pain and fear, her skin paper white. "There were only six other girls."

Chapter 40

THIS TIME, I didn't look or think. I let my fists and feet fly almost independently as I fought my way back up the stairs. These weren't people I knew, these were things standing between me and my duty. The only time I hesitated was when Aunt Jewel came at me with the punch ladle. It killed me to do it, but one quick elbow thrust to her temple sent her sliding harmlessly to the floor. Stepping over her prone form, I swore to myself that I'd go visit Aunt Jewel every single day when this was all over, and make her as many cakes as she could ever want.

The house shook as I moved toward the bedroom. I heard a distant crash, and realized it was the chandelier in the main hall falling to the ground. Light was pouring out from underneath the bedroom door, golden and searing, and all I could hear was the pounding of my heart and the constant repetition of *Too late, too late*.

Throwing my shoulder against the door, I forced it open, and immediately threw my hands up to shade my eyes.

David stood stock-still in the middle of the room, bathed in light, glowing with it. It poured from his fingers, filled his eyes, spilled out of his open mouth. The other girls were all huddled together against the far wall, heads down, while Blythe, clad in a white dress, a blond wig crooked on top of her head, stood on the bed. Her eyes were closed, nose still a little swollen from our fight, and she held both hands open at her sides. Words in a language I'd never heard fell from her lips and seemed to fill the room. Both windows shattered, and I heard high, thin screams.

I launched myself at Blythe, knocking her back on the bed. She gave a grunt as the air rushed out of her lungs, and started to shake. At first, I thought she was crying, but as I rose up on my knees, straddling her waist, I realized she was laughing.

"It's too late!" she yelled as the house continued to shake and sway. "Look at him! He's beautiful!"

David was still standing there, still covered bright light. He didn't look beautiful. He looked beautiful in his stupid sweaters and dumb glasses and unfortunate pants. Now he looked terrifying and unnatural and . . . not human.

As I watched, he lifted one glowing hand toward the girls against the wall. I saw Bee lift her face, saw her wide, horrified eyes.

"No!" I heard myself shout, and then a bolt of light flew from David's fingers, crashing over all of the girls.

The light was blinding, and my blood was churning, and Blythe was still laughing, laughing, laughing in my ear.

Someone grabbed me from behind, yanking me off Blythe. Even as I struggled, all I could think was, *I failed*. All that training, all that trying, and I'd locked David in with Blythe. I'd let her turn him into a weapon. And my friends. Abigail, Amanda, even Mary Beth. And Bee. Oh God, Bee. My attacker had me turned away from the wall, and I was glad for it in a way. I didn't want to see what that bolt of power had done to them.

I reached back, trying to dig my fingers into eyes, but clawed empty air. And then suddenly, there was a thump and I was landing on the ground, hard.

Whirling around, I saw that it had been Headmaster Dunn holding me, and standing over him, hands on her hips, was Bee.

I said her name, confused and relieved. She was okay? But I'd seen David blast her with that lightning thing, seen waves of power crash over her and all of the girls.

Mrs. Catesby, my old Sunday school teacher, ran into the room, wielding the ladle Aunt Jewel had dropped. I braced myself, but then Blythe grinned and said, "Show her what you've got, girls."

Twisting my head to look at Blythe, confused, I almost missed seeing Mary Beth's hand shoot out and grab the ladle. With a neat flip, she used the hook at the end of the handle to catch Mrs. Catesby's ankles and the ladle's bowl at the other end to knock her out. Grinning at her handiwork, Mary Beth brandished the long silver spoon at me. "*Hard Fists!*" she cried, and I could only shake my head.

Two more people, women I recognized from Junior League, raced in. Abigail and Amanda, working together, clotheslined them before spinning and using the inertia of the women's bodies to push them back out of the room.

"Oh my God, we are *ninjas!*" Amanda squealed. "How did that happen?"

They weren't ninjas. They were Paladins. All of them. David had made them Paladins.

David!

As my fellow debutantes kicked the ass of every person who walked through the door, I looked back to the middle of the room. David was on his knees now, no longer surrounded by light. But when he lifted his face to me, his eyes were still bright gold, like coins, behind his glasses.

"David?" I asked, kneeling down with him.

He blinked, and the light faded for a moment before growing bright again. "Pres?" he murmured, and I flung my arms around his neck.

"Oh, you're still you," I breathed. "You're still in there."

"I-I think so," he said. "But—what did I do to them?"

We looked over to where Amanda and Abigail were wrestling with their escorts, and Mary Beth was using her ladle to great effect on the owner of the Dixie Bean.

"You made them Paladins," Blythe said from the bed.

I had almost forgotten about her. She sat in the middle, legs crossed, hands clasped under her chin, grinning like a little kid. "I told you the ritual would work," she said. "You made Paladins, just like Alaric! And this is merely a handful of girls. If you had focused harder and if I hadn't been interrupted"—she glared at me—"you could've made this entire town an army. The whole state, if we tried hard enough."

Breathing hard, David stared at her. His eyes were still filled with light, the effect disturbing. "Why would I want that?"

Giggling, Blythe shook her head. "Oh, if you knew what was coming, you wouldn't ask a question like that."

I stood up, reaching under my dress for the knife strapped to my thigh. I was officially over Blythe. Whipping out the blade, I made my way to the bed, but I only got about three steps when a vise-like grip closed around my wrist.

I glanced back, stunned. "Bee?"

She blinked at me. "I . . . I can't let you hurt her. I don't know why, but I can't."

Mary Beth was at my other side, her fingers tight on my arm. "Me, either. If you try to kill her . . ." She didn't finish, but her hands squeezed tighter. Even Amanda and Abigail were standing by the door, eyes wary.

Delighted, Blythe clapped her hands. "Even better! See, Paladins can't harm their creator. And since I had a hand in turning David into a personal Paladin factory, that makes me a creator!"

"Bee," I pleaded. "Override it or something. I can't let her go."

Everything in Bee's face was anguished. "I really want to, Harper, but I *can't*. Now please put the knife away or I'm going to have to hurt you, and I really don't want to." Tears pooled in her eyes, spilling down her cheeks. "Except I *do* want to. What the heck is going on?"

"It's going to be okay," I told her. "This is what I am. This is what I haven't been telling you, but now you know! And now you're one, too, and we can train together. But let me take care of—"

I didn't finish the words before Bee wrenched my arm,

throwing me off balance. With a well-placed kick to my chest, she sent me tumbling back against the bed. "Oh God!" she cried. "Harper, I'm sorry, I didn't mean—"

"It's all right," I told her, even as I wheezed for breath. "We can fix this."

Blythe got off the bed, her dress bunched up in her hands. "Oh, this is nothing that needs fixing. This is perfect." Her sweet little face practically glowed with excitement. "All these Paladins, and my very own Oracle. Now." Holding out one tiny gloved hand, she crooked a finger at David. "Come along."

His eyes still blazing, David struggled to his feet. "No." The words sounded like they were being forced through broken glass, but he got it out. And then, again, stronger. *"No."*

Blythe fisted her hands on her hips. "Now isn't the time for stubbornness. I said—"

A thin bolt of golden light shot out from David's finger, striking Blythe in the middle of her forehead. Shrieking, she stumbled back, landing on the little settee at the end of the bed.

"I am not yours to control, Mage," David said in a voice that didn't sound anything like his own.

Blythe slowly rose, staring at David with a mixture of shock and wonder. "Oh," she breathed. "This is . . . unexpected."

David's hand shot out again, and Blythe winced as another bolt of light took her in the chest. "Very unexpected," she said through gritted teeth.

Moving away from the settee, Blythe stepped behind Bee. "Well, if I can't have an Oracle, at least I'll have a Paladin."

Before I could think, she had an arm around Bee's waist. Blythe was so tiny, she barely came up to Bee's shoulder blades. Sticking her head out from behind Bee, Blythe winked at me.

"I think I like this one best," she said and then, almost instantly, they both vanished.

Chapter 41

"Bee!" I cried, staring at the spot where she and Blythe had been. Behind me, David put a hand on my shoulder.

"Pres," he said softly, but I shook him off, leaping to my feet.

"No! They can't be—*she* can't be—"

But they were. She was. My best friend was gone, and I had no idea where Blythe might have taken her. Greece? To the other Ephors?

David reached up, brushing the tears off my cheeks, and I let myself lean into him for a moment. His eyes were still too bright to look directly into, so I focused on his hair, the places where it stood up in peaks and tufts. "If I'd known she'd take Bee, I would've gone with her," he said, sounding like himself again.

I held on to his jacket tighter, the material wrinkling under my fingers. But as I held on to him, I could only be happy that at least David was still here. At least I still had him.

"Whoa," Amanda said, glancing out the door. "What happened?"

David and I walked out onto the landing, the other girls trailing us. Downstairs, the main room was covered in bodies.

"Are they dead?" Mary Beth asked, but I shook my head.

"They were being mind-controlled. Now that Blythe is gone, it's over. Everyone will wake up in a few hours with fuzzy brains and . . . probably a lot of bruises."

We made our way downstairs, stepping over people as we went. It wasn't until we were halfway downstairs that David asked, "Where's my Aunt Saylor?"

"She's in the kitchen," I said, speeding up. "She was hurt, but she said she had a potion to heal it, so hopefully she's okay now."

I moved for the kitchen, but David caught my arm "Harper, there's no such thing as a healing potion."

"What?" I looked up from my skirt. There was a huge splash of red across the front that, thanks to the fruity smell rising up from it, I was pretty sure was punch. My hair was falling in my eyes, and when I went to push it back, I saw another splash of red on the back of my hand. *That* was definitely blood.

The light was beginning to dim from his eyes, but they were still more gold than blue. "She told me that healing is the one thing Mages can't control. Minds, sure, protection, yeah, but healing the human body is way beyond them."

My heart thudded painfully as his hand grabbed my arm tighter. "How bad was she?"

I didn't answer. Instead, I opened the kitchen door.

Saylor was slumped against the cabinets, her eyes closed, her face surprisingly peaceful. Brandon still lay on the floor in front of her, the knife he'd killed her with a few inches from his foot.

And kneeling next to her, shaking and holding one of her hands, was Ryan.

When he saw us standing there, he looked back and forth, his eyes wild. "I . . . I decided to come back because I wanted to see you do Cotillion," he told me. "But when I got here, the place was shaking, and I thought there was an earthquake. I c-came through the back door, and I found her. Brandon—"

Ryan's throat worked convulsively, and I went to him as David knelt down on the other side of Saylor. "I never told her," David said, his voice flat. "I never said thank you for everything she did."

"She knew," I told him, gently prying Ryan's hand from Saylor's. "And she loved you."

"I . . ." He shook his head, and tears splashed onto his black pants. "I should have told her. And she shouldn't have died like this. Alone."

At that, Ryan looked up. "She didn't. I was with her."

His mouth worked again and his hand, still in mine, was ice cold. "That's the thing. I was sitting here with her, and she—she said she hated to do this, and she knew how complicated this would make things for everyone, and then she . . . she . . ."

"She kissed you," I said, not sure if I should laugh or cry.

"Kind of," Ryan agreed. "More like she blew something in me, and I got really cold, and suddenly, I felt like I could . . . I don't know, do stuff. Weird stuff. And I really wanted to find the two of you." He nodded at me and David.

David raised his tear-streaked face to mine. "I feel like now would be a good time to use the F-word."

We spent the next few hours trying to repair some of the damage to Magnolia House. People left in uncomfortable positions were gently moved to the floor. I found my aunts and was relieved to see that with the exception of a scrape on Aunt May's forehead, they were pretty much unharmed.

Finally, I found Bee's parents, slumped at the bottom of the staircase. I went back to Saylor's body, getting the little tub of lip balm out and handing it to Ryan. "You have to put this on your fingers, and then—"

"And then I touch them," he said in a dull voice. "Tell them that Bee is away at cheerleading camp. Be fuzzy on the details."

"How did you know that?"

Ryan seemed to have aged ten years in the last half hour, but there was still a little bit of the sparkle I knew in his eyes as he shrugged and said, "I just know."

"You'll have to do the same to Brandon," I told him, and he just nodded.

That taken care of, we moved to the last task.

All of the girls were gathered back in the bedroom. Their white dresses were streaked with sweat and punch and blood, but they were all yammering excitedly, a couple of them practicing flips and spin-kicks.

"You're sure you can do this?" I asked David, and he nodded, flexing his fingers. A shower of golden light raced along the backs of them.

"Yeah. I hate to, though. I mean, for one thing, it would take some of the Paladin pressure off you. For another, they just . . . . they look really happy."

They did look happy. Happier than they'd looked in all of the months prepping for Cotillion. But I couldn't risk Blythe having five girls—six, I thought, my heart aching for Bee—who were willing to fight and die for her.

One by one, David drew the power back from them, until his eyes were bright gold again and he was shaking. That done, Ryan moved down the line with the lip balm, erasing their memories of this night. When he got to Mary Beth, I saw the way his finger didn't so much smudge the balm on as caress her palm, and something in me eased. Maybe Mary Beth would be good for him. And—I glanced at David—hopefully, uncomplicated.

Eventually, they all lay slumped on the bedroom floor, and the three of us stood over them, watching.

"So are we done?" Ryan asked, and it was so close to the words he'd used breaking up with me that I wanted to laugh.

"We haven't even really started," David told him. "The three of us, we're . . . connected. We will be forever, and—"

Ryan held up his hands. "Whoa, what do you mean forever?"

I was exhausted and heartsick and wrung out, and I wanted Saylor here so badly I ached. But she was gone. There was no one left to explain things, to offer guidance. We only had each other.

David reached out and squeezed my hand, and I saw Ryan's gaze drop to it. "That was . . . fast," he said, and David dropped my hand like it was on fire.

"It's not like that," he said, but I shook my head.

Taking David's hand in mine, I held it tightly and faced Ryan. "Actually, it kind of is. And if the three of us are going to work together, Ryan needs to know that."

Ryan looked between the two of us before heaving a sigh that seemed to come from his toes. "I can't," he finally said. "I can't deal with any of this. Superpowers, and Brandon murdering old ladies, and the two of you, I . . ."

He pushed past us. I went to grab his arm, but David stopped me. "Let him go," he said. "Give him time."

I didn't want to. Blythe and the Ephors had Bee, and we had to get her back somehow. We'd need all three of us, working together. But Saylor had let me go once. I had to do the same for Ryan.

The earthquake that hit Pine Grove the night of Cotillion was destined to be a legend. It almost destroyed Magnolia House, and nearly everyone there had some kind of injury, from scrapes, to bruises, to a couple of broken bones. Luckily, no one died. But the house would probably have to be torn down, and no one who was there that night had an especially clear memory of what happened. They all agreed the trauma had probably rattled them all.

Bee's parents were glad Bee had decided to go to cheerleading camp instead of participating in Cotillion this year. No, they weren't sure when she'd be back. Soon. They knew it was soon.

The Aunts mourned the loss of their mother's punch bowl, damaged by falling plaster that night, and Aunt Martha blamed Aunt May for not putting it in a more secure location. Aunt Jewel only knew she never wanted to make punch for Cotillion again, but she didn't know why.

And that Monday, I went to school like nothing had happened. I wasn't surprised to find David in the newspaper room. No one else was in there, and I stood in the door for a while, watching his back as he sat at the computer, typing. "I know you're there, Pres," he said at last.

Smiling, I leaned against the doorjamb. "Could you sense me with your awesome new superpowers?"

He snorted, but didn't turn around. "No, I could actually feel you staring at me."

Wheeling around in his chair, he gave me a truly sad excuse of a grin. "No one's stare is quite as piercing as yours."

When I folded my arms and gave him a look, he sighed. "I knew you'd come. And not because I saw it. I mean, I *did* see it, but . . ." He trailed off, tugging at his hair.

I walked across the room and covered his hands with mine, gently pulling his loose from the top of his head. As I did, he watched me very carefully, and I felt that same fire, the one from the Cotillion, curl in my belly. We held each other's gaze, our hands still tangled up as I stood in front of him.

"You know what's awkward?" David asked, the corner of his mouth lifting.

"Our entire existences?"

Now the grin was real. "That," he acknowledged. "And when you make a big, dramatic gesture because you think you're going to die, and then you—"

"Don't die," I finished for him, and he nodded.

"Exactly. Not that I'm not one hundred percent psyched that we didn't die, but . . ."

"I get it," I told him. "So . . . that's why you kissed me, then? Because you thought we might die?"

"More or less," he said, dropping my hands and turning back to the computer. "It was a heat of the moment thing. I mean . . . you and me, as a couple? Could that even work?"

He typed for a few more seconds, and when I didn't answer, he turned around. There was still the teeniest speck of gold in his eyes, but you had to look for it to know it was there. "Do you . . . Pres, do you want it to work?"

Saylor had said that Blythe's spell could make David dangerous. It could mean I'd have to kill him for his own sake. But he'd controlled it the night of Cotillion. He'd used incredible amounts of power, and he was still here, still David.

The gold dot in his eye seemed to flame brighter for a second, and I felt a little shiver.

Still, I straightened my shoulders and looked into his eyes. "I'd like to try."

David sat in his chair, staring at me for the space of two heartbeats. And then he was on his feet, and his mouth was on mine. It wasn't as intense as the kiss at Cotillion, but it had the exact same effect on me. In fact, kissing David in the newspaper room at seven thirty in the morning, I could almost forget I hated PDA.

He pulled back, giving a breathless laugh. "We're so stupid for doing this."

"It will probably end in murder," I agreed, but we were both grinning. Then David's smile faded. "Have you talked to Ryan?"

I sighed, moving back against a desk. Brushing a few wadded-up pieces of paper off its surface, I perched on top. "No. He's not returning my texts or calls."

"It's a lot to deal with, Pres. Suddenly having superpowers forced on you is rough."

"Is it?" I asked, raising my eyebrows. "I had no idea. Please tell me more, and let me subscribe to your newsletter."

At that, David gave a real laugh, sinking back into his chair. "Okay, now this is the Harper Price I'm more familiar with."

I smiled back at him before looking around the classroom. "So . . . what now?"

David turned around again, propping his head on the back of his chair. "Are you asking me what I've seen?"

"I was actually wondering if you'd had any ideas," I said, shaking my head. "I know this sounds totally stupid, but . . . it's like I keep forgetting you can fully see the future now. That is totally stupid, isn't it?"

Still studying the ceiling, David said, "No. Because I keep forgetting, too. I'll have a dream, and wake up thinking, 'Huh, weird dream.' You know, like I have every day of my life. And then suddenly I have to remember that, no, it might not have been a weird dream. It might have been a-a vision."

"But not everything you see will come true," I said. *We were fighting, but we weren't angry. We were sad. You killed me.* The words spun in my mind.

"That's the whole thing." David dropped his head, looking at me. "The worst part. If not everything you see will come true, how do you know what to do? What's the point of even having your head full of all this . . . this stuff?" He ran a hand over his eyes, and I saw that it was shaking.

Now it was Saylor's words looping through my mind. *That much power, it will burn him up and eat him alive until he's not David anymore.*

I'd spent the past seventeen years thinking David was annoying and mean, but he wasn't. He was smart, and dedicated, and loyal, and completely him. The thought of his powers turning him into someone else, of killing him, hurt too much to even think about.

But I wouldn't let that happen. I knew what Saylor had said, but, hey, I was a Paladin. My job was to protect the Oracle and I'd do that, even if it meant protecting him from himself.

"Anyway," David said, closing the laptop and wheeling his chair over to me, "as for what comes next, Saylor had some kind of in case of emergency spell set up. As far as I can tell, everyone in town thinks she's gone on some kind of extended vacation, and I'm totally fine here by myself."

He didn't sound totally fine, and I took his hand again. "I miss her, too."

David just nodded, pressing his lips together, and I squeezed his fingers. "I don't like the idea of you in that house by yourself."

"It'll be okay," he said. He was wearing a ketchup-red sweater and houndstooth pants. When I glanced down, I saw that, sure enough, he had on one brown sock and one black. He could not have looked any less like someone who would be okay on his own.

I stepped closer, our joined hands between us. "Are you saying that in your usual patronizing sense, or in the 'I can see the future and know how this all turns out' way?"

He grinned at me. "It was definitely more the former than the latter. The whole vision thing . . ." The grin faded. "It's like Saylor said. It needs three of us for me to see clearly. And without Ryan, we're kinda screwed."

"Funny, because Ryan himself is feeling kind of screwed by all of this."

David and I both turned. Ryan stood there in the doorway, chin lifted. He looked like he hadn't slept in days, and I think his hair may actually have been worse than David's, but he still could have been posing for a cologne ad.

"You're here," I said, wondering if the relief I felt was because we had our third part, or just because it was Ryan. Ryan, who may not have been the guy I got all fluttery for, but who had been a rock for me for such a long time.

He gave an easy shrug. "I'm here." Stepping into the classroom, he gave us both a wary glance before closing the door.

"So."

"So," David and I echoed in unison.

"The three of us, working together to save the world. Me, my ex-girlfriend, and the guy she dumped me for." His mouth twisted into a half smile. "This has to be the most screwed-up situation three teenagers have ever found themselves in."

"I think I saw an episode of *Gossip Girl* like that once," I offered, and while both boys chuckled, their hearts clearly weren't in it.

"We can do this," I told them, using my SGA president voice. "Is it awkward? Sure. Will it require sacrifice and hard work and probably get even *more awkward*?"

"No doubt," David said, just as Ryan muttered, "Yup."

"But . . . I believe in you guys. And I hope you believe in me. So." I took a deep breath and held out my hands. "Why don't we see what's coming for us next?"

The school was still quiet. Teachers wouldn't start arriving for another half hour, and the janitor who had replaced Mr. Hall was on the other side of the building.

Ryan took my hand and then, with a little more hesitation, took David's. "What's going to happen?" he asked. "Are we all going to stand in a circle and sing 'Kumbaya'?"

David held my eyes for a long moment before rising to his feet. "Not quite," he replied.

And then he placed his palm in mine.

Acknowledgments

HUGE THANKS to Jennifer Besser for loving this weird little book first, and to my agent, Holly Root, for not blinking an eye when I said the words "it's like *Legally Blonde* meets *The Terminator!*"

I'm also massively grateful to Ginny Bakkan, Hunter Chapman, Ashley Parsons, Andrea Poole, and Rachel Waters for sharing everything they knew about debutante balls with me. Sorry I took your memories and covered them in Hawaiian Punch and violence, but such is the risk of being friends with a writer! Thanks too to Jennifer Sauls for coming up with the perfect tagline!

Thank you as always to my mom, who signed me up to be an Azalea Trail girl when I was six and had a special dress made just for the day (even if a fever kept me being an Azalea Trail girl in what I like to refer to as the Most Tragic Thing That Ever Happened to Me). Mama, no one is as rebellious and belle-a-licious as you, and I love you.

Hugs and snuggles and kisses to John and Will for being the best little family a girl could have, and for understanding when I locked myself in the dining room during our vacation to Scotland so that I could finish this book. There are not many men who would be patient when a visit to the Loch Ness Monster is on the line, but y'all didn't complain once.

And lastly, huge, obscene, downright embarrassing amounts of gratitude to my editor, Arianne Lewin, who helped me knock this book down to its foundations and rebuild something much more befitting a Queen Bee like Harper. You may be a New Yorker, but you will always be an honorary belle to me, and I am so, so thankful that I get to work with you!

HARPER MAY HAVE SAVED THE PLANET, BUT SHE'S NOT
DONE WITH THE SUPERNATURAL DRAMA YET. TURN THE
PAGE FOR A LOOK AT THE SERIOUSLY FUN SEQUEL—

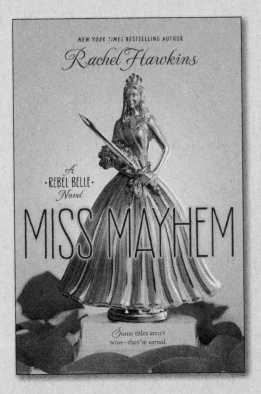

Chapter 1

"THIS IS going to be a total disaster. You know that, right?"

There are times when having a boyfriend who can tell the future is great. And then there are times like this.

Rolling my eyes, I flipped down the visor to check my makeup in the little mirror.

"Is that your Oracle self talking, or your concerned boyfie self?"

David laughed at that, twisting in the driver's seat to look at me. His sandy blond hair was its usual wreck, his blue eyes bright behind his glasses. "Seriously, you have got to stop calling me that."

The visor smacked back into place with a snap as I smiled at him. "But you *are* an Oracle," I said with mock innocence, and now it was his turn to roll his eyes.

"You know which term I was objecting to."

The windows in David's car were down, letting in the breeze as well as the faint smell of beer and the pounding bass coming from inside the Sigma Kappa Nu fraternity house across the street. It was getting late, and there were a million places I would rather have been, but I had a job to do tonight.

Still, I could mix a little business with pleasure. Leaning over the seat, I tipped my face up so he could kiss me. "It'll only take a sec," I promised once we parted. "And besides, this is what we're supposed to be doing."

David's lips were a thin line, and there was a little wrinkle between his brows. "If you're sure," he said, and I paused, hand on the latch.

"What do you mean?"

David pushed his glasses up the bridge of his nose. "This whole changing-the-future thing. Sometimes I wonder . . . like, what if you can't change the future, Pres? What if you're only delaying it a little while?"

My hand fell away from the door as I thought about that, but before I could answer, a loud *bang* from the front of the car had us both jumping.

Two dark-haired guys in polo shirts and pastel shorts chortled as they walked past, their faces washed out in the glow of the headlights. "Nice car, asshat!" one of them shouted before they did some kind of fist-bumping move that made me want to bump my fist, too.

Right into their faces.

At my side, David heaved a huge sigh. "Well, if we're supposed to be fighting evil, I'm not sure guys like that qualify." He turned to look at me, one corner of his mouth lifting and making a dimple appear in his cheek. "Although I am a little more excited about watching you pound them into a pulp now."

I settled back into my seat, fussing with my hair. "Hopefully there won't be any need for that. I'm going to get in there, get the twins, and get out. And you won't be watching anything, since you need to stay in the car."

David scowled. "Pres—"

"No." I turned back to him, the streetlight overhead outlining him in orange. "There's no way those guys will let you in. Because you're . . ."

Wearing an argyle sweater and lime-green shoes, I thought to myself. "A guy."

He was going to argue again, I could tell. That V between his eyes was getting deeper and his knee was jiggling, so I hurried. "You've already done the Oracle thing, so let me do the Paladin thing, and then we can get the heck out of here as quickly as possible, okay?"

Not even David Stark could argue with that, so he gave a terse nod and leaned back in his seat. "Okay. But please make it fast. This place is already starting to have a bad influence on me. I feel the need to buy polo shirts and shorts. Maybe some Man Sandals."

Grinning, I unbuckled my seat belt. "Anything but Man Sandals! Although, not gonna lie, a polo shirt wouldn't be a bad addition to your wardrobe."

David made a face at me and tugged at the hem of his sweater. "This is a classic," he informed me, and I leaned over to give him one more quick kiss.

"Sure it is."

Across the street, a group of boys came stumbling out the

front door of the redbrick Sigma Kappa Nu house, one of them breaking away to puke in the azalea bushes.

Charming.

"Abigail and Amanda, the things I do for you," I muttered as I got out of the car, shutting the door behind me.

Pushing my shoulders back, I did the best I could to saunter across the lawn, projecting confidence while also trying not to draw too much attention to myself. That's why I'd picked this dress. Should things get . . . out of hand, "girl in a black dress" wasn't all that memorable of a description.

The door to the frat house was hanging open as I approached, thanks to the puking guy and his friends, so I was able to slip inside unnoticed.

If the bass had been pounding from outside, it was like a physical presence in the house, rattling my teeth and starting an immediate headache behind my eyes.

And the smell . . .

Beer, boy, old pizza, and carpet that probably hadn't been cleaned since they'd built this place back in the sixties.

Ugh. Frats were the worst.

But I was here on a mission, and I switched my purse from one shoulder to the other as I scanned the crowd, looking for Abigail and Amanda's twin blond heads.

A few months ago, I wouldn't have been caught dead here. I mean, don't get me wrong, there are some fraternities worth hanging out with, but Sigma Kappa Nu was not one of them. These were, on the whole, big dumb party boys, and I was not into that. At all.

But back in October, I'd killed my history teacher with a shoe, and everything had changed.

It turned out I was a Paladin, a kind of superpowered warrior, charged with protecting the Oracle, aka David Stark, aka my new boyfriend. Being an Oracle meant that David could see the future, which obviously made him a pretty valuable commodity to a lot of people. And not good people, either. The Ephors were a group of men who had owned Oracles for years, using their visions to get ahead in the world. To predict the outcome of everything from wars to financial investments. Because David was a male Oracle, the Ephors had wanted to kill him—the only other male Oracle had been nowhere near as powerful as the traditional female ones, plus he'd become super unstable. But David had been rescued by his first Paladin, a guy named Christopher Hall, and by his Mage, Saylor Stark.

I hadn't exactly done a bang-up job of protecting David at first—people had died, including Saylor, and David had undergone a spell that gave him stronger powers than ever. Not only did he have much clearer visions, but also, he'd been able to make Paladins, giving the same powers I had to a group of girls at Cotillion. Oh, and did I mention my ex, Ryan, was our new Mage? So, yeah, complicated, but we were all trying to make the best of things.

That's part of why I was here, walking carefully among plastic cups and Ping-Pong balls, dodging puddles of beer. Before she'd died, Saylor had told me there was a possibility of David becoming a danger to himself, that the world-changing, super-intense visions would "burn him up."

Ryan and I had only helped him have two of those big types of visions. The first one, in the newspaper room at our school, had started a fire in a trash can, and short-circuited every computer in there. The second had resulted in David staying home for nearly a week, his eyes glowing brightly, his head aching. After that, I decided we should start small. Besides, it's like my mom always says: Charity begins at home.

What better way to use David's powers than to check on the futures of friends and family, and see if there was anything I could do to help them should those futures turn out not so great?

So far, we'd kept my Aunt May from accidentally using salt instead of sugar in a batch of brownies for the Junior League bake sale (an act that would have gotten her kicked out of Junior League), and we'd saved David's friend Chie from forgetting to save the final copy of *The Grove News* to her hard drive.

And now Abigail. Her future would take a hard left turn tonight when she met some douche-y frat brother named Spencer. They'd date for the rest of Abi's high school career, then she'd marry him instead of going to college. From there, David hadn't been able to see much more, only that Abi's future with Spencer felt "sad," and would lead to her and her twin, Amanda, becoming estranged.

Saving people from future earthquakes or volcanoes seemed daunting—not to mention almost impossible to get people to believe—but keeping a friend from falling for the wrong guy? Oh, that I could handle.

Provided I could find Abigail, of course. A set of French doors opened into a big backyard, and I headed in that direction, hoping to see the twins. As I kicked a crumpled Bud Light can out of my path, my phone vibrated. Pulling it out of my purse, I saw it was a text from David. "This is how I feel about fraternities right now." Underneath was a picture of him pulling the worst face—nose wrinkled, mouth turned down in a huge frown, eyes narrowed. I smiled, unsure of what was funnier: the picture itself or the idea of David Stark taking a selfie.

"Goofball," I texted back before sliding my phone into my purse and stepping outside.

A giant keg had become a sort of fountain in the middle of the yard. Two boys were holding another guy up by his legs so he could attempt the dreaded keg stand, and I sighed, wondering what the appeal of these dudes even was.

And then, thank God, I saw two identical blond heads close together by a cluster of coolers.

"Abigail! Amanda!" I called, making my way over to them. That involved stepping over more beer cans, and at least two unconscious dudes, and I frowned. *Ew.*

The twins both raised their eyebrows at me, surprised. "Harper? What are you doing here?" Abi asked. She wore her signature fishtail braid loose and over one shoulder, while Amanda's hair was pulled back from her face with two little clips. They were both wearing red dresses, so I was glad the hair made it easy to tell them apart.

I gave them my sternest look, propping my hands on my hips. "I should ask the two of you that. Now come on. We're leaving."

This is a secret I learned from cheerleading and SGA. If you act like you're in the right, people will fall in line without really questioning. I'd never bothered to come up with an excuse as to why I was looking for the two of them at Sigma Kappa Nu, and it wasn't like I could say, "My boyfriend has psychic powers, so tonight I'm saving one of you from a terrible future." Instead, I relied on two years of being their head cheerleader to make Abi and Amanda follow me.

And it worked.

They both studied me for a minute. Abi screwed up her mouth like she might argue, but Amanda shrugged and took her twin's arm with a muttered "I'm over this place anyway."

I made my way toward the French doors, pleased. That had gone so much easier than I'd—

A figure suddenly reared up in front of me. "Whoa, whoa, little lady, what's the rush?"

The guy who blocked the doorway looked a lot like my ex-boyfriend, Ryan. Tall, nicely built, reddish hair that was just a little too long. But while Ryan's smile was charming, this guy's was smarmy, and I was not in the mood to deal with him right now.

"We're leaving," I said, smiling but saying the words firmly enough for him to know I meant business. "My friends are ready to go."

"No, I'm not," Abi said, one strap of her red dress sliding off her shoulder. Amanda kind of shook her head, too.

Man, what I wouldn't have given for Ryan and his mind-control powers right about now. But all I had were my powers of persuasion, which *I* thought were still pretty great.

"This place is super gross, Abi," I told her, gesturing around at the crushed cups on the lawn, the stained couches inside, the random depressions knocked into the walls by heads or fists, "and if your parents knew you were here, they'd die. Heck, you're not even related to me, and *I* kind of want to die. Now let's go."

But Frat-enstein over here was still looming in the doorway, arms braced on either side of the frame, a red plastic cup in one hand. "'Super gross'?" he repeated. He pressed a meaty paw over the Greek letters on his shirt, and his blurry eyes tried to focus on me. His cheeks were red, and his nose was kind of shiny. Honestly, what did Abi even see in a guy like this? "Sigma Kappa Nu is the best frat on campus."

I snorted. "Please. Alpha Epsilon is the best frat on campus. You guys are the *biggest* frat on campus, and that's because there's so many of you without the grades to get into decent fraternities. Now get out of our way."

He was blinking down at me, like my words were taking a while to penetrate the haze of beer and dumb that clearly clouded his mind. Then, finally, he slurred, *"You're* super gross."

"Zing," I muttered, turning back to Abigail and Amanda with eyebrows raised. "Can we please go now?"

Amanda nodded this time, thank God, but Abi was still chewing her lower lip and looking at the guy. "It's not even eleven," she said, fiddling with the end of her braid. Now the guy was looking back at her, blinking, and, ugh, this was going to be harder than I thought. "I mean, we could stay for a little while."

Biting back a sigh, I made myself smile at Abi. "No, we can't. Now kindly get out of our way . . ."

"Spencer," the guy offered with a flick of his hair. "And I think your pretty friend is right—she *could* stay for a while."

There was no real danger here, but everything in me ached to go super Paladin on Spencer's fratty butt. And then, thankfully, he gave me the chance.

His hand came down on my shoulder, hard enough that I actually winced. "Hey, there—" was as much as he got out before my fingers curled around his hand, holding him in place while my other hand shot out, heel of my palm smacking him solidly in the solar plexus.

He let out a whoosh of air that smelled like stale beer and sour apple Jolly Ranchers, making me wrinkle my nose even as I hooked my foot around his ankle and sent him crashing to the ground. The dude was built like a tree, so he went down hard, and I didn't give him the chance to get up again. Still clutching his hand, I pressed my shoe to his chest and slid my fingers down to circle his wrist. I only had to pull the littlest bit before he whimpered. And, I mean, I didn't want to break his wrist or anything.

I just wanted to scare him a little bit. It occurred to me that once upon a time I could do that with a mere icy smile or an eye roll. These days, things were a lot more . . . physical.

"When a lady says she's ready to leave," I told him, applying pressure, "she is ready to leave. And you do not get in her way. Is that clear?"

When he didn't answer, I gave another little tug that had him nodding frantically. "Right, yes. I'm sorry, I—I won't do it again."

I tossed his hand down, dusting my palms on the back of my skirt. "I would hope not."

Lifting my head to the twins, I saw them watching me with mouths agape. Luckily, most of the party was still outside, so only a couple of guys—also dressed in the maroon and blue of Sigma Kappa Nu—saw me with Spencer, and they were so drunk that they barely noticed me.

I glanced back at the twins. "Self-defense class," I told them with a little shrug. "Now can we please go?"